THEY WERE FIGHTING AGAINST TIME——AND EACH OTHER——IN A DESPERATE ATTEMPT TO SURVIVE . . .

Andrew Held, world-famous physicist, whose guilty secret could destroy him.

Felicia, his beautiful, socialite wife, who had a taste for young lovers.

Donald Campbell, a brutal, sexually starved ex-convict, whose only law was that of the jungle.

Norma and *Blake Mansfield*, whose "perfect marriage" concealed an aching void of need.

Warren Brock, a celebrated, witty and effete homosexual sculptor.

Carlo, an almost too-handsome Hawaiian musician whose specialty was love-starved women.

Diana, a lovely young girl desperately afraid of her own wakening sensuality.

Rolf, torn between the white man's world and that of his American Indian forebears.

All of these people would be forced to discover the primal truth about themselves and each other in the ultimate struggle for survival on—

PHOENIX ISLAND

Big Bestsellers from SIGNET

PHOENIX ISLAND

a novel by

Charlotte Paul

A BERNARD GEIS ASSOCIATES BOOK

A SIGNET BOOK

NEW AMERICAN LIBRARY

TIMES MIRROR

Copyright © 1975 by Charlotte Paul Reese

Published by arrangement with Bernard Geis Associates, Inc.

SIGNET, SIGNET CLASSICS, MENTOR, PLUME AND MERIDIAN BOOKS
are published by The New American Library, Inc., 1301 Avenue of the
Americas, New York, New York 10019.

FIRST PRINTING, JANUARY, 1976

1 2 3 4 5 6 7 8 9

PRINTED IN THE UNITED STATES OF AMERICA

To the very special friends whose love of the islands and knowledge of island living inspired me during the writing of this book.

—CHARLOTTE PAUL REESE
Lopez Island, January 1976

PHOENIX ISLAND

John Gulbransen

BOOK I

Chapter One

ACCORDING to ancient mythology, there is a monster imprisoned in the center of the earth. When he sleeps, the great seas are quiet and the land is at peace. But once awakened, he is angry, and in anger he is violent. When his ferocious power is unleashed, the earth quakes, mountains explode, and the oceans rise and crash against the land in murderous waves.

Far below the land mass of Pater Island in French Polynesia, the beast within the earth lay undisturbed. But his sleep was restless. For the moment, the terrible energy within the earth's fluid outer core, molten rock boiling at 10,000 degrees Fahrenheit, was trapped between the solid inner core and the layer of rock that overlies it, the 1,800-mile-deep earth's mantle. But the earth's crust, the top layer resting upon the mantle, is only two or three miles thick under the oceans, and no more than twenty-five miles deep beneath the continents. At intervals, for thousands upon thousands of years, this thin crust has been cracked and deformed by gigantic upheavals that the ancients attributed to the fury of the monster within the earth. Nowhere has the ocean floor been more tortured by the rage of the beast than in the Pacific; nowhere is the equilibrium between crust and mantle and core more precarious.

Geologists do not talk of monsters. They tell us that gigantic fissures rim the Pacific Ocean floor. Along these faults, the edges of crustal rock press against each other with unimaginable force. As the pressure builds, the ocean floor bends until it can bend no more, and then, along the great cracks, the earth slips, rising or dipping, sliding sideways or up and down. The monster within the earth shudders and awakens angrily from its slumber. And this expression of the monster's cosmic rage we call earthquake.

Even so, this thunderous movement in the earth's crust may not satisfy the imprisoned beast. The cracks in the ocean floor may go much deeper, through the earth's thin crust and on down hundreds of miles into the mantle below. Beneath the mantle, processes at the core of the earth may generate such heat as to melt the mantle's solid rock; this white-hot fluid will well up through the crustal fissures, creating new ridges and new valleys in the ocean floor. And if cold ocean water rushes downward through the widening cracks and meets the molten rock as it rises from the mantle, there will be an explosion. This demonstration of the mythical monster's fury, we call volcano.

Earthquake and volcano—they may be disasters, but they are not the master killer. Separately, or together, they are parents of *the* killer, the great wave oceanographers call "tsunami." The word is from the Japanese: *tsu*, a small bay, port, or harbor; *nami*, wave. . . . We call it a tidal wave. If the equilibrium between the earth's layers is disturbed, the shifting and upheaval of the ocean floor triggers the earthquake, the earthquake triggers the tsunami, and the deadly tsunami is the wave that kills.

Tsunami is born at the epicenter of the earthquake. While the mother is still shuddering with the convulsions of labor—five minutes, perhaps, six or seven minutes at the most—the destructive infant is already moving out from its birthplace. Like ripples across the surface of a pond when a stone is dropped into the water, the series of long, low sea waves begins its predatory journey.

It is ironic that a "tidal wave" isn't a wave and has little or nothing to do with tides. It is energy. As great blocks of the ocean floor are thrust upward or drop suddenly, as the land trembles and cliffs slide into the sea, the downthrust and upheaval of the tortured earth's crust projects its energy into the water, generating the catastrophic waves. But a "tidal wave" is not a body of water traveling across the surface of the ocean. The sea remains in place—the wave is energy passing through it. Consider what happens when you crack a whip. The force of the movement ripples along the length of the whip from the handle to the tip. The motion travels, not the leather.

In open ocean, tsunami pretends innocence. The waves are only a foot or so high, and each wave is so long that it may be a hundred miles from crest to crest. Traveling at 400 to 600 miles an hour, the deceptively shallow ripples follow each other at intervals of ten to forty-five minutes. A few hours hence, these waves may kill thousands of human beings and destroy millions of dollars worth of property, yet they cannot be spotted from an airplane, and in open water they will pass harmlessly under an ocean liner. It is when the path of the potential murderer is blocked by a land mass that the true lethal nature of tsunami is revealed.

As the wave approaches the coast, the depth of the ocean decreases, and the killer slows down proportionately. At an ocean depth of 25,000 feet, tsunami travels at 600 miles per hour. At 12,000 feet, 425 miles per hour. At 3,000 feet, 200 miles per hour. But the retarding of speed is not an indication of weakness. When the ocean is sixty feet deep and the destroyer is advancing at only thirty miles an hour, the wave that raced so innocently across open water is actually preparing for the kill. The shallower the ocean, the higher the wave. With the victim in sight, tsunami collects itself into a striking force that may smash the shoreline with a wall of water hundreds of feet higher than normal high tide.

A steel and concrete lighthouse 150 feet above the water may be ripped from its foundations and cast into the sea. Shoreline installations are smashed; docks, warehouses, and fuel depots dismembered. Ships in harbor are swamped, overturned, and tossed against each other like wood chips. And when the wave recedes, heavy machinery, lengths of railroad track, and blocks of limestone or granite weighing ten tons or more will be strewn among the wreckage as if a careless child, finding something better to do elsewhere, has suddenly run off and left his toys.

Having destroyed, the diverted killer wave moves on, once more gathering speed as it passes the obstructing land mass and rolls back into open water. But woe to those survivors who think the danger is over and return to the shore from their place of refuge on high land. For another wave will follow, perhaps in fifteen or twenty minutes, perhaps in an hour. There is no way of knowing how many successive waves will strike at any particular spot, nor how much time will elapse between them. There is no way of guessing whether the next wave will be more or less destructive than the last. For above all else, tsunami is deceitful and unpredictable.

On a beautiful August morning in the late 1970's, the day the French tested their revolutionary new giant nuclear warhead, the *Victoire*, nothing had happened to disturb the monster within the earth. Pater Island, the tiniest and most remote outpost in French Polynesia, was a green dot in a sparkling sea, 2,400 miles south of Hawaii and 2,400 miles northeast of New Zealand. All preparations for the bomb test were complete. In concrete shelters, observers counted off the minutes. The slender palm trees rimming the test site swayed gently with the summer breeze. Far below Ground Zero, deep within the core of the earth, the awful forces were in balance. The monster slept, the ocean was quiet, and Pater Island was serene.

It was fourteen minutes and twenty seconds before Shot-Time. In the last hour, this bombproof chamber of steel and concrete had become a sinister place. At one time the Directeur du Bureau des Essais Atomique had considered it an engineering triumph, but now the grim, gray walls seemed to be closing in on him. As if to clear his head, he swallowed several times, hard.

Only fourteen minutes and twenty seconds remained before the most powerful nuclear warhead in the history of the world would be exploded here on Pater Island. Not merely a bigger and better hydrogen bomb, such as the People's Republic of China had tested last year. No, in this weapon, French physicists had created a fusion device with a destructive potential one and a half times greater than the super-bomb built only the preceding year by the Red Chinese. And *he,* the Directeur, had the key, the key that opened the line to the control point aboveground. He alone would unlock this line and give the order to detonate the bomb.

Victoire—the Directeur himself had given the mammoth explosive its proud name. Some of the more Francophobic journalists had been calling it "the Armageddon" and had refused to come to Pater Island to observe the test. But what did they know of the exhaustive preparations, since only sketchy bits of technical information had ever been released to the press? The safeguards were absolute—that's what the Directeur had emphasized repeatedly. In an effort to calm himself, he reviewed them now, like a man in silent prayer counting off the beads of a rosary.

Ground Zero, where the bomb was buried deep in the rock, was at one end of Pater Island. The underground observation post and the control point were at the other. Sixty kilometers separated the two areas. That distance was in itself such a safety factor that "Control" had been built aboveground. It was a steel building, the size of several large trailers joined together on the long side. It housed all the equipment for detonating the bomb and recording the results of the test, and was connected to the installations at Ground Zero and to the nearby underground observation post by a highly sophisticated system of electrical and television cables.

Numerous technicians were in that ground-level control center now. The Directeur could not remember hearing them express fears for their safety. In fact, several government officials had elected to view the test from Control rather than going underground with the other observers. So this vast chamber within the rock was probably an unnecessary precaution. And a costly one, the Directeur reflected. Sleeping quarters for two hundred, cooking facilities, plumbing complicated by the courtesy of providing separate comforts for the ladies—and that was all in addition to the closed circuit television, the seismographs, the maps and charts, and the telephone system that connected the bunker with Control. Ah, yes, it had come very dear.

As for the installation at Ground Zero . . . Again, they had been cautious in the extreme. The bomb was buried in a hole eight thousand feet deep. This vertically drilled shaft was lined with steel casing and the casing firmly cemented to the wall of the hole. Two years had been spent on this construction alone. Meanwhile, numerous calibration tests of small-yield exposives had been conducted, and the findings from each carefully studied by members of the Directeur's special "Containment Evaluation Panel."

The panel's unqualified approval had been required before the Bureau could even set a date for testing the *Victoire*. During this past week on Pater, the Directeur and his full advisory panel had reexamined every aspect

of the preparations. Yes, the *Victoire* was capable of
demolishing the biggest city in the world, but through
this kind of underground test her appalling potential was
to be measured without risk of deadly fallout.

When the bomb was detonated, the shock would crush
and melt the surrounding rock and, within a few hun-
dredths of a second, create an underground cavity hundreds of feet in diameter. But the radioactivity and the
unimaginable heat would be contained in the ground.
Victoire was trapped in the bowels of the earth, for the
vertical hole in which she was buried had been thoroughly "stemmed." From the bottom of the hole to the surface, the shaft was packed with sand, gravel, and
numerous poured concrete and plastic plugs. Any other
man-made holes created in the process of drilling or construction had also been carefully sealed.

The Directeur's thoughts were distracted by the approach of one of the Bureau's consultants, the graying,
soft-voiced Paul Clicquot. Clicquot always tried his patience. He had an absentminded but total dedication to
science and never considered the political side of things.
Today, he had irritated the Directeur even more than
usual by speaking during the early morning press conference about the efforts of the Australian and New
Zealand governments toward stopping this Pater Island
test. Today, of all days! And in the presence of scores of
journalists! Incredible.

"Yes, Paul," the Directeur said curtly, clasping well-
groomed hands over his bulging abdomen.

Looking up into the Directeur's florid face, meeting
his commanding gaze, Clicquot's faded blue eyes blinked
rapidly. "Jean," he said hesitantly, "please excuse me.
But I must ask you once more. Reconsider, I beg of you.
For an hour, the word 'Armageddon' has been sounding
in my head."

The Directeur was suffering from his own inexplica-
ble fears and said snappishly, "You have been listening
too much to those American journalists. The name is
Victoire."

Clicquot smiled tremulously. "I have to remind you,
Jean, that it was not American journalists who gave our
warhead the terrible name of Armageddon, it was our

old friend and colleague, Dr. Andrew Held. The news-paper people were simply quoting him."

"Aaahhh . . ." The Directeur's right hand clenched and struck irritably into the open palm of his left. "Here we are, back again to Andrew Held. You *know* all his objections to this test have been studied conscientiously."

"Yes, but we have considered only what is *probable*, not what is *possible*. Dr. Held is not a foolish man."

"He *was* a brilliant man," the Directeur replied sharply. "Even perhaps the most brilliant physicist of our time. But that was the old Dr. Held, of the fifties and sixties and early seventies . . . *Pardon*. I do not wish to offend you, Paul, but I have no time now for pointless debate. I must call together my advisory panel. However, I will say that since Dr. Held changed from the greatest weapons expert in the world to the loudest messiah of world disarmament, I *do* find him a foolish man."

"There is still time!" Cliquot's voice was husky with fear. "You have the authority to stop the test. You have the key!"

"You are crazy," the Directeur whispered angrily. "Lower your voice. And please, no more about Dr. Andrew Held!"

Andrew Held, whose name excited the Directeur to dyspeptic fury, was in his home on Phoenix Island, 5,000 miles to the north and east of Pater Island. He was moving about restlessly, frustrated by two events he could neither prevent nor control.

One was the imminent arrival of his second wife. Two hours hence, his skipper and general mechanic, Donald Campbell, would be steering the cruiser *Trident* into the bay below the house. Among the passengers would be a woman Dr. Held had not seen in almost two years, a woman he loved but was apprehensive about seeing, his second wife, Felicia Stowe Held. He wanted her here, he did not want her here. . . . It didn't matter which side of his ambivalent feelings dominated. There was nothing he could do either to hasten her arrival or to prevent it.

The second reason for this pointless pacing of the living room was the French bomb test on Pater Island. If his calculations were correct (and his calculations always were, at least when the issues were scientific) the device he called "Armageddon" would be detonated in the next five minutes, and he could do nothing to stop it.

He had tried, God knows he had tried, but his new position on nuclear arms had so startled his enemies and so confused his friends that neither group really listened. Could he blame them? Maybe not. For thirty years, he had been the country's most vocal advocate of armed preparedness. Then, at a point in his career when he was secure in an important post in the capital and the government had never been more supportive of his philosophy, he had become an earnest Isaiah, pleading loudly and publicly for total disarmament.

Insofar as it had been analyzed in newspapers and magazines, the metamorphosis from hawk to dove was based entirely on scientific reason. In truth, Andrew Held's thirty-year campaign to arm the United States with the deadliest weapons ever invented was rooted in strong emotions, and so was his sudden conversion to the ministry of disarmament.

During the long years when he preached that the only way to insure peace was to win the international arms race, his reasoning was riddled by obsessive fear and suspicion of Russia. The feeling went back to early childhood. As a little boy in Budapest, he had overheard the servants whisper about unimaginable horrors. Solemn conversations between his elders had ceased abruptly when he came into the room. Pogrom. He knew the bloody meaning of the word, for Hungary sheltered thousands of refugees from the east and north, and many of those who escaped told their frightening stories in the drawing room of his home. Though he was too young to visualize the exact shape of the terror, he recognized grief and fear, and he knew it had been caused by Russia.

When he was six, the fear came closer to home. The Galician fortress of Przemysl, defended by 100,000 men, mostly Hungarians, surrendered to the Russians after a long siege had exhausted all supplies. Among those defeated men was his uncle, his mother's brother.

Andrew had never before seen his mother cry. It shocked and distressed him, for adults, as he knew them (not counting the servants) were consistently dignified and regally calm. He had assumed that crying was only for little children. Trembling, he watched his mother sob uncontrollably against his father's shoulder. The terrible something that had befallen his uncle Laszlo and reduced his mother to a weeping stranger was all the fault of the Russians.

Even as a child, Andrew Held had *langelme,* a "flaming mind." When he emigrated to the United States as a man of twenty-seven, his genius was already fired by a passionate desire to explore the unknown territory of atomic physics. And it was a dramatic triumph when he stepped up to a blackboard at Princeton University in 1951 and scrawled out the breakthrough formula that cleared the way for the development of the hydrogen bomb, for he had been obsessed for ten or twelve years with the conviction that atomic fission was a preliminary step toward production of unlimited energy by means of fusion.

When the H-bomb became a reality, a feeling of tremendous relief swept over Andrew Held. Members of his family and their friends had been rendered destitute by what was called "communization" when Russia set up its puppet government in Hungary. For Andrew, as for most Hungarians, the word ever after meant "rape."

And reprisal, death, hunger, and poverty. These were the four horsemen who had galloped into Andrew Held's life carrying the Red flag. But now there was an all-powerful weapon to hold the horsemen at bay—and he, Andrew Held, had forged that weapon.

The Directeur had had enough. His peace of mind, indeed his very sanity, seemed to depend on isolating himself from his trembling consultant, Clicquot. He walked across the room to a corner unoccupied by any observers because the monitoring equipment faced the other way.

There would be shock waves, of course, as the bomb's unleashed energy moved outward through the layered rock of the ocean floor. Considering the fantastic power of the *Victoire,* seismic signals would undoubtedly be picked up as far from Pater Island as 1,000 to 1,500 miles. The bomb might even trigger a shallow earthquake, but on the basis of preliminary tests, they estimated it would hit somewhere between five and six on the Richter scale, and in the highly seismic Pacific that was a commonplace. There would be aftershocks, but they wouldn't last for more than twenty-four to thirty-six hours. As ecologists had charged, some sea life would perish in the immediate vicinity of Pater. That couldn't be helped. The matter of importance, the Directeur reminded himself, was the protection of human life.

The small native village on Pater had long since been removed and the people resettled at government expense on the island of Bagatea, one hundred miles away. At that distance, they would barely feel the motion of the earth. Here on Pater, observers would feel strong vibrations for a minute or two, nothing more.

"Like riding on a train," his press aide, Henri, had told the children at the press conference yesterday when they arrived by plane from Papeete. "The Directeur's children," Henri had pointed out. "Would he have brought his own children to Pater if it were not completely safe?"

At the thought of the children, the Directeur was gripped again by the sensation of being trapped. Perhaps it was the walls without windows and the low, heavily reinforced ceiling that aroused these irrational fears. They were so deep in the ground. The Directeur imagined he could actually feel the pressure of the rock above him. And he wasn't breathing naturally. The air wasn't real. It was a manufactured air-like substance and he could fill his lungs only with great effort. . . .

Ah, there they were, on the other side of the room, with their governess. Jean, Marie, and Toinette, ages six, eight, and ten. Cameramen from several countries had already photographed them, and Henri had the Bureau's staff photographer alerted to catch them precisely at Shot-Time. Clapping their hands with excitement, laughing together, something like that. . . . Automatically the Directeur looked again at his wristwatch. Twelve minutes, fifty seconds—and counting.

Chapter Two

AFTER a few minutes at his desk, Dr. Andrew Held threw down his pen, got to his feet, and walked across the room to the windows opening onto a deck above the water. His basset hounds, Mike and Lili, had been sleeping in the sun. They lifted their massive heads, following their master's movements with large, sorrowful eyes. Moments later, Dr. Held recrossed the room, looked down at what he had written, growled a wordless sound of displeasure, and then went back to the window. The dogs, disapproving of all this activity, dropped their heads onto their paws and closed their eyes.

Normally, Andrew Held did not pace the floor. He had known fear, anxiety, and frustration in abundance during his sixty years, but he had vented these feelings in other ways, usually by taking some sort of action. He scorned pacing as a form of brooding, a substitute for action but not its equivalent. Moreover, he could not walk without limping. It had been more than forty years since the accident that resulted in the amputation of one foot. Despite long practice with various combinations of steel, wood, and rubber that were devised to replace it, he had never entirely accepted the loss and never ceased resenting the limp that betrayed it. His thick black eyebrows came together as he glanced once more at his wristwatch. Toni, his gentle, passive first wife, in one of her rare efforts to express herself, had said he wasted his strength when he fought things he could not control. "If you can do nothing about it," she used to say, "you must forget it."

To give up graciously—that had been Toni's mode of life. But Andrew's way was different. Many a project beyond his control had ended up under his control simply because he had been too stubborn to give up an unequal fight. In one sense, his fight to prevent the testing of the *Victoire* had been a fight to preserve a small remote island called Pater. In the name of another island, called

13

Balegula. And in the name of an old friend, Aaron
Salinger, whom he had, in good conscience, mortally
wounded.

When the creature Andrew Held had fathered was exploded in a full-scale test, the peaceful little Pacific island
of Balegula, selected as the shot site, was transmuted into
a submarine crater 175 feet deep. This violent destruction had raised no doubts in his mind. Other than his
scientific genius, lack of self-doubt was Held's greatest
strength. But when his long-time friendship with another
brilliant physicist, Dr. Aaron Salinger, broke up in the
heavy seas of controversy, a curious depression took root
in his mind.

Aaron Salinger and Andrew Held had been students
together at Gottingen. Later they worked side by side on
the first experiments with atomic energy, but they came
to a philosophical crossroads. The path toward disarmament and test bans went one way, and that was Salinger's.
The path towards super-bombs and massive retaliation
went another, and that was Andrew Held's.

For a time, the balance of opinion was in Salinger's
favor. But then it shifted, and Salinger, suspected of having close ties with Communist Russia, was called before a
government hearing board investigating evidence that he
was now a security risk. Andrew Held had been openly
opposed to Salinger's views ever since Salinger had attempted to prevent development of the hydrogen bomb.
As a result, the government called Held as a witness.

It had been a bitter experience to testify against his
colleague, though it was Held's honest opinion that
Salinger should not be granted clearance, and under the
grueling questions of the security board, he had no choice
but to say so. Afterward, Salinger had resigned from
government service and virtually dropped out of sight.
His supporters, the entire fraternity of scientists who had
always opposed Andrew Held's ideas on philosophical
grounds, now became bitter personal enemies. Their hostility sapped his strength, but Dr. Held could have accepted even that if it hadn't been for the terrible effect
on Toni.

For Toni hadn't been a fighter. Every snub, every de-
nunciation had wounded her, and she had no instinct for
retaliation. When a trio of prominent scientists—old

friends, to Toni—deliberately ignored them at the annual conference in Denver, Toni's reaction was to retreat to their hotel room and remain there until Dr. Held packed their suitcases and telephoned to change plane reservations; they left two days before the conference ended. When a student organization called "Soldiers For Peace" marched around their home, shouting obscenities, waving banners, and trampling flower beds, Toni hid behind drawn shades and cried uncontrollably when Andrew Held opened a window so as to address the angry crowd.

He was able, within a few days, to have a high steel wire fence erected encircling their property, and the students were held back by its locked gates. Nevertheless, Toni kept heavy drapes across the windows and refused to leave the house. The demonstrations subsided, but even then he often saw her thin, pale face peering through a narrow crack in the curtains when he came home in the evening. The home she loved gradually became her prison. He suggested a boat cruise, but she refused tearfully. He asked her to come with him on a business trip, and her refusal verged on hysteria.

The doctors had explained her death in pathological terms, but Andrew Held knew that his testimony against Salinger had caused the fatal injury. True, an organic illness had eventually overtaken her, but by then she had already given up.

At noon one day he decided impulsively to leave the laboratory early, and on the way home he stopped at a fruit stand and bought a box of warm, fragrant peaches. The nurse he had hired to stay with Toni during the day opened the locked and bolted door, and he went quickly into the shadowy airless bedroom where Toni lay, small as a doll, in their ornately carved oak bedstead. He placed the box of fruit on the bedside table, sat down on the bed, and gently took her hand between his own.

They talked for an hour, all about their childhood in Budapest. Then she went to sleep, and Andrew Held, shaken by premonition, retreated to the empty living room, pulled back the drapes, and threw open the windows. Gusts of air laden with the green smell of freshly cut grass washed over his face. He dropped into a chair, covered his face with his hands, and wept, not only for the dying woman but for the little girl in the starched full-skirted dress and pinafore, with thick white stockings and shiny black pumps, and bright hair ribbons tied in bows at the ends of two long plaits of coppery brown hair. A little girl who often joined the games he played with her two older brothers in the beautiful park in Budapest, and whose favorite fruit had been peaches.

Chapter Three

THE Directeur's glance moved nervously around the room, seeking proof that, in spite of his turbulent emotions, he was not attracting attention. The four members of his advisory panel were close by, talking together quietly, awaiting his summons to their final conference before Shot-Time. The observers and journalists had arranged themselves in clusters so that everyone had a clear view of one of the six closed circuit television sets installed in a wide convex arc along one side of the bunker. An hour ago, the room had buzzed with their conversation. Now their voices were hushed, their attention focused on the big electric wall clock or the television screens.

For the third time in as many minutes, the Directeur raised his left arm, pushed back his immaculate shirt cuff, and squinted at the dial of his wristwatch.

Only twenty seconds had passed since he last checked the time....

Was it the presence of the children that disturbed him? The Directeur frowned and once more looked at his watch. Twelve minutes. He would make another call to Control....

With an occasional nod to a colleague, the Directeur pushed past the small groups that had been impeding his view of the telephonic communications system. He alone carried a key to the gray steel box containing the telephone. An ordinary metal box. And locked inside, a telephone that would have looked natural in the humblest atelier in Paris.

He stepped up to the box and withdrew the key from his coat pocket. All around him, conversation stopped. He could feel a hundred eyes fixed on his back. Were they wondering, as he was, if *this* time the report from Control would be reason to postpone the test? The weather might have changed? They might have detected a dysfunction in some part of their equipment? Something

wrong with the pipes or cables from the bomb emplace-
ment to the surface at Ground Zero?

Subduing a nervous tremor, the Directeur inserted the
key, opened the box, and dialed Control.

The response was quick and unqualified. Everything
was in readiness. All was well.

"Jean, Jean?"

The Directeur turned quickly, startled by a voice so
close to his ear.

Clicquot again! *Merde!* Well, he wasn't going to permit the little man's fears to infect him or even to be expressed. "Ah, yes, Paul. It won't be long now." He
cleared his throat, for it seemed to him that his voice was
unnaturally high. "About twelve minutes."

"Jean, I beg—"

Ignoring him, the Directeur nodded to the members of
his advisory panel. "Well, well, my dear colleagues. Shall
we retire for a minute or two?"

A private conference room, as small and plain as a
monk's cell, opened off the central chamber. With a determined step, the Directeur turned away from Clicquot
and walked into it. One by one, four men followed.

As the door closed, the Directeur caught a glimpse of
his consultant. Poor Clicquot! He was motionless, staring
at the locked telephone box as if the sight of it had
paralyzed him.

The final conference of the advisory panel was as brief
as the Directeur's last call to Control. All reports were
favorable. No adverse circumstances had arisen to delay
the test. In four minutes and twenty seconds the Directeur would make his last call to Control, and this call
would authorize the beginning of the countdown.

When the Directeur opened the door and stepped back
into the main chamber, the room was so quiet he could
hear the soft hum of electronic equipment. The gray steel
boxes were like living creatures, pulsing with electricity,
straining to receive messages due now in less time than a
man could light and smoke a cigarette. Silent and
watchful, the observers waited for the Directeur to speak.
Their faces, even those that were familiar, seemed
strangely distorted. The bluish artificial lighting stained
them all the same hue and cast dark shadows under their
eyes. He was expected to address them, just a few words

from the top official, the man with the key. . . . His fingers fumbled in his coat pocket and nervously clutched the chain to which the key was attached. He was about to speak when, without warning, his children broke through the crowd.

The two younger ones, Jean and Marie, ran to him and tugged excitedly at his sleeves. "How much longer, Papa?" That was six-year-old Jean. "Papa, how long do we have to wait?"

He freed his hands and awkwardly patted the tops of their heads, noticing that the eyes of many observers were focused solemnly on this little family group. "Not much longer, little ones. Here, look at my watch . . . Two minutes . . . You have had your pictures taken, eh? How many times—did you count?" Bending to their level, he gave Jean and Marie an absent-minded hug. Then he straightened up, the key on its heavy chain still dangling from his fingers. As he did so, he found himself directly in front of his eldest child, his firstborn, Toinette. She was standing absolutely still, looking into his face with wide and frightened eyes.

"Two minutes . . ." he repeated. He had never before noticed how much she resembled her mother. The fear he had been trying to deny swept through him like an electric shock. *My God!* the Directeur thought. *Could I have been wrong?*

Numbly, he looked again at his wristwatch. Almost a hundred men and women were waiting for him to speak. "Gentlemen. . . ." He swallowed and cleared his throat. "Gentlemen, if you will arrange yourselves so that you can all see the television screens. I am about to call—"

A man's voice, strident with terror, screamed, "No!" and Paul Clicquot burst from the group. Lunging at the Directeur, the gray and aging Clicquot grasped the hand that held the key.

Confused, little Jean looked from Clicquot's stricken face to his father. "Papa, Monsieur Henri said it would be like riding on a train . . ."

The Directeur jerked his hand free and secured the key in a tightly closed fist. "Clicquot!" he commanded. "For the love of God . . ."

The consultant's mouth was open, his tongue protruding slightly as if his face had frozen at the moment he screamed. Wordlessly, he struck again at the hand holding the key.

This time the Directeur's attention was diverted by his effort to push the children out of the way. With a grimace of surprise, he let the key drop to the floor.

Like a small demented hawk, Clicquot swooped onto his prey. Key clutched against his chest, he looked wildly around a room from which, clearly, there was no escape.

The Directeur stepped forward and placed a restraining hand on Clicquot's arm.

Clicquot cried hysterically, "No! Stop the test! It is not too late to stop the test!"

"There is *no reason*," the Directeur said hoarsely. "I cannot stop the test, I *will* not stop the test, because there is *no reason!*"

Some observers had retreated. Others moved forward, closing in around Clicquot. He fought, striking out with both hands.

"Henri!" the Directeur commanded. "Henri . . ."

His press aide stepped through the ring around Clicquot. The men holding Clicquot relinquished their captive and backed away. Henri was a young man. Clicquot was old and frail but fired by desperation. As they struggled, both Jean and Marie broke into frightened sobs.

"What are they doing that for, Papa?" Marie begged tearfully. "What's *wrong* with that man?"

Clicquot's resistance lasted less than a minute. Henri secured the key, handed it to the Directeur, and then, pinning the older man's arms behind his back, half lifted, half pushed him into the small side room where the Directeur had held his meeting with the advisory panel.

Just before the door closed, the Directeur noticed that a cut had been opened on Clicquot's forehead. Blood was streaming from it, clouding one of Clicquot's eyes and coursing down his cheek.

Shaking uncontrollably, the Directeur turned to the telephone box, inserted the key, signaled Control, and issued the order for countdown. Behind him, little Jean's shrill childish voice rose above the wordless murmuring of the observers. "You promised, Papa. Like riding a train, is it not?"

Chapter Four

WHEN Andrew Held renounced his platform as "Father of the H-Bomb" and began to campaign for disarmament, there was no visible reason for the change. He was respected in his field. Twenty years had passed since the terrible day he testified against Aaron Salinger. Held was now employed by the Pentagon at a generous salary. He was the friend of influential senators as well as key Administration figures. Even a respected U.S. Ambassador to the Soviet Union supported his views in public statements emphasizing that the United States must keep its defenses so strong that Russia would be deterred from yielding to the temptation of a first strike.

Rather to his astonishment—for physics professors do not ordinarily grow rich—Held was also wealthy. In addition to his own lucrative salary, he had inherited an unbelievable sum of money from a childless uncle in Europe who chose him as heir because he was himself even more fanatically anti-Soviet than his famous nephew.

To complete the picture of a man who is happy despite the burden of a brilliant mind, he was enjoying his second marriage.

Felicia Cabot Stowe was beautiful, wealthy, and a good many years younger than he. It was proof of his self-confidence that he had married her, for she was a passionate woman who could be too much of a challenge even for a man her own age. And she was not only as different from Toni as a bright color print is from a black and white negative, she was in most ways temperamentally different from Andrew Held.

Felicia was sophisticated, while Andrew was direct and even at times antisocial. She was soignée; he looked as if he had been caught in a high wind. She was a skillful manipulator in situations where he had a tendency to charge into like a mad bull. She was one of the two or three most photographed Washington hostesses, whereas theater parties and formal balls made Dr. Held restless.

Yet they had been drawn together as if everything that had happened to them separately had prepared them for recognizing each other now. They were each secure in their own abilities; they hadn't competed with each other nor even bothered to analyze their differences. From the beginning they had a strong common bond of mutual desire. Felicia excited him, and he was excited not only by her body and her need but by the discovery that he could fulfill such a passionate woman.

They did not have to go to bed together to decide whether they were in love. The knowledge overtook them one evening when she was caressing his hand, her head bent low. Suddenly, for no reason, he thought: Felicia Stowe, you're in love with me, and I, Andrew Held, am in love with you, and what, really, do we know about each other?

He said softly, to the top of her head, "Don't look up."

"Why not?"

He laughed. "Is that typical? Do you always ask 'why?' "

Her muffled voice replied, "Absolutely. I won't take an order, but I'll do anything you ask, if I understand your reason."

"All right, I'll tell you. A little scientific research. What color are my eyes?"

"Why, they're brown, of course."

"Now look up."

"Not yet," she said. "First, you tell me. What color are mine?"

"They're—" He stopped abruptly. He knew her eyes were bright and expressive, he knew they shone with amusement and grew soft with sympathy—but he didn't know their color. He chuckled. "All right, you win the first round. Now look up, please."

She lifted her head, looking directly into his penetrating blue eyes, and her own eyes, green as the sea, began to sparkle. "Oh, well," she laughed gaily. "I was right, in a way. You *think* brown. As for you, Dr. Held. Be advised, *I* think green."

Yes, they had married for love, even if they didn't know the color of each other's eyes. And because at the time he had been so supremely confident of himself, the demands of the marriage were easy to meet. Much later, after he had fled Washington and barricaded himself behind the lonely isolation of Phoenix Island, he was able to look back and see when the first small crack had opened in the fortress-like confidence that had been his strength for thirty years.

It was Toni's death. Long after, during bleak early morning hours, every incident that had hurt her surfaced in his sleepless mind as if it were a spirit message from long-dead Toni, and he wrestled with the thought that he himself, if only indirectly, had been the cause of her destruction. In daylight, the ghosts of guilt faded, and after some months, left him in peace even at night. And then, a year or so after he had married Felicia, when his sense of well-being had never been more secure, a series of events reopened the old wound, and in the raw emotion that was uncovered were planted doubts like dragon's teeth.

First was the report that the French were experimenting with a thermonuclear weapon infinitely more powerful than the hydrogen bomb they had tested in 1974. No public announcement was made, but the scientific community had its own grapevine, and it quivered with the message that this great super-super-bomb, to be called the *Victoire,* would carry a load unprecedented in nuclear history. Which meant it would be the greatest potential destroyer in history.

Andrew Held did not fear France as he did Russia. He had attended university with one of France's top physicists, and several consultants with their Bureau des Essais Atomique had been long-time friends of his. But gradually, a curious fear began to stir in his mind.

The United States had always refused to share its knowledge of atomic weapons. Thus French scientists were being forced to go through the long, hazardous series of experiments and tests which could, because of the smallest error, result in accidents, injuries, and failures. The *Victoire* was a warhead with unimaginable power. More and more often, Andrew Held found himself wondering—had Salinger been right? In harnessing nuclear energy, had they really created a keeper of peace and protector of mankind, or had they unleashed a monster? The *Victoire* would be tested on a remote island. Surely there would be safeguards. But he was troubled by the recurring memory of another island, beautiful little

Balegula, which a bomb—*his* bomb—had reduced to a useless hole.

To his growing concern about the French bomb was added bitter disillusionment with the President of the United States. Once Andrew Held had been proud of his contacts with the country's chief executives and his part in forming Administration policy. He had always liked to tell about the sunny afternoon in the summer of 1939 when he and another young Hungarian drove to the Long Island home of Albert Einstein and there, while they sipped tea, obtained the great man's signature on a letter to President Roosevelt. That letter, stating that the power of the atom could be used to make an incredibly powerful bomb, had been a moving force in the President's decision to authorize work on the first atomic bomb.

Ten years later, Andrew Held had sought and obtained President Truman's support in his battle to develop the H-bomb. When his whole program was threatened by a ban on testing, he had convinced President Kennedy that such a moratorium was idiotic, and the President had ordered that tests be resumed. Roosevelt, Truman, Eisenhower, Kennedy—they had all commanded his respect even when they did not share his views.

But at the time France began work on the *Victoire*, the President of the United States was a man Dr. Held disdained. Yet this man, arrogant beyond belief, pious and mealy-mouthed, had authority to order an all-out nuclear attack without concurrence of the Congress or the people. Andrew Held, knowing as few of his countrymen did how dreadful was the hydrogen bomb's potential, was sickened by the realization that such a weapon was under the control of a man so lacking in intellect or integrity.

The final step in his conversion was caused by India's announcement of an underground bomb test. He was incredulous. The United States, Russia, China, France—these were military powers. But India, where the million dollars New Delhi claimed as the cost of its first nuclear blast—obviously a preposterously low figure—could have fed 25,000 people for an entire year?

That night he was tormented by hideous dreams. Of his own visit to New Delhi, where child beggars looked up at him with large dark eyes and an old man had asked fifty rupees for the moribund body of his starving baby. Of Aaron Salinger, calmly smoking his pipe during his security hearing, while at the other end of the room a cold-eyed chairman of the board kept repeating, "I will ask you again, Dr. Held. In your opinion . . ." And of Toni, dying in a huge oak bed. . . . In the morning, his head cleared. He was exhausted, but he had finally arrived at a decision.

To Felicia, he said simply, "I've changed."

She raised her eyebrows. "Yes, Andy? I didn't know you ever bothered."

"Salinger was right after all."

Her green eyes lit up with a humorous twinkle. "Ah! Now at least I know the general area of discussion. Well, perhaps he was. But that incident is buried in the past."

Andrew Held's bushy eyebrows drew together in an inward-looking frown. "The incident, but not the issue. I have no influence in India. I do in France."

Felicia's attention had already turned to the engraved invitation in her hand. "Very good," she said absently, as she studied the elegant raised script. "Then you will come along willingly to dinner at the French Embassy."

Reluctantly he agreed, and during the dinner had suffered through the sort of conversation that by unwritten code skirted every subject of keen or immediate interest. But after dinner his restraint collapsed. In conversation with a French official, he began to talk about the Pater Island test and the more-than-super-bomb, the *Victoire*.

"I am concerned about my old friends in the Bureau des Essais Atomique. They are moving ahead too fast. You must tell the Directeur, or perhaps Paul Clicquot is the man, that it is one thing to invent a bomb, but it is another to develop adequate safeguards. When it comes to tests, they are more important than the bomb itself. I wish . . ."

"Yes? Dr. Held, you wish?"

Dr. Held answered sincerely, and in a louder voice than he intended. "I wish it were possible to protect you from error. I have done so much work in that regard. Yes, I think I could help."

A few days later he expressed the same thoughts to one of his associates in the Pentagon. "Wouldn't we be wise to cooperate with the French? After all, France is an ally, an important part of the anti-Soviet bloc. By helping them develop their potential for retaliation, we would be protecting ourselves."

The man looked at him curiously. "Are you suggesting that we divulge atomic secrets to a foreign country?"

Andrew Held shook his head impatiently. "To the *French,*" he said, scarcely noticing the inconsistency. "Before it is too late."

Almost a year later, Andrew Held learned during interrogation by the Chairman of the Atomic Energy Commission that his remarks to the French official, as well as his comments to his friend in the Pentagon, had been reported. The Chairman would not say by whom.

The message from the Directeur of France's Bureau des Essais Atomique had come as a complete surprise. The Bureau had been advised of Dr. Held's interest in their current project. Would he be willing to assist the government of France?

He had replied that in view of the United States policy on secrecy, he did not know how he would be able to do so. There followed a series of telephone calls, letters from France, and visits from officials at the embassy in Washington. In each stage of communication, the offer became more specific. At length, Andrew Held saw clearly what the future might hold.

He would, of course, have to resign his present position with the United States military. He and Felicia would move to Paris. In a country that was not restricted by treaties or test bans, he would be free to pursue his work with thermonuclear weapons far beyond the point where the United States had called a halt—in fact, without limit.

That was the moment Dr. Held recognized fully that a revolutionary change had taken place in his own philosophy. He *feared* what the French were doing. He feared what India was doing, small as their first effort might be, for now he saw all nuclear weapons as a threat to the survival of the human species. Thinking of the nature and power of the French bomb, he became agitated and blurted out, "It ought to be banned!"

Felicia smiled. "It? To what do you refer, my dear? Not connubial bliss, I hope sincerely."

He shook his head, overcome by the realization that after a battle that had engaged all his strength for all his adult life, he had joined the other side. He seldom disclosed his professional concerns to Felicia, and had said nothing at all about the developing contact with the French. So of course she could not know what he was talking about now.

She laughed softly, rose from her pink velvet chair, and came toward him with outstretched hands glittering with her favorite emerald and diamond rings. "Well, it's past midnight," she said, brushing his cheek lightly with the tip of her beautiful straight nose. "Let's go to bed, where, I assure you, nothing is banned."

That was the first night Andrew consciously tried to satisfy her. And perhaps because he was determined to satisfy her, he failed.

The first time Andrew Held recognized that his personal and confidential mail was being intercepted, he called himself a fool for not having anticipated it. He began to check his telephone. Just as he thought, the faint sound of the electronic device was distinct, once he listened for it. Somewhere in the building, a recording device was automatically tripped into action when he lifted the receiver.

There was undoubtedly a minute microphone planted somewhere in his private office. He did not bother to search for it. And when he stepped into a taxi and gave the driver an address, he felt insulted—but not surprised —that a blue car pulled out from the curb at the same time and followed the cab all the way down the parkway to his apartment on the river.

He knew of these things. Being spied on had been a reality of life when he was a young man in Hungary and power-hungry Admiral Horthy had established himself as dictator. "Surveillance" was too abstract a word for what he had experienced in Germany before he fled to England in 1933. Now it wasn't the indignities of his own early years that came back to him, it was the Aaron Salinger affair.

Salinger had been spied on. He had been followed by two or three Secret Service men, his letters read and copied, and his telephone conversations recorded, and he,

Andrew Held, had considered such affronts to his friend to be "necessary precautions." The memory was an ulcer on his conscience. The sound of the telephonic bug, the discovery that his private secretary was sending memos to the FBI, logging the identity and length of stay of every visitor to his office—these things did not infuriate him, they made him feel guilty.

After several weeks, Felicia tried to get beneath his brooding and his impotence. She moved into his bed, and touching him, whispered, "Tell me what's happening."

Until this whole French affair had blown up, the pressure of her hand had been enough to arouse him. She had always been the aggressor. That in itself had excited him. Now the insecurity he was feeling in relation to his work seemed to have imbedded itself in his groin.

"What's happening . . ." Why, everything he had believed in had been turned inside out. He hardly understood it himself, and as for telling Felicia about the FBI and the Secret Service men and his offer from the Bureau des Essais Atomique—he was totally incapable of communicating those sorts of things to a woman who was his wife.

"What's happening . . ." Felicia's hand was stroking him gently, and all he could think of was that the last time he had tried to respond, he had failed dismally. Her hand was not exciting him, it was arousing fear. . . .

With a flash of cruelty as foreign to him as self-doubt, he said, "When I want you, I will come to your bed."

For an instant, Felicia lay rigid at his side. Then she stepped out of his bed and returned to her own. Already ashamed, Andrew Held thought: Toni would be crying. Felicia will not.

He was right. Across the dark gap between their beds, Felicia's voice was cool and steady. "When you do, *if* you do, *I* will decide whether *I* want *you*."

A moment later, he heard her slide out of bed, walk barefooted to the bedroom door, and go out. As the door clicked shut behind her, he restrained his immediate impulse to follow and apologize. Felicia was angry, and in anger she would be unyielding. She was not the kind to feel hurt. He doubted that she knew how to cry; how pointless therefore to offer to comfort her! He turned over and closed his eyes, determined to sleep.

In the living room, Felicia lighted a small crystal lamp and proceeded to the sideboard. She was trembling with anger. She stood at the sideboard, both hands gripping the edge of the serving area as if she were about to push it through the wall, her eyes fixed in a furious and sightless stare on the row of cut-glass decanters.

She stood that way until her hands ached and the cold air began to settle around her bare feet. She would pack up, leave, tonight . . . No, that was childish. She would stay, and take a sleeping pill . . . Damn it, no, that was weak and foolish. She disdained people who relied on pills. She would pour herself a drink.

She released her grip on the sideboard and, with a curious stab of panic, realized that anger was draining out of her. Stay angry, she told herself, it feels better than falling apart.

Shivering, she picked up a decanter of cognac, removed the heavy stopper, and poured a generous amount into a cocktail glass. Have a drink, she whispered, have a good stiff drink . . . She picked up the glass, lifted it partway to her mouth, and stopped.

Anger had deserted her, and she felt bare. She looked blankly at the glass in her hand. The shadowy room was still except for the rhythmic ticking of the marble mantel clock; the clock's faint voice seemed to echo the beat of her own pulse. She looked pleadingly at the hand that held the drink, waiting for it to act independently and lift the glass to her lips. For long, trembling seconds, the hand was motionless, and then it moved, carefully returning the untouched glass to the sideboard.

She turned, dropped into the nearest chair, and covered her face with her hands. The fingers were cold compared with the tears that welled up, spilled through them, and flooded her cheeks, tears she could not control and did not bother to wipe away.

Chapter Five

On Pater Island, the moment of Victory had come. The countdown ended, the signal was given, and in the shaft 8,000 feet below the surface the most powerful nuclear device in the world was detonated by the pressure of a man's forefinger on a lever no bigger than his thumb.

In the bombproof chamber of concrete and steel, two hundred observers stared fixedly at the television screens. The only voice was that of six-year-old Jean, asking, "Now, Papa?" while a photographer from the Associated Press took his picture.

It happened almost instantly. At precisely ten in the morning in the time zone for French Polynesia, the great bomb released its energy. Raised to a temperature of several million degrees, its contents vaporized. A tenth of a millionth of a second had passed . . .

Then the first shock, as the pulse of the bomb moved outward and downward from the unimaginably hot high-pressure region. The earth melted. A cavity formed and expanded. Four-tenths of a second had gone by . . . And instantly everyone knew that something had gone horribly wrong.

The fury of the explosion rumbled from one end of Pater Island to the other, shattering solid rock, heaving up the overlying earth in a series of monstrous regurgitations. Shocks gripped the concrete vault of the observation post, crushed it, spewing out the dismembered bunker in a hot black vomit that, moments later, sank down into the widening crater where Pater Island had been.

In the last millisecond, a child screamed, a little girl sobbed "Papa!" The Directeur of the Bureau des Essais Atomique clutched his abdomen and reached for the telephone to Control. The press aide Henri stared blindly at the seismograph, his face ashen and both hands covering his mouth. The observers' faces froze into death masks as they watched television sets record the lethal blackness of disaster.

Locked into the anteroom by order of the Directeur,

Paul Clicquot dropped to his knees. He had no time even to weep.

The floor trembled and cracked, the walls imploded. Observers were thrown into the center of the room and crushed under the battery of electronic devices.

In the last fraction of a second before the underground observation post exploded into unidentifiable fragments of steel and concrete and human flesh, the Directeur saw the face of his firstborn, the solemn, wide-eyed Toinette, and he thought he was looking at her mother.

It would be contained, the scientists had said. The chimney would be plugged. There would be some vibration, some minor upheaval of the land at Ground Zero, perhaps a few landslides along the coast, no more. They were brilliant men, but their calculations had been too small for the unleashed power of the super-bomb.

The terrible force of the *Victoire* penetrated downward as well as laterally, breaking through all structures man had built to control it. Not as a victory but as the Armageddon that Andrew Held had predicted, it bit deeply into the shallow crust of the earth, striking down through the ocean floor to invade the underlying mantle. And there, along the dangerously seismic region of the Pacific rim, the man-made bomb opened the gate and freed the monster inside the earth.

All along the network of faults that scar the ocean floor, the explosive force found weaknesses. The equilibrium between layers of the earth was jolted, the balance between opposing pressures was lost. The earth's crust contracted violently, crinkled, and ruptured. Old cracks widened, and the earth was ripped apart as new wounds opened. Through the torn and crumpled surface, the molten content of the earth surged upward to create new land masses less than a mile from where the old land mass, the island called Pater, had been.

In Japan, in Guam, in Alaska, in Peru, the ground shook, and at two dozen stations around the Pacific rim the needles of the seismographs jerked spasmodically. Their ordinary course along the cylinder was an even, barely wavy line. As the first shock arrived, the line changed abruptly into a frenetic scribble of acute angles, sharp peaks, and sudden precipitous drops.

Earthquake!

For hundreds of miles around Pater, great blocks of the ocean floor heaved upwards ten to twelve feet, and other blocks as suddenly dropped down. Along the shores of islands near Pater, rocky cliffs were shattered, and the land for miles up and down the coastlines sheared off and fell into the sea. For nine minutes, a vast area of the South Pacific groaned and cracked with the spasms of a mammoth quake. Then, as if the monster's anger had been exhausted, the earthquake subsided . . . but her offspring, the aftershocks and the tidal waves, now came alive. Her life was short. Theirs were just beginning.

From birth to death, tsunami confuses its prey. Tsunami's deadliest deceit is to give warning in such a way that few people recognize the sign. When the threat to life and property is greatest, the killer wave prepares to strike not by rushing up onto shore but by pulling back. As if all the water along the coast were being sucked back into the ocean, the tide recedes slowly and steadily. When it reaches the normal low tide level, it inexorably continues its menacing retreat, until reefs are uncovered and fish flap wildly on rocks never before exposed.

This quiet but steady pullback may continue for ten, fifteen, or twenty minutes. Then the great wave reverses its course and rolls back toward the land at twenty to thirty miles an hour, a ferocious and implacable mountain of water. The only protection against tsunami's deadly ruse is to recognize the terrible meaning of the pullback. The retreat of the water is a ten- to twenty-minute warning. Ignore it, misunderstand it, and you are lost. The only defense against the killer wave is escape to high land. When you can see the mountain of water coming, it is already too late.

Where will tsunami strike? When will tsunami strike? How hard will tsunami strike? . . . Seismologists study tsunami behavior as clinical psychologists analyze the pathology of a demented child. They cannot avert his furious outbreaks; no oceanographic device for preventing tsunami has ever been invented. But they can observe the nature of his tantrums and, based on their severity, estimate how long it will be before they run their course. Above all, their understanding of the child's dementia makes it possible to warn those near him that it is time to get out of the way.

In essence, this is the purpose of the Tsunami Warning System, the TWS, a network of seismograph and tidal stations all over the Pacific with headquarters in Honolulu. TWS technicians cannot prevent earthquakes, nor stem volcanic eruptions, nor limit the size of nuclear devices to be exploded on test sites in the Pacific. But with seismographs and teletypes, and tide gauges so sophisticated they are capable of making their own telephone calls, they can spot the first evidence of a disaster, natural or man-made, within seconds of its happening. Within thirty minutes to an hour, they can ascertain the magnitude of the shock and identify the epicenter. And as they piece together reports from warning stations all over the Pacific, they know whether the shock of the disaster has awakened the monster within the earth and whether, as a result of his terrible wrath, tsunami is on the move.

Near the epicenter, it may already be too late. Tsunami's birth often comes too fast to send warnings to settlements within two hundred miles of its birthplace. Even at greater distances, no warning system, not even the new and improved TWS with its thirty-three seismograph stations and fifty tide stations, can move docks and schools and warehouses and hospitals out of the path of the killer wave.

Tsunami's first target will be Bagatea, only 100 miles north of Pater. Next it will strike Tolui, 150 miles beyond Bagatea. From there, the waves will rush on to Hawaii, then curve across the open sea toward the vulnerable coastline bordering the cracked and deformed submarine floor of the Aleutian trench.

It will be ten or eleven hours before the first of the killer waves can travel from Pater Island to the coast of North America. The first victims at the end of this long journey will be offshore islands, such as the Outer Islands of Washington State and British Columbia, a chain of remote islands reminding us that, millions of years ago, a mountain range stretched out across the water we now call the North Pacific. At the far end of the chain, the most remote of the Outer Islands, lies Phoenix Island . . .

It was ten-fifteen A.M. in the zone where the black remains of Pater Island protruded grotesquely through a turbulent sea. Only fifteen minutes since Shot-Time. It

was twelve-fifteen P.M. on Phoenix Island, where Andrew Held, a genius in the invention of mechanical devices that could blow up the world, was glowering at a
simple little contraption called a radio.

No matter what he did to it, it wouldn't work until
Donald Campbell arrived with the mail, which, Dr. Held
expected, would contain the replacement part necessary
to repair it. Another frustration in a day that was crushing him with things he could do nothing about. He wanted
to listen to the news, he *demanded* of the defective radio
that it give up its waywardness and broadcast the news.
If Toni were alive, she would be urging him to accept
what he was powerless to change. But his second wife,
Felicia . . . ah! Felicia was a different sort. Felicia scorned
passive attitudes, she accepted *nothing*.

Andrew shook his head fiercely, as if he could clear
it of these disturbingly persistent reflections. He would be
courteous, even friendly, when she arrived, but also . . .
well . . . a little detached. He did not even know her reason for coming. Murmuring his favorite Hungarian ex-
pletive, Dr. Held walked unevenly down the hall. He
would ask Mary, his cook, to make a fresh pot of coffee.
The two basset hounds were at his heels, ever loyal to
someone headed for the kitchen.

When the alarm sounded at Tsunami Warning System
headquarters, Ewa Beach, Hawaii, was in peaceful midmorning slumber. Inside the brick rectangle housing the
seismic recording center and the communications department, a battery of seismic recorders was producing the
nearly smooth lines that showed all was well. The two
men in the office were sitting quietly, at ease, when the
alarm went off.

Startled, the younger man muttered, "Holy Christ!" and
ran across the room to the bank of seismographs. His
veteran partner followed at a normal pace, unruffled by
the familiar sound of trouble.

The message on two of the seismographs was unmis-
takable. Like polite, well-mannered people who suddenly start waving their arms, the needles were jerking errat-
ically from side to side.

The older man studied the machines with the quick
and knowing eye of the expert. There had been an earthquake—an earthquake of terrifying proportions. The

worst was probably over. The spasms of aftershock might go on for hours, even days. But the machines had not told him precisely where the initial quake had occurred, and this he had to know as quickly as possible. If the earthquake had triggered a tsunami, the waves would already be on the way. Pinpointing the epicenter was essential to calculating the wave's travel time across the Pacific and predicting arrival time at any given coastal point.

He recognized the bitter fact that *if* a tsunami had been unleashed by the convulsions of the quake, it would have started on its disastrous course even before the initial quake subsided. That meant settlements near the epicenter would undoubtedly be struck by waves before they could receive a warning. Beyond the area of such immediate disaster, there was hope. Figuring 500 to 600 miles an hour in open water . . . The veteran seismographer's thick fingers were swift and agile as they touched the teletype keys. "REQUEST IMMEDIATE READINGS FROM ALL STATIONS . . ."

The race was on.

Chapter Six

DR. Andrew Held went out onto the sundeck overhanging the water, where his cook, Mary, had placed a lunch of dark rye bread and strong cheese on a table next to his lounge chair. His bushy eyebrows drew together as he faced the open sunlight, and for a moment his blue eyes teared. He disdained dark glasses; they altered color values. He also scorned the lotions and unguents with which civilized people anoint themselves before going out into the sun. He was a dedicated sunbather—his compact, heavily muscled body was evenly tanned, head to toe— but he went about it methodically. X minutes per day, calculated by the exact number of days he had been exposed to the sun. He had never been sunburned.

He sat down, and the two hounds, Mike and Lili, took up positions at a respectful distance, waiting for the signal to come forward for the last bits on the plate.

Dr. Held ate slowly, savoring the simple food. Now that his eyes had adjusted to the light, they moved restlessly along the horizon, trying to project onto its smooth unbroken line the image of the cruiser *Trident* on her way back from Wolf Island. She wasn't due for two hours, but Dr. Held had never waited patiently for anything he really wanted. The *Trident* was carrying the part he needed to repair the radio, and he wanted it urgently. In fact, he had been frustrated to the point of frenzy by his inability to pick up news broadcasts covering the bomb test on Pater Island. And yes, the *Trident* was also bringing Felicia.

Did he *want* Felicia? In one sense, yes, and desperately. For all his determination to shut her out of his mind, he had yearned for her repeatedly over the past two years, but always as she had been during the first years of their marriage. Restless, demanding, passionate. When he saw her body, it was as it had been created for him, the beautiful long thighs opening to receive, the back arched slightly as she drew his head down to her breasts and whispered, "Gently, lick me gently . . ."

Often another scene came to mind and, like a terrible avenging angel, drove out the first. The scene in the darkened bedroom when Felicia had come to his bed and he sent her away. "When I want you, *I* will come to *you.*" How could he have rejected her so cruelly? And above all, how could he have reassured his conscience with the thought that Felicia would not suffer as Toni would have!

After that night, the structure of Andrew Held's life was shaken to its foundations by a series of events occurring in such rapid succession that, later, everything seemed to have happened simultaneously.

First, he was summoned to the White House, where a Presidential aide issued a warning. "We have no reason to doubt your loyalty, Dr. Held. But I would like to remind you that a close association with any foreign power could be misinterpreted."

With difficulty, Dr. Held controlled his indignation. "I am a scientist, Mr. Kreuzner. I have what you call 'close association' with physicists all over the world. But I am an American. When I became a citizen in 1941, I swore to protect and defend the United States. For me, this was and is and always will be my primary obligation."

The aide was a lean young man, tall and athletic, with a military haircut and cold blue eyes which did not match his smile. "We have given you the highest security clearance. We trust you."

Andrew Held's indignation hardened into anger. "What do you mean, sir, when you say 'we'? Do you speak of yourself and the President of the United States, or yourself and God? You say, *'We* trust you.' Why, then, the wiretapping? And enlisting my secretary in your spying, and the two Secret Service agents who follow me wherever I go?"

The young man's condescending smile dropped from his face. "I have no knowledge of such things," he said smoothly. "Be assured that we—" As if the regal pronoun had burned his tongue, he stopped abruptly. When he began again, the smile was once more applied to his face. "Remember these two things. Policy may be determined by vote of the entire Atomic Energy Commission, but ultimately it must be approved or disapproved by the President. The President, on his own authority, without concordance of any agency or commission, can order an all-out attack with any or all nuclear weapons in our possession. Secondly, remember that anyone who divulges military secrets to a foreign power is violating the security of this country, and *that* is called *treason*."

With that, the aide turned his back and pressed a buzzer on his desk. The office door opened, and a Secret Service agent with a noncommittal expression appeared, to usher Dr. Held from the office to the White House door. There, a second agent accompanied him all the way through the gates to a taxi.

The command performance at the White House embittered him. An interrogation at the Pentagon the next day did even more to change the course of his life. The military men did not cover their threats with smiles. They gave him chapter and verse, including reports from the FBI in Washington and from a CIA man in Paris. Whatever indecision still clouded his understanding of his new position was suddenly cleared away. His role was crystallized.

He was by now unalterably opposed to the use or further development of thermonuclear devices. It was his duty as a loyal citizen to say so. That France was developing a super-bomb deadlier than the hydrogen bomb was his immediate concern. He could not accept the French Bureau's offer. But he was obviously respected by the French. He would use all his influence, and as much technical data as he dared, to persuade them that the weapon they were developing was potentially disastrous and that such a monstrous invention should never be tested.

For the world as a whole—for scientists, politicians, heads of state—he would write a book justifying his new position. He would call it *The Noble Truth*.

He wrote the book at home, most of it late at night after Felicia had gone to bed. They slept in separate rooms now. More and more Felicia was going out alone to various dinners and benefit balls, the nature of which he did not remember even when she bothered to tell him. At the same time, he wrote letters to France, first to the Directeur of the Bureau des Essais Atomique, and then to his old friend Paul Clicquot.

They replied courteously but questioned his arguments,

primarily on the grounds that he had not included enough specific technological data to support them. Of course, if he would accept a post with the Bureau and thus assist the republic of France . . .

His sense of urgency grew. Now there were reports that an island in French Polynesia had been selected for the first test of the super-bomb. Andrew Held began to address his pleas to French newspapers and scientific journals. This effort brought a letter from the Bureau's Director, asking that he fly to Paris so that they could talk personally.

By then he had finished his book and voluntarily submitted it to the Pentagon's public information officer. The day after the French asked him to fly to Paris, the Pentagon verdict was rendered, not by the PIO but by the General himself.

His manuscript, *The Noble Truth,* expounded views contrary to United States policy. No clearance. However, in consideration for the long hours he had spent writing it, the book would be purchased by the government and kept on file.

"And if I submit my manuscript to a publisher?"

"You would be violating a Defense Department directive. If the book were accepted for publication, you would be dismissed."

Dr. Held returned to his office immediately. There he dictated a formal letter of resignation. When he got home that evening, he found a note from Felicia. She would be out until quite late—a meeting of the program committee for an important charity ball.

He felt unaccountably relieved. He was taking a night flight to the Pacific Coast, for he was to be the main speaker at a conference in Vancouver, British Columbia. He packed quickly and left for the airport by taxi, much earlier than was necessary.

After the conference, a Canadian physicist, Dr. Harvey Stapleton, approached him. He was a quiet man with soft brown eyes, large hands and feet, and a benign smile.

"Dr. Held, you have been under considerable strain. I have a boat. Nothing elegant, but she's seaworthy. I'm about to take her on a cruise through the Outer Islands. Will you come along?"

A cruise on a comfortable boat? Once Dr. Held would

have rejected the suggestion as frivolous, compared to the serious work it would force him to postpone. But everything was changing now. His former convictions lay around him in a hundred jagged pieces. A new Dr. Held was emerging painfully from the wreckage, but somehow in struggling to find himself, he was losing Felicia . . . A cruise on a boat? Why not? For the moment, he could not bear to go back to Washington and the big apartment overlooking the river, and Felicia.

They cruised west and a little south of Vancouver, moving at a leisurely pace through the blue waters of the Pacific Ocean on to the archipelago of small islands known simply as "the Outer Islands." Evenings, after a sun-filled day of cruising, they dropped anchor offshore or in the shelter of a narrow bay. Held slept as deeply as he had when he was a boy in Hungary. At low tide, they went ashore in the dinghy and picked oysters off the rocks. In the afternoon, they fished for cod and snapper, drifting the length of rocky reefs where seagulls, cormorants, and puffins perched and nested, and hair seal and sea otter slid into the water at their approach.

After four or five days, the sunshine and the peace had invaded Held's body like a sedative. But his mind seemed to be tuned to the twinkling brilliance of the water, for it was quivering with an impossible dream.

"You said many of the smaller islands are owned privately?"

"Yes, indeed. In fact, a neighbor of mine bought an island two or three years ago. One of the Canadian islands . . . By the way, we're in the United States now." With a sweeping gesture, he included all the bright water around them and the three islands nearest to them. "Forgot to mention it."

"Over there?" Dr. Held asked, pointing due east.

Stapleton nodded. "That land mass you can just barely see along the horizon, that's the American mainland. Coast of the state of Washington. Good many islands between here and there." Stapleton sat up straight. "See here, Andrew. You sound quite serious. Do you really want to buy something? Leave Foggy Bottom forever, chuck the whole thing?"

Andrew Held's voice was bitter. "I cannot. I am only dreaming."

"Nevertheless . . ." His friend swiveled around and

looked back thoughtfully in the direction of Canada. "Nevertheless," he repeated, "let's take a look." He reached for the detailed chart he had followed in navigating their course south from British Columbia. "See this, here? Furness, isn't it? F-U-R-N-E-S-S. My friend who owns an island to the north of it tells me it's for sale. Estate matter. There was a small farm on it, maybe forty years ago, but when the farmer died his widow left the place. It's terribly isolated. Not one of the heirs has ever wanted to use it. Second generation of heirs trying to get rid of it now . . ." He put down the chart and looked at Andrew with a boyish smile on his face. "It's off course, really a far place, but we'll do it, on the way back to Vancouver."

To reach the island identified on the chart as "Furness," they crossed a seemingly endless stretch of open water. Looking back toward the American mainland, the irregular outlines of a hundred land masses became dimmer and dimmer as they proceeded out to sea. The Outer Islands had vanished over the horizon when, to the west, the profile of a single island was suddenly outlined against the sky.

"There she is!" Stapleton cried. "Curious shape, don't you think?"

Andrew Held agreed. He had a feeling that the island had just emerged from the sea and at any moment might vanish beneath the surface. At one end, cliffs rose 200 feet above the water and were crowned by heavy forest. This high section sloped down to a plateau only thirty or forty feet above sea level and then rose again on the left to a lesser hill, gently rounded and covered with pine, alder, and madrona. Andrew thought of a crouching animal, haunches high, head resting on its paws.

"Furness," he mused. "If I owned this island, I could call it Phoenix. Phoenix, the resurrection. Phoenix, rising not from ashes but from the sea."

His friend nodded in understanding. "We all dream of one day owning an island. The island mystique. But this one, so far from everything? What would you find here?"

Without hesitation, Andrew Held answered. "Escape, my friend. And in escape I would find peace."

Chapter Seven

On his return from Vancouver, Andrew Held had his first bitter argument with Felicia.

He told her he had resigned, and she called him a headstrong fool. He tried to explain why he had reversed his stand on nuclear weapons, and she said he could have done it quietly and kept his job. When he revealed the indignities of "surveillance" which he had borne patiently for many months, she criticized him for having committed the acts that brought it about.

"You confided your wonderful idealistic thoughts to a French official at a party, and you were overheard!" She laughed derisively. "Even *you* should know that in Washington you don't discuss ideas at a social function!"

Andrew looked at her for several seconds before he could speak. He had thought she was so beautiful. Dark auburn hair, swept up into an elaborate but completely suitable hairstyle, rather like the coiffure of a mid-Eastern princess. High cheekbones, a straight, perfectly proportioned nose, wide-set green eyes with heavily painted lashes, and a mouth in which the upper lip curled a little and the lower lip was a little fuller than the upper. He thought, She *is* beautiful, perhaps too perfectly beautiful. If you drew a line down the center, both sides of her face would be exactly the same. She looks lacquered . . .

"Well?" Felicia's voice was sharp. "Now that you have resigned, what do you intend to do? Run away to Paris, work for the French?"

He answered solemnly, "No, though I still have that option."

"You realize that I would not go with you?"

"To be honest, I had not thought about it. No, I am sure you would not."

"Ah . . ." Her green eyes blazed. "But you *have* thought about what to do with this book of yours?"

"Yes," Held replied wearily. "I have, indeed. Now that I have resigned from the government, I am a free agent.

The publication of my book is an issue that lies between me and a publisher. The Pentagon kept my manuscript, but I have a carbon copy. I will go to New York in the morning."

Felicia turned angrily and walked away. The heavy green satin of her hostess coat made a whispering sound as she crossed the thick white carpet. At the sideboard, she dropped two ice cubes into a crystal highball glass and poured vodka over the ice. "Hemlock, anyone?" she asked over her shoulder. "May I serve you, Dr. Held?"

"Thank you, no."

She turned around, lifting her glass in a toast. "Here's to the New Evangelism. Viva Jeane Dixon, and Isaiah, not to mention Cassandra. Well, I have certain modest talents as a prophet, and I hereby foretell, with apologies to Genevieve Tabouis, et al., that the only way your so-called campaign for peace will get a majority vote is if you retreat to a desert island, alone."

Island . . . Her sarcasm didn't divert him from the picture that word evoked. Furness, which he would rename, calling it Phoenix . . . "Not a desert island," he said thoughtfully. "An island of cliffs, and a long narrow bay. Dark green evergreens, seagulls screaming—"

"My God," Felicia breathed, taking another sip of chilled vodka. "You sound serious. Where is this island? Where the waters of the farthest ocean fall over the edge of the earth?"

"Off the coast of British Columbia, northwest from the coast of Washington State. I saw it when I went to the Vancouver conference."

"Who lives there?"

"No one."

"A house?"

"I would build one."

Suddenly she was as serious as he. She looked at him thoughtfully, then set her empty glass on the sideboard and, turning very slowly, surveyed the elegant room. When her glance came around to her husband, she shook her head.

"I couldn't, Andy. *This* is what I want. This is where you found me, this is where I belong. *I* have not changed. If sometime, somehow, you were to make this insane dream come true and move to your island in the Pacific, you know I could not come with you. I would not survive. I would not *want* to survive."

Andrew said gently, "It is only a dream, Felicia. Now, I am very tired, and I am going to catch the ten o'clock shuttle to New York tomorrow. I'll say good night . . ." As he walked past her, he had an impulse to embrace her and ask her to come to his bed. But the day had exhausted him. He would be no good. So he patted her perfectly smooth cheek and, limping badly, went off to his separate room.

In New York, the editor expressed enthusiasm and promised a decision in two weeks. Dr. Held flew back to Washington, taxied to his office, and there, without a thought for electronic monitors or telephone bugs, called his travel agent and made arrangements for a flight to France.

Felicia's weapon was sarcasm. "Are you naïve or just plain stubborn? Why do you refuse to believe they distrust you? Just because you have not violated the trust? And they are right, you know. If you were not considering the French offer, you would not be making a trip to Paris."

"I'm going to Paris only to try once more, in a different way this time, to persuade their Bureau that they should stop work on this terrible bomb. The *Victoire,* they are calling it now. I think a better name would be Armageddon."

"The French want your brains, not your principles." She stopped abruptly. "Did you say you called your travel agent from your office?"

Dr. Held said absently, "What? Oh, yes. Yes, why not?"

"Dear God," Felicia moaned. "You *are* stubborn, as well as naïve. Be prepared."

A few days later, when he was waiting at Dulles airport for his plane to Paris, her words came back to him in a rush.

At the gate, the regular security guard examined his attaché case and topcoat with such thoroughness that the people behind him demanded that he step aside and let them take their turn. Satisfied at last, the guard closed his case, returned it and his topcoat, and signaled to someone who had apparently been waiting in an unlighted corner of the security area.

A middle-aged man in business suit, white shirt, and dark tie stepped out of the shadows and approached them. He was carrying the suitcase Dr. Held had deposited earlier at the ticket counter to be checked through to Paris. The noncommittal expression, the conservative dress, the athletic physique, and, above all, the steady unsmiling eyes—Andrew Held knew instantly that the man was a Secret Service agent.

"Would you mind coming with me?" the man asked politely, somehow leaving no alternative for the person who *would* mind, and mind very much.

Dr. Held looked at his watch and frowned impatiently. "The plane leaves in twenty minutes."

The agent's answer was to place a hand under Dr. Held's elbow and guide him firmly across the lobby to a door marked "Private."

The door opened at his knock, and more or less propelled by the elbow, Dr. Held went in.

It was a small room, brightly illuminated by a battery of fluorescent ceiling lights. The furnishings were coldly clinical—three or four plain chairs, a glass cabinet containing medical instruments, a washbasin and paper towel rack, a standing lamp with adjustable gooseneck. And in the center of the room, a stainless steel examination table, covered by a two-foot-wide strip of white paper.

At the far side of the room a door opened, admitting a young man in starched white jacket and white trousers. "I am Dr. Youngman," he said pleasantly. "Dr. Held, would you be kind enough to remove your clothing."

For several seconds, Dr. Held was immobilized by disbelief. He looked at his wristwatch and the figures meant nothing to him. All at once his perceptions came into focus. His accent, usually faint, became more pronounced in anger, but his voice was level and cold. "I had not anticipated the pleasure of your acquaintance, Dr. Youngman, and have not allowed time for it. My plane leaves in less than twenty minutes. I have no intention of taking off my clothes."

He turned to the Secret Service agent. "This is a democracy, I believe? If you have a warrant, I will comply. If not, I expect you to escort me to the boarding area, along with the luggage you had no right to take from the airline."

The agent spoke without emotion. "I do not have a

warrant, but I can easily get one. If you refuse to submit to a body search, I will hold you here until I do."

"Body search . . ." Held turned back to the doctor.

The doctor had curly red hair, pale lashes over pale blue eyes, and white skin stippled with large orange freckles. He spoke in a disconnected way, as if determination to do his job were pushing the sentences out of his mouth in random-size chunks. "I believe that through . . . your, uh, cooperation that . . . we can get you . . . onto your plane . . . on time." His face was flushed with the effort. "If we don't find . . . anything, that is."

Again, the imperial "we." Dr. Held exploded. *"We?* You and this insolent Gestapo agent? You and the Pentagon? Or you and God?" At that point, perversely, Dr. Held decided that nothing, not even a body search, would prevent him from keeping his appointment in Paris. In furious silence, he took off his clothes.

The young doctor was not at home in a dialogue, but when it came to physical examination, he yielded to none. Every orifice was a possible hiding place.

He started with the head. He probed inside the ears, ran a finger along the wet valley between gums and cheeks, put a light up each nostril. Then his fingers moved to the armpits, scratched through the hair, slid down the body to probe in the pubic hair around the genitals. He next tested the tip of the penis as if he believed it a logical spot for a circumcised male to conceal contraband.

When he came to the feet, the prosthesis seemed to give promise. The doctor removed it, examined it minutely, shook it, and finally, almost reluctantly, reattached it to the leg.

He straightened up. "Ah, well . . . If you will please climb up on the table. That's right, that's right . . . No, no, not to sit. Please turn over. Rest on your elbows. Yes, yes, knee-chest position. Knees a little forward, please."

An angry protest rose in Dr. Held's throat as the white-coated demon he couldn't see spread his buttocks and, with an uncompromising thrust, inserted a cold metal object into the anus. Held choked back the words and closed his eyes in an effort to shut out the insult and the pain.

"We won't be long," the doctor murmured. "Relax, please . . ."

In silence, Dr. Held fought the undignified attack that

the metal tube was launching against his body. With all his power to control his muscles, he tried to close the anal entrance, but the probing metal continued relentlessly, past all obstruction, until it had advanced beyond every sphincter the human mind can command.

Dr. Held's eyes were still closed when the tube was withdrawn, bringing with it the primeval odor of human waste. The doctor carried it to the washbasin, dropped it with a clatter, and noisily washed his hands. "Nothing," he pronounced, addressing himself exclusively to the Secret Service agent. "Sorry."

The agent's voice betrayed no feeling one way or the other. "That so? It wouldn't have to be very big."

The doctor replied impatiently. "Nothing, I said."

"Well, okay . . ."

Only then did they seem to notice Andrew Held. Together they helped him to his feet, and while he dressed, the agent telephoned the boarding area and advised the guard at the other end of the line that their passenger would be there in three minutes and they were to hold the plane.

When Andrew Held flew back from Paris, he was prepared to tell Felicia that she had been right in her judgment. The French did want his brains, not his principles.

One consultant, Paul Clicquot, had shown interest in his arguments against testing the *Victoire,* but the Directeur of the Bureau had listened for only a few minutes before he rose from his chair at the head of the conference table, thrust out his ample belly, adjusted his cufflinks, and in tones bordering on rudeness, said he hoped his old colleague Andrew had not traveled so far to discuss irrelevancies.

"Irrelevancies!" Held regarded the Directeur with a long, thoughtful stare. Was it possible that this eminent scientist was satisfied to assess his monstrous super-bomb on technological grounds alone and to close his mind completely to its human and social implications? Incredible, inhuman. And yet, Held reflected with a sickening surge of guilt, a year ago I would have spoken just as he is doing now. "I came to Paris because you requested it," Held said with dignity. "And because I assumed your request was based on appreciation, or even need, of my particular skills."

"I am sorry, my friend." The Directeur toyed with his right cufflink. "We all acknowledge your scientific genius. It is the art of persuasion that seems to elude you."

"It cannot elude me, because I do not pursue it." Dr. Held smiled wryly. "I know all about the art of persuasion. It consists of telling one's listeners what they want to hear. I have told you the exact opposite of what you want to hear, so you feel threatened in your cherished ambitions, and you repudiate me."

Dr. Held planned to recite this conversation for Felicia's amusement, even at the risk of hearing a note of malicious glee in her laughter. He was also prepared to confess that he had been searched at the airport, apparently for a roll of microfilm. The Americans had insulted him; the French had rejected him. He had been shocked and he had been disappointed. But Andrew Held had never recognized a defeat, however obvious it might be to everyone else. A colleague had once remarked, "Mortals yield. Andrew Held does not." Even before the mammoth airship landed at Dulles airport, Dr. Held's spirits were regrouping and he was forming a new plan.

He could not, would not, go back into government service. But he could always teach. In fact he had received three excellent offers as soon as news of his resignation appeared in the papers. In addition, there was his writing. Judging by the comments of the editor in New York, *The Noble Truth* was sure to be published, and he would want to start work on a second book.

Actually, he would not have to teach. Financially, he was free to spend all his time writing. How wonderful it would be if he could concentrate on creative work in an atmosphere unpolluted by the intrigue and caste system and tension of Washington.

Fleetingly, the memory of a distant island popped into his mind, like a picture suddenly illuminated by a spotlight. But of course Felicia would not consider such a wild scheme, and part of his regrouping and gathering of purpose was a resolution to rebuild his marriage.

Felicia was still uppermost in his mind when he emerged from customs and walked into the lobby of Dulles airport. She was not in the crowd waiting to welcome passengers. However she seldom met him, and in this case, she couldn't have done so because he had not known when he left that he would stay in Paris only three days, nor had he cabled.

The thought struck him that he should have brought her a gift. He could at least have picked up something in one of the shops at Orly. When he stepped into the taxi, he instructed the driver to make a stop at a liquor store, where he bought a bottle of excellent *brut*.

Thus it was that Dr. Held was holding a bottle of champagne when he walked into their bedroom and startled his wife in the act of making love to a young man he had never seen before. He had not meant to enter quietly, but the door was ajar, and the carpets throughout the apartment were deep and soft.

He stood in the doorway, gripping the bottle of champagne. The young man was darkly beautiful, with long black hair waving back from a smooth, unwrinkled forehead. The back of his head was resting on the cushioned back of the chair. His eyes were closed, his nostrils a little dilated, his full lips slightly parted. His naked body was as finely sculptured as his head, and smooth but for the fine dark hairs on his chest and calves. His groin was concealed by the back of Felicia's head, and for the hundredth part of a second before he wheeled and fled to the living room, Andrew Held noted that the young man was stroking her breasts in rhythm with the slow forward and backward movement of her head.

Six months later, he had purchased Furness Island and somehow persuaded the twelve bureaucrats who made up the United States Board of Geographic Names that it could be renamed "Phoenix" without doing violence to their policy on local usage. Nine months later, the first boatload of building materials arrived at Phoenix, and construction began.

It was 2:24 P.M. in Phoenix Island, where Andrew Held lay on a canvas deck chair beside the pool and let the August sun relax and warm him.

It was 12:24 P.M. in Hawaii, where the shriek of sirens was warning the residents of coastal towns that all sea-level areas must be evacuated. Tsunami was on its way!

Chapter Eight

ON the island of Bagatea, the natives lived in cottages scattered through groves of palm and pandanus trees rimming the shallow harbor. Their guests from Pater had been housed in the old military barracks on the hill, where they could look down on the village, the harbor installations, and the frame cottage of "Monsieur," the local government official.

When Pater Island exploded, the shock hit Bagatea instantly. Native huts swayed like paper houses caught in a crosswind. Flimsy walls fell apart, and corrugated roofs slid to the ground. Frightened women and screaming children pulled themselves out of the wreckage, and the grove vibrated with human cries.

On the hill, the barracks shuddered and groaned in a rhythmic convulsion that instantly severed the power line. While terrified Pater Islanders huddled in the yard, clutching their children, mumbling broken prayers, the old building swayed in its dance of death and the raw end of the power line, snapping sparks, whipped about like a maimed snake.

In the garden adjacent to his cottage, Monsieur's reactions were swift. His small tide station was not a regular subscriber to the Tsunami Warning System, but it was his duty to report to Honolulu should his gauge show any unusual rise or fall.

At the front of his house, the porch had collapsed. The building hung over the bay, unsupported. He ran to the back of the house. The back door was jammed into a crooked frame, and he could not open it. The kitchen window had been broken. Disregarding the shards of glass, he crawled through it and ran across the dipping floor to the workroom where his equipment was set up.

His guess had been right. The tidal gauge was rising dangerously. It screamed—*tsunami!* Report to Honolulu . . .

He swung around toward the teletype, but at that

point, the power went off. There was no tidal gauge, no communication. He drew in his breath sharply. The people in the barracks on the hill were lucky; up there they would be safe, but his own villagers lived right on the edge of the water.

He ran from house to house, calling out the warning. Some villagers had been injured by falling roofs or timbers, and they all were confused and frightened, but they respected Monsieur, and they fled the village and made their way toward the hill.

The first group of fifteen or twenty villagers was halfway up the hill when a wailing and shrieking mob of Pater Islanders rushed down the hill from the barracks.

"Fire! Fire! Run!"

They looked up, and it was true. At the top of the hill, flames were leaping higher than the barracks roof, and smoke billowed out through broken windows.

The hysterical cries of "Fire, run back, fire!" doubled as the pressure of the Pater Island people was thrown against the group from the village. Panicked, the Bagatea natives turned around, and with their visitors from Pater hard on their heels, ran down the hill toward the village. In their frenzy to escape the fire, no one heard Monsieur's shouts, nor interpreted his gestures as he tried to make them look out to sea.

When the first wave struck, most villagers had their backs to the water, still staring at the tall flames on the hill above. The great wall of water soared over the reef. They turned around, and screams of panic burst from a hundred mouths. Like stampeding animals, they ran back toward the hill.

It was too late. The wave swallowed the *proas* and small boats in the harbor, spewed them out in shreds, and rolled forward, overtaking all but a few people before they could reach the safety of the hill.

One person in the village had escaped the killer wave by a miracle. It was a young girl, the most beautiful of all Bagatea's dark-eyed and smiling young people, and already spoken for by a fisherman. She had struggled against the wave until, as if some benign power were intervening in her behalf, she had been lifted high on the wave, carried forward, and deposited gently on a grassy spot above the village, inches away from the highest water mark. The turbulent water spared her life but stripped her of all her clothing. Her lovely naked body, wet but pulsating with life, lay stretched out on the hill above the village, like an offering to the sky. She was unharmed, but she was unconscious, and for that reason she did not see, and could not run from, the fire now moving out from the burning barracks across the sunburned field.

When the second wave roared in a half hour later, it claimed only a few lives, those of the people who lay unconscious on the beach. It was the third wave that lifted Monsieur's painted house off its shaky supports and carried it forward a hundred feet above the beach. Casting the house onto the clearing at the top of the hill, the wave drew back. The house settled down on the mud, only a few feet from the smoldering remains of the barracks.

One hundred miles north of Bagatea, on the island of Tolui, the elderly government official was experiencing an uncomfortable sensation: a strange pressure in his ears. Was it his new medication, perhaps?

Frowning nervously, he applied the palms of his hands flat against his ears, pushed in, and then suddenly released the pressure, more or less as he had done as a young man when water had gotten into his ears while swimming. But there was no relief. All at once the idea struck him—*air* pressure. He hurried across the room to his barometer.

The instrument was acting strangely, indeed. In a few minutes, it fell three millimeters. Then for half a minute it held steady. Then a fast rise of about seven millimeters, and again a short lull, again a fall . . . A typhoon? The thought filled him with dread.

The pressure in his ears seemed to follow the changes of the barometer. When the needle indicated a rise, the pressure was worse. When it fell, he felt better. He stared dumbly at the instrument, as if it were a tribunal with power to save him or condemn him. Gradually, the time between the rise and the fall grew longer. The difference between high and low narrowed, and the barometer settled quietly on a point and stayed there.

The elderly man sighed deeply. An earthquake, not a typhoon. The worst was over. What he had been feeling was the impact of the aftershocks. Now his ears felt better but his arthritic knees cried out for rest. So he crossed the office and lowered himself carefully into his easy chair . . .

He was sound asleep when the first wave of the tsunami slammed against the island.

The voice of his male servant awakened him. "Wave, big wave!" The man's face was constricted by terror.

Still half asleep, the government's man on Tolui pushed himself out of his big chair and stumbled across the room to the door. His only coherent thought was that something was happening and it was his responsibility to do something about it.

The administration building stood on a slope above the port, fifty or sixty feet beyond the docks and warehouses that rimmed the bay. The old man looked down unbelievingly at a scene worse than any typhoon in his experience.

The wave had deluged all the buildings at the water's edge. One or two had been knocked off their pilings and had fallen sideways. Others had held firm, though their windows were smashed. Several roofs had been dislodged, swept away, and dropped at crazy angles in the mud. As for the villagers, some had escaped entirely and were running up the slope toward higher ground. Those caught in the buildings but not drowned were struggling to free themselves. Cut and bleeding, they were trying to crawl through broken windows or cling to floating rubble.

Several bodies were floating in the bay. Far out, the port building was bobbing on the water like a small Noah's ark. A native woman was clinging to the peak of the roof, screaming at the running figures on shore.

The government official stared while his servant pulled on his arm. "Run, run!" the man shouted in his face. "First wave go out. Next wave come, maybe soon, maybe higher! Hurry, please!"

He followed numbly after the servant, who had already bounded yards ahead of him. He wasn't much of a weatherman, but he knew that another wave was sure to follow. He might have ten minutes . . . He struggled painfully up the hill, conscious of the ache in his knees. Then he heard a voice, the voice of a woman. Like Lot's wife, he turned.

It was the storekeeper's wife, crying out from a spot about halfway down the slope. She was thoroughly wet, and appeared to be wedged between a tree trunk and the hill in such a way that she could move only her arms. She beckoned to him, calling his name.

Without a thought for the second wave, the old man slid down the hill to the spot where the woman seemed chained to the protruding tree trunk. Her terrified explanation was incoherent, but he understood at a glance. The first wave had gone over her, lifted her, thrown her against the hill, and receded, leaving her alive. But she was, indeed, chained to the tree trunk. Her long black hair was hopelessly wrapped and tangled around the tree's lowest limbs.

He tried to sort out the strands, but she would not hold still. After he made a few clumsy efforts, she began to scream and point toward the bay.

He did not need to look around. He took his penknife from his pocket, pulled out the blade, and holding a handful of the woman's hair in his left hand, cut her hair free with jerky sawing motions of his right. She was free . . .

The instant he cut the last strand, she leaped back and, on hands and knees, clawed her way up the hill.

An old man with arthritic knees can slide down a hill more easily than he can climb it. The government man tried to escape the second wave, but it was no use. It swallowed him, cast him out into the bay, rolled him over and over like a balsa log, pounded him against the wreckage of the port authority office, and then pulled back, dragging his unconscious body out into the depths of the sea.

When the Tsunami Warning System headquarters in Honolulu broadcast its first advisory bulletin, it was already too late for Bagatea or Tolui, and tsunami was back on its course across the open water, racing north at 500 miles an hour. At 11:45 A.M., Hawaiian Standard Time . . . 1:45 P.M. on Phoenix Island . . . tsunami is ninety minutes old and has traveled 600 miles. Ahead are the islands of Falatopa, Markham, Ile de Ciel, Thompson, Davis Reef, Simpson, Mauritius. . . . In another 600 miles, tsunami will cross the equator. Then for the most part it will be open sea all the way to Hawaii.

Tsunami was slowing down as it approached Markham Island, approximately 150 miles northeast of Tolui.

The freighter *Wotan*, just departing Markham, had cleared port and was a mile beyond the mouth of the harbor when the helmsman exclaimed, "Sir!" The captain automatically wheeled around and looked at the sea dead ahead. He saw a high broad bank of water rolling in from the ocean.

The quartermaster had just poured coffee and was standing with a thick white mug in each hand. The first mate shouted, "Tidal wave!" at the very moment the wave reached the *Wotan's* bow.

At twenty to thirty miles an hour, the great bore of water moved under the freighter, lifting her straight up. On this broad, nearly flat crest, the *Wotan* rode forward. The captain prayed to God and tensed himself for the moment his ship would drop into a trough and be swallowed by the sea. "Hold on!" he shouted hoarsely, and the quartermaster nodded, as if the skipper were talking about coffee mugs.

But there was no trough, no sudden drop. Having passed under the *Wotan's* stern, the steep front of the assaulting wave rolled toward land. Ahead of the ship, the surface of the sea was level, and in less than a minute the *Wotan* had been lowered gently and was proceeding steadily out to sea.

"Coffee, sir?" the quartermaster asked. He hadn't spilled a drop.

There were no protecting reefs to divert tsunami as it closed in on Markham harbor. By the time it reached shore, the first wave was forty feet high. It swept over the town, picking up buildings, trees, automobiles, people, and livestock.

On the hill above the harbor, a young marine biologist ran to the telephone to call the port administrator. Four, five, six rings. No answer. He hung up the receiver, checked the number, and dialed again. It rang once, and then silence. The line was dead. His hand shook as he replaced the receiver. He was no seismologist. It was up to Markham's port administrator to notify the Mission Hydrographique at Papeete. Papeete would forward the message via radio telegraph to the station at Nandi in Fiji, and from there it would be transmitted via FFA communications to headquarters of the warning system at Ewa Beach, Hawaii. But it had to start with the port administrator, and his office was on a pier only a few feet above sea level.

The biologist tried to telephone again, but the line

was definitely dead. He replaced the useless receiver and repressed a shudder, not letting himself think of what kind of death had swept over the people at the other end of the line. So there was no telephone, no radio. But someone had to get a message to Papeete, and fast.

Ah! Suddenly he remembered his most treasured possession—a fine, modern shortwave transceiver, a unit that transmitted messages as well as receiving them. In three strides he crossed the shabby parlor and examined the control dials, like great shiny eyes in the gray-green steel cabinet. But of course, even this ham operator's dream was as useless as the telephone, now that the power lines were down. He turned away, and through the window, saw the hood of his old Fiat parked just outside the cottage door.

The car battery . . .

In fifteen minutes, he was ready. He had disconnected the radio, carried it outside, and placed it on the ground where the antenna cable from the roof could be attached to the transceiver and the radio to the battery. The old Fiat was idling smoothly. It should keep the battery charged, he thought, at least long enough to get out a warning. *"Deus volente,"* he murmured as he picked up the small microphone. He began with the vocal equivalent of S.O.S.: "Mayday, Mayday, Mayday. This is F08VZ, F08VZ, F08VZ . . ."

He listened, signaled again, waited . . . Finally . . . a slight murmer of replies, one stronger than the others. "This is XE3QQ, XE3QQ . . . Roger, Roger, go ahead . . ."

In a shaking voice, the biologist began his message. "XE3QQ, this is F08VZ. Qth is Markham Island. We have been hit with a tidal wave. . . ."

At Ewa Beach, the men at the Warning Center were preparing to send out a second information bulletin when a report bearing on Markham came in:

MARKHAM ISLAND EXPERIENCED SEISMIC SEAWAVE AT 2205 Z. WATER LEVEL 40 FEET ABOVE MEAN SEA LEVEL. PAGO PAGO TIDE GAUGE INDICATES ABNORMAL HIGH TIDE. WILL ADVISE.

"Tsunami warning," the senior seismologist said. "And fast!"

Within minutes, this message went out from Honolulu to all warning stations in the Pacific:

THIS IS A TSUNAMI WATCH/WARNING. A SEVERE EARTHQUAKE HAS OCCURRED AT LAT. 24.9 S., LONG. 154.6 W. VICINITY OF PATER ISLAND, AT 2015 Z, 3 AUGUST. A TSUNAMI HAS BEEN GENERATED THAT IS SPREADING OVER THE PACIFIC OCEAN. THE INTENSITY CANNOT, REPEAT, CANNOT BE PREDICTED. HOWEVER THIS WAVE COULD CAUSE GREAT DAMAGE. IT MAY BE FOLLOWING ELONGATED AFTERSTOCK PATTERN NORTH AND EAST TOWARD PACIFIC COAST. THE DANGER IS EXTREME AND MAY LAST FOR 12 TO 14 HOURS.

The message concluded with a list of estimated travel times:

ETA HAWAIIAN ISLANDS 0145 Z, 4 AUGUST. ETA ALASKA 0715 Z, 4 AUGUST. ETA BRITISH COLUMBIA 0615 Z., 4 AUGUST . . .

For Hawaiians, about four hours. For Phoenix Island, about nine hours. But there was no warning system on Phoenix, and because electronic devices are not infallible, there was no radio on which Dr. Held would be able to pick up news from the distant mainland.

Chapter Nine

At last Dr. Held had finished his lunch, except for the scraps he always saved for his dogs. He snapped his fingers, and the hounds struggled to their feet and lumbered across the deck to his chair.

The male, named Mike after the world's first hydrogen bomb, swallowed the bread and cheese in a gulp. Lili accepted the food from Dr. Held's extended hand, but the pungent odor of the cheese assaulted her sensitive hunter's nose. She placed the scrap carefully between her big webbed paws, sneezed, and looked up at her master apologetically.

Dr. Held nodded. "Ah, yes, Lili. Either you eat it, or Mike will. It is your decision."

The air was soft, carrying a mélange of warm seashore scents from the gravel beach below the house. Dr. Held adjusted his lounge chair to a semi-reclining position. Lying back with arms outstretched and eyes closed, he invited the August sun to reach inside and melt his anxieties.

Anxiety, he reflected, is a noncreative emotion. Unlike anger, which produces action, it weakens and deprives one of a sense of direction. It struck him that his four house guests, due to arrive this afternoon, might be experiencing its debilitating effects right now. How could they know they were coming to gourmet meals and most of the bodily comforts to which they were accustomed in Manhattan and Washington, D.C.? Just the process of getting to Phoenix would be enough to make them uneasy.

As urbane Easterners, they undoubtedly thought of the Pacific Coast as a resort area extending several miles north and south of Los Angeles. To them, Seattle would be a last outpost. But even then they would have to make a hundred-mile drive north to the town where the ferry departed for the Outer Islands. After that, a long ferry boat ride past islands betraying little or no human habitation. And when they got off at the very end of the line and found that, lonely and isolated as it was, Wolf Island was still only a way station on the route to Phoenix . . . Dr. Held smiled. By the time Donald Campbell got the house guests aboard the *Trident*, they would be visualizing Phoenix Island as something rather like a French penal colony. The idea amused him.

It amused him, too, to reflect on the curious composition of this little house party. He hadn't really selected his guests. They were coming separately, each for his or her own reasons. Their simultaneous arrival was an accident he had decided to memorialize with a dinner party. Besides his guests, the *Trident* was bringing six cases of champagne, a young musician by the name of Carlo, and a young girl named Diana who was to help Mary with the cooking and housework. It was a luxurious ratio. Four hired servants, four guests.

Among the latter was Warren Brock, the fashionable sculptor from San Francisco. He had a summer home and studio on Wolf Island and had accepted a commission to do a large figure for the corner of the living room. Witty, eccentric, homosexual—Warren was a hedonist who would not have agreed to come to Phoenix if he hadn't been assured that the cuisine was excellent and the pool was heated to eighty-five degrees.

There would also be a young couple, Norma and Blake Mansfield. Their customary habitat was New York City, with an occasional foray to the north shore of Long Island. Mrs. Mansfield was the niece of a physics professor Dr. Held had first met when Held came to the United States in 1935 to teach at George Washington University. He'd never met the Mansfields, but his old friend Professor Sterling had asked that he invite them, and had done so in a way Held couldn't very well refuse. Why? To check up on the well-being of the old hermit? Well, they would find him healthier and more cantankerous than ever.

And then there was Felicia . . .

Andrew Held sat up straight and opened his eyes. Looking from the house to the adjoining outbuildings to the boathouse and the swimming pool, he tried to anticipate what Felicia's reaction would be. She would be impressed, probably surprised, by the size of the house. As for the interior—the walls of clear grain cedar, the floor-to-ceiling fireplace of blue basalt, the slate floors—she might consider it dark as compared to the apartment in

Washington, which was all white and gold and crystal. But the bedroom . . . He frowned, uncomfortable at the thought of Felicia's seeing that bedroom. She would know instantly what he had done: designed and decorated a room to duplicate, as closely as possible, her bedroom in Washington, hoping, as he had at first, that she would change her mind and come to live with him on Phoenix.

He stood up and glanced at his wristwatch. Two o'clock. They wouldn't be here until four. With his lunch digested, it was time for his afternoon swim.

Dr. Held believed in physical fitness, more as discipline than as pleasure, and swimming was an exercise well suited to a man with one foot. He swam twice a day, on schedule. "Mike, Lili . . ." he called. The dogs followed him from the sundeck down the long ramp between the house and the pool area to the dressing rooms.

Andrew Held went into the first dressing room. There was a bench along one wall and a shelf above it, where brightly colored beach towels were stacked in two neat piles. His swim trunks were draped over a towel bar where he had left them to dry after yesterday's swim. On the opposite wall there were clothes hooks and hangers so that his slacks and sports shirt would not get wrinkled.

His personal habits were as orderly as a mathematical formula, but ironically, the compulsive neatness failed utterly in giving the great scientist a neat appearance. He had been widely, and justly, publicized for his "rumpled look." His fastidious cleanliness showed. His thick brown hair always looked as if it had just been washed and towel-dried. The skin on his wide forehead and across his high cheekbones shone with the frequent use of soap and water. Everything he wore was spotless and smelled faintly of the old-fashioned cologne, 4711. But his hair tended to fall into his eyes, and his clothes, no matter how expensive, appeared to have been selected at random from the bottom of a steamer trunk.

Systematically, he removed his shirt, slid it on a hanger, unzipped his slacks, and in one gesture pulled slacks and undershorts below his knees. Then he sat down on the bench, untied and removed his shoes, and placed them on the bench beside him. Though he was not a young man, bending was no strain. His abdomen was flat, the muscles firm and the skin taut. He leaned forward easily and drew off the left pant leg. Now there was only the right leg and the right foot.

Automatically, he looked up to make sure the dressing room door was closed and locked. Being nude did not concern him; for the simple act of taking off his clothes, he wouldn't have bothered to close the door. But for him, the final act of undressing was to remove the prosthetic device that for forty years had served him as a right foot. During this ritual, he had an uncontrollable, fanatic need to guard his privacy.

He was twenty years old. He had just taken a degree in chemical engineering at the Institute of Technology in Karlsruhe and had gone to Munich for further study. He was not the classical Munich student. He had carried the burden of mathematical genius from the age of four or five, and even in the playful *Trinkverein* atmosphere of the Bavarian capital, he thought more about quantum mechanics than he did about the Hofbrauhaus. Yet, he was twenty and gregarious, and when it was time to play, he played with a natural ebullience that made him popular with his peers even after they discovered he was brilliant.

The game of jumping onto a moving streetcar was as old as singing in a *Bierstube*. They all played it, at least when there were other students on hand to observe. Of course the last one to jump had to leap at the worst possible moment, when the platform was already crowded, the streetcar was picking up speed, and his friends, being safely on board, had nothing to do but cheer and jeer.

Young Andrew Held had been in a soaring mood that day. He'd received a long, surprisingly intimate letter from the sister of a schoolmate in Budapest, then had a stein or two at a noisy *Ratskeller*. Bursting with vital juices, he held back so that he would have to be the last to leap onto the streetcar.

He ran forward and grasped the metal bar as he leaped onto the first step. But something caught on the edge of the step. The sole of his shoe, the cuff of his trouser— he never knew. He was jerked backwards, and as his hand slipped off the vertical bar, he lost balance and fell sideways. The shouts of his friends could not stop the car in time, nor blank out the searing pain as the heavy iron wheel rolled over his foot.

The amputation of his mangled foot was accomplished that same day. The injury was three months in healing. The trauma—well, he supposed, that would last the remainder of his life.

At twenty, in Munich, he had made three decisions that were to shape the course of his life. One was to marry his classmate's sister, Toni. The second was to cease his concentration on chemistry, which had been at his father's insistence, and to pursue his interest in physics.

The third decision was born during those grim and lonely hours when he tried to visualize the life of a man with one foot. He decided it would not be enough to accept his handicap philosophically. His interests had always been chess, music, and poetry; but his injury would not affect any of them. If he was to accomplish something, he must select some sort of recreation he had seldom if ever attempted, and he must not only pursue it, he must excel.

He chose waltzing, horseback riding, swimming, and driving a car. He had had no experience with any of them, but in time he did them all, and well. Only a slight lurch to the right when he went into a pivot during a Viennese waltz betrayed him as a man with one foot.

Held swam vigorously for several minutes, and then flipped over on his back. How peaceful it was to float in the sun, to hear only the murmur of the wind and the discourse of the birds. How right he had been to leave everything behind and, through the alchemy of civilized devices, convert this lonely island into his very own Shangri-la. If only he could have Felicia back to share it with him.

In less than two hours, she would indeed be with him, at least temporarily—providing Donald had handled the arrangements for the guests competently. But then Donald handled everything competently. A strange man, Donald Campbell. Held could never quite figure him out, but then sometimes it was better not to ask oneself too many questions about one's employees.

Chapter Ten

ALTHOUGH Donald Campbell had been out of prison for eighteen months, the carbolic acid smell of the cell block was still imbedded far back in his nasal passages.

La Tuna, Texas. Something in the supplies he had just loaded onto the deck of the *Trident* was sending a message up his nostrils and calling out "Federal Correctional Institution, La Tuna, Texas . . ." The chow line, that was it. Big steel trays loaded with beet greens and fatty pork, or slices of meat loaf drowning in a sauce that looked like congealing blood.

He grunted, sniffed, spat over the side of the boat, and wiped his mouth with the back of his hand. God damn. Someday Dr. Held would be with him when he got one of these remembering spells and blurted out something about a cellmate or the warden or VT shop. There was a lot he didn't want Dr. Held to know, but one thing for sure was the fact that he had done three years for auto theft and right now was a fugitive from a warrant accusing him of assault with intent to kill.

Donald Campbell, whose real name was Henry Jackson Riley, stood six foot four and weighed 240 pounds, all bone, muscle, and guts. He was barrel-chested and short-legged for his height, a strong, barroom build. He had one scar, a jagged white line about six inches long, cutting across his ruddy face from cheekbone to upper lip. That time he won the fight but lost the girl . . .

Girl . . . Jesus, how he needed a girl. Living on Phoenix Island, he was almost as bad off as he had been in prison.

Donald pulled a folded sheet of paper from his hip pocket, opened it, and checked down the list of errands he was to complete during the trip to Wolf Island.

Six cases of champagne, in addition to the usual whiskeys and vodka. Fresh eggs and a dozen chickens. A hindquarter of beef and a spring lamb, cut and wrapped for the freezer. Three cases of assorted groceries from the store in the village, including a dozen boxes of dog biscuits for Mike and Lili. Two gallons of raw milk from the dairy farm. Miscellany such as lubricating oil, kerosene, soap . . . And, of course, the mail.

The mail was in a large canvas rucksack, stowed with the other supplies under the *Trident's* ample bow. Dr. Held wasn't going to be happy about the mail. It included several packages, but nothing from the electronic supply house from which he had ordered a radio part. With a touch of malice, Donald thought of how indignant the old man was going to be when he learned he wouldn't be able to repair his radio . . .

What a character! No interest in television or even radio, except for news broadcasts. He spent hours at the big grand piano in the living room, which wasn't Donald Campebell's idea of fun. God damn it, he was going to buy his own TV. Dr. Held had agreed. He had even suggested that Donald take the ferry to the mainland and buy what he wanted. But Donald didn't want to show his face on the mainland, not for a good long time.

The *Trident* was moored to a float attached at right angles to a long, narrow pier. Four other pleasure boats were tied up nearby. Their skippers and passengers had all gone ashore, probably to the Harbor Inn, a motel/cocktail lounge/dining room complex above the beach near the pier. All except for a girl in a bathing suit, stretched out on a mattress on the bow of a twenty-footer near the gas pump. For a delicious moment, Donald thought of approaching her, then decided against it. She might squawk, and this was no time to get into trouble.

Besides, he had something lined up. At least he hoped he did. Diana Lindgren, Minnie Lindgren's granddaughter, was coming to Phoenix to help Mary with the housework. She was sixteen or seventeen, still in high school. She was about the most beautiful chick he had ever seen. Close up, he got the feeling no man had ever done it to her. He liked the idea; he often daydreamed about the times he had been a girl's first.

He had heard she had a boyfriend—that young Indian, Rolf. But Rolf wasn't going to be on Phoenix, and on Phoenix, Diana wouldn't be able to run away . . . Donald's wide mouth tightened. He ached for a girl. Jesus, what he could do to a girl. .

There would be five passengers on the *Trident* besides Diana Lindgren. Mr. and Mrs. Mansfield, the couple from New York. Carlo Minatti, the Hawaiian who played guitar and sang at the Harbor Inn. He was a paid entertainer, but if Donald knew Dr. Held, he would be seated at the dining room table along with the other guests, like that artist, Mr. Brock . . .

Donald grinned. That kind of sex was all right in prison. Jesus, he'd had it whenever he wanted it. There were always some willing younger men, and Donald was big and strong enough to take his pick. In return, the boy had a protector. He never had to worry about other guys ganging up on him at night or trying to make him in the showers. But that didn't make Donald a fag! Hell, no. "Situational homosexuality" was what his caseworker called it. In the streets, Donald wanted girls, preferably with big tits. And he wanted them flat on their back.

For Phoenix, Diana was his first choice. He licked his lips and looked across to the boat where the sleeping girl was stretched out in the sun. Her almost naked body made him think about the third woman who would soon be making the trip to Phoenix. Mrs. Held, Dr. Held's wife. God damn, what he knew about her!

Mrs. Held had been staying at the Harbor Inn for the past two nights, and each evening she spent several hours in the lounge. Donald watched her from an excellent voyeur post, a stool at the bar. She was an elegant bitch, all fancy hairdo and rings on her fingers. He thought, First I'd take her, and then I'd take the jewelry, but even as he was trying to imagine what such a high-class dame would be like in bed, he knew he was afraid to try. Something about her made him see himself as he was, big and ugly with a crooked nose and bulging forehead.

But she didn't scare Carlo Minatti. Donald had burned with envy as he watched Carlo introduce himself to Mrs. Held. The first night, she complained about her cocktail. The bartender mixed a new one, and she complained again. At that point, Carlo put down his guitar, turned off the mike, stepped behind the bar, and made a third cocktail. He carried the drink to her table, and while she was thanking him, he sat down.

On his weekly trips to Wolf Island, Donald had had
ample opportunity to admire Carlo's self-confident technique. Carlo smiled, he laughed, he listened more than he
talked, and the girls followed him out of the Inn as if
they'd been hypnotized. Of course, he had the looks—
large dark eyes with just a little slant to them, wide
smiling mouth, glistening white teeth, smooth deep-tan
skin that never showed the stubble of a beard. Donald's
usual attitude toward other human beings was both doubt-
ing and hostile, but Carlo was so natural, so lacking in
conceit, that Donald envied him without a trace of resentment or dislike.

He was no beginner, that Carlo. Before the evening
was over, he had bought Mrs. Held another drink, and
she had returned the favor. But he was too smart to push
his luck. When the bar closed, Mrs. Held went to her
room alone.

The second night, Donald took up the same post at
the bar. At midnight, Mrs. Held stood up, shook Carlo's
hand, and like a queen, walked out of the lounge without
so much as a glance to the right or left. She passed so
close to Donald that he saw that her eyes were sea-green
and her upswept red hair was caught and held by a pair
of diamond pins.

Fifteen minutes later, Carlo turned off the microphone,
locked his guitar into its case, and came over to the bar.
He ordered two big snifter glasses of cognac. One in each
hand, he walked out of the lounge toward the motel.

Donald already knew the number of Mrs. Held's room.
That morning he had called her from the reception desk
to tell her the time the *Trident* was leaving the next day.
Room 12. An even number, so it would be on the bay
side of the corridor. He gave Carlo five minutes, and then
he, too, walked into the motel.

At the door to Room 10, he stopped and tried the
doorknob. It was locked, maybe occupied. He continued
past Mrs. Held's room to Room 14. Very gently he turned
the doorknob, prepared to apologize and explain that he
had the wrong number, his room was down the hall . . .
But Room 14 was empty. Light from the hall shone on
an empty clothes rack, a freshly made bed. A break for
him—the maid had forgotten to lock the room, and at
this hour, there wasn't a chance it would be rented for
the night.

He entered quietly, then closed and locked the door. Though it was dark, he knew the layout. A big double bed would be on the north wall. On this side of the corridor the rooms were L-shaped opposites. In Room 12 the entrance hall was on the north side, in Room 14 it was on the south side, so that the furniture was arranged back to back. The headboard of the bed in 12 and the headboard of the bed in 14 were separated by a thin inside wall and were actually only inches apart.

Donald took off his shoes, set them beside the door, and moved stealthily to the wall beside the bed. The voices in the next room were indistinct. They must be drinking the cognac at the round cocktail table on the far side.

He waited, his ear pressed against the wall. His mouth was dry. Hurriedly, he went into the bathroom and drew a glass of water. Fresh bath towels were stacked on the shelf beside the washbasin. He pulled one loose, hardly noticing that he knocked the rest of them onto the tiled floor. Pulse throbbing he went back to the bed and very carefully eased his big body down until he was lying on his back full-length, his head turned slightly so as to keep his left ear close to the wall.

The voices were coming closer, maybe to the bed. Then a faint but distinct "whish" as the mattress was depressed by the weight of their bodies and a dull knock as the bed moved a fraction of an inch and the headboard hit the wall.

Carlo's voice, deep and soft, was so close that the separating wall seemed to conduct the sound rather than muffle it. "Beautiful lady, beautiful lady . . ."

Mrs. Held's voice, higher but husky. "Leave the light on . . ."

Donald's fingers fumbled with the zipper of his jeans. Jesus, oh sweet Jesus . . . He had left the room dark. Now he wanted light, too. Trembling, he reached for the bedside lamp, found the switch, and a golden glow poured over him as he pulled down the zipper.

They were still talking, in single words, murmured together like a duet. "There . . . yes . . . there . . . slowly . . ."

Donald spread his legs, thrusting his pelvis forward urgently as if there were a body there to be entered. Jesus, oh Jesus . . . He moaned out loud, and could not stop. The bed creaked rhythmically with the movement of his hand and the thrust of his hips. On the other side of the wall, the bed was alive with sounds. The bedsprings sang, and the bodies thumped the mattress in an ever faster beat. The slippery sounds of sex oozed through the walls, blending with the rising murmur of their hungry voices.

Donald's frenzied motions quickened as the images communicated by the sounds swam around him. In the bright light from the lamp, he watched his own strong organ sliding furiously between his fingers. The whole whirling dance came to its violent end. Carlo's voice, "Now! Now! With me, baby, with me!" A second later, the voice of Dr. Held's wife, rising in a prolonged but wordless sob. Donald was with them, all the way.

It was quiet on the other side of the wall. Donald sank back into the soft bedcovers, reached for the towel, and turned off the light.

The young man from New York City was the first to board the *Trident*. Blake Mansfield was tall and slender, with broad and smoothly muscled shoulders. A tennis player's build. In fact, tennis was his game, whenever he could get away from his law office in Lower Manhattan and spend a little time at his country house on Long Island. The only contradiction to his image as a slender, well-tailored athlete were his eyeglasses. He was extremely near-sighted, and without glasses he was, for all practical purposes, blind. His intensely blue eyes were screened by thick lenses in a heavy black frame. He surrendered his luggage to Donald, eyes blinking against the bright sunlight, and said apologetically, "Sorry to burden you with so much luggage. I'm afraid Dr. Held will conclude we're staying for the season."

A few minutes later, Norma Mansfield appeared at the top of the pier. Even from a distance, it was obvious that she was not comfortable in this place. At the end of the pier, she hesitated, studying the ramp that sloped down to the float. Grasping the wooden railing, she descended carefully, as if the whole thing might tip over or sink. At the *Trident* she acknowledged Donald Campbell with an impersonal nod and addressed herself to her husband. "I couldn't find the mailbox. They said it was right outside. I walked a mile . . ."

Her oval face was framed by straight brown hair parted uncompromisingly in the middle and falling almost to her shoulders. Her dark eyes looked unhappy, and her thin eyebrows were drawn together in an impatient frown.

Blake Mansfield stroked his wife's hand. She had been opposed to his "romantic impulse" to explore the Pacific Northwest, and even more dubious about her uncle's request that they look up his anchorite friend Andrew Held on some remote island. She was being a dutiful niece, but for all her Puritan credo, having a hard time being a good sport about it. Blake could guess what had happened when she tried to post her letter. The "mailbox" to which she had been directed was a weather-beaten gray tin rural mailbox on a wooden post beside the gravel road. Norma would have walked right by it, looking for a big red-white-and-blue postbox like those on city streets.

"I know where the box is," Blake said gently. "Give me your letter, Norma. I'll mail it."

"No, no, it's all right." She gave him a tentative smile, an apology for her peevishness. "It's for my uncle. He'll want most of all to hear about our visit with Dr. Held. I'll add onto it tomorrow and mail it when we get back from Phoenix."

"I'll add a postscript, if I may."

Norma looked at him in surprise. Her uncle was her favorite and only remaining close relative, but Blake did not know him well. "Yes, of course. But you don't, usually—"

Blake leaned forward and pressed her hand. "I just want to tell him that I love you."

For an instant her thin mouth relaxed and her eyes were wistful. Then the softness vanished and a look of irritated hauteur settled over her face like a mask. She withdrew her hand. "I wonder," she said coldly, turning her head away.

The next arrival was Carlo Minatti, carrying a small canvas bag and a large guitar case. He jumped aboard, introducing himself with a wide friendly smile. His dark hair shone with coppery lights, his dark eyes with the natural friendliness that disarmed and engulfed anyone he directed it toward.

As Carlo seated himself across from the Mansfields,

Donald saw that Mrs. Held was on her way down from the Inn. At her heels was—Donald wanted to laugh out loud —it was the deputy sheriff, Frank Schmidt. How had she managed *that?* She probably spotted good old Frank drinking coffee in the coffee shop—it was a regular stop on his rounds of Wolf—and before he knew it, he was playing bellhop.

Mrs. Held proceeded with quick, confident steps, a tall, elegant figure in bright green pants suit with a green and gold headscarf wrapped around her hair, the loose ends fluttering in the wind. The young deputy sheriff, carrying a bright red travel bag and a matching cosmetics case, trailed behind.

"Mr. Campbell," she said regally, inclining her head. "Mr. and Mrs. Mansfield, nice to see you again. Mr. Minatti . . ."

Jesus, Donald thought. The way she carries it off! As he helped her into the boat, he looked directly into her face, his small pale eyes shining with secret knowledge. She barely nodded, turned her back, and began a conversation with the Mansfields.

Donald thought bitterly, Don't treat *me* like dirt, lady. You don't know what *I* could tell your husband.

Warren Brock was a short man, thin and narrow-hipped. His face had an aging prettiness to it. Though his upper lip was straight, the lower lip was full and curved in at the center like an archer's bow. His eyes were large, dark, and luminous beneath thick bleached eyebrows. His sun-streaked brown hair was thinning, but his head was well-shaped, with a broad forehead and a short nose that went straight down from the forehead without indentation, a classical Greek bust of Apollo at age thirty-eight.

"Well, well, well," he said pertly as he reached the *Trident.* "Beautiful people, all." He himself was clothed in faded bluejeans and a loose-fitting pullover sweater, in curious contrast to the expensive saddle-stitched leather case in his hand. He stepped lightly into the boat and began speaking to the Mansfields, an impish master of ceremonies. "*You* are the people from New York. I can see *that.* All Sulka's, Lord and Taylor, Abercrombie and Fitch." He turned slowly. "*You,* of course, are Mrs. Held."

Diana Lindgren was the last, and her boyfriend Rolf was with her. Donald stared rudely as they stopped a few feet from the *Trident* and said good-bye.

He had to concede that Rolf was a good-looking kid, for an Indian—shiny, thick black hair, curling just a little where it rested on his shoulders, a clean-looking gold-colored skin, and a well-shaped mouth under a wide black mustache. Donald saw him touch Diana, saw her draw back. That pleased him. Damned if he wanted that breed to get to her before he did.

Rolf wheeled around and rapidly walked away. Diana, an old brown suitcase in hand, watched his retreating back. Her long dark hair concealed her face until she half-turned and continued to the *Trident*. Then Donald saw that her large gray eyes were filled with tears and her soft mouth was trembling.

The sight of her crying filled Donald with desire, not pity. He'd have her, by God, he'd have her before she ever got off Phoenix Island. "All aboard," he said, looking hungrily at her damp cheeks. "Next stop, Phoenix Island."

Chapter Eleven

IT was four hours and thirty minutes since the imprint of disaster had first appeared on the seismographs of the Honolulu Observatory. During that time, messages from outlying tidal stations had pieced together a true portrait of the killer. Stations within a 250-mile radius of Pater Island had not responded to the Observatory's urgent requests for information; it could be assumed they had already been obliterated. Farther from the epicenter, reports had been coming in.

SEAWAVES AT 2105 Z, 38 FT; AT 2155 Z, 40 FT; AT 2220 Z, 44 FT . . .

Such a message was recorded on the headquarters map like a communiqué from the battlefront. It meant tsunami was *there*. Later, the same station would report SEA WAVES 35 FT AT 2310 Z; SEAWAVES 28 FT AT 2345 Z; SEAS DIMINISHING. WATER RECEDING . . . Tsunami had struck and run. The monster was outward bound, racing toward its next victim.

ETA HAWAII 0145 Z. . . . ETA HAWAII 0145 Z. . . .

On all the islands, coastal settlements trembled with the shrill blasts of sirens. All radio programs were interrupted at regular intervals for the broadcast of numbered civil defense disaster bulletins. By local time, the first wave would hit shortly after 3:30 P.M. It would strike Hilo first, on the east coast of the "big island," Hawaii.

Hilo was ready. The tugs in the harbor had put out to sea. Fishing sampans moored along the Wailuku River had been lifted and dragged to high ground. Police cars patrolled the streets, loudspeakers bawling the order to evacuate to designated disaster centers three miles back from shore. And the local mortician had donated two ornate black hearses for the transportation of hospital patients from Puu Maile . . .

The administrator for the leper colony on Molokai received the tsunami warning in a telephone call from the state health department in Honolulu. It was 2:30 P.M., Hawaii time. He and the tiny Kalaupapa police force had at most one hour in which to remove hospital patients and residents to safety—one hundred and ten people in all.

There was only one possible escape route, for Kalaupapa is a low-lying point of land jutting two miles into the sea and surrounded on all but the beach side by cliffs over 1,600 feet high. The small Cessna and Beechcraft that made the regular mail and supply run, charter boats, helicopters—they were all out of the question, for there wasn't time. It had to be the old mule path that zigzagged up a nearly perpendicular cliff more than a quarter of a mile high, the narrow, now-neglected path, *kapu* to the lepers, by which a postman on mule or horseback had once brought the mail. Even for the young and healthy, it was a forty-five-minute climb to the locked gate and heavy steel mesh fence at the top.

And Kalaupapa was a colony of old people. The average age was 58, but many residents were much older— "clean," thanks to the sulfone drugs and to the later discoveries of clofazimine and rifampin, but crippled, disfigured, weak. Some would have to be supported, even carried. So the strongest would help the weakest, and the rest would pray and go it alone.

Within minutes the superintendent had completed his calls, and the orderly flight began. Those not well enough to walk to the base of the cliff were driven there by the colony's fleet of rattletrap cars. With a half hour remaining before the first wave was expected to strike, the column of lepers was moving slowly up the trail.

It was overgrown with weeds and littered with chunks of lava rock. A heavy rain had fallen the night before, converting disintegrated lava into black mud. Some lepers had lost toes and had difficulty keeping their balance. Some had ulcerating leg sores, so that every step was painful. Many stumbled on the slippery path. Many fell. Hands with only one or two fingers clutched at a bush or tree as they pulled themselves upright and went on.

A young medical student started up the trail with an elderly patient on his back. The old man was too weak to hold on, and he slipped off into the mud. A young woman was next in line, a woman whose beauty lived in her eyes though her nose was sunken and she had lost one ear. She pulled off her cotton shirt, tore it into two pieces, and wrapped and tied them securely, binding the old man to the student's back.

A middle-aged man, his face mottled with purple nodules, carried a ukelele. His special role in the colony was to lead the singing at the social hall. If they all survived tsunami, they would want to sing.

Slowly, torturously, the long line advanced.

The wave rolled onto the Kalaupapa peninsula in a massive bore of turbulent water. Gigantic blocks of black lava were tumbled furiously and carried forward to help in the destruction. Coconut palms were uprooted and flung against the lighthouse. The lighthouse, torn from its foundation, rode the crest of the water as it roared over the airfield and slammed against two beach shacks, flattening their walls. Still greedy, the wave hit the Catholic church, breaking its windows and ripping off the porch.

Kalaupapa is a place of many cemeteries. Rows of headstones extend in many directions, a tragic vineyard of marble and granite and wood. The destroying wave rolled over the burial grounds, maliciously exhuming the wooden caskets of long-ago exiles. Boxes, headstones, broken church timbers, huge chunks of lava, splintered trunks of palm trees—all were hurled forward together. A dozen caskets split open, spilling their content of bones and withered flesh.

The wave crashed against the cliff, clawing up the trail in a last furious effort to claim the stubborn human beings who had now barely dragged themselves beyond its reach. Then it receded, pulling heavy objects with it but casting aside everything light or buoyant.

As it withdrew, corpses and pieces of corpses, skeletons and parts of skeletons were deposited on the dormitory steps, on the courthouse lawn, beside the social hall, at the door of the post office. One of the bodies it left was that of Father Mike, a Catholic priest only recently buried. He was curled around the gasoline pump at the filling station, like a sleeping child who has found his favorite pillow.

On the path, halfway up the cliff, trembling voices joined the ukelele in the singing of an old, old song.

As if it were tiring of Hawaii, the killer wave veered to the east, ignoring Kauai and racing along the east coast of Oahu, an angry monster hungry for new victims. Soon incoming reports began to suggest to the men at Tsunami Warning Headquarters what tsunami's latest caprice might be.

"I'll make a prediction," the veteran technician said grimly. "The Aleutians, then the Alaskan mainland, then the coast of British Columbia and Washington State. That's not a prediction. That's for sure. Where I'll stick my neck out is about the mood this killer is going to be in when it hits the continent. There's nothing to break it up between here and there. I say ugly, very ugly. Let's get back to the teletypes."

In the Federal Aviation Administration office in San Francisco, a man turned to a special telephone and pushed the black button on the side of it. Simultaneously, emergency calls came into offices in California, Oregon, and Washington.

In Washington, the message was received at Washington state patrol headquarters in the capital city of Olympia. Five officers were on duty in the radio room and adjoining law-enforcement teletype center. The gigantic "Access" computer, six feet tall and fifteen feet wide, was alive with blinking lights and moving knobs and dials. The room was filled with its steady hum. Like the attendant officers, the all-wise machine was quiet, disciplined, and confident.

STAND BY FOR TSUNAMI MESSAGE . . . Within fifteen minutes, the patrol had relayed San Francisco's message to twenty-six primary warning points, and all twenty-six had reported back.

The Whatcom county sheriff received the message from state patrol headquarters without excitement. There hadn't been a tsunami warning in eight years, and even then his territory had seen nothing more than an unusually high tide. Nevertheless, the sheriff was not the kind to analyze his orders and select only those he personally thought made sense.

Deputy Rankin was standing at attention.

"Okay, Rankin. You say you checked with Bellingham Fire Department?"

"Yes, sir."

"Mayor's office? Civil defense?"

"Officer Gardner doing it now, sir."

The sheriff nodded approval. "Looks like you covered all bases. Except Discovery County."

Officer Rankin's earnest blue eyes took on a look of bewilderment. He could recite the first and last names of all sheriffs west of the Cascades, but he couldn't recall ever having known the name of the Discovery County sheriff, nor even, for sure, the name of the county seat.

"Yes, Officer Rankin, *Discovery*. Made up mostly of the Outer Islands. County seat Cristobal, population four-fifty, counting the sheepdogs. Sheriff DeLancey."

"Yes, sir."

"Hold it, Rankin. Don't forget that you can't get Discovery by Access. That stubborn bunch out there refused to ante up matching funds. So you'll have to get the sheriff by regular telephone."

Actually, the sheriff admired the people of the Outer Islands. In his own way, he was complimenting them.

The sheriff of Discovery County was having coffee with two cronies, the veterinarian and the manager of the county bank. From the front of the Seaside Cafe, the waitress waved a telephone receiver over her head and yelled, "Hey, Hugo, it's for you."

The sheriff heaved himself reluctantly out of the booth, threw two quarters on the table to cover his coffee and apple pie, lifted his broad-brimmed trooper's hat off the rack, and walked heavily to the telephone.

"*Hal*lo . . ."

His deputy responded with a high-pitched torrent of words from which the sheriff extracted the term "tidal wave."

"Calm down, Brady," he growled. "I'm coming."

Back in his office, Sheriff DeLancey sat down at his desk, lit a cigar, and began to give instructions. Call the mayor of Cristobal. Call in Deputy Smith. Call or car-radio the deputies on all the other islands.

Almost as an afterthought, he said, "Hey, Brady. Don't forget Frank Schmidt, out there on Wolf."

Deputy Sheriff Frank Schmidt had been up most of the night. Somebody ran a car into the ditch. Someone's pigs broke out and were rooting up another farmer's wheat crop. A horse was lost, a horse was found. A dog chased sheep, a dog was shot. Fire, heart attack, a runaway child, or a fist fight in the tavern—whatever it was, "Call Schmidt," and since he was the only law-enforcement officer on Wolf Island, he was on twenty-four-hour duty. Most of the time, fatigue was his greatest challenge.

Today his wife, Leona, had taken things into her own hands, though he didn't know it. After lunch, she persuaded him to lie down on the soiled and threadbare sofa in the living room. The moment he fell asleep, she went softly to the spot in the wall where the telephone was plugged into a jack. She took it firmly between her fingers and pulled it out. That would take care of *that*. No telephone to wake him and send him on some stupid errand, like this morning, chasing Mrs. Goodman's geese halfway across the island. The sheriff's office on Cristobal might try to get him through the two-way radio in the patrol car, but it was parked in the back of the house and they could yell, "Come in, Wolf . . ." all they wanted to, he wouldn't hear it. He needed sleep. He deserved some time off. For once, he was going to get it.

Chapter Twelve

WHEN Donald Campbell brought the *Trident* into Phoenix harbor and tied up at the pier, Andrew Held was waiting. The two bassets were with him, tails wagging, poised to welcome the new arrivals with yelps of pleasure. Once Donald had secured the boat fore and aft, Dr. Held came forward, attention focused on the deck where his house guests would be seated.

Instantly, his eyes picked out Felicia. The others were a blur around her. He took a few more steps, acutely conscious of his limp. He felt like a foolish young lover, absorbing his returning sweetheart with his eyes.

She looked up at him, and for a moment, she was a young girl. Her green eyes softened, and her lips parted slightly with an excited smile. But the others were in the way. They climbed out, one by one. Carlo, Diana. He nodded in recognition. Warren Brock. They shook hands. The Mansfields. They introduced themselves and moved along the pier. Finally, Felicia.

She waited for Donald to set her cases onto the dock and to steady her for the step from the *Trident* to the landing. This accomplished, she turned toward her husband and extended her hand. He grasped it eagerly, and she kissed him lightly on the cheek.

"Well, Andy, you are looking very well indeed." Her voice was businesslike, as if she were telephoning the banquet manager at the Shoreham to compliment him on arrangements for a benefit ball.

Andrew Held searched her face for the little-girl look that had been on it, just for an instant, when they first caught sight of each other. It was gone without trace. The private Felicia was hidden once again behind the amused, partially lidded green eyes. As nearly as he could, he said what he felt. It wasn't his fault that it sounded banal.

"I have thought of you a great deal, Felicia. I am glad you are here."

She pulled off her headscarf and smoothed her coppery

78

hair. "Dear Andy, that is very nice of you to say, but I must tell you honestly, you won't be glad at all. No, indeed, you will not like my reason for coming." With that, her bright eyes turned away and directed their examination to the big house and sundeck over the water.

"Phoenix, is it? I know, something about the taste of ashes. Well, Andy, come along. Show me what you have made here." With a light step, she proceeded toward the house. Dr. Held followed slowly. The dogs, strangely subdued, stayed close behind.

On Wolf Island, Deputy Sheriff Frank Schmidt was waking from his nap. His eyelids felt gritty and his mouth was dry. Groggy with sleep, he sat up and squinted at the face of his wristwatch. Christ, it was going on six o'clock!

He stood up, stretched, and walked across the room to the kitchen. "I must've slept for damn near four hours," he told his wife's back. "Never heard the phone once."

She turned down the burner, set the cooking fork on the sink, and with a secretive smile, walked past him into the living room. He watched her curiously. She was bending over, fiddling with the telephone jack.

"Leona! Did you disconnect the telephone?"

"You bet I did!" She straightened up and faced him, daring him to find fault. "You got to get some sleep, one way or another. Let people chase their own geese."

"I'm supposed to be on duty, Leona. A deputy just can't do that. It don't matter how tired he is."

"I'm not sorry," she said defiantly, and went back to the kitchen.

He would have followed her—he had to get the idea of "duty" into her head, even if it ended up in a fight—but the telephone rang. It was the sheriff himself.

"Hey, what the hell's going on over there? We been trying to get you all afternoon. There's some kind of warning about a tidal wave."

"Tidal wave?" Schmidt was a native of Montana. He had read about such things, just as he had read that Mount Vesuvius was a volcano that erupted and wiped out a town, but the idea that a tidal wave would flood Wolf Island was completely unreal to him. However, his sense of duty, which he thought of as vaguely sacred, something like his marriage vows, took over. "Yes, sir. What's the procedure?"

"You know your island. The idea is to warn everybody. You know what to do."

Deputy Schmidt replaced the receiver. Frowning, he tried to drag from his life experience some precedent for this emergency. He had to cover an island fifteen miles long and three to five miles wide. He had to convince five or six hundred people that something as fantastic as a tidal wave was a real danger. He had four hours. He couldn't do it alone.

Frowning, he picked up the telephone and dialed the volunteer fire department's emergency number. It automatically rang telephones in twenty-four different shops and homes. To the twelve or fifteen persons who answered, most of them the wives of the volunteers, he repeated the message he had received from the sheriff on Cristobal Island and asked that all firemen drive to the fire hall as fast as possible. Then he strapped on his holster with its heavy .38 Magnum and picked up his wide-brimmed felt hat. At the kitchen door, he said, "Leona, you heard what I was just telling the firemen."

"Yes, Frank." She made a gesture that said clearly, Watch what you say in front of the kids.

"Send them out in the yard. You stay by the telephone. Take the book, start at the A's. Everybody you get, give them the message. *Just* the message. Don't let them get to talking and hold up the line."

He put on his hat, adjusting it carefully so that it was secure and level, and ran to his patrol car. By the time he had started the motor and turned the car around to go out, Leona was beside the driveway. "Here, take this," she said, handing him a brown paper bag that felt warm and smelled of fried chicken. "Tidal wave or no tidal wave, you got to eat something."

Twenty men met at the fire hall: the butcher, the postmaster, the one resident minister, the barber (one day a week), two carpenters, five farmers, three commercial fishermen, two auto mechanics, two truck drivers, the owner of a sawmill, and an artist. On the map of Wolf, the deputy marked out twenty territories. In minutes, a curious fleet of squad cars—all models, all makes, all ages—was on its way.

From the fire hall, Schmidt proceeded to the Harbor Inn, where he advised the manager to evacuate the Inn and motel and to warn everyone aboard the boats moored to the Inn's floating pier.

The manager was incredulous. "Tidal wave? *Here?* Well, I guess I would be liable . . ." Halfheartedly, he promised to follow instructions.

The deputy ran out to his brown-green car with the horizontal gold stripe and raced to East Harbor, where Wolf's commercial fishing fleet was moored. At this time of year, gill netters were in harbor during the daytime, scattered across the bay as thick as cars in a shopping center parking lot. They fished at night, usually from five in the afternoon until five the next morning.

Half the boats had already put out to sea. The most the deputy could do was warn the operator of the Company fish tender and the ten or fifteen fishermen still tied up at the pier. But what to do about the boats at anchor in the harbor? A young boy in a dinghy solved the problem.

His outboard had a lot of speed, he said proudly, and he agreed enthusiastically to cruise the bay and pass along the warning. "They'll hear me, all right," he assured the deputy, his freckled face glowing with a happy grin.

In the time he had, Deputy Schmidt covered every side road, following every rutted lane to its dead end. He was chiefly concerned about the people in houses without telephones, the people in the fields and on the beaches, and the isolated cabins in the woods. As he searched, the flat voice of the radio operator in the sheriff's office beat against his eardrums.

ALL UNITS, EMERGENCY PROCEDURE. FIRST REPORTS FROM ALEUTIANS INDICATE SEVERE DAMAGE. ETA ALASKA MAINLAND, ETA COASTAL AREAS BRITISH COLUMBIA, ETA WASHINGTON . . .

He reached the Lee Corners general store at a few minutes after eight o'clock. Normally the rotund storekeeper, "H.P.," would have locked up and gone home, but the door was wide open. The deputy bolted through it.

A shoulder of lamb lay on the chopping block, a slab of beef and a knife and meat saw beside it. "H.P.?" The deputy's voice bounced off shelves of canned goods and drifted like a wisp of smoke to the far corner where bolts of printed cotton were stacked on an old oak dining room table. A volunteer fireman had been here, or maybe Leona had called. . . .

A telephone hung on the wall above an old black ice cream freezer. As he dialed his home number, a burst of unintelligible dialogue came up from the patrol car into the abandoned store. His radio . . . The line was busy. He put down the receiver, looked uncertainly toward his car, waited, tried again. Line busy . . .

The deputy was sweating. Damp circles stained his shirt, spreading under both arms as he dialed, waited, dialed again. The heavy twill fabric of his shirt was sticking to his chest.

On the fourth try, Leona answered. His voice was tight in his throat as he told her to put blankets and food in the Chevy and a gallon jug of water, and to drive the children up to Justin Heights and stay there until he came for them.

"What for, Frank? Our place is far back from shore. Nothing's going to come up *this* far."

"Listen, honey," he said urgently. "That's what I thought. But reports are beginning to come in from Alaska, and they sound bad."

"That's *Alaska!* I've been talking to people who lived in the Outer Islands all their lives. They just laughed when I said tidal wave."

"Tomorrow, they can laugh at me all they want to. But right now, Leona, you do what I say. Fast!"

Chapter Thirteen

AT nine o'clock Pacific Standard Time on the night of August fourth, the first wave of the tsunami was 500 miles off the coast of British Columbia and the state of Washington. On Phoenix Island, which lay directly in its path, Andrew Held's house guests were sipping Benedictine and cognac in the living room while Carlo strummed his guitar and sang the rippling melodies of Hawaii.

In the kitchen, Mary surveyed the conspicuous waste of a four-course dinner. Dr. Held himself had chosen the menu. When she protested that everything on it was "foreign," he took a notebook from his pocket, sat at the kitchen table, and wrote down the recipes from memory.

"If you can read," he said, handing her the notebook, "you can cook."

So it had been lobster from South Africa, artichokes and endive from California, cheese and candied chestnuts from France, olive oil from Italy. The beef was the only item that hadn't been flown in from 1,000 to 6,000 miles away, and by Dr. Held's order, even that staple had been tricked up into a center-cut filet basted with dry Madeira and cognac and garnished with filled mushroom caps. Mary viewed the whole meal as an exercise in useless complication. What would those poor rich people do if they had to get by just eating food?

She had no criticism, however, of Dr. Held's choice of bourbon, and she'd had quite a bit of it. Brushing a strand of gray hair back from her face, she calculated her chances of getting a little more.

Jimmy, the "helper," was still unloading the *Trident.* But he could catch her with a shot glass in hand and he'd look the other way. Jimmy was her brother's boy, and the same as her own. His mother had died before the child was old enough for school, and her brother spent most of the year in Alaska.

Mary had reared Jimmy in her own rough Outer Island tradition. He got his first buck deer when he was twelve years old. He could run any tractor made, and he knew how to bring out a calf born in breech position. If they had been poor, who noticed? They weren't the only family that used a rifle to keep meat on the table, and Jimmy always had special clothes for school and a good pair of boots. He was a good boy, a bright boy. Right now he was hipped on electronics, but when she offered to write his father in Alaska and ask for tuition to trade school, Jimmy had backed off. He didn't want to leave the island. He'd be satisfied to do a little farming and a little fishing, and cut a little cordwood, if in that way he could stay on Wolf Island for the rest of his life.

Mary knew the feeling. As a young girl, she had been a bright student and, with the encouragement of her parents, had gone to the mainland to take a secretarial course. In six months she fled the competition and the pressure and returned gratefully to the comfortable poverty she had always known. If Jimmy was really interested in electronics, she would help him, but she would not force him to go to school. If he was only dreaming . . .

She chuckled tipsily. She could guess why Jimmy was taking so long to clean up the *Trident*. He was fiddling around with the boat's radio and ship-to-shore telephone system, as he did whenever he figured Donald Campbell wouldn't catch him at it. That was *his* secret. Hers was that she raided the liquor cabinet whenever Donald forgot to lock it.

Tonight, she was in luck. When Donald left the kitchen to show Diana the swimming pool, he forgot the keys lying on the pantry shelf. Mary hurried to the back door and peered across the yard toward the pool. No one in sight. A wide smile wrinkled her lined brown face as she hurried into the pantry.

"It's a beautiful pool," Diana said politely, avoiding Donald Campbell's small, staring eyes. It was hard to keep her mind on what he was showing her. The quarrel with Rolf possessed her, a deep physical pain blurring all other impressions.

It had begun when she told Rolf it was foolish to buy Johnson's gill netter. According to her grandmother, Minnie Lindgren, the equipment was poor and the price too high. Rolf had not really disagreed about the boat. He had been working it for Johnson ever since the gill-net season opened. He knew its condition and had often cursed Johnson for being too tight-fisted to put in a radio. But he was fiercely independent, consumed with the need to have a boat of his own. And so he had countered by telling Diana she shouldn't go to Phoenix. While she was gone the manager at the Harbor Inn would give someone else her job. More important, he had only a few weeks on Wolf Island.

Actually, these were small differences, easily resolved if it hadn't been for the emotional issue that had gathered around them like an invisible storm cloud. She let Rolf kiss her, but lightly. When his mouth lingered, she tensed. If he rested his hands on her back, she trembled uncontrollably. There had been times when Rolf embraced her so demandingly that she felt every contour of his body. Even as desire flooded through her, she had panicked, pulled free, and run.

Rolf asked *"Why?"* with pain and longing in his dark eyes. She could not even begin to answer. She knew, and she could face it squarely when she was alone. Rolf wanted her, and she wanted him, but she was afraid. Ever since that night in her sister's house, when she had been awakened by the pressure of hands on her bare shoulders and in the dark heard her sister's husband whisper, "Lie still, baby, just lie still . . ."

And so, because she did not know how to reach inside herself, wrench out the tumorous fear and show it to him, Diana had assailed Rolf's desire to buy Johnson's gill netter. Rolf retaliated by saying he would be gone for good before she got back from Phoenix. And so she had been crying when she boarded the *Trident* . . .

Donald Campbell's voice demanded, "Hey, Diana, are you listening? I said, did you bring a swim suit?"

"I . . ." She hesitated, and then told the simple truth. "Mine is too old. It was one of my sister's. I didn't think it was good enough."

Donald's eyes fastened hungrily on her lips, the lower lip softly rounded, the upper lip short and curving. Her dark hair parted over her shoulders and fanned out over her breasts, and the nippled peaks thrust through the silky covering.

The tip of his tongue moved across his lips as he

imagined what it would be like to pull off her clothes. He had been aching with such images from the moment she came aboard the *Trident*. Those big eyes of hers, so wide open between the thick dark lashes. He'd like to show her what a real man looks like; those eyes would get even bigger. If he guessed right and she had never had a man between her legs, she might be afraid. That was the day-dream he liked best. Diana crying, Diana struggling while he held her easily . . .

Diana backed away and started toward the ramp lead-ing up from the pool to the house.

"Wait a minute. First, you oughta see that building there, the one Dr. Held calls a cabana." He cupped a big hand under her elbow and guided her up the ramp to the bath house. Opening the first door, he pulled her into the shadowy dressing room. "Some place, huh?"

His little eyes moved from her lips to her throat to the smooth tanned skin showing above the top button of her shirt. The shirt was bright blue, and as she looked up at him, her wide eyes held shimmering reflections of the blue.

"Towels, shower, everything you need except a bathing suit. But who needs a bathing suit, huh?" His attempt at a friendly laugh turned into a gurgle deep in his throat.

She tried to leave, but his massive body blocked the door. "Don't be in such a hurry, Diana. Listen . . ."

Now she was really scared. Her mouth opened, and her eyes shone. More than ever, she reminded him of a trapped animal. God, he wanted her . . . Dizzy with need, he looked into her frightened face. "You think I'm going to hurt you, don't you, Diana?"

She whispered, "Yes."

"I want to. Jesus, how I want to. But I won't." He stepped aside, clearing the doorway. "Go on back to the house. Right now!"

For a second she was motionless.

"I said, get the hell out of here!"

That broke the paralysis of fear and she was past him, out the door, running up the ramp toward the house.

"You're beautiful!" Donald cried huskily after the fleeing girl. In a burst of furious loneliness, he pulled a large terrycloth beach towel off the shelf and, with one en-raged motion, ripped it in two.

While Carlo sang, Andrew Held rested his head against the back of the overstuffed throne that was his favorite chair and reflected on his good fortune in bringing this disarming young Hawaiian to Phoenix.

Superficially, the dinner party was a success. The food had been excellent, for all of Mary's grumbling. Though Diana was a native daughter, a child-woman who should have wild flowers in her hair and the juice of wild berries on her lips, she had served all four courses without a gaffe. In short, the stage props had been in order. Nevertheless, Dr. Held reflected, there had been a brittle edge to the well-bred conversation, and the atmosphere at the table had snapped with invisible tensions. It was more peaceful now, for while Carlo played, the others were relieved of the burden of communicating with each other. Everyone, Dr. Held mused, has retreated across his personal moat and hoisted the drawbridge.

His glance moved in speculation from guest to guest. He liked Blake Mansfield. He was everybody's Best Friend in college. Loyal, courteous, sensitive, eager. When Andrew Held called him "Mr. Mansfield," the nice blue eyes had smiled myopically through the thick lenses, and the young man said earnestly, "Blake, if you don't mind, Dr. Held." The inconsistency hadn't struck Andrew at the time. He was "Dr. Held" to all his students, and there was a distinctly collegiate air about this young attorney. Now he recognized it, and smiled. Yes, Blake Mansfield was charming, and so was his wife.

It was their way of directing their charm toward everyone else, scarcely speaking or even looking at each other, that broadcast the tension between them. When Blake spoke of escaping New York City, Norma's altogether proper image had split open.

"*I* don't want to leave New York," she had objected. Her eyes teared and her voice was unsteady. "I like a modern apartment with a doorman and a sauna bath on the roof and the laundry and the garbage and the cleaning taken care of by someone else."

Carlo had been the one to intercede, with such easy good humor that the conversation resumed its civilized course. Andrew Held couldn't remember what he had said. Just a few words, softly spoken, a gentle laugh, somehow sympathizing with Blake and Norma at the same time. Carlo, he thought, is the one with the truly unassailable charm. It's not something he studied and acquired, like an academic degree.

Dr. Held's attention turned to Warren Brock. He is not a man I like, he decided, though he is amusing, and admirable for his ability as a sculptor. But at the dinner table his witty commentaries on women had been almost too discerning, and he was too open, too militant about his homosexuality.

The obbligato of his thoughts was interrupted by Mike, the male basset, who strolled across the room on stubby pronated legs and laid his damp muzzle on his master's knee. With a long guttural sigh, the hound rolled his bloodshot eyes in frank admiration.

Dr. Held dropped one hand onto the dog's head and began to knead the satiny hide. Composing thumbnail analyses of his guests was simply an exercise for a curious mind. The truth was that only one person in the room really interested him. Stroking Mike's ear, Held looked up again, and this time his glance settled on Felicia.

How elegant she was in her dinner gown of white silk, cut with the high bodice and low circular neckline of a medieval robe. Her heavily jeweled fingers were tapping the arm of the chair in a quick, nervous rhythm. At the dinner table she had radiated a queenly self-assurance as she described her current project, a benefit ball at the Shoreham. Now, when the music was forcing them all into at least a pretense of repose, he sensed that Felicia's composure was a fragile cover for emotions she wanted to conceal. Was it possible that the regal Felicia was actually unhappy?

With the shock of revelation, Andrew Held realized he had been listening to his wife as he never had before. He had always been bored by social conversation, and he usually retired from the lists, silent and restless. Whereas in professional circles, he was a spirited conversationalist. He had once pointed this out to Felicia when she criticized his moody behavior at a dinner party.

"In the presence of people who are capable of understanding what I am saying, I talk a great deal."

Felicia nodded. "Yes, I know. I have seen you with your fellow scientists. You do *all* the talking—but I suppose that's because you have a great deal to say."

"At this point," he had retorted, "I have more to learn from my enemies than I do from my friends."

"Ah, Andy. If I were only an enemy . . ."

Andrew Held closed his eyes, shutting out the dinner party on Phoenix in an effort to plumb the meaning of that long-ago conversation. Had he ever really listened to Felicia? Had two years of solitude taught him something that would have saved their marriage? He had always been secure in his belief that he was a "sensitive" person. Tonight it struck him that most people who profess sensitivity are actually thinking only of how they themselves are affected by others, and not at all about how "sensitive" they are toward anyone else.

Mea culpa, he thought unhappily. Was it now too late? He did not know exactly what Felicia's purpose was in coming to Phoenix, but he did sense, with gloomy foreboding, that whatever she had to reveal would destroy all his foolish hopes that she might someday come back into his life.

On the fishing grounds off the coast of Wolf Island, the twinkling lights of the gill netters cast cheerful streams of gold across the black sea. Rolf Morgan was late. By the time he steered Johnson's old tub into the area, two dozen boats had already taken positions. Without a radio, he couldn't query other boats, and it was too early anyway. They had just made their first set, and it would be at least two or three hours before they pulled their nets and discovered if this was to be a good night. But the broad swells, the smell of the wind, and the size of recent catches told him the sockeye were running. With any luck —or, more exactly, without any bad luck, such as wrapping his net around a buoy or fouling it up on his reel— he might haul in a thousand dollars' worth of salmon before six o'clock in the morning. This was the night. This was going to be a big one. And still he kept thinking, I don't care.

He had felt better when he was angry, as he had been when he said good-bye to Diana at the Harbor Inn marina. Anger had smothered the guilty knowledge that he could have avoided their quarrel; anger blacked out the image of Diana crying. But at last his anger deserted him. From the beach he had watched the *Trident* back away from the pier, circle slowly, and put out to sea. Long before she was out of sight his natural honesty had risen like a clean fresh wind and blown away the last ugly wisp of indignation.

It had been a lonely and aimless afternoon, frustrated as he was by his impossible wish to see Diana—not next week when she was coming back to Wolf, but right now. At five o'clock, he rowed out to his gill netter, lifted the skiff, secured it on the roof of the cabin, and slid his lunch bucket and bad weather gear under the bow. Fifteen minutes later he had checked his equipment and gasoline supply, and the winch motor was humming as it rotated the spool and hauled anchor. As he left the harbor in the nightly parade of fishing boats, he was still obsessed by his desire to see Diana, to touch her, to somehow make things right.

On the fishing grounds, he threw the clutch into neutral and looked around. Some of these boats would return to harbor in the morning with salmon spilling out of both fish pens and flopping around in the hold. He could be one of them, and there wasn't a fisherman out here who needed money more than he. Old Johnson was asking seven thousand for this aging gill netter, but a catch of two or three hundred sockeye would make a good down payment. Yes, this was the night . . .

He never unreeled his net.

The practical realities were clear to him: He had to fish to make money, and he had to wait to see Diana. But reality was no match for the glorious moment of youthful rebellion that surged through him, throbbing in the blood vessels in his neck and tightening in his chest. "You crazy Indian nut!" he said out loud as he put the boat into gear, and with all the speed the aging scow could muster, he put out to sea and headed for Phoenix.

In an hour, the last companionable lights of other boats had faded away. The rhythmic chugging of the engine floated out across empty seas. The water peeled back from the stern in long straight parallel rolls that spread out behind the boat until the ripples flattened and melted into darkness. He was totally alone, moving out of blackness into blackness. He was excited, but not by fear. To have his blood race through him was a good feeling, like winning a tough canoe race. He did not doubt himself, his boat, or his absolute need to see Diana. During the long dark ride across the empty sea, the only fear he knew was a tremor when he realized that he might not have decided to go on to Phoenix Island.

The sun had been down for two hours. Directly ahead, the moon was rising. As the pale disc lifted above the horizon, a silver glow spread out across the water. In the distance, the dark silhouette of an island rose out of the sea. Rolf jumped to his feet. Laughter burst from his throat like a song.

Chapter Fourteen

It was after ten o'clock, and Andrew Held's guests were in a euphoric mood induced by excellent liqueurs and Carlo's lilting melodies. No one spoke of going to bed.

Felicia listened with her eyes partly closed. She was secretly amused that so many of Carlo's songs were already familiar to her. In fact, the whole situation piqued her sense of the ironic . . . that her partner in a *petite affaire*—or unpremeditated roll in the hay, to quote Alfred Lunt in the long-ago *Reunion in Vienna*—should be under her husband's roof. That she should be sitting equidistant from husband and lover, free to observe them both under half-closed lids. The situation, however, was potentially dangerous. She intended to be extremely cautious.

She had come to Phoenix on a mission for which she must secure the utmost of Andrew Held's goodwill. Though their marriage was by now a technicality, her husband had refused to cooperate in obtaining a divorce, clinging obstinately to the notion that their multiple problems would magnetically dissolve, and, here on Phoenix Island (Heaven forbid!), they would reunite. Rationally, Andrew might know that she hadn't been celibate for two years, but emotionally he would react furiously if he stumbled across the tracks of another man. So Felicia was grateful to Carlo. He was not only an artful lover but, not surprisingly for a man with an innate sense of the fitness of things, he also had a gentlemanly respect for protocol. Here on Phoenix, he had skillfully avoided any word or action that might suggest they had ever met.

Her attention moved from Carlo to Andrew. Yes, there was beauty in Andrew's face. Refinement to the narrow high-bridged nose, a compelling vitality in the bright blue eyes. She had been attracted by the intensity of the eyes and touched by the hint of vulnerability betrayed occasionally in a sudden softness around his mouth. She had even liked his shaggy look—the bushy eyebrows, the rumpled tangle of brown curly hair. Yes, she had loved him almost as much as she had admired him. But how did she feel now? She didn't know. Even her memory of loving him once was confused and dimmed by the scars of their mutual failure.

As if such reflections had struck a nerve, her head jerked to the side, just enough to remove Andrew Held from her line of vision and bring the Mansfields and Warren Brock into view. An amusing man, this Brock. His effeminacy did not repel her. Every mature woman needs one close homosexual friend. The malicious edge of his wit did not hurt her because she recognized the game. During cocktails, he had opened a portfolio of sketches and photographs of his sculpture. A number of photographs showed wood carvings of a slender male figure that Felicia guessed—as it turned out, correctly—were made from the same model. "On Wolf Island?" she asked.

The sculptor's round mouth pursed into a perfect O as he framed a silent "no." Then in a brittle tone of voice, he amended it. "Until recently. I sent him back to California."

Felicia had thought, Aha, a lovers' quarrel.

Focusing her half-closed eyes on the Mansfields, Felicia decided that Brock was interesting because he was unpredictable—totally candid one moment, devious the next —whereas the Mansfields were almost stereotypes. Very nice stereotypes. Literate, patrician, politically conservative, clean good looks, suitably athletic and yet holders of season tickets to the symphony. Their bodies were slender and well cared for. Felicia guessed that they went through a prescribed series of exercises for at least fifteen minutes every day. Their clothes were expensive but restrained.

Felicia thought, No wonder Norma, pretty and so well-brought-up, is so obviously uncomfortable in a strange environment. Her patterns are inherited, tested, and set in concrete; they protect her from having to deal with the unfamiliar. If her husband was serious in his heretical thoughts of leaving New York City, then Norma's world was under siege and the controlled hostility that shot back and forth between them like an electric charge was understandable. Well, *I* wouldn't leave Washington, Felicia reflected. If I were you, you good-looking blond tennis player with the lucrative law practice, I'd romp right back to New York as fast as possible. Some growths can't be transplanted. If you try to move your wife, she will shrivel up, like a plant without water or sunlight.

Carlo's song ended. Andrew Held rose and limped across the room to the carved teakwood sideboard. The hounds, Mike and Lilli, had been sleeping beside his chair. They lifted their heads, following their master's movements with sleepy speculation. Having decided that crossing the room was impractical, they dropped their heads onto their paws and closed their eyes again.

At the sideboard, Dr. Held picked up a cut-glass decanter filled with a gold-brown liquid that glowed in the muted candlelight. "I suggest we give Carlo a half-hour break. I'll refill the glasses."

His guests murmured agreement. Carlo pulled the guitar strap over his head, set the instrument on his chair, and slid open the glass door leading out onto the sundeck. He closed it gently and disappeared down the steps toward the boat dock.

Felicia rose. "I'd like to finish the evening with champagne. If you have it, Andy. First, however, I'm going to my room. Just for a moment. I'll be right back."

Dr. Held pressed the buzzer connected with a bell in Donald Campbell's quarters at the back of the house. There was no answer. He tried three times, and still no response. Frowning, he pressed the second button that sounded in the kitchen. Not Campbell but Diana answered the summons. Still wondering why his manager was not on the job, Andrew Held told her to fetch the champagne, wine bucket, and glasses.

Felicia opened the bedroom door, flipped the light switch, and closed the door. As she approached the dressing table, an alcove containing a small writing desk came into view. Donald Campbell, with a flashlight dangling from one hand, was standing between the desk and the wall.

Felicia's reaction was not to retreat but to advance. "Explain yourself, Mr. Campbell," she said icily. "And then—*get out!*"

Campbell's scarred face stiffened with surprise. After the scene with Diana he had felt ugly and rejected. His impulse to come looking for Mrs. Held's jewelry was the conditioned reflex of a self-hating human being; he had always rid himself of bad feelings by "getting back" at someone. But his mind worked slowly, He had been in the bedroom for several minutes before stumbling onto the fact that stealing on Phoenix was impossible.

There weren't enough suspects. Diana and Mary and the boy, Jim, had stayed in the kitchen all evening and could alibi one another. Besides, who would suspect them? When Felicia surprised him, he had already decided to wait until he ferried her back to Wolf Island. The burglary of a motel room would be hard to pin on him. In a hoarse voice, he spoke the truth. "I was just leaving anyway."

She kept coming on, her head lifted up high and mighty and her bright mouth drawn down in an expression of disgust he recognized all too well. He thought bitterly, Damn you, lady. Rich bitch who screwed Carlo Minatti and thought she could get away with it. His small eyes narrowed. "Well, I *was* going to leave. But I ain't, until we have a little understanding. Like about you and Carlo last night."

Carlo was standing on the end of the boat dock, smoking a cigarette. His half-hour break was up. It was back to the living room, more music, more songs. He was reluctant to go because far out, beyond the mouth of the U-shaped harbor, the masthead light of some sort of fishing boat was twinkling like an orange star. As she yawed around, the port and starboard lights blinked red and green and the white glow on the top of the cabin swung from side to side. She must be a small boat, for the lights were close to the water. And she must be headed for Phoenix, if only because this was the only possible destination, unless the skipper was headed for the Aleutians.

As the boat came nearer, moonlight pulled its shape out of the shadow. A large reel was mounted at her stern. Obviously, a gill netter. Carlo smiled. That crazy young Indian! Who else but Rolf Morgan would be putting into Phoenix Island on a night when every other fisherman on Wolf Island would be making his grubstake forty miles to the east? Carlo's intuition quickly supplied the answer. He himself had never in his life gone to so much trouble to see a girl, but he sympathized with the impulse that spurred Rolf to follow Diana all the way to Phoenix.

He would have called out, but the gill netter was still too far away, and Rolf couldn't possibly hear his voice over the thudding beat of the engine. Carlo turned, still smiling, and strolled toward the house.

When he first came down to the dock, Carlo had noted automatically that the tide was out. As he walked back, something about the tide began to bother him.

He stopped, turned around, and surveyed the harbor with a growing sense of uneasiness. The *Trident,* tied to the pier fore and aft, rolled gently from side to side. This afternoon the deck had been even with the pier. Now, it was out of sight until he leaned over the edge of the dock and looked straight down.

He did some simple figuring. This month, there was a difference of nine or ten feet between the early morning Highs and Lows, but only a three- or four-foot fluctuation between flood and ebb tide in the late afternoon and evening, and a shorter period before the tide turned. So with high water about three P.M., add approximately five hours for the water to go out. What was it now—10:30 P.M., more or less. For at least two hours, the tide should have been *rising.* Yet even as he was standing here, trying to figure out what seemed wrong, Carlo could see the water get lower. Very slowly, but steadily. Not like the flux, the swishing forward and back, forward and back, of a normal tide. It was receding as if the whole bay were going to empty, as if some huge invisible suction pump was drawing all the water out to sea. It reminded him . . .

Hilo! Hilo in 1960, when the sea had pulled back, just as it was doing now, and a half hour later the mountainous bore of raging water roared back into the harbor, swamping and crushing small boats, pounding the larger craft against the docks, drowning or maiming those who ignored the warning and stayed to watch. Of course! *Tsunami!*

Tsunami! . . . For a fraction of a second, Carlo looked helplessly at the approaching gill netter. He muttered a prayer to Pelé to have mercy on a young fisherman who was too far out from land to hear a warning. Then he raced for the house.

He did not see the boy, Jimmy, who had been hiding in the cabin of the *Trident* ever since Carlo came down to the dock and lit his first cigarette. Jimmy was fascinated by the ship-to-shore telephone and marine band radio. Donald Campbell had forbidden him to touch them. So tonight, as on other nights when he figured he wouldn't get caught, he had left the kitchen, presumably to go to his room, but instead he crept through the dark, around the boathouse and onto the pier. When Carlo ran past the boat on his way to the house, Jimmy thanked his lucky stars and went back to his loving study of the radio. So far, he had never quite dared to turn it on.

Carlo's clattering footsteps on the wooden pier were also heard by the cook, Mary. Since she was stretched out on a lounge chair beside the swimming pool, she could not see who it was, but then she didn't want to be seen, either. The moment she had found herself alone in the kitchen, Donald Campbell gone goodness knows where, and with Diana serving champagne in the living room, Mary had focused her cunning on "borrowing" a fifth of bourbon from the pantry and making off with it to a nice quiet corner where no one would think of looking for her. The swimming pool. Who would think good old fat Mary the cook would be sitting beside the swimming pool? What the devil, she had put in her day's work. They could yell for her all they wanted, she was going to stay right here, drinking whiskey and having a right good time.

Felicia looked squarely into Donald Campbell's grinning face. "That's blackmail, you know. You won't tell Dr. Held I was in bed with Carlo if I don't tell him you're a thief."

Campbell shook his head. "You know I ain't stole nothing."

"You entered my room. Your intent was to steal."

Campbell's little eyes were shrewd. "I'm the maintenance man. I had to check the electric heaters."

"You expect Dr. Held to believe that?"

"Even if he don't, I can sure get him to believe what I know about you."

She spat furiously. "He'll fire you! You'll lose your job!"

"Huh! What'll he do to *you?*"

She stared at him, repulsed by his brutish strength and panicked by the raw threat of an ugly scene to come. She had acted impulsively, stupidly, indulging in a night of lovemaking with a young and beautiful man. But her husband hadn't been in her bed for three years. He had deserted her, and her occasional affairs since that time should be judged on the basis of aesthetics, not morals. She did regret her act, and in fact was badly frightened by the prospect of this infuriating little melodrama being played out to its unpleasant conclusion. This clumsy oaf had not half-imagined the harm he could do her and her plans. In a subtle way, Andrew could be so much more punishing than Campbell's simpleton version of aggrieved husband confronting unfaithful wife.

For a moment she felt like a small child trying to see how long she could hold her breath as she balanced the meanness of bargaining with Campbell against the destruction of her entire purpose in coming to Phoenix. Her head cleared. If she had any pride, there was only one possible course. She walked to the door, opened it, and said curtly, "Follow me."

Bewildered, Donald Campbell trailed her down the hall. "What the hell," he grumbled at her heels. "I told you, I won't say nothing if you don't."

She swept on, her long pointed white sleeves floating out behind her like banners. "You bungler," she threw back over her shoulder. "You're not going to tell him. *I* am."

Campbell's voice rose to a nervous whinny. "Listen, lady, there's no use to—" He reached out to stop her. His big hand barely grazed her shoulder, for now she was running. Together, with Campbell almost losing balance as he tried to block her, they burst into the living room.

The three men were near the front windows. On the other side of the room, Diana held a tray of champagne glasses while Norma Mansfield transferred glasses to the sideboard. Dr. Held came forward, threw a puzzled look at Felicia, and then at Donald Campbell. "I wanted you, Donald. You didn't answer my ring."

"I was checking the heating system."

"He's lying." Felicia's voice, very low, stung the air like the crack of a whip. "Andy, I have something to tell you."

Dr. Held's bushy eyebrows met in a worried frown. "Now?"

Felicia gestured toward the french door opening into the garden. "I'd prefer, Andy, that you and I and Mr. Campbell step outside. I can promise you that what we have to say will be excessively boring to your guests."

"Yes, of course." With a polite nod for Felicia, Dr. Held moved toward the open door, but he did not reach it. On the opposite side of the living room, the glass door to the sundeck slammed open and Carlo Minatti burst into the room.

Carlo was breathing heavily. His dark skin shone with perspiration. "Dr. Held! Tsunami!"

They stared, absorbing neither the strange word nor the terror that was so obvious in his dark eyes.

"Tsunami!" he cried again.

In uneven, rapid steps, Dr. Held crossed the room. "Tidal wave, Carlo?"

Carlo answered with two emphatic nods.

"You are sure? You know the signs?"

Still fighting for breath, Carlo described what he had seen in the bay and what, as a boy of twelve, he had seen when a tsunami swept into the town of Hilo. Buildings knocked off their foundations, buses overturned. Sixty-one people drowned because they refused to heed the warning.

It was a brief and frantic recital, spilling ugly brutal pictures. Shocked, Norma Mansfield automatically turned toward her husband, waiting for him to call it all nonsense. Instead he murmured, "Frightening . . ." in the same detached tone of voice he would use to find fault with the opera's new baritone.

Warren Brock's thick sun-bleached eyebrows were raised in skepticism. He remembered newspaper accounts of a "disaster" in Hawaii, but those people loved them. Look what they did every time Mauna Loa erupted. They chartered planes and rushed to fly over the crater . . .

Felicia did not understand "tsunami" as a scientific reality. Her eyes kept straying to the frosty wine bucket and its unopened bottle of champagne.

With Carlo's first gasping word, Dr. Held's mind had raced backward from effect to cause, mentally tracing the links from tidal wave to earthquake, earthquake to submarine landslide or explosion, explosion to the fearful potential of the "Armageddon" bomb test on Pater Island. In seconds, all pertinent elements had been fed into his lightning calculator of a mind, and the smoothly functioning machine had ejected the answer. Knowing the cause, he fully appreciated the danger.

With one simple gesture of his right hand, Dr. Held cut off Carlo's monologue. His commanding tone made it clear to everyone: Andrew Held was in charge. "Carlo, how much time do we have?"

"Maybe twenty minutes, maybe only ten. The pullback acts differently, different places."

"The house, the dock, everything is at sea level. We'll leave instantly and climb to higher ground."

His alert blue eyes reviewed the troops. "We're all here, except Mary and Jimmy. Donald, go fetch them. I'll lead the others to the path up the hill. You know the way, Donald. You, Mary, and Jimmy will go directly there. On your way. Hurry!"

Donald disappeared through the dining room.

Norma Mansfield was on her feet, plucking nervously on the sleeve of her yellow linen dinner dress. With a small frown, she turned to Blake. "Climb a hill? In this? Shouldn't we change?"

Blake said politely, "I'm afraid there may not be time."

Andrew Held limped to the door opening onto the back yard. The two basset hounds struggled to their feet and followed him, tails wagging with pleasure because their master was going to take them for a walk. "All of you, quickly. But *do not run.* You would stumble and hurt yourselves, and that would slow us all down. The hill is steep, and the path is rough. We use it very little. It is going to be a hard climb."

In the back yard, they knotted around him. "No," he said sharply. "Form a line."

With Andrew Held in the lead, the dogs in tandem at his heels, they proceeded across the back yard, down a grassy slope framed by rose bushes, then up again to the base of the hill. Here, the gardens, well-kept shrubbery, and clipped lawn ended abruptly. Ahead lay a narrow path barely visible in the pale moonlight. It followed a steep upward course between monolithic boulders whose gray granite surfaces were obscured by a heavy growth of scrubby madrona trees and twisted pine.

Dr. Held stopped and looked around. This was the spot where Donald, Mary, and Jimmy were to join them. But the only shadowy figure at the rear of the column was that of Felicia, flowing white silk rippling out behind her as she ran back to the house.

"Felicia! No!" But the white figure kept running. Andrew Held muttered in Hungarian. In English, he gave the order for the night. "Blake, will you proceed, please, with Mrs. Mansfield and Mr. Brock. Diana and Carlo, you, too. When you reach the top of the first hill you will be in dense woods. Moonlight will be cut off. You will have to feel your way carefully. Whatever happens, do not leave the path. In one or two places, there is a precipice on each side. Now, quickly but carefully—"

Carlo spoke. "I have to go back, Dr. Held."

"In the name of God, why?"

"A friend from Wolf, a gill netter. He was pulling into the bay when I first noticed the way the tide was acting. He was too far out to hear me so I ran for the house. By now he's closer, and he might have turned off his engine. If he's caught in the harbor, on his boat . . ." The sentence was left unfinished as Carlo turned to go back. Diana cried "Rolf!" and followed.

Dr. Held shouted "No, Diana! I say, no!" His answer was the rapidly fading image of a slender girl in white running downhill toward the boat dock.

From the hill above came the sounds of stumbling footsteps, the crackle of brush, the plop of rocks dislodged by a footfall and rolling down the path. Dr. Held was alone, except for Mike and Lili, waiting expectantly, tails thumping on the hard ground.

Other than Carlo, he was the only one burdened with the knowledge of what was really happening. The girl Diana ran out through the night calling "Rolf!" but she did not entirely comprehend what sort of disaster threatened Rolf, only that he was in danger. The Mansfields and Warren Brock had accepted his instructions because he was the host and they were well-brought-up. As for Felicia . . .

The unusual exertion was already stirring up the pain in his bad leg. From the first, he had recognized that once everyone else was on the path, he would place himself at the end of the line. But he had to go back for Felicia, and the extra price this repeated descent and ascent would cost him could not be a consideration. He began the descent and then he saw her, walking unhurredly across the moonlit yard.

At the edge of the lawn, she halted and tucked some sort of sack into her bodice. Then she lifted her long silk skirt and continued carefully up the slope.

When she was beside him, she said simply, "I went back for something."

He was angry. "Something of greater importance than your life?"

She laughed. "Bosh, Andy."

Another figure left the house and moved up the slope. It was Donald Campbell, alone.

Dr. Held called, "Where are the others? Mary? Jimmy?"

Donald Campbell stopped ten feet below them. "I went through every room in the house. I looked all around the yard. I can't find them."

"They can't have disappeared. Go back and look again."

Far below, a shout from Carlo broke the peaceful night. "I see the wave! I see it! Run!"

Donald Campbell advanced on Dr. Held, looming over him like a crazed giant. "*You* go back and look again!" With that he pushed the older man off the path. As Andrew Held fell, Donald dropped to the ground and scrambled up the dark hillside on his hands and knees.

The crest of the killer wave glistened in the moonlight. It rolled into the harbor at twenty-five miles an hour, deliberate and unhurried in its attack.

Its first victim was Rolf Morgan's gill netter, which it picked up like a piece of cork and pitched against the end of the boat dock. The cabin burst free of the main body of the boat and tumbled end over end onto the deck of the *Trident*.

The *Trident*, festooned with splintered parts of the fishing boat, rode high on the water until it reached the walls of rock around the swimming pool. Like a frightened traveler trying to gain entrance to the inn, the sixty-foot cruiser knocked on the swimming pool walls. Glass shattered and oak timbers cracked as she beat uselessly on the rock. The great mountain of water roared over the concrete sea wall and into the pool. Trapped and angry, the water flooding the pool picked up chairs and tables, crushed them in a furious eddy, and spit them out, far over the wall and back into the bay.

In five minutes, the entire complex of buildings—house, powerhouse, cabana, covered moorage—had been reduced to wreckage. Some of it was carried out to sea when the first wave receded. Some was abandoned on the beach, lifeless plunder for the series of waves to follow. Some was cast up onto the bank, for the first thrust of tsunami had clawed hungrily at the hill Andrew Held and his guests were climbing.

The last to save themselves were Diana and Carlo. Hoarse from screaming, weak from crying, the two had waited until the white bore of the tsunami was visible at the mouth of the harbor. They escaped it by such a narrow margin that the edge of the murderous water was licking at their legs and thighs before it withdrew, pulling back with an angry hiss.

They had seen Mary's body lifted and hurled over the sea wall and tossed into the roaring blackness on the other side. They had seen Jimmy's slender figure on the bow of the *Trident*, still as a stone figure while the wave smoothly ripped the boat from its mooring and pitched it against the wall of the swimming pool.

They had never seen Rolf at all.

The wave was as capricious in retreat as it had been in attack.

Most of the *Trident* was left for the second wave, but the hull of Rolf's gill netter rode out of the harbor as if it were on a track. The first wave also captured the bodies of Mary and Jimmy. Jimmy was sucked down by the force of the undertow. He would have been killed by drowning if he hadn't already been thrown against the hull with such violence that his neck was broken.

Mary, drunk and buoyant, tossed like a rubber doll on the top of the wave. At some point outside the mouth of Phoenix harbor, where the surface of the sea had flattened out, she was thrown against the hull of the gill netter. She had the presence of mind to grab the piece of anchor chain still suspended from the battered vessel, and to hold on until she had the strength and wind to pull herself up over the side. Instantly, she passed out.

In the battered remnant of an old fishing boat, Mary was carried out to sea, still unconscious, still drunk, lying on her back in three inches of sea water—but alive.

They were safe on top of the hill. They had bruises, cuts, and scratches, for they had all stumbled on the rocks or fallen into thorny underbrush, but they were alive and dry, except for Diana and Carlo, whose clothes were soaked almost up to the waist.

They dropped wearily to the ground, stunned by a disaster they still couldn't believe. Too spent to try to communicate, they sat as far apart from one another as they dared wander in the dark. With nothing to say, they listened to the sounds of destruction, not really visualizing the destruction nor wanting to see it. The only human sound that carried into the strangely separated encampments was Diana's weeping.

After the first wave receded, the sound from below diminished to the whispering pulse of normal waves, breaking gently against the cliffs at their feet. Andrew Held, after conferring briefly with Carlo, announced that no one was to go back down the hill. They accepted the order mutely. Why shouldn't they? Even if he was wrong, they had no taste for seeing what had happened. They all expected to be rescued first thing in the morning and so, until dawn, this hilltop was the safest place to wait out the night.

If one of them had kept a journal, two events would have closed the report for that day.

The first took place just before the second wave roared into the bay and carried off the carcass of the *Trident*. They heard a voice, a young man's voice, calling weakly but distinctly from below.

Diana jumped to her feet. "Rolf!"

"No! Not you!" Dr. Held's voice rang with authority. "Carlo, Blake, you find him."

Carlo spotted Rolf on a ledge of rock some seventy-five feet above sea level. His body was wedged between the cliff and the one crooked and deformed pine tree that had managed to take root on the shelf of rock. He was too weak to climb. By moonlight, Carlo sought precarious footholds on the cliff's irregular face and worked his way down to the ledge. One arm around Rolf's waist, he made the upward climb, half dragging, half guiding the injured youth.

In the dark clearing at the top of the hill, the others made room for Rolf to lie down. The roar of the second killer wave rose from the beach as if an angry monster were calling to them. Diana sat down beside Rolf, but they did not speak. Much later she lay down beside him, and

Rolf drew her into his arms. That was the second of the two notable events with which that first night on Phoenix Island came to an end: For the first time in her life, Diana fell asleep, innocent though it was, in a man's arms.

BOOK II

Chapter Fifteen

ON the steep hill above Phoenix Island's harbor, eight sleepless people waited tensely for the roar of the next incoming wave and the malignant hiss of receding water. Only Andrew Held retained a sense of time. When sounds from below reached the crescendo of a new assault, he referred automatically to the illuminated face of his calendar watch, clocking the time gap between waves. Twenty minutes. Then thirty minutes. Forty minutes . . .

Pale moonlight filtered down through the pine trees to outline the figures huddled around him. Like separate armed camps, they kept their positions several feet apart, walled off from each other by the shock of the disaster. Except for Rolf and Diana, sleeping in each other's arms, they were all sitting up, their backs braced against the trunks of trees. In the moon-streaked dark Held was able to make out their profiles. Most of the time they stared straight ahead, as if to avoid even the small commitment of looking at each other.

Shortly after midnight, Held struggled to his feet and limped to the spot where Felicia was drawn together, arms around her knees and head resting against a tree. A wisp of moonlight shone in her wide-open eyes.

He asked, "Are you warm enough?"

Without looking up, she answered, "Would you give me your coat?"

"Of course." He began to pull off his dinner jacket.

"No, no . . ." She laughed wearily. "Keep it, Andy. I'm not cold."

He touched her bare arm, testing the warmth of the smooth skin. She drew back. "Just leave me alone." Her voice was low and unsteady. "I am enduring, and I'm not very good at it."

"I'll sit with you."

"No!" Her head lifted defiantly. "Thank you, but I prefer to be miserable in private."

109

He dropped his dinner jacket at her feet and retreated to his own small lonely territory.

Some time later, the last great wave crashed against the cliffs of Phoenix, clawing peevishly at the remnants in the bay and then subsiding. The monster's fury was spent. For hundreds of miles along the Pacific's rim, tsunami died on dark and mutilated beaches.

On the hill, Andrew Held checked his wristwatch and noted that this peaceful lull was continuing far longer than any of its predecessors. He waited, looking frequently at his watch, listening not to any sound but to the lack of it. He was instinctively cautious about interpreting the prolonged stillness, but after two hours he was sure. "It's over," he said quietly. "The last wave has come and gone."

Their heads turned toward him but no one spoke.

More loudly, he repeated, "It's over. The tsunami, the tidal wave. It's passed."

Warren Brock's voice inquired pettishly, "Well, what do you recommend? A toast to tsunami? That would suit me, but someone neglected to bring the champagne. How about blending joyful voices in a fine old hymn? Praise God from whom all blessings flow . . . tra la . . ."

A brittle laugh from Felicia, a muttered, "Shut up, you crazy fag" from Donald Campbell, and then Dr. Held's firm voice took charge. "We mustn't leave the woods until daylight. It wouldn't be safe. I suggest we try to sleep."

Blake Mansfield spoke for the first time. "That's very sensible." He might have been applauding an opponent's serve.

For a few minutes the little encampment on the hill rustled with movement as they sought comfortable positions on the hard ground. One by one they settled down, still apart from one another. Felicia was next to last to submit to sleep. When she finally lay down full-length on the pine needles and covered herself with his dinner jacket, Andrew Held was still upright. Fifteen minutes passed and she had not moved. He, too, lay down and closed his eyes.

As they slept, clouds gathered, dimming and shutting off the pale light of the moon. The wind changed its

course, and a fresh young breeze from the southwest
came—carrying rain.

Andrew Held was the first to awaken. The rain was
harmless, yes, but it seemed almost the last straw. His
right leg throbbed, but it was a familiar pain and did not
deter his precise scientific mind from evaluating the circumstances of this strange new day. Daybreak. The strip
of pink and orange sky visible through the trees shone
with reflections of the rising sun. The thick green roof of
overlapping branches had pretty well deflected the raindrops from the others. In any event, damp clothing would
dry quickly once they went down the hill and out into the
open. He thought, Ah, yes, once we go down the hill! On
three hours' sleep, we will have to face the true nature of
the calamity. Which of us, he thought grimly, has the
slightest idea of what we are going to find when we go
back to the house? Carlo, perhaps, because he has wit-
nessed the disaster of a tsunami before. But even Carlo
may not have thought beyond the disaster to the next
questions: Now that we have saved our lives, what happens next? And if we aren't picked up soon, how do we
continue to save our lives?

Dr. Held pushed himself up onto one knee and rose
stiffly to his feet. As if his movements broke a spell, the
others began to stir. Disoriented, drugged with sleep, their
eyes moved anxiously from one member of the group to
another. As they came fully awake, their faces showed
embarrassment and, yes, hostility. Except Diana, Dr.
Held noted. When she looked at Rolf, there was no tension in Diana's sensitive face. She kneeled beside him,
examining his cuts and gently pressing her fingers along
his bruised and swollen thigh. "I don't think it's broken,"
she said quietly. Putting one arm around him, she helped
him to sit up.

He smiled, teeth very white under his dark mustache,
dark eyes bright. "Did you sleep?"

She smiled back, and to Andrew Held, it was a perfect
answer because it expressed some sort of bond—of love
and acceptance and sympathy all at once—and for the
young couple Diana's smile expressed it so well that
words would have been superfluous.

A few feet away, Warren Brock was massaging his

eyelids with delicate strokes of his forefingers. *"Don't* tell
me I snored, *please,"* he said to no one in particular.

Donald Campbell stumbled into the underbrush, obviously intent on relieving himself. Blake Mansfield bounced
to his feet and began brushing pine needles from his
mud-soiled and rain-spotted garments, while his wife
smoothed her hair with the palms of her hands and inquired, "Did you bring a comb?"

Felicia, looking like a queen whose crown is on
crooked, extended one arm in Andrew Held's direction.
"Give me a hand up, will you, Andy?"

In weary silence, the group descended the hill. At the
spot where the heavy growth of pine, fir, and salal bushes
opened onto the sloping lawn, where the night before
they had started their ascent of the narrow path up the
hill, they came to a halt. Norma Mansfield gasped. Donald
Campbell swore under his breath. Dr. Held thought, My
God, do I deserve this calamity? and closed his eyes.

The destruction was total. Timbers that had supported
the wooden pier were still in place, rising above the
peaceful surface of the bay like parallel rows of stumps.
But the pier, the *Trident,* and every structure on shore—
everything was gone. Everything Andrew Held had built
had simply vanished.

The house, the cabana, the powerhouse, the boathouse
—all had been erased. On the far side of the bay, the
face of the hill had been cut back to raw blue clay, and
the ledge on which the house had stood was scoured
down to hardpan. Layers of sand and gravel had been
swept off the beach, exposing the underlying shale and
creating new pools in the rock. The cement bulkhead
that had walled in the swimming pool was smashed. In
the pool itself, now open to the sea, was a grotesque assortment of splintered boards, plastic bottles, and twisted
machinery. One bright blue flotation pillow bobbed
peacefully on the water.

In place of everything civilization had brought to
Phoenix were the rejects of the sea. Strewn the length
of the crescent-shaped beach were mutilated fragments of
man-made devices. The wheelhouse of a boat, a torn gill
net hopelessly tangled around a bedspring, a tennis racket
impaled on a gaff hook, a badly bent galvanized five-
gallon milk can, men's clothing snarled in a mat of eel

grass and kelp. Hundreds of useful objects in wood, metal, and glass had been so twisted and broken by the process of being ripped loose, tumbled out to sea, and thrown back onto the land that their original purposes were hard to identify.

The rose garden had disappeared under a thick layer of sand and gravel. Shattered remnants—a pot handle here, a coat hanger there, the top half of a dining room chair—protruded through the surface of the ugly dune.

Sniffing the ground, Mike and Lili, the basset hounds, padded cautiously across the coarse sand. They went directly to a silt-covered lump, and there they stopped. Lili's candlewick tail wagged excitedly. Mike reared backward, lowered his head to a menacing point, and growled.

No one had spoken since their first paralyzing view of the destruction. Still numb, they turned automatically to see what was exciting the dogs. As the object came into focus, Felicia's anguished voice split the air with a prolonged high-pitched scream.

It was a human hand, reaching up through the blackish ground as if the corpse below were signaling for help.

Andrew Held put his arm around Felicia. "Donald," he said quietly.

Donald went ahead, dropped to his knees, and with a few scooping motions, cleared away the covering sand. "It's Jimmy," he called over his shoulder. "I better cover him up again, huh?"

"Yes, please." Andrew Held glanced quickly at the stricken faces of this little cluster of people. Warren Brock almost looked as if he were laughing, though muted sobs emerged from his twisted mouth. Felicia was clutching a little leather sack hanging on a ribbon around her neck and staring blankly at the telltale mound. Norma Mansfield was weeping helplessly.

Andrew Held's mind leaped forward. At this point, the first numbness had not worn off. They were horrified by the sight of the dead boy, but they saw him as the victim of a disaster that had ended. Now, before this small band of civilized, well-bred human beings began to recognize the danger they were in, he must assume leadership.

His voice was calm but clearly authoritative. "Listen a moment, please. We will take care of the boy later. Right now, we need to talk about what we are going to do. Let's find a place to sit down."

Years before, General Curtis LeMay had been a good friend of Andrew's. As if his mind had been programmed to produce the memory when needed, Held suddenly recalled a conversation he had had with the General when the Air Force School for Survival was founded in 1949.

In survival, the General had remarked, the greatest enemy is not hunger, climate, or terrain. It is fear. Fear can paralyze human beings into passive acceptance of their fate, or it can shock them into panic. The one dependable antidote is purposeful activity. Make a plan, keep busy, keep trying.

But these people, Dr. Held reflected, do not yet realize survival is the issue. They have no idea how isolated Phoenix Island is from the rest of the world. He thought, If a helicopter suddenly swoops down to pick them up, or a Coast Guard cutter appears in the harbor, they won't recognize a miracle. It's what they are expecting. They are so confident that the nightmare of the past six hours is about to end with their timely rescue that they aren't yet aware of the outlandish picture they make. Bizarre little figures in evening dress, surrounded by hellish destruction, waiting for rescuing angels to emerge *deus ex machina* from the nothingness of the empty sky or the endless sea.

They sat on driftwood logs which the men rolled and dragged to form a rough circle. Since, disaster or no, they were obviously still thinking of him as their "host," Andrew Held was the first to speak. "Well, my friends, we haven't been shipwrecked on a desert island, à la Robinson Crusoe, but our situation is not very different. We have lost our transportation to the mainland or to Wolf, the nearest island. We have lost all means of communication. We can *expect* to be rescued, and we can *hope* to be rescued soon, but meanwhile, I think we should analyze our immediate needs."

He paused, sensing that they weren't really paying attention. The Mansfields, for example, were trying to remember their manners, but their eyes kept wandering to the spot where Jimmy lay covered by sand. All right, Dr. Held thought, let's face it. Let's start with Jimmy.

"You're wondering about the boy. Blake, Donald . . . Will you two take charge of burying him?"

Blake looked at Dr. Held curiously. "I will, of course,

but I think . . . that is, as a lawyer, I question whether it's advisable. His family will want the body, and so will the authorities. When we're picked up, the body will have to come with us."

Dr. Held hesitated. Facing the reality of a bad situation was like swimming in icy cold water. Entering slowly was torture, but plunging in could produce dangerous shock. He remembered the instructions his father had given him. Walk in until the water comes up to your waist, then go back to the beach. Your body will react to that first chilling assault, and within a minute you can go back and swim without feeling the cold. It was time for this group to enter the water, but only up to the waist . . . Held said carefully, "What to do with Jimmy depends on what we expect will happen to us. If we are picked up soon, it would be pointless to bury him. If we remain on Phoenix for some time, it's a different story."

Warren Brock sniffed delicately. *"Obviously."*

"Oh, for heaven's sake, Andy," Felicia exclaimed. "Why are we sitting around like children during story hour? Someone will be coming after us. Much as I admire the scenic wonders of Phoenix Island, I have no intention whatever of spending another night on top of that hill."

Dr. Held said patiently, "I don't blame you. You want to get back to Washington before the benefit ball at the Shoreham. Everyone here wants to be rescued. Except you, perhaps, Donald." Held's blue eyes twinkled brightly under his bushy eyebrows. He patted the heads of his hounds. "Mike and Lili are in this, too. I'm sure our present condition is not *their* idea of a dog's life."

Felicia snapped, "Get on with it, Andy. You agree, we all want to be rescued. What must we do?"

Andrew Held smiled. "A moment ago, you were demanding that some outside force or agency descend on Phoenix and save us all. Now you seem to be saying that we ourselves must do something if we are to achieve what we want. Perhaps I shouldn't quote Sophocles at a time like this, especially since I can't remember the words exactly. But almost twenty-four hundred years ago he told us *why* we will survive and *how* we will survive. He said, 'Of all the wonders of Nature, surely the most wonderful is man. For he has caught the birds of the air and the fishes of the sea, first in his mind and then in his net.' And that is what we will do right here and now. We will devise our means of survival, first in our minds and then with whatever tools our minds tell us we must use. I think, Felicia, that your marvelously practical mind is already working along those lines."

Momentarily Felicia was confused. She had meant to be disagreeable, and he had retaliated with a compliment, albeit one tinged with irony. Fingering the little pouch now hanging unconcealed on the outside of her dress, she murmured, "Well, there must be some way we can send distress signals."

"No electricity, no telephone or radio or shortwave, no ship-to-shore."

Warren Brock giggled. "*I* know. A note in a bottle."

Dr. Held looked at him evenly. "Do you even have a pencil and paper?"

"No, no, certainly *not*," Warren Brock replied brightly. "I wouldn't *dream* of throwing the game."

Norma had been studying her broken fingernails, moody and silent. At the sculptor's quip, she looked up and said disapprovingly, "This is anything but a game, Mr. Brock. I for one am beginning to realize we are in a very serious situation. The first step toward being rescued is being missed, isn't that so? But no one knows Blake and I came to Phoenix. Blake's office, our personal friends, our relatives—they knew we were flying to Seattle, but no more. I did write my uncle that we had looked up Dr. Held . . ." She turned to her husband and gave him a small rueful smile. "That's the letter I brought to Phoenix with me."

Who knows we are here? Like an invisible grinning specter, the question hovered over the circle.

"Now that's a pretty thought," Brock said soberly. "No one looks for us because no one knows where to look."

Dr. Held turned to Carlo. "You, Carlo?"

"The manager at the Harbor Inn would have been angry if he knew I took time off to come here." He shrugged and smiled. "So, I didn't tell him."

"Rolf?"

"All anyone knows is that I went out with the other boats to go fishing."

"Diana?"

With a faint smile and a glance at Rolf, she said, "I told Rolf." They both laughed, like children overcome by a private joke.

Rolf said, "But your grandmother knows."

"Oh, yes." She turned back to Dr. Held and said cheerfully, "My grandmother knows where I am. She'll get someone to come and get us."

"Oh, pshaw," Brock said. "I liked the bottle idea."

Andrew Held started to speak and then stopped. Should he point out that the tsunami which struck Phoenix had undoubtedly rolled on to strike Wolf Island and might have brought more horror to that long flat land mass . . . No, he decided, not yet.

Blake Mansfield said uncertainly, "Excuse me, but it seems to me . . ." He looked toward Rolf and then Carlo, apologizing in advance to persons who probably knew more about these things than he did. "Shouldn't we build a signal fire?"

Heads nodded, and a chorus of approval echoed around the circle. Dr. Held lifted one hand. "In daylight, would a fire be seen at a distance? I rather doubt it."

Rolf said, "Not the fire. The smoke."

"Good. We can begin to act. Let's collect driftwood."

"First," Felicia said firmly, "I'd like a drink of water."

It was a simple statement of one of the commonest of all human needs, but it shocked them. Water. Yes, of course. They all wanted a drink of water. They looked at each other expectantly, each waiting for the next person to do something about it.

Blake Mansfield broke the uneasy silence. "I remember reading someplace, years ago, that you can go without eating for forty days but you can't live a week without water." He looked around the silent circle and added apologetically, "Sorry. I should have remembered something more cheerful, right?"

Chapter Sixteen

DONALD Campbell had maintained and repaired all the machinery on Phoenix Island. Far more than Dr. Held, who had refused to learn the operation of the power plant or the jet pump because he considered them too simple, Donald fully realized how dependent they were on equipment that had vanished with the storm. "Jesus God," he said fervently, like a man coming out of a deep sleep. "We haven't got any water."

"No water?" Norma's tone was incredulous. Even "out in the country," which was the way she described the heavily populated settlement on Long Island where she and Blake maintained their second home, water was something supplied by a utility company and paid for by the fifteenth of the month. Out of the right faucet it ran cold and out of the left faucet it ran hot.

"But I thought . . ." Blake turned to Dr. Held. "I think you said during dinner last evening that you have your own water system? There must be a well."

Donald guffawed rudely. "Sure there's a well. Three hundred and fifty feet down in solid rock. You need a pump to bring water up, and we ain't got a pump. With the power plant gone, it wouldn't make no difference if we did." He rubbed his lips with the back of his hand. "I'm already thirsty as hell."

"This is getting ridiculous!" Felicia's haughty posture was only half convincing. To Andrew Held's practiced ear, her voice carried an undertone of honest fear.

Blake Mansfield blinked behind thick lenses. "I believe I have read you can drink small amounts of sea water."

Carlo shook his head vigorously. "You can drink a little sea water, but only when you don't really need it. Right now, our bodies aren't dehydrated. A little salt water wouldn't hurt us too much. But after a while it would, because we'd get twice as thirsty."

Donald regarded Carlo with a mixture of admiration and suspicion. "How come you know all that?"

Carlo's wide white smile was no less charming for Donald than it was for anyone else. "I was born and brought up in the middle of the Pacific Ocean."

Rolf's voice, deep and low, said, "Those pools in the rocks probably have something we could use in place of water. There may be fish. There's water in the spine of a raw fish. You just have to suck it out."

"Raw fish! No *thank* you." Brock's tongue licked his full lower lip. "Of course," he said less disdainfully, "I do like *ceviche*, the way they serve it in the bars in Panama. Grated corbina, lime juice, hot sauce. *Tops* for a hangover. And I *am* getting thirsty. Why do you suppose that is? I wasn't the *least* bit, until you brought up the subject, Felicia."

Diana said quietly, "When you're afraid you can't get water, you get even thirstier."

"Water," Blake said thoughtfully. "Strange. This is the first time in my life I ever really thought about water."

Brock sniffed. "This is the first time in my life I ever wanted any except with Scotch."

"There must be water on the island," Diana said. "There was a farm here a long time ago. The old Furness farm. They would have located it near some kind of water, like a spring or a creek, or maybe a lake or pond."

Felicia grimaced. "I don't want polluted water."

"What would pollute it?"

The question came from Norma Mansfield. Dr. Held looked at her with surprise. Perhaps there was more inside her finely sculptured patrician head than rigid conventions.

"It might be muddy," Norma insisted, "but not polluted."

Felicia wrinkled her nose. "Who wants to drink muddy water?"

Dr. Held smiled. "*You* will, my dear. When you are thirsty enough."

"Mud settles out of water," Rolf said simply. "Or we could use one of our shirts to filter it. What we need is something to put water in when we do find it. I saw a milk can on the beach. If it doesn't leak we could take it when we go to the farm." He turned to Dr. Held. "I'd be glad to go. Where is the farm?"

Dr. Held pointed toward the high north end of the island. "I've only seen it by air when a hydroplane brought me here on my first trip. There's nothing left, as far as I could see. I'm ashamed to plead ignorance, but on account of this—" he tapped his right foot— "I have never explored that part of Phoenix."

Rolf's dark eyes moved to Donald Campbell.

"Hell, don't look at me! I came here to handle the boat and keep the equipment running. I ain't no nature lover, and that farm lies somewhere along the top of the island, high up and maybe three miles beyond the woods where we camped last night. So go ahead, Daniel Boone. I'll stay here and pile up wood for our fire."

Felicia said sarcastically, "Rolf's leg is badly cut and bruised, whereas you, Mr. Campbell, appear to be in the pink of condition. In any case, we should *all* stay right here, because this is where they will come looking for us. When they arrive, I don't want to be romping through the brush in evening slippers and a thousand-dollar Aldano original. Besides, I'd be no good on a water hunt. The only sign of water I am prepared to recognize is a chrome-plated drinking fountain with a sign over it saying *'Eau Potable.'* " In a softer voice, she addressed herself to Rolf. "Couldn't you find water right around here?"

"Maybe. Like along that clay bank over there. Dark stains usually mean underground water. Or if you see someplace in a field where everything is growing greener than any place else—that means water under the surface. If you dig down, it will collect at the bottom of the hole. But the nearest and the easiest, for right now, would be rain water, if we can find any."

Rain water! Another of General LeMay's precepts of survival jolted Andrew Held's memory: You can't afford to make mistakes, for even the smallest may endanger the lives of others.

He, the host and leader at least *pro tempore*, had made a mistake. When it rained during the night, why hadn't he anticipated their need for water? If he was going to assume responsibility, he should also assume the blame. "We should have collected rain water last night," he said apologetically. "It was my mistake, and we can't afford mistakes. Before we stumble into another one, let's sort out priorities. I guess we all agree that water comes first, even before we collect wood for a signal fire. Shall we divide into two groups, and one look for water while the other gathers driftwood?"

"Dr. Held . . ." Norma's smooth forehead drew into a worried frown. "I suppose it was a mistake not to catch rain water last night." She cast a frightened glance at the raw ground where the house had been. "I know water is important, but aren't we about to make another mistake? About tides. I know a little about them because of our place on Long Island. Wasn't it a low slack when we came down to the beach?"

Carlo nodded vigorously. "Yes, yes it was." He jumped to his feet and looked appraisingly at the quietly lapping water. The night before he had anticipated the tsunami because he understood the cycle of tidal rise and fall. With Norma's question, last night's timetable came back in a rush. Normal high tide about three in the afternoon when the *Trident* came into Phoenix harbor. Normal low about five hours later, and next high about one o'clock in the morning . . . Yes, it figured. At dawn, the water had been as far out as it would go until the next low tide sometime in the afternoon, and in between, the water would rise and flood the beach. He turned and looked at Norma, frank admiration in his dark eyes.

"If it was low slack about an hour ago," Norma said with a small thoughtful frown, "then the tide is turning. When it comes all the way in, won't it carry away all the things we see lying around? Like some sort of containers for water?"

Blake exclaimed, "Norma, of course, you're absolutely right!"

With a new positive ring in her voice, Norma continued. "Before we do anything else, I think we should search the beach and carry everything useful to higher ground."

Brock jumped to his feet. "I *love* to beachcomb."

Blake stood up. "How much time do we have before high tide?"

"One moment . . ." Andrew Held pushed himself to his feet, pain pricking at his right leg like a series of small electric shocks. "Norma, I'm grateful for your foresight. Yes, before anything else, let's comb the beach. But let me put in a few words of caution.

"Beachcombing is certainly the right thing to do, but we could go about it the wrong way. The day is getting warmer. If you run, if you exert yourselves so that you perspire, you'll dehydrate your bodies and increase your need for water. Blake, please don't experiment with sea water. You would probably vomit and that would dehydrate you dangerously. Remember, our bodies are already weakened by loss of sleep. Being overtired and thirsty at the same time is bound to affect us emotionally. Let's get busy, but slowly and deliberately."

Felicia tucked the little leather pouch inside her bodice and stood up, an imperious figure in spite of the fact that her formal hairdress was disintegrating and several long strands of red-gold hair were hanging down her back. "God, Andrew," she murmured, "you always manage to sound as if you were standing at a blackboard with a slide rule in your hand."

"I've always been a teacher," he said quietly, "but I've never pretended to know everything. Right now I am very much aware of my own limitations."

"You're saying that I'm not." She flushed. "Forgive me, Andy. This . . . this crisis, or whatever it is, ought to bring out the best in me instead of the worst. But all I can think is—what silliness is this, hopping around the beach like a horde of maddened pack rats? I'm thirsty and I want a drink of water, and then I want to sit down and wait. You see, I told you, I'm not good at enduring. You are. You're admirable."

Before he could reply, she had turned away and retreated toward the beach.

The ledge where the house had been was designated as the warehouse for their curious treasures; it was a good twenty feet above the level of a normal high tide. At Blake's suggestion, Andrew Held acted as storekeeper, sorting out the objects they brought to him and stacking things of a kind in separate piles.

When the others were busy on the beach, Donald Campbell seized the opportunity to talk to Dr. Held alone. "I'd sure like to know what you meant when you said I was the only one might not want to get rescued. How come? You think you know something about me?"

Dr. Held shrugged. "No, not really. In any case, it doesn't matter."

"Well, you're right about me not wanting to go to the mainland. I got into a little trouble . . ."

"I said, it doesn't matter. Relax. Phoenix may turn out to be a better hiding place than you ever imagined."

"My real name—"

Dr. Held broke in impatiently. "You are Donald Campbell to all of us. A different name would only cause confusion. You have been very helpful to me. I've depended on you, and you've never disappointed me. So forget the confessional. It's not important now. What *is* important is the fact that, right now, I need you more than ever. We all do. You're stronger than any of us."

Donald's pale eyes narrowed suspiciously as his mind tried to assimilate the idea of being needed. "Well, I am strong," he admitted finally. "Look, it don't seem right to leave Jimmy where he's at. If we have an extra high tide . . . How about I pull him out while the others aren't too close and bury him right, someplace up there in the woods."

"Can you do it without a shovel?"

"Huh!" Donald held out his hands, presenting them proudly for Dr. Held's inspection. "I can do more with these than the average man can do with a god damn shovel."

Dr. Held nodded solemnly. "I don't doubt it. But remember what Mr. Mansfield said about taking the body with us when we're picked up? I gather you aren't as confident as he is that we'll be rescued soon."

Donald's eyes narrowed in a look both shrewd and secretive. "I got a good idea what our chances are, but I won't say anything to the rest of them. Like they say, what you don't know won't hurt you."

"I'm afraid I can't agree," Dr. Held said with a deep sigh. "We are very much in danger of being hurt by what we don't know. Well, anyway, Donald, you have the right idea about Jimmy. You might break off a sharp piece of shale from the cliff over there and use it to help you dig. We're going to need those hands of yours."

Donald said gruffly, "Yeah, sure. Well, there's a lot I can do." He took several steps, stopped, and turned back. "Mr. Mansfield told me to call him by his first name. What do you think of *that?*" He wheeled around and hurried down the slope to the beach, not waiting for an answer.

Chapter Seventeen

FELICIA knelt to examine a shiny object half-buried in the sand. With a slender, enamel-tipped forefinger, she uncovered a sterling silver fork, undoubtedly part of a three-piece carving set. What a crazy collection, she thought as she added the fork to her pile of bric-a-brac. A gallon jug with a severed neck. A pair of men's swimming trunks. An electrical extension cord. Several bits and pieces of broken china. A screwdriver with a yellow handle.

She had collected all she could carry at one time. If she only had a shopping bag . . . Instantly her practical self reminded her of the way she had carried apples when she was a little girl visiting her uncle's farm. In her skirt. So this thousand-dollar original was good for something, after all. With deft motions, she drew the skirt together at the hemline, lifted the gathered edge with one hand, and with the other picked up her discoveries and dropped them into the cradle of her skirt. She was revealing her panty hose, but they were all too busy to notice and, in any case, it didn't seem to matter.

Her streaked makeup and smudged mascara disturbed Felicia a little, especially when she caught a glimpse of Diana bounding over logs and rocks like a wood nymph, her skin clear and radiant, and her loose unlacquered hair falling softly around her face. Of course, Diana was so beautiful anyway . . . surely the epitome of true natural beauty. Felicia's elaborate coiffure had finally collapsed around her shoulders. But I did save the hairpins, she thought, and she thanked the god of the sea for not coughing up any mirrors or even parts of mirrors. If she looked as if she had just won the world championship for female wrestlers, so be it, it would all be over soon.

One of the first finds had been Rolf's discovery of a large stainless steel mixing bowl, scratched and dented but fortunately right side up. It was partially filled with rain water, enough to give all nine castaways several swallows.

So Felicia was not actively thirsty, and her hunger pangs were not much worse than those she had experienced during periodic campaigns to lose weight.

She did not know what the others were feeling and did not particularly care, except for Andrew. Andrew . . . Wasn't she a little relieved that this search of the beach was preventing her from talking to Andrew? Felicia was honest about being honest. Yes, she *was* relieved, she *was* glad. The truth was that she dreaded the moment she would say, "Andy, I want a divorce because I am going to marry another man."

Curious that the "other man," the key to her future happiness and comfort, had become such a misty figure during the past two days. Perhaps it was because Andrew was so very real and so very near. Her awareness of Andrew as a vital, physical human being threatened to reduce the man in Washington, D.C., to a faceless figure, a theory rather than a man.

Damn Andrew! During the years of separation Felicia thought she had rid herself of the reactions that once made her so vulnerable. The desire for his approval. The strong physical attraction. The knowledge of his body and the sparks of excitement he lighted with the smallest gesture of tenderness. She had thought these feelings had died when the two of them pulled back within themselves, like knights retreating to their own castles, pulling up the drawbridges, safe because they were separate. But yesterday, when she got off the boat and saw him standing on the pier with the two dogs at his feet, remembered feelings had come back in a rush.

Of how deeply they had been in love. Of their first lovemaking, when he came to her apartment late at night, shaken by some sort of incident during an evening meeting of government officials. He had hardly spoken. When she put a drink into his hand, he studied it curiously, as if he were trying to identify it. Then he looked up at her, and his intense blue eyes spoke so eloquently that she said, "Bother the drinks. We'll have them later."

Taking his hand, she led him into her bedroom. She had undressed very slowly. The bright bedside lamp illuminated every part of her body as she stretched out on the bed and, cupping her full breasts in her hands, said, "Andy, I want you. Oh, Andy, I want you." Oh God, how

sweet the moment when he had entered her, as strong
and as gentle as his tongue was in her mouth . . .

For a long terrible moment yesterday on the pier at
Phoenix, Felicia had been afraid she would burst helplessly into tears. And now, approaching Held with her
skirt full of crazy bits and pieces, she felt ridiculously
excited.

She held out her skirt and looked down at its contents
so as to avoid his bright analytical gaze. "The bounteous
gifts of the seas," she said gaily. "I lay them at your
feet."

The tide was rising. By ten o'clock they had collected
everything the beach offered. Silence engulfed them as
they dropped to the ground and surveyed the pathetic
piles of broken boards, shattered glass and pottery, wire
and string and net.

Andrew Held's voice brought the drowsy circle fully
awake. "You may think that gathering these things has
been a childish pasttime. But bear with me just a few
minutes longer. We know what the storm gave us, but
these piles of junk don't constitute our entire wealth as a
community of nine. I've been thinking that everything
we're wearing, everything we're carrying, is potentially
useful and should be considered as part of our inventory."

Felicia laughed. "God love the orderly, scientific mind.
Andy, you're truly unique."

"I'm trying to remember things I may never have
known."

"I don't know what you mean, but let's get on with
the game. I'd hate to be sitting here playing Show and
Tell when the Coast Guard arrives."

"I'll start with myself." Andrew Held tapped his watch.
"Calendar wristwatch, in good condition. In my pockets,
one handkerchief, and that's all. Everything that usually
makes them bulge is . . . that is, *was,* laid out on the
chiffonier in my bedroom. Clothing includes a jacket,
trousers, undershorts, shirt, necktie, socks, shoes." He
stopped abruptly. His mechanical foot. Since it contained
metal, it was undoubtedly more valuable than anything
he had mentioned. But even Felicia had never seen him
attach it to his leg and, except for a quick glance in the
bedroom or beside a swimming pool, she had never really observed the pointed footless stump which was his

right leg without the prosthesis. It would be easier to expose or discuss any other part of his body. At the thought of uncovering his maimed leg, Andrew was suffused with a feeling close to grief. During his long-ago trip to India and the Far East, a beggar had displayed an amputated leg, whining pitifully as he extended a pleading hand. Dr. Held had filled the dirty palm with all the money in his pocket and fled, limping, from the fellow human being he could not prevent himself from despising with all his heart.

Carlo, smiling warmly, said, "You've forgotten something, Dr. Held. Something metal."

Dr. Held started.

"Your tie clasp."

"Ah . . ." Held exhaled deeply. "Yes, of course. All right. Would the next person . . . ?"

Around the circle they spoke with varying degrees of embarrassment. Carlo showed none at all, even when it came to the athletic supporter he wore with lightweight summer slacks. When it was her turn, Norma flushed and for the first time tried to pull together the open seam of her dress. Blake produced a second wristwatch in addition to his clothing, leather wallet, and wedding ring. Brock quipped about his gold fillings. Rolf's voice was so low he could hardly be heard, while Diana seemed perfectly natural and at ease. "My sandals, my panties and bra, and my dress. That's all. I don't have any rings or jewelry or even hairpins. It isn't much, is it?"

Donald Campbell reached into his hip pocket. Grinning broadly, he pulled out a sturdy jackknife. "Three blades," he said proudly. "That ought to be some help, huh?"

Dr. Held smiled approval. "That knife makes you the millionaire of this group."

Felicia's right hand flew to the little leather pouch hanging on a ribbon around her neck. She was the only one who hadn't spoken.

"Felicia?"

Her fingers tightened convulsively on the little sack. She took so long to answer that by the time she said, "Just the usual skimpy female raiment," the attention of the entire circle was fixed on the mysterious object around her neck. "Oh, and these . . ." She opened her left hand, revealing a dozen large bronzed hairpins.

Andrew Held had never squandered his powers of observation on the details of feminine self-adornment. The total effect registered, and for him, that had always been enough. But suddenly he knew what that leather pouch contained, the object so precious to his wife that at the risk of being overtaken by a tidal wave she had run back to the house to get it. He thought, What an insane sense of values! Then he instantly corrected himself. For Felicia, who had been unwilling or unable to understand the peril of tsunami, going back to save a sackful of precious gems was perfectly consistent with a practical sense of values.

Donald said belligerently, "Well, go on, Mrs. Held. What's in the leather bag? The rest of us didn't hold nothing back." With his three-blade jackknife displayed on one big rough palm, he seemed to be challenging Felicia to match his prize.

Dr. Held said quickly, "It's not important. This was all voluntary, Donald. She doesn't have to show—"

Donald interrupted with an angry roar. "She don't, don't she! How come *she* don't? Carlo here was offering to give up his jock strap for a slingshot."

"Mrs. Held has a right to privacy."

"Huh! When she goes into the woods to pee, she does. But not when we're trying to put all our useful stuff together, things we need to get along on this island. That means things *all* of us need."

Felicia's haughty resistance crumbled abruptly as her face broke into a smile. Slowly at first, then with more and more abandon, she was taken by bursts of laughter. When she could catch her breath, she gasped, "Here, do have a look!" She pulled the ribbon over her head, opened the pouch, and shook the contents into her lap.

In silence, nine people stared at a tangled mound of necklaces, bracelets, earrings, and brooches. Diamonds and emeralds winked in the morning sunshine, a string of pearls glistened wetly, a topaz ring shone like a comet. "There, you see? I do have something to contribute to the general good. Whenever we are hungry or thirsty, we'll just rub one of these little magic stones."

"Oh for Chrissakes . . ." Donald's hungry eyes moved from Felicia's lap to his own open palm. Contemplating the jackknife, he began to smile. "God damn. It's funny, at that, all right. God damn, it sure is enough to make you laugh. If we were in the city, that stuff of hers

would be worth fifty thousand dollars and you couldn't
get three bucks for my knife. But here, the way things
are . . ." He chuckled. "Want to trade, Mrs. Held?"

"Thank you, Mr. Campbell. At the moment, that gadget
of yours may be worth more than my jewelry, but *I'm*
going back to the city. You can play millionaire for a
day, but I have no use for your knife."

Donald looked at her boldly. "I wonder. Don't that
depend on how long we're stuck here?"

Felicia pointedly turned her back and began to refill
the leather pouch. Pulling the cord over her head, she
dropped the sack into the crevasse between her breasts.
"Well, now, Andrew, I'm getting awfully hungry. We
haven't eaten in twelve or fourteen hours. What are we
going to do about it?"

Andrew Held wanted to say, "We'll rub one of those
little magic stones," but he decided not to. Somehow it
didn't seem funny anymore.

Chapter Eighteen

ROLF lowered two strings of fish onto the upper beach. "These were flapping around in the swimming pool, or what's left of it. They must have come in with high water and when the tide went out, they got stranded. They're good and fresh."

Warren Brock's short upper lip curled with distaste. "*Horrible* eyes! Are we going to *eat* those ugly creatures?"

Rolf said quietly, "That's what fish look like before they're cooked. But you don't have to eat them if you don't want to."

"But I'm *famished*. What else is there? All right. Just this once. But not raw, *please*." Daintily he dusted his palms against each other and backed away.

"No, I'll cook them. The way my grandmother used to, on sticks beside a fire."

Fire . . . As the word "water" had struck them dumb a few hours earlier, the word "fire" hung on the air while they looked at one another expectantly.

Andrew Held spoke first. "Warren, Felicia. You both smoke."

Warren Brock shrugged elaborately. "Yes, but I use matches. I can't abide those fussy little gadgets that are always running out of fluid."

"Matches are fine."

"But that's what I mean. I used the last one an hour ago."

"Felicia, your cigarette lighter?"

"It was on the table in the living room." She laughed shrilly. "It probably still is."

Brock snickered. "All we have to do is find the living room."

Dr. Held turned to the others. One by one, they shook their heads. "Sorry," Blake said earnestly. "Neither of us smoke."

"I see . . ." Dr. Held looked around the group. At this point, Felicia and Brock, the specialists in facetiousness, were as sober as the Mansfields. Held felt a little sorry. For both of them, a sense of the ridiculous was an important defense. "We do need fire," he began, his mind automatically sorting and grading their various needs. "Right now, to cook by. Later, for our signal fire. Eventually, for warmth, because it will be cool by evening." He smiled wryly. "Or it might rain, which would solve one problem and create another."

Felicia crossed her arms over her breast. Her long painted fingernails tapped impatiently on the bare flesh of her upper arms. "I'm really *very* hungry, Andrew. Don't Boy Scouts learn to make fire without matches? Who was a Boy Scout?"

Blake said, "I was, for a while. I remember trying to get a spark by rubbing two sticks together. It never worked. At least, not for me."

"The sun's rays through a convex lens . . ." Dr. Held looked thoughtfully at his wristwatch. "If we had a magnifying glass. Or a flashlight, or binoculars or a camera . . . Well, forget it, we don't. There's broken glass in our warehouse here. The bottom of a bottle, or a piece of broken bottle might work." He touched the crystal of his watch. "I have never tried it, but I think two watch crystals, with a little water between them . . . Blake, you're wearing a watch."

"Excuse me . . ." Rolf's tone was friendly but faintly defensive. "You don't have to take your watches apart. That way of making fire only works when you've got a bright sun. If the fire went out and the sky was cloudy . . ." He shrugged. "Don't waste your watches. I can make fire without them."

Felicia looked at Rolf in open admiration. Probably, Andrew Held decided, as much for his physical beauty, with his characteristic high cheekbones, as for his knowledge of firemaking. "Fine, Rolf. What's your method?"

"A fire drill."

Dr. Held nodded. "I should have thought of that. I've seen it done in a native village in Africa."

Rolf gave him a level and unsmiling look. "My grandfather taught me, in *our* native village."

Dr. Held heard and accepted the rebuke. "Do you want help?"

"Only to stack up driftwood. We should have a lot of

firewood before I even try to get a flame. I'll go look for tinder."

The spot for the fire was chosen under Rolf's direction. It was well above high water so that the incoming tide would not extinguish it, but as close as possible to a ready supply of firewood. It was out in the open, not only to make it visible from a distance but to eliminate the danger of forest fire. Then, while the others collected driftwood, Rolf began his search for tinder.

He went into the woods with two implements—a sharp piece of broken glass and the stainless steel bowl that had earlier contained rain water. His first find was a dead cedar log. He pulled off several long strips of bark. Under the bark, the log was infested with insects whose threadlike trails honeycombed the rotten wood. With the shard of glass, Rolf scraped the powdery dry rot into the bowl.

Moving on through the woods and out into a field, he had soon collected handfuls of dead bracken fern, long grass, and small dry twigs. When he came upon a pine tree oozing with golden sap, he had another idea. Nearby, greenish-gray moss hung in festoons from the limbs of a dying tree. He tore handfuls from the lower limbs and rubbed it into the sticky aromatic juice of the pine tree. Like the rotted wood, the dried fern and grass and cedar bark, the pitchy moss would help produce a quick, hot fire. His last acquisitions were to be used in the making of the fire drill: a branch from an alder, and a dry willow stick about a foot long.

Back at the spot selected for the bonfire, Rolf rolled the strips of dry cedar bark between this palms until they were reduced to a reddish brown dust. Beside this mound of bark dust he set down the bowl of powdery wood rot. These two substances were his tinder.

Next was the kindling. He broke small dry twigs into pieces several inches long, and that made one stack. In another, he heaped handfuls of dried bracken fern and the moss sticky with pine sap.

One by one the wood gatherers gave up their plodding round trips to the beach and formed a silent, curious group around Rolf and his neatly organized firemaking. He looked up, smiled, and said bashfully, "So far, so good. But now comes the fire drill. I hope my grandfather was a good teacher."

Diana's hand touched his shoulder. "What I remember is, you were always a good student."

Slowly, testing each one as he picked it up, Rolf assembled the five parts of the drill. An alder branch a yard long and an inch in diameter—that was the bow. For the bowstring, he used a leather lace from one of his own boots. The fireboard was a lucky find in the warehouse of refuse. Though it was splintered at one end, the other end was flat on both sides and square on the edge, and it was about the right size—five or six inches wide, a half-inch thick, about a foot and a half long.

With the sharp piece of broken glass, Rolf gouged out a cone-shaped hole not far from the squared edge of the board and halfway through it. Then he cut a V-shaped notch from the hole to the edge of the board, the sharp point of the V extending nearly to the center of the hole.

The fourth part of the fire drill was the spindle, a dry willow stick about a foot long. Once more, Rolf used the glass, this time as a plane, and shaved the stick lengthwise until it was no longer round but six-sided. With the same crude implement, he tapered one end of the stick so that it looked like a blunt pencil. The other end he rounded off.

Finally, he selected a small chunk of wood suitable for the knob. Stroking his mustache, he gave all parts another careful inspection. "Well," he said, "I guess I'm ready to put it together."

He tied the bowstring to one end of the curved and flexible alder branch, wrapped it twice around the spindle, pulled it taut, and wrapped it around the other end of the bow. The knob fit over the rounded end of the spindle. This done, he inserted the tapered blunt-pencil end of the spindle into the hole in the fireboard.

On the spot where the fire was to be, he placed the fireboard on top of a plain board selected at random from the warehouse, and then filled the V-shaped hole with several pinches of the tinder. Again he looked up, and his dark eyes sparkled. "Ladies and gentlemen," he said to the attentive audience, "you are about to find out how good an Indian I am."

Rolf kneeled with one foot firmly on the fireboard.

With one hand, he grasped the wrapped end of the bow; with the other he held the bow itself, thumb between the shoelace thong and the curving alder branch. Placing the pointed end of the spindle into the notched hole in the fireboard, he began sawing back and forth, forcing the spindle to revolve.

At first his strokes were long and the pressure light— a cellist playing a slow waltz. Gradually, the hand on the wrapped end of the bow increased the tension by pressing the thumb toward the palm. At the same time he speeded the rhythm of his sawing strokes, the cellist was working up to a *schottische*.

Rolf's long black hair bounced on his shoulders, his bare back glistened, and his breathing kept pace with the rapid movement of his arms. In a few minutes, a tiny wisp of smoke rose from the notch in which the spindle was revolving so frantically. He accelerated, breathing hard. Suddenly the smoke tendril burst into a small, billowy cloud.

He dropped the bow, picked up the fireboard, and quickly poured the smoking wood dust onto the small pyramid of pulverized bark and punky wood. Dropping to his knees, his face was only inches from the smoldering tinder as he blew gently, caught his breath, and slowly blew again. The smoking dust ignited with a tiny, orange spark. Rolf grabbed a fistful of sticky moss and, holding it against the spark, continued to blow. The live spark caught, and the moss erupted into flame. He reared back, reaching for a handful of small dry twigs.

Fire! He *was* an Indian, after all. Rolf dropped a second handful of twigs and grass and fern. As the uncertain orange tendril exploded into a sturdy flame, a chorus of cheers sounded at his back.

Felicia could not understand why they should not eat all the fish for lunch. "I tell you, I'm *starved!*" she protested when Andrew Held insisted they divide Rolf's catch into two parts and save half for an evening meal. "I don't know why, but I've never been so hungry in my life, and after all, we have nothing to eat but the fish. No salad, no vegetables . . ."

The fish were already cooking. Using Donald's jack-knife, Rolf had gutted, beheaded, and split them, and then skewered the thick filets on green sticks which he planted around the fire, each stick leaning over the heat at a slight angle. The outer skin was charred but the white flesh inside was exuding a fragrant juice.

Diana sat near Rolf with her legs drawn up and chin resting on her knees. "I could find some roots or greens that would be like vegetables. But the fish is almost cooked. I'll do it this afternoon and we can have it tonight."

"Roots?" Norma's pale face brightened with interest. "Do you mean, like burdock roots?"

Felicia threw a glance at Norma that dismissed her question as ridiculous. "Those are *weeds*."

Norma hesitated but then said firmly, "At one time, Mrs. Held, everything was."

Felicia laughed. "Oh, I suppose so. But thistles, or the roots of thistles? What foolishness. We'll poison ourselves."

Norma's respect for good manners kept her from contradicting someone who, in relation to her own age, would be classified as an "older woman," though she was only in her late thirties. With considerable spirit, she replied, "Admittedly, I don't know much about it. There's a health food store on Sixty-third, where I go occasionally to buy honey. I saw a book there called *Eat the Weeds*. I just glanced through it." She threw Diana a rueful smile. "Now I wish I had read it, because I'm hungry, too."

Diana's soft mouth curved into a smile. "I guess being hungry had a lot to do with it when my grandmother used to pick nettles and pull up cattails in the swamp and things like that. She often took me with her. I learned quite a lot."

Norma said eagerly, "When you look for greens and roots, may I go with you, Diana? I took botany at Wellesley."

"Oh my dear Aunt Maude," Warren Brock snorted. "When I get marooned on an island, it has to be with a Wellesley girl."

As the sun began to settle on the horizon, Andrew Held sensed that even Felicia had accepted the fact that they were going to spend another night on Phoenix Island.

Once they had finished an evening meal of bass and

dandelion greens, weary silence engulfed the group around the bonfire. Though they were physically near each other, they retreated within themselves once more, hugging their disappointment in the nameless authorities who should by now have plucked them off this wild place and transported them quickly to clean sheets and hot and cold running water.

Night was overtaking them. The last scrap of food had been eaten, the last portion of water drunk, and they were exhausted. Still they sat around the bonfire, dumb with fatigue but clinging to faith in the "signal fire" that earlier in the day had seemed to be a guaranteed beacon.

Donald was the first to stumble up the hill toward their camp. A little later, Blake Mansfield said, "Norma, it will be easier while there's still a little light."

As they left the circle around the fire, Blake put his arm around his wife. It was a commonplace gesture, and yet it struck Andrew Held as odd. What was surprising about such an ordinary show of affection? And then he realized it wasn't Blake's gesture that seemed different, for Dr. Held had observed several of his efforts to pat Norma's shoulder or to hold her hand. It was Norma who had acted differently. She hadn't pulled away this time, and as they disappeared into the shadow of the hill, she slipped her arm around Blake.

Andrew Held looked around at the somnolent figures huddled beside the fire. "Well?" he asked. "Don't you think we'd all better get ready for another day?"

There were a few sleepy murmurs, but they all stood up. While Carlo banked the fire, the others fell into line and began to move slowly over the logs and rocks toward the path leading up the hill. Only Felicia hesitated, still expecting a search party to spare her a second night in the woods.

Andrew Held said gently, "I know, dear. I agree with you. It's hard to give up."

"You never do," she said bitterly, "except at the wrong times." She walked away alone, not waiting.

With Carlo's strong hand guiding him, Andrew Held limped across the dark beach and began the painful climb.

Chapter Nineteen

THE sound dragged Andrew Held across the no-man's-land between sleep and awakening. At first it was more of a vibration than a sound, a steady rhythm of blows muffled by distance which his sleep-drugged mind could not translate into any recognizable entity. It grew louder, as his growing consciousness struggled harder and harder to free itself of the persistent hold of sleep. The dream images fled, his waking mind groped for light, and he opened his eyes.

All around him they slept, still figures under patchwork coverings of salvaged cloth. Far above him, the source of the sound hovered invisibly, hidden by the entwined branches of pine trees. A loud whir, chopping the air . . . Wide awake now, Dr. Held shouted, "Helicopter! Donald! Rolf! Blake! Run for the clearing!"

In seconds, they were all on their feet, and Rolf was racing barefoot along the path to the beach. Diana was only a short distance behind him, lithe and sure-footed as a doe. The others followed, Felicia and Norma lifting long skirts above their knees. Andrew Held loped along unevenly at the rear of the column.

Felicia's triumphant voice floated back to him. "They've come, Andy! Didn't I tell you? Thank God, they're here."

Dr. Held overtook the others at the top of the hill, where the path broke into the open and descended toward the beach. On the ledge below, Rolf had uncovered the banked fire, and pale flames were beginning to lick at the driftwood he laid on hot coals. Diana had pulled off her white dress and tied it to the end of a long stick. In miniscule underpants and bra, her slender young body whipped from side to side as she waved the improvised flag in a frantic semaphore. But they were too late—Andrew Held knew it instantly. The thudding beat of the blades was already diminishing.

In silence, the Mansfields followed the strange bird's

retreating outline. The excitement in their faces faded as
the sound of the helicopter, and then the sight of it, was
swallowed up by the unending sky.

Blake reached for Norma's hand. "Bad luck. But another will be along soon."

Norma pulled her hand free and continued down the
path to the fire.

The noise and vibration inside the helicopter ruled out
normal conversation, but as they took their last look at
Phoenix Island, the three men on the search and
rescue team exchanged meaningful glances.

"Wipeout!" the co-pilot bellowed, and the pilot and
paramedic nodded their agreement.

The pilot made a circular gesture that said clearly,
Want to make another pass?

The co-pilot shook his head, shrugged, and shouted,
"Seen all there is to see! *Nobody* could have lived through
all *this!*"

The pilot looked over his right shoulder into the sober,
frowning face of the paramedic. The young petty officer
was staring back at the island, though it was already
diminishing in a vast expanse of empty sea. "Joe!"

Startled, the young man drew himself together at the
sound of his name and facing front, mouthed his answer:
"Nothing for me to do there, sir."

The co-pilot was scrawling notes on a pad braced
against his knee. The pilot tapped his arm and wiggled
a beckoning finger in a clear message—*Let me see what
you've written.*

Grim-faced, the co-pilot picked up his notepad and
held it out at an angle so that both his companions
could read. Pilot and petty officer looked thoughtfully
at the words which were to appear many times later,
first in official Coast Guard reports, and soon thereafter
in newspaper and magazine accounts of the tragic toll of
the August fourth tsunami:

"All buildings and installations destroyed. Shoreline altered significantly. No evidence of survivors on or near
the island. Devastation total."

The paramedic leaned back in his seat and wearily
closed his eyes. The pilot forced himself to focus his attention on the chart and the next area to be searched,
and the co-pilot, rereading his notes, wet the tip of his

pencil on his tongue and, with one heavy black stroke, underlined the key words: *Devastation total*. Then he looked out the window, but Phoenix Island was only a blur on the misty horizon.

Dr. Held did not have to suggest that they gather and talk things over. Like a well-trained team responding to a familiar signal, they sat down on logs around the bonfire and waited dejectedly for their leader to interpret this new disaster.

Blake cleared his throat. "Coast Guard, I think it was. I made out a number. And it was the right color. Kind of a silvery aluminum, with the international orange band around the fuselage."

"Well, that's good," Felicia broke in. "That means they're searching for us. They'll be back."

"You may be right, Felicia. But I think we've got to face another possibility." Andrew Held sighed deeply. He had assumed leadership because that had been his role throughout his adult life, but in a desperate situation authority had its price. Hope was healthy, as essential to survival as oxygen is to breathing, but if the level of hope were raised too high, the realities of the situation would inevitably cause a sudden and potentially dangerous drop, a kind of spiritual hypoxia. How often would he have to risk the antagonism of these stubborn believers by drawing a line between hope and self-delusion? He said, carefully, "Phoenix is way outside the boundaries of any routine patrol, so that helicopter was undoubtedly on a search mission. Now that they've checked the island and observed no signs of life, they have no reason to come back."

"Yeah!" Donald was making an awkward attempt to stifle a grin. "You're right, Dr. Held. Them guys already covered their run. They won't be back."

Donald's big face shone with childish glee. He enjoys knowing that everyone else is more anxious to leave Phoenix than he is, Dr. Held reflected. He glanced around the circle, trying to gauge the temper of these tensely silent people. "I'm sorry, but the truth, as I see it, is that our chances for early rescue are now greatly diminished."

Felicia jumped to her feet. "What did we do wrong this time?" she asked furiously. "What was our mistake?

You said we should build a signal fire. We built a signal fire. Then some brainless idiot puts the fire out—"

Carlo said quietly, "I am the brainless idiot. But I didn't put it out. I banked it, which is the right thing to do if you want to have fire in the morning."

Felicia ignored him. "Well, Andrew? You were right here when Carlo banked the fire, whatever that means. Why didn't you stop him?" Her voice rose into an angry sob. "They *came* for us! They would have taken us off this godforsaken rock. I want to *leave* Phoenix, can't you understand that? I *must* leave Phoenix. And I'm asking you, what are you going to do about it, just exactly what are you going to *do*?"

Warren Brock's mouth formed a small O as he waggled his forefinger at the angry woman. "You're getting a little shrill, dear heart. Try for medium range. Nothing over high, C, *please*."

Felicia sobbed, "You stay out of it, Brock," and sat down on the log. Tears left glistening trails as they rolled down her cheeks and dropped onto her hands.

"Stay out of it?" Brock retorted. "Look, lovey, I'm in it just as much as you are. And *I'm* not screaming and pointing fingers."

Norma said coolly, "You're doing something worse. Mrs. Held is frightened, and you respond with ridicule."

Brock made a half-turn so as to stare mockingly into Norma's face. "Fiddle dee *dee!* Felicia screams like a fishwife, and you explain that she's frightened. What priceless pearls of insight do you have to cast in *my* direction?"

"You're frightened, too. But you handle it in a different way."

Brock's composure cracked wide open. "Don't bother to analyze me, you Boston bitch!" he retorted shrilly. "I've been dissected, identified, and catalogued by the best of them, and still no one knows *me*."

Blake Mansfield crossed the circle in one stride and dropped his hand on Brock's shoulder. "Your language is offensive, Mr. Brock. It wouldn't give me any satisfaction to hit you, but you *are* going to apologize."

Donald growled, "It would give me plenty of satisfaction," and he began to rise.

Andrew Held's voice broke in commandingly. "Sit down, Donald. You, too, Blake."

After a second's hesitation, Blake released Brock's shoulder and returned to his place. "Sorry. You're right, of course. An apology from him would be as meaningless as the insult."

They fell into weary silence, but the cross-currents of hostility were clearly visible. Felicia was scornful, Blake was superior, Norma was defensive, Brock was cruel, Donald was brutal. Across the circle Felicia began to wipe her tears with the corner of her long white skirt. At the same time, as if a storm had passed, Diana turned to Rolf and smiled.

Thanks to their mattresses of fern and cedar boughs, they had all benefited from a good night's sleep, but as the second day on Phoenix stretched out ahead of them, that was their only asset.

They needed water—at least a quart per person per day, Blake thought he had read someplace, sometime. They were hungry, but they had gathered no food. While it shone, the August sun would keep them warm, but, particularly in the case of Felicia, whose fragile white silk dinner gown was already ripped in half a dozen places, the problem of clothing could be held in abeyance for only a short time. It seemed to Dr. Held that the worst aspect of their situation was not these primitive physical needs, but that they lacked the spirit to go out and find ways in which the needs could be satisfied.

The furious exchange of insults and accusations had ended abruptly. More alienated than ever, they sank into a mute depression, responding in monotones to Andrew Held's efforts to get them talking. The passive acceptance of one's fate—that was one of the dangers his friend General LeMay had warned against. Yet they weren't passive people. Even Norma, who had seemed at first to be the helpless captive of her Upper Manhattan conventions, had shown surprising spark. How to shake them up and get them moving, when undoubtedly all they could think about was the little dot of the helicopter disappearing into the distance?

"It wasn't a mistake to bank the fire," Dr. Held began.

Carlo said quickly, "Mrs. Held didn't mean what she said. We're all nervous." He threw Felicia a gleaming smile. "I'm not an idiot, but I have done crazy things. Some of the nicest things that ever happened to me were at least a little bit crazy." Addressing the group as a whole, he said seriously, "If we want to keep the fire up tonight, we can set up watches."

Blake said eagerly, "I'll certainly take my turn."

"So will I. But it won't work." Rolf's dark face became animated as he talked. "Patrols don't go out at night without a special reason. They must be checking out the damage done by the tidal waves. They're looking for the wreckage of boats, and for bodies. They wouldn't try to spot things like that in the dark."

"Awful," Felicia murmured. "Oh, how awful . . ."

"But there are a couple of things we can do. One is what we did yesterday. Make smoke by putting wet wood and weeds on the fire. That'll make white smoke instead of black, but that shows up best against rocks and gravel." Rolf's eyes sparkled as he turned to Diana. "That was a good idea, waving a flag. If we cut down a sapling and set it up as a flagpole, in the clearing at the top of the hill . . ." He hesitated, then went on. "But we wouldn't have to use your dress for the flag. There's some cloth over there, that we found on the beach."

Donald Campbell put in gruffly. "Say listen, you two kids can't do that alone. If your flagpole is big enough to see, hoisting and planting it is going to take some muscle. I'll work with you."

All at once they were all talking, and apathy had vanished like fog dissipated by the heat of the sun. Brock announced he would look for water. Rolf had described what to look for. Dark stains in a clay bank, patches of especially green grass.

Felicia said wryly, "Well, Brock, you haven't mentioned a pond or a brook. In your diligent pursuit of dark stains and green patches, I hope you won't overlook the obvious."

"I am never *obvious*, sweet one. Only infuriating." With surprising strength for a man with such a delicate, small-boned body, Brock swung the five-gallon milk can onto his shoulder and proceeded jauntily across the beach.

Carlo examined the warehouse of beach debris and selected the yellow-handled screwdriver and a plastic pail with a hole in the bottom. "My specialty is seafood. Maybe not the kind you're used to. Chitons, limpets, mussels, snails, barnacles. I'll go along shore and see what I can find." Waving and smiling, he went off alone.

Andrew Held thought, And now we are four. The Mansfields, Felicia, and I . . .

Standing together, Blake and Norma discussed what they should do. Search for edible roots and greens? Try to make fish hooks out of Felicia's hairpins? Weave honeysuckle vines and bracken fern into room dividers for the dormitory? Dr. Held, who considered himself objective, even emotionally detached from other human beings unless they were part of his intimate family circle, caught himself wishing fervently that these over-nice young people would quit sparring with each other and go off on some project they could do together. It gave him a ridiculously poignant feeling of satisfaction when they agreed that first Blake would help Norma collect wild foods and then Norma would help Blake construct green walls to separate their sleeping areas.

When they had gone, Felicia said drily, "Andy, you're beaming like Mama at her eldest son's bar mitzvah."

"They're all right, those two. I like them."

"You sound downright maudlin. For you, that is. I thought you never let yourself get involved in other people's problems."

Andrew said thoughtfully, "That's true, I never have. At least, not in their personal problems. I think it's been a way of saving myself for things I consider more important."

"More important than personal problems?" Felicia's voice was wistful. "Is that possible?" She laughed, recovering her poise and her distance. "Well, I'd say that Blake's desire to build a wall around their beds is a good sign. I, too, like privacy in the bedroom."

It was a mistake, a slip of the tongue, a cruel reference he was sure she made carelessly with no intention of invoking the mental picture that shot into his mind. Andrew Held looked down at his hands, thinking that if men were allowed to cry . . .

"Andy . . ."

Her tremulous voice, the impulsive movement of her hand to his shoulder, told him she had hurt herself, too. "Andy . . ."

"It doesn't matter," he said unsteadily. "I agree that Blake's idea of bedroom walls is a good one. But we'll have to wait and see, won't we?" He looked up directly into Felicia's unhappy, sea-green eyes. "We don't know yet whether he'll build a wall around them—or between them."

"Oh, Andy . . ." Her fingers pressed urgently into the hard shoulder muscle. "I'm so sorry, so desperately sorry."

"It doesn't matter, Felicia," he said quietly. As if they were moved by feelings of their own, his fingers reached out and caressed her cheek. "It was a long time ago. A very long time ago."

The flagpole had been raised and Diana and Rolf had gone off together, looking for roots and berries. "What the hell," Donald Campbell muttered audibly, staring jealously after the retreating figures. They wanted him when he took hold of a dead pine and cracked it off at the roots. He was an okay guy when he was carrying boulders to the center of the clearing and hoisting and planting the tree in a base of fieldstone. But they didn't want him now. Disgruntled, he turned and began to make his way back to the beach.

He was alone in the woods when he saw Felicia. She startled him, moving through the timber like a ghost in her long white dress with her hair hanging loose and wild. He ducked behind a tree. He didn't exactly know why. If it had been Dr. Held or Mr. Mansfield, he would have charged through the underbrush and made himself known. But Mrs. Held—Jesus, he hated Mrs. Held, but he liked to look at her when she didn't know he was looking. Those beautiful big boobs, hanging full inside that thin white dress. Hiding out on Phoenix had always meant living without a woman, and that was bad enough. But to have three half-naked women running around all day and sleeping near you at night—Christ, that was driving him crazy. The worst of it was that each was a beaut in her own way. If he didn't hate this Mrs. Held so much, he'd try to make it with her.

What in hell was she doing in the woods alone? Going to meet Carlo? The thought excited him. That would be something to see, wouldn't it? The two of them making love, seeing it instead of just hearing it. The idea hit his pulse and his groin almost as fast it came into his head. He'd follow, keeping out of sight.

But Mrs. Held wasn't acting as if she was going to meet

someone. She was moving slowly from bush to bush, examining each one. Looking for something to eat, that was it. Berries, or hazelnuts, or some of those things Diana and Rolf had been telling them about. God damn. She wasn't meeting Carlo at all.

Still he watched her, hidden by the big trees and shifting his position just enough to keep her in sight. Her skirt caught on a twig and she lifted it, wound it around her waist, and tucked the end inside the folds over her stomach. God, this *was* something to see. She was as good as naked from the waist down. Panty hose did nothing but blur the outlines of her rounded thighs and the dark V between her legs. And then she dropped to the ground to examine something, and bent over like that, her white breasts were bare right down to the nipples. Oh Christ, he thought, oh Christ . . .

She stood up and looked around, still searching for something to eat. She don't know nothing about wild berries, Donald thought smugly. He might not have picked up a lot since he moved to the Pacific Northwest, but he wasn't as ignorant as this elegant broad from back East. Her attention was drawn to a big-leafed shrub as tall as she was, and he wanted to laugh out loud. He knew *that* one. By God, you couldn't hang around the Pacific Northwest without sooner or later meeting up with a devil's club. Every stem was covered with vicious barbs. Take hold of one of them and your hand would throb with a dozen wounds. Felicia had seen the brilliant red berries. She was going right up to the big plant. By God, she was reaching out with both hands like she was going to hold the stem with one hand and pick the berries with another!

The thought of calling out and warning her flashed across his mind, but just as quickly faded. If he did, she would know he had been watching. Besides, it was just an accident that he was here. Dumb, gad, she was dumb. Dumb, dumb, dumb, he said to himself, and grinning, waited for Felicia to touch the devil's club.

"Don't touch that plant!"

The high-pitched voice exploded right at his ear. Donald froze, too shocked to drop to the ground or to run. Mouth agape, he turned his head. Warren Brock was only a few feet away.

"Felicia, pet, back away from that monster and don't

touch any part of it." Brock's voice had returned to normal. "And remember what it looks like, because if you're going to go gamboling about in the woods you could run into it again. Donald, you should recognize a devil's club when you see one."

Felicia withdrew her hand, doubly startled to hear Brock's voice and to see Campbell only a few yards away. As always, she recovered quickly. "Thank you, Warren. Thank you very much." She loosened her skirt and let it fall. "I thought the berries might be edible. I'm so *damned* hungry."

"So am I, lovey. But let's leave the food gathering to our more knowledgeable companions."

"I'm not ready to give up." Felicia lifted both arms, pulled her long hair back from her cheeks, and began to braid it into a single plait. "I'll admit I don't know anything about wild berries, but I should be able to recognize a hazelnut, and Diana says they grow wild in these islands." She had finished the braid. Holding the loose end, she asked, "You don't happen to have a rubber band, do you, Warren?"

"A rubber band?" He uttered a wispy laugh. "No, sweet. And I left my hair ribbons at home."

"Here . . ." With her free hand, Felicia lifted the hem of her skirt. "Tear off a piece for me, please. About an inch or two wide."

"Your *Aldano?* That greedy Italian wouldn't sell a two-inch strip for less than three hundred dollars . . . Oh, all *right,* Felicia. As you say, dearie . . . Here we go . . ." Brock knelt delicately, and with hands posturing like a ballerina's he ripped off the bottom of the white silk gown. With a quick twist, he tore enough for a hair ribbon, rolled the rest into a neat silken pellet, and deftly thrust the extra silk down the front of her dress.

To Donald's astonishment, she didn't object, nor even seem to notice. "I'm on my way." Her amused grimace was for Brock alone. Donald was excluded as definitely as if she had pushed him aside.

The moment she left them, Brock wheeled toward Donald. Like an angry bantam, he glared up into the face of a man strong enough to crush him. "You cold-blooded, rotten son of a bitch!"

"Hey, watch your mouth, buster. I don't have to take any shit off you."

"You were grinning, actually *grinning*. You knew she was going to hurt herself, and you were *enjoying* it!"

"Oh, shut up. What's it to you? You mind your own business and I'll mind mine."

"Ducky, just *ducky!* That's what I intend to do, especially when I see you backing up to the edge of a cliff."

Donald lowered his head and scowled into the little man's flushed face. "Listen, you, don't get me riled. I could break you in two and you know it. You know something else? I hate fags."

Brock's derisive laugh rippled out through the shadowy woods. He picked up the big milk can, gave Donald a long, knowing look, and still laughing, walked away.

They had had no breakfast, and they were all back at the beach by the time the sun was overhead, drawn by the hope that the others would have found food and water. But Brock's milk can was empty, and there was nothing to eat but dandelion greens gathered by Norma, the salmonberries Diana and Rolf had picked, and the bucket of strange shellfish Carlo had plucked off the rocks.

"Chinaman's hats," Carlo explained, picking up a conical shell no larger around than a quarter. "Limpets. I'll show you." Crooking his forefinger, he scooped the morsel of raw seafood out of the shell, popped it into his mouth, and swallowed. "Like that," he said, smiling. "Very good."

Felicia had already finished her small share of the salmonberries. She looked hungrily at the strange food and slowly shook her head. "We'll do better this afternoon. I can wait."

Andrew Held picked at a limpet, rolled it on his tongue, and with some difficulty, swallowed it. It tasted like a particularly salty oyster. His shaggy eyebrows lifted. "Not bad at all, Carlo. I suppose we could cook them."

"We could, but in Hawaii we think it spoils them."

"Oh, let's not wait to cook them," Brock said with his mouth full. "Not until we have more than this."

The meager meal was over in minutes. As they looked at the empty pail and dry milk can, Donald's announcement that a signal flag was now flying on Phoenix Island brought almost no response. Food, drink—these needs

consumed and distracted them. Ignoring Donald, they
began to make nervous disconnected statements about
all the things they would collect during the afternoon.
Now that she was equipped to recognize salmonberries,
Felicia was sure she could find another bush. Carlo had
discovered a gravelly beach that might yield clams at low
tide. Diana and Rolf were going to search for the old
Furness farm . . . One by one they promised each other
they would have plenty to eat when they came back in
the evening.

They were still sitting on the beach, their mouths dry
and stomachs contracting with hunger, when the two
basset hounds, Mike and Lili, came bounding down the
slope. Mike was in the lead, and he was carrying something in his mouth. Lili, yelping anxiously, was making
a futile attempt to overtake him. Mike raced across the
sand and came to a sudden halt a few feet in front of his
master.

A gray, white-tailed rabbit hung limply from his
mouth, the head with round staring eyes flopping on one
side and the furry hindquarters on the other. Panting and
wagging his tail, Mike looked up at Andrew Held.

Lili made a quick experimental foray in the direction
of the rabbit. Without relaxing his hold on his prize,
Mike sounded a low warning growl. Lili backed away
and stretched out on the ground. Dropping her head on
her front paws, she fixed sad bloodshot eyes on Mike's
mouth.

Donald Campbell exclaimed, "Hey, that's a fresh kill!"
He jumped up and approached the dog. "Okay, Mike.
Good dog, Mike."

Mike rolled his eyes upward, and through clenched
jaws growled again, more menacingly than before.

Andrew Held spoke up. "That's his, Donald."

"That's meat! Fresh meat!"

Dr. Held said quietly, "Mike knows that."

"But we could cook that rabbit. It's a good size. It
would give us all something solid to chew on."

Rolf said very quietly, "He hunted for it. We can hunt
rabbit, too. The best time is dawn. I'll go out tomorrow
morning."

There was a murmur of agreement from the other
men, and then a heavy silence.

Donald looked around the group, blinking uncomprehendingly at their disapproving faces. What the hell. Rabbit meat right at their feet, and they didn't have the guts to take it away from a dog. What the hell . . . Scowling, he retreated and sat down on a log. They were as hungry as he was, he knew it. Mike had carried his kill to a safer spot and was settling down to eat it. Look at them all, Donald thought angrily, staring at the damned hound like the sight of raw meat put them in some kind of a trance. Staring and drooling. Their stomachs were growling as loud as his. How did they get off looking down their noses at him? God damn hypocrites. If he had taken the rabbit when they weren't looking and roasted it over the coals and offered them all a piece of it, not one of them would have asked where he got it. Not one.

Blake welcomed the task of gathering firewood, for the monotonous physical exercise diverted him from the pain of hunger. After an hour, he stopped and surveyed the fruits of his labor.

"Curious thing," he said to Andrew Held. "That's nothing but a pile of wood, yet at this point it looks to me like a pile of gold. I'm almost ashamed of how proud I am that I collected it—but I feel I've stored up something more valuable than money."

Dr. Held smiled. "Well, you're right. It *is* a lot more than driftwood. It's energy."

Norma looked at him thoughtfully. "It's been your life work, hasn't it, Dr. Held? Energy. Atomic energy."

"Atomic energy in particular. But I've also had a lot to say about coal, oil, solar electricity generation, and so on. And I've been a little schizophrenic, I guess. On the one hand I've played Cassandra, foretelling in awesome tones, at least I *hoped* they were awesome, that our entire industrial system is doomed as long as our production is tied to imported oil at ten to fifteen dollars a barrel. But I've also taken the role of Pollyanna, and I prefer it. Because I believe there *is* a cure to our ailing economy."

Felicia exclaimed, "*A* cure! Only one? It seems to me that our brilliant chief executive has prescribed at least three. Turn off the lights. Turn off the air conditioner. And don't drive your car."

"Well, we *do* use too much power." Norma's voice was

primly defensive. "Or I should say, we use power un-necessarily. Don't you agree, Dr. Held?"

"Oh, yes, of course. We should conserve. We've been importing forty percent of our fuel. Through conserva-tion we could reduce our fuel consumption by twenty-five percent and make up the remaining fifteen percent by reopening abandoned oil wells, converting coal into nat-ural gas, and so on. Austerity, self-control—they unite people, if the cause is just. What better common cause than to reduce the level of our self-indulgence?"

Felicia's laugh was faintly derisive. "After only two days on this island of yours, I am *not* in the mood for self-denial." With a significant glance in Norma's direc-tion, she added, "And I suspect that doing without would hardly be the tie that binds. Forty-eight hours with no comforts whatsoever have *not* made me love my fellow man."

"But they have made you work with him," Dr. Held said.

"Out of necessity, not desire."

"The end result is the same. You're surviving." With a reassuring smile for Norma, Dr. Held began to walk away.

Serious-minded Norma cut off his retreat. "Dr. Held? You said there is a solution to the energy crisis. You didn't mean conservation, did you?"

"Oh, no. That would satisfy our immediate needs. But in the long run our survival, at least our survival as a great industrial power, may well depend on what you see right there." He turned and pointed west. "It's all around us. Sea water. An almost limitless source of energy. A nation that can put men on the moon can turn sea water into fuel."

Warren Brock said cheerily, "I *adore* riddles!"

"I don't." Felicia's tone was sharp. "They make me feel inferior. And that makes me nervous."

"Tonight, when we're together around the bonfire," Dr. Held said. "I'll explain. Right now, it's back to work."

"Tonight," Felicia echoed, frowning as her glance trav-eled from the beach to the hill above where they had slept the night before. "We'll still be here tonight?"

No one answered her question. Like Andrew Held, they were all intent on getting back to work.

The freighter was bound for Alaska, cutting a clean straight line in the smooth sea and making her seventeen knots and no more because the captain believed in the economical use of oil. The seaman on watch in the bow narrowed his eyes against the setting sun and gave himself thirty seconds to decide whether the floating blur off the starboard was really a boat or an extra large piece of drift.

As he adjusted his binoculars, the dark object came into focus. The hull of a boat. Wide in the stern, high in the bow. A commercial fisherman, or as much as was left of it. He let the binoculars hang around his neck, opened the telephone box at his elbow, and rang for the bridge. "Floating object one point off the starboard bow, sir."

In the absence of the captain, who was in his quarters dipping into the ship's stores of Scotch, the second mate was conning the bridge. He instantly translated "floating object" into "wreckage of a boat" and that raised the possibility that a person or person might be inside. The freighter had been at sea and out of reach of the tidal wave, but radio reports ever since had supplied a continuing story of tsunami disasters. To check the "floating object" they would have to change course, and that meant calling the Old Man.

"Hell's fire!" the captain observed as he looked lovingly at his shot glass and reached for the telephone with his free hand. His orders were delivered quickly and clearly. Steer for the object, alert the boat crew, pull alongside the derelict, and cut the engines.

Within minutes, the freighter lay in the water and the lifeboat crew, headed by the boatswain, had lowered a lifeboat and was descending the long rope ladder. The men didn't bother talking until they reached the splintered hull, and the engineer exclaimed, "Christ, it's an old woman. A dead old woman, if you ask me."

A half-hour later, Andrew Held's cook Mary had been put to bed in the stateroom designed for the occasional use of the freighter's wealthy owner. Since he had a tendency towards *mal de mer* as well as a deep-seated repugnance for all things maritime except the company's profit and loss statements, the room was seldom occupied.

"She's alive, all right." The first aid man, the freighter's only medical officer, was comfortable with cuts, bruises, and severe hangovers, but this old woman baffled him. She was breathing, but something had given her a terrible shellacking. Her clothing was half torn off, her body was covered with bruises and scratches, and a large swelling suggested she had taken a monumental blow on the head. Concussion? Fractured skull? Internal injuries? He really didn't know, and he said so.

The captain nodded. The boat crew had completed the rescue and hoisted the wreckage onto the deck. The first aid man had given the best diagnosis of which he was capable. In addition to her injuries, this woman was obviously suffering from exposure. Her face, arms and legs were badly sunburned, and her lips were cracked and bleeding and rimmed with dry salt. It would be four days before they made port. Should they continue on course?

That would be the economical thing to do, and the Company was all for economy. But this woman was hurt, and they didn't know how badly. Inasmuch as the Company would be very touchy if one of its ships docked with a corpse on board, and the Coast Guard could get downright mean if he didn't make a prompt report of a rescue at sea, the captain hesitated only briefly. "Radio the Coast Guard . . ."

Once the message was sent, and a copy of it and the time of transmission entered in the ship's log, the captain returned to his quarters, refilled his shot glass, and sat down to wait for the whirring beat of the Coast Guard chopper. In the guest stateroom, Mary moaned, rolling her head to one side, and once more sank into a warm engulfing blackness.

Chapter Twenty

Diana and Rolf came out of the woods into the clearing and stopped as if by agreement. They had found the old farm, but there wasn't much left to see. A pile of rotting logs overgrown with blackberry brambles and wild roses—that would be the farmhouse. Not far beyond it, some sort of barn or shed had disintegrated, scattering rough timbers like jackstraws. Grass, ferns, and wild currant had repossessed the clearing, almost smothering even the huge stumps which some early Furness, long since dead, hadn't been able to burn or pull after the land was cleared.

Diana imagined that if she looked hard enough, the soft summer haze would evaporate like a mist and reveal the last Furness farmer, carrying a bucket to the cow barn, or the last Furness woman hanging clothes on the line. If she listened, listened deeply, she would hear voices, a woman calling to her child, a man shouting "gee" and "haw!" as he guided his draft horse along the single furrow . . .

"Seeing ghosts?"

She looked up, and knew Rolf had been watching her. Laughing, she made a joke of rubbing her eyes with her knuckles. "Have they gone?" she asked, keeping her eyes closed.

"No, I think they live here all the time. But they aren't looking." Rolf bent his head and his lips touched hers in a gentle and lingering kiss.

A tremor went through her body. It was a good feeling, a free, happy feeling of being excited and comforted at the same time. And it had been a good feeling to lie innocently in his arms the first night on Phoenix while the thunder of the waves sounded on the beach below. Last night she had retreated to her separate bed, pretending not to see the question in Rolf's eyes. Why? How could most of her want him so badly—like this kiss, which she had halfway expected, or to be honest

153

about it, halfway asked for—and still have inside her a
secret fearful self who screamed in panic at the thought
of being held and uncovered and seen and touched?

Diana turned her head, rested her forehead against
his shoulder and once more closed her eyes. When Rolf's
arms went around her she felt enclosed but not frightened. Somewhere in the peaceful clearing, a meadowlark
sang on Phoenix.

Against her ear, Rolf said, "Diana, I want to tell you
something. Look at me."

She shook her head. "I don't want to move."

"All right. I'll tell you anyway. I love you. You're my
girl, and someday, you're going to *be* my girl, all the
way."

She squeezed her eyes closed and fought the impulse to
pull free of him and run.

He continued to hold her, but his arms made no demands, and one hand gently stroked the back of her
head. "You don't have to be scared of me, Diana. You
don't have to be scared of anything we do together.
Someday we will make love, but it won't be until you
want it as much as I do."

In a choked voice, she whispered, "I love you, too."

He laughed softly. "Oh I know that, or I wouldn't be
talking like this."

In her surprise, she lifted her head and looked into his
face.

"You're funny-looking," he said. "Your eyes are too
big, and they're gray or purple or purple-gray and what
kind of color is that for eyes? Besides, you've got those
funny-looking long eyelashes and your nose is too short
and covered all over with freckles."

In mock anger, she raised a small brown fist. He caught
it and simultaneously jumped to the side so that she lost
balance. Together they fell to the ground in a squirming
tangle of arms and legs.

They lay in the long grass, half-winded, laughing. The
old fear stirred but quickly subsided, for Rolf made no
attempt to touch her other than to reach out and hold
her hand. Someday, he had said, they would really make
love, but not until she wanted it as much as he did.
Silently, Diana added her own qualification: Not until
the ugly memory of Julie's husband loses its power to
scare me and turn me cold.

His name was Bud. "Bud," he explained, "because I'm your buddy, just like a brother." Her sister Julie and Bud had come home to the farm because Julie was carrying a baby and the doctor said that with her history of miscarriage, she ought to spend most of the seventh month in bed. Julie and Diana's mother had left Wolf years before—not even their father or grandmother knew where she was—so Julie came to the Lindgren farm to stay with the three of them, Diana, her father, and Minnie Lindgren. Bud came over from the mainland every weekend.

It had been a Saturday, a cold rainy Saturday, when sometime late at night Diana was awakened by the pressure of a hand clamped over her mouth. She tried to turn her head, and the pressure increased. She pulled her hands free of the bedclothes and struck at the arm. Another hand grabbed her right wrist while the dark body above her dropped to pin her left arm against her side. Bud's voice sounded low and rough. "Don't fight me, little girl. Just take it easy. I'm Bud, your buddy-buddy, remember?"

Diana's attic bedroom was wedged under the slanted roof. Raindrops echoed her frightened pulse.

"You're fifteen, sweetie. You're a big girl now, I been noticing that. Look what we got here . . ." His hand slid inside her nightgown and settled over her breast. While his thumb and forefinger played with the nipple, he whispered, "That feel good, Diana, don't that feel good?"

She struggled against the weight of his body, against the rough palm clamped so tightly across her mouth. "Don't do that, Diana. I'm not going to hurt you. I'm going to make you feel good, sweetie."

In the darkness his body was a weighted shadow, crushing the breath out of her, and his voice was a pleading whisper. "I promise you, it won't hurt, only a little bit. You promise you won't yell, and I'll take away my hand. You don't want to yell, anyway. You know how sick your sister is . . ."

The thick voice went on and on, picturing the terrible things that would happen to Julie if she got upset. She would bleed, and lose the baby, and die. For two weeks, Diana had been seeing her sister pale and weak and scared of losing her baby. She was too frightened now to doubt what Bud said.

Slowly, Bud removed the hand that covered her mouth. Now she was free to cry out. But she didn't. Instead, she begged him, "Please go away, please. Leave me alone, please . . ."

"In a little bit, sweetie. In a little bit." He pulled the bedclothes down to her waist and the cold black air washed over her breasts. He said hoarsely, "No one ever touched you before, did they? Sweet little virgin baby."

Desperately she jerked one hand free and tried to hit him. He caught and held it. "I told you, don't do that. Remember your sister. Remember what you would do to Julie."

She lay back, defeated, hot tears stinging her eyes.

"That's a good girl. Sweet little girl. Someday, somebody's going to give it to you. I'm going to make it easier for them. I'm just going to fix that sweet little virginity of yours."

That's when the worst part began, the part she had never told anyone. With his body and one hand he held her fast while his second hand moved under the covers and slid along her belly. The hand found the warm and secret place, pressing down hard on the patch of soft curly hair. He whispered, "There, there, there . . ." Each time a strong finger entered her body and, with each stabbing motion pushed a little deeper, until the words "There, there . . ." were flooded out of her mind by the pain.

It went on forever, and then he said, "Ah . . ." like a long sigh, and he stopped. Slowly he took his hand away. "Don't forget, nobody knows about this but you and me. But *you* know, sweet Diana. I got into you, in a way." He stood up, crossed the room, and the door closed softly behind him.

Diana lay alone in the dark, fear and shame hitting her in convulsive waves. The only coherent thought she could pull from the turmoil was that her sister Julie must never know. And in the morning the same resolution came back to her with first consciousness. Her body ached, and her arms were sore, but she concealed it from the shrewd eyes of her grandmother. She even managed to wash the blood out of the bedsheets when no one was around.

This morning, raising the flagpole and flying a table-cloth flag had been a great accomplishment, but now that they had located the old Furness farm, Diana and Rolf weren't searching the sky for the Coast Guard helicopters. Their eyes were on the ground. Hunger and thirst had pushed rescue out of their minds.

Somewhere, the Furness family had drawn water from a well or dipped it at a spring. Somewhere, they must have planted an orchard. Grains and corn had once grown in this stump-cluttered clearing, and a vegetable garden would have been located near the house. If there were no traces of the many growing things they had cultivated here, at least wild berries and edible weeds would have increased naturally wherever heavy timber had been cut and the land opened to the sun.

Methodically, Diana and Rolf began the hunt. Three kinds of fruit were growing all around them. The pinkish-orange globes of wild rose hips, the dusty purple clusters on the wild currant bushes, and the large blackberries on vines that nearly enveloped the old stumps. They would pick these later, on their way back to camp. It was more important to explore beyond the clearing in order to get a more complete idea of the sources of food and water on this end of the island.

Their first discovery was a second clearing, hidden from the first by a grove of alder that fifty years of undergrowth had made into an effective screen. As soon as they had passed through the woods, the land began a gradual slope and, at the far side of the meadow, it rose again so that the center area was a natural bowl.

"Look, oh look!" Diana exclaimed as they saw what lay at the bottom of the hill. A pond! A dark, still pond, rimmed by cattails and skunk cabbage and overgrown in some places by floating clusters of yellow pond lilies. Water! Muddy, streaked by green scum, but water. And on the other side of this miniature lake, a dozen gnarled apple trees rose above a field of wild grasses and stalks of fireweed.

"Let's go!" Diana shouted.

They ran down the sloping field, Diana in the lead with her long hair streaming and bare arms lifting and dipping like the wings of a glider.

"Hey, we're not supposed to run," Rolf called. "Dr. Held told us not to use up our energy." But he was right behind her and right beside her when they both reached the edge of the pond and dropped to their knees. With

short skimming motions of both hands they cleared away
the bright green growth that lay on the surface of the
water and, without hesitation, cupped their hands together and scooped the dark water into their mouths.
Then they fell back on their buttocks, legs stretched
straight out, and laughed with brownish trickles of water
still rolling down their chins.

Diana's eyes were bright with amusement. "It smells
bad. I can just see Mrs. Held . . ."

Rolf smiled. "It smells muddy, but it tastes wet." He
reached across the bank to a clump of skunk cabbage
and pulled off one of the large shiny leaves. In one swift
motion he rolled the leaf into a cone-shaped cup, dipped
it into the pond, and held the leaf-cup up to Diana's
mouth. "Have another drink, Swinomish style."

Rolf remembered a great deal that some of the older
coastal Indians had said about the uses of wild plants and
trees. Just the one plant at his feet, the rank but plentiful
skunk cabbage, was useful as a vegetable, as material
for lining berry baskets, and as a medicine—for the cure
of carbuncles, to purify the blood, and to bring about an
easier childbirth.

Diana's knowledge of wild foods had come from her
frugal grandmother, who had also taught her that the
first lesson in gathering nature's bounty was to recognize
what would poison her. Very soon, she and Rolf had
gathered enough roots and berries to provide several
meals for the whole group, and, in addition, the old
orchard had yielded a surprisingly bountiful crop of small
hard green apples.

Their problem was how to carry what they had found
across fields without paths and through woods without
trails, and to do this with virtually no containers. From
the junk pile, which they were already calling the
warehouse, they had picked out a man's shirt, a plastic
bucket without a handle, and a bundle of fishnet. With
these, and with Rolf's shirt, they improvised their packs.

By twisting green honeysuckle vines, Rolf fashioned a
kind of rope that he tightened around the top of the
pail as reinforcement and then looped across the top as
a handle; this was for carrying water. If it held, this pail
would transport as much pond water as they would need

until they could return the next day with the five-gallon milk can.

Diana folded the fishnet into several thicknesses so that nothing would fall through the holes. Then she picked apples to put into it, leaving enough room for half a dozen pond lilies whose rootstalks could be roasted and the green seed pods sliced as a salad. Rolf waded into the pond and broke off several skunk cabbages, which he tied up in his shirt and hung at his belt. In one hand he picked up the pail of water, in the other the fishnet sack of apples and pond lilies. With a long, sure stride he started up the slope toward the farm. Back at the old farmhouse, he rested while Diana used the extra shirt as a container for blackberries and currants, separating the layers of fruit with mustard greens.

"How about those over there, at the edge of the clearing?" Rolf pointed to a tall bush covered with clusters of tiny red berries.

Diana shook her head. "My grandmother said never to eat them. They don't hurt some people, but they make other people deathly sick, and she said there wasn't any percentage in finding out which kind of person I am."

"They *look* good," Rolf commented as she picked up the shirt with its load of berries and gathered the edges to form a sort of sack. They smiled at each other, turned south, and began the long trek back to camp.

Chapter Twenty-One

By the time she reached the clearing, Felicia was desperate. Her mouth was dry, her head throbbed, and she was obsessed by the desire to find something to eat. All afternoon she had been thinking of her favorite dishes. Filet of sole with green grapes. Breast of chicken amandine. Soft-shell crabs. Asparagus with hollandaise . . . At first she had tried to blot out such thoughts, for they made her even hungrier, but as the hours passed her mind reached out in spite of her and enveloped the succulent images as greedily as a carnivorous plant closing on a particularly fat fly.

How long had it been since her confrontation with that beast Campbell? How long had she been struggling against underbrush and falling over logs? For two hours at least, perhaps longer, but if she had finally reached the old Furness farm, it was worth it. Diana and Rolf had said if they could only locate the farm, that was their best bet for finding food and water. And here was an open field, a broad field dotted with charred stumps and sprouting all kinds of unrecognizable ferns and weeds and vines. There in a clump of brambles and tall grass was a pile of logs and the remnant of a wall. Yes, surely, she had found the Furness farm. Now, to search.

But search for what? Even the few "natural foods" she had experimented with had come to her from a store, so dried, toasted, crumbled, and ground that she could not have guessed what the product looked like as a growing thing. As she hesitated at the edge of the clearing, a bird flew by and settled on the branch of a large dark-leafed bush. Berries! The bush was covered with clusters of red berries. Like the dove who appeared to Noah, the little gray and black bird had brought her a message. Moreover, he plucked a berry and flew off with it, so it was obviously edible.

Picking up her long skirt, Felicia ran across the field and raked her fingers through a bright cluster so that the berries fell into her palm. She put four or five into her mouth, chewed and swallowed them, once more reassuring herself with the thought that they could not be poisonous because a bird had eaten them. They were seedy and they were tasteless, but they weren't bitter, and that, surely, was another good sign. Something to eat, something to ease the cramp of hunger . . . All restraint was gone as Felicia reached out with both hands and in feverish haste pulled the berries off their stems and pushed them into her mouth.

While she was eating, she thought of the others. They might not have been as lucky as she was in finding something to eat. She should pick the berries and carry them back to camp. Carlo had found those strange little shellfish, Norma collected dandelion greens, Diana picked salmonberries, and they brought it all back to camp. In just a moment, she would stop eating and begin to harvest the remaining berries to take back for the others. That's what she had planned when she brought along a rusty coffee can from the warehouse. In just a moment, after she had eaten just a little more . . .

But if there was this bush, wouldn't there be others? She hadn't really explored. She would find another bush and fill the coffee can before she returned to camp. In any case, why had she been so naïve as to assume that Carlo had shared *all* the shellfish he found, or that Diana hadn't eaten more salmonberries than she brought back for the rest of them? *Sauve-qui-peut*, Felicia said to herself, filling her mouth and reaching for more. The coffee can was too small, anyway. What little it would hold wouldn't be worth dividing. The sensible thing to do was eat all these berries and come back tomorrow with a larger container and look for another bush.

Their meal that evening was primitive, but to people who had been suffering hunger for the first time in their lives, filling the stomach was deeply satisfying.

Carlo had found an abundant supply of small white clams. "Ah, the *pièce de résistance!*" Warren Brock sang out merrily, for he had been studying Rolf and Diana's produce with obvious distaste. "Gorgeous, with *lots* of melted butter."

For the first time, Norma was not offended by Brock's deliberately ridiculous postures. She looked his way and smiled. "I was just thinking, how strange it is that even when I'm grateful to have something to eat—anything *at all* to eat—I'm so terribly conscious of what we don't have. No butter for the clams. No salt for the vegetables. No sugar for the berries. No spices or oils or dairy products. I'm ashamed of myself."

Brock's bleached eyebrows lifted. "Oh, tsk! *Ashamed.* Isn't it enough to cope with your disadvantaged digestive system without trying to appease your Puritan conscience at the same time?"

Norma's precise features stiffened for an instant, and then relaxed into the same moody half-smile. "One of my Puritan mother's lessons should be a help right now, not a burden. I had to eat whatever was served, and whenever I resisted, she said, 'You don't have to like it. You just have to eat it.' "

"My *dear*, how *repressive.* Didn't you ever rebel and simply throw your food on the floor?"

"Never," Norma said wistfully. "Never . . ."

Without being asked, Carlo, Diana, and Rolf had taken charge of preparing the food. High on the beach they dug a pit about two feet across and covered the bottom with small stones they had heated in the bonfire. On top of these they arranged layers of seaweed Rolf called "dulse," then the clams, then dandelion greens, and continued alternating layers of seaweed, clams, and greens until the hole was packed. A top layer of heated stones put a lid on the cooking pot. While the contents steamed, the three cooks turned their attention to the rest of the meal.

"Skunk cabbage!" Warren Brock shrugged elaborately and turned his head. "Oh, well, I'll eat it if I don't have to see you do whatever you're going to do to it."

Diana broke the plant apart and set aside the small inside leaves. "It's the oil that makes it smell skunky," she explained. "After I've boiled these tender leaves in three waters, they'll taste like regular cabbage."

"Well, dear, that's not exactly *gourmet,*" Brock observed, "but at this point I'd eat the skunk, too, if I didn't have to catch him."

"Skunks are edible," Rolf said. "But there aren't any in these islands." He was sitting cross-legged on the ground, with a board across his knees and Donald's jack-knife in his hand. Using the board as a chopping block, he cut the stems and seed pods of the yellow pond lilies until they looked like cole slaw. Then he scraped the yellow-green bits into a badly cracked mixing bowl. To this green salad he added a handful of finely shredded dulse. "For flavor," he said. "But it's also full of vitamins and minerals."

Carlo wrapped skunk cabbage roots in thick green streamers of kelp and buried them in the hot ashes. While they baked, he cut a dozen green sticks, sharpened the ends, and on each of them impaled a small, hard apple. "If they're halfway cooked, they'll be softer and sweeter," he explained, thrusting the sticks into the sand as close to the heat as possible without burning the skins.

The blackberries and wild currants needed no treatment. Or rather what they needed, Brock pointed out, was sugar and cream. "Oh, well," he chirped, his large round eyes moving appreciatively from the roasting apples to the bowl of salad to the boiling cabbage. "Sugar and cream is another do-without."

"It's a do-without situation," Norma Mansfield responded and then the thin line of her mouth softened as she giggled. It was a totally spontaneous, childlike giggle, and so unlike his reserved and proper wife that Blake Mansfield turned and stared. She met his startled look and giggled again. "Think of it, Blake. Of everything we can do without. And you're the man they're talking about in those advertisements saying 'For the Man Who Has Everything.' "

"It *is* funny," he agreed uncertainly, wanting to but unable to join the nonsense. "I guess when we eat we'll do without plates and do without forks."

"There you go!" she said gaily. Blake, still perplexed but trying hard, slowly began to smile.

To be playful, even briefly, was so unlike Blake that Andrew Held could not repress a responsive chuckle. Rubbing the stubble on his chin, he decided not to offer his own "do-without." A reference to their lack of razors would only remind Blake that he hadn't shaved for two days, and that would undoubtedly distress such a fastidious person more than going hungry. We may have some fine beards around this campfire, Dr. Held mused, before some sort of rescue team gets around to Phoenix Island.

They had finished dinner when Felicia began to feel ill. She had eaten very little. The berries had not satisfied her hunger, but they seemed to have taken away her appetite.

They ate on thick outer leaves of the skunk cabbage supported by boards, and when Diana offered her a "plate," Felicia accepted it with every intention of dipping into the strange buffet with her fingers just as the others were doing all around her. Yet even the steamed clams, which were a familiar food and one she had always been fond of, filled her with revulsion. She was hungry, but she wasn't hungry. Her stomach was crying for food, but an unpleasant tightness gripped her throat, and it was hard to swallow.

She tried a bite of apple, and it was no better. She looked around surreptitiously. Had anyone noticed she wasn't eating? No, they were concentrating on the contents of their plates. She sat among them, steadying her plate with both hands, and wondered how she could explain that she wasn't hungry. Because she had filled up on berries—no, she certainly wasn't going to tell them that. Thank God that for the moment, at least, no explanation was necessary. Only Diana looked at her curiously, as if to ask what was wrong.

Felicia shook her head.

"Are you all right?"

Felicia nodded. She longed to put down her food and leave the circle, but that would attract attention.

"Would you like something more?"

Diana's concern irritated her. "No, no!" Felicia snapped. "I have always been a slow eater."

For a moment Diana's thoughtful eyes lingered on her, and then the girl looked down at her own plate and continued eating.

Slowly the gripping sensation in her throat spread to her stomach. Felicia bore it in silence until the painful churning settled in a lump inside her rib cage. As inconspicuously as she could, she set her plate down on the sand and leaned forward, both arms crossed over her stomach to press against the pain. Now she had attracted Andrew Held's attention, as well as Diana's. Though her hands felt icy and her face was burning, she tried to ignore them both.

Andrew Held was standing over her. "Felicia, are you ill?"

She shook her head violently. But she was, of course. Ill, terribly ill, and obviously from eating all those berries.

"I think you are." He sat on the log beside her, gently touched her forehead, and pressed fingers against her wrist. At his signal, Diana crossed the circle and dropped to the ground at Felicia's feet.

"Her pulse seems fast," Andrew Held said quietly. "Are you sure that nothing we've eaten is poisonous?"

"I'm sure." Diana pointed to Felicia's plate. "It can't be anything we've had for dinner. She's hardly touched it."

A half-hour earlier Felicia would have ordered them to mind their own business, but now the agonized cramping in her body and the secret knowledge of its cause were frightening her. With each jolt of pain, the fear grew. Instead of pushing Andrew Held's hand away, she clutched it.

"What *is* it, Felicia?" he begged, putting his arm around her. "You're shaking. Your hands are cold and the palms are damp. Where were you this afternoon? What happened?"

She meant to whisper, but her voice got caught in a wave of nausea, and when it broke loose it came out in such a loud agonized cry that everyone around the campfire abandoned their plates and closed in around her. "Poisoned! I ate some berries. They must have been poisonous!"

An excited murmur went through the group. Warren Brock cried, "Oh, my God, I *knew* it. We'll all be dead before nightfall."

"Take it easy." Carlo put a firm hand on Brock's arm and led him across the beach. "Sit down and stay here. There's nothing wrong with you, or any of the rest of us, except Mrs. Held."

Diana stood up. "Please . . ." she said quietly. The men fell back, but Norma remained, and Diana turned to her as if they both understood that she would. "What do you think, Mrs. Mansfield?"

"We should induce vomiting. Isn't that what you'd do?"

"Yes. As quickly as we can."

Felicia moaned. "Vomit? Throw up, in front of all these people?" In desperation she pulled free of her husband's supporting arms and tried to stand. Her legs buckled, and she fell to the ground. Clutching at the log, she made a futile attempt to pull herself up, and then Andrew was on his knees beside her, helping her.

Even as the fear and the pain attacked her in spasms, and her helplessness was as clear to her as the hammering of her heartbeat, Felicia fought against the brutal exposure of emptying her stomach in the presence of others. "Let me go!" she sobbed, though without Andrew's arms she would have slipped to the ground. "Away from here. I can't vomit! I won't vomit! Leave me alone!"

Diana called out, "Rolf, would you stir up the fire . . ."

Dimly, through half-closed eyes, Felicia watched Diana's slender but strangely authoritative figure. She moved quickly, dipping the stainless steel bowl into the bay, carrying the bowl to the fire and setting it over the brightest flame. Felicia was aware of Norma lifting the skirt of her dinner dress to blot Felicia's forehead and cheeks, aware of the slippery cold moisture oozing from her pores and collecting between her breasts, aware that Carlo had somehow rounded up the others and drawn them to the far end of the beach. She saw everything through a mist, and she knew that she must be crying.

And now Diana was dipping one finger into the bowl of water. Now she had picked up the bowl and was bringing it to her and telling her to drink from it. Felicia's last fight was a weak attempt to turn her head away, and then she gave up, and Diana was holding the bowl to her mouth.

It all blurred together after that. The taste of the salt water, the uncontrollable spasms of her stomach as it reacted to the lukewarm liquid, the tears streaming from her eyes so that she could not see but only feel, that Norma was holding her head down and Diana was in front of her with the empty bowl in her hands. Her head was throbbing as if it would burst by the time the crescendo of contractions reached its awful climax, and she opened her mouth and let the gaseous evil-smelling contents of her stomach pour out into the bowl. By then, she had lost all control. She surrendered herself to her body and all the ugliness it was visiting on her and, gasping, prayed for the agony to end. Andrew was speaking to her, but she did not understand the words. Norma and Diana were close, but she could not make out their faces.

At last, it stopped. There was an ache under her ribs but it was quiet pain, and her body was still. Andrew was wiping her face with a warm cloth and everyone else, even Norma and Diana, had disappeared.

Felicia leaned against him, too exhausted even to cry.

"You'll be fine." Andrew's fingers, awkward but gentle, brushed her hair back from her face. "Strange, isn't it, that not one of us is a comb carrier? Nine persons, and no one with a comb in his pocket. Tomorrow we'll have to see what we can do about that. I'll bet on Rolf to know what Indians did before they could buy combs at a dime store."

Felicia said, "Oh, Andy, what a disgusting sight I must have made."

Andrew Held chuckled. "My dear, none of us saw anything we hadn't seen before or won't see again."

"Awful, awful."

"I know," he said soothingly. "I understand your feelings. The queen has no legs, neither does she vomit."

Felicia laughed weakly. "Exactly. And the queen got her comeuppance."

"Never mind. You didn't do it in the grand ballroom of the Shoreham Hotel. And here, on Phoenix, we're a do-without society, remember?"

"Like do without pride?"

"Oh, no, not at all. Just *that* kind of pride, the kind that makes you too good to be human."

Felicia sighed. "Don't preach, Andy. I'm human."

Andrew's arm squeezed her affectionately. "I think I am, too. But I'm not sure. How does it feel?"

Weak and aching as she was, Felicia lifted her head and looked into her husband's steady blue eyes. "Humble," she said softly. "Terribly, terribly humble."

At Andrew Held's request, they collected around the beach fire. The waning moon was hidden by a misty overcast; darkness enclosed them. They drew together instinctively, sitting nearer to one another than they had in daylight.

"Perhaps we should get together before we try to sleep,

if only for a few minutes." Andrew Held glanced around the circle of faces turned so gratefully toward the orange glow of the fire. "I know how tired you are, but I think we'll all rest better if we have agreed on definite plans for tomorrow. In fact, I wonder if we shouldn't meet together every evening."

"Whatever for?" Felicia murmured wearily.

"To exchange ideas. To ask questions. To share."

"Coo!" Warren Brock said weakly. "That sounds like the minister I had to listen to every Sunday. He was always asking to *share*. 'I want to *share* this thought with you . . . ,' or 'Let us *share* this moment . . .' He had a puffy face and buck teeth and a nervous tic in his right eye. I didn't know what else he had, but whatever it was I didn't want to *share* it."

Andrew Held smiled. "You may not want to share, Warren, but the fact is that you have to. We have shared a disaster. For two days we've shared the experience of finding food and water. Sharing may be an offensively ministerial word to you but we may as well recognize that in our present circumstances any one of us, individually, would perish. As a community we may survive."

Blake Mansfield said uneasily, "You make it sound rather desperate, Dr. Held. Actually, some sort of search party is bound to discover us long before it's a question of survival. We may have to wait a little, of course. Two, three days. Perhaps a week."

"And while we wait?" Andrew Held's busy eyebrows came together in a thoughtful frown. "I worry about that word. I have seen our country wait, instead of planning ahead. Wait to negotiate for disarmament until the world is committed to an arms race. Wait until the water is poisoned with industrial waste and the air is thick with smog and we have too many people and not enough fuel. Two hundred million persons can survive for a long time without anticipating the future, but on Phoenix Island we are nine. I fear for us if we do not plan ahead."

"Aren't we?" Blake asked. "We're going to keep a signal fire going. We've erected a flagpole so that we can fly a distress sign. What more can we do?"

"You are still speaking of rescue. I'm talking about *living,* and for that, we can't count on anyone but ourselves. There are nine of us. We have different skills. We've got to use them."

Norma said thoughtfully, "Some skills are more practical than others. I think it's far-fetched to be talking about survival. As Blake says, it isn't going to come to that. But if it did, Donald would be better off than any of us. He's the strongest. He's used to working with his hands." She shrugged. "And he's got the jackknife."

For a moment Donald's battered face softened into a grin of pleasure, but as his eyes moved to Andrew Held, the pleased look disappeared and he said soberly, "Well, yeah, I got a knife, but I don't know how to organize nothing. I never been a foreman or a boss. I ain't no leader, like Dr. Held."

It was the first time Andrew Held's leadership had been acknowledged out loud. He said tentatively, "We *do* need a leader, simply because we need some degree of organization. But I may not be the one you want. Rolf, for example, knows more about living out of doors than all the rest of us put together."

Rolf's smile showed white teeth under his full black mustache. "That doesn't make me a leader, Dr. Held. You *think* faster than all the rest of us put together. That's what counts."

There was a general murmur of assent. "All right, I'll take charge, *pro tempore*." Dr. Held's eyes twinkled humorously as he added, "On the understanding that I can be deposed by majority vote. As my oath of office, I'll adopt this precept: Leaders always follow where their followers lead them." Dr. Held paused and smiled. "I will not, however, go so far as Mahatma Gandhi, who said, 'There go my followers; I must hasten to catch up to them, for I am their leader.'" Nods of agreement seemed to close that issue.

Held continued, "Well, then, we'll meet regularly every night and everyone will be given an opportunity to speak. I say *regularly* for a reason. Some of you may find it hard to express yourselves, and you'd hesitate to call a special meeting when you have something to say. By establishing a nightly routine, we're creating a kind of 'system' which spares us a nightly decision as to whether we ought to meet and gives all of us, whether shy or aggressive, an equal chance to speak out." He paused. "Well?"

Norma was the first to speak. "I'd like to suggest two rules that I think we should agree to follow. Concerning what we eat."

They listened attentively as she documented her case. Tomorrow they would be hunting for food just as they had today. Since most of them knew little or nothing about what they might find, they were likely to make two mistakes—one was to eat something poisonous, the other was to overlook something edible. Both mistakes could be avoided if they made two simple rules and followed them conscientiously. First, bring everything back to camp. Second, subject every questionable berry or root or plant to the six-bite test.

"I've never hunted wild mushrooms," Norma explained with a small, self-deprecating smile. "They aren't abundant in the East Sixties. But my friend Lucy is an amateur mycologist. She told me that whenever she picks mushrooms she hasn't identified previously, she goes through a six-bite test. That is, she cooks one of the mushrooms and eats one bite every hour for six hours. If no symptoms have developed by the end of that time, she knows the mushroom is edible. We could use the same test on wild plants and berries."

Norma's rules were quickly agreed to, but when Blake Mansfield made a suggestion, the group was divided.

"This morning, when we saw the Coast Guard helicopter fly away, we talked about setting up watches on the beach so as to keep the fire going overnight. I think we should do that tonight."

The line of division was instantly clear. Those who knew the Outer Islands, Andrew Held observed, considered Blake naïve. No search planes or ships would be roaming around Phoenix at night. But the Mansfields, Felicia, and, to a lesser extent, Warren Brock were still unable to grasp the fact that they were beyond the jurisdiction of authorities duly constituted to account for (as well as to number, fingerprint, list, photograph, and catalog) all of its members. One side had faith in a signal fire, and the other thought it was a silly waste of firewood.

Only Donald had nothing to say for or against Blake's proposal. If they were stranded for any length of time, Dr. Held decided, he ought to put some thought into analyzing the big man's motivations. But now there was an immediate issue and it would have to be settled before they climbed the hill to the dormitory. "It isn't possible for all of us to agree on every issue," Dr. Held put in quickly, "and it isn't necessary. We can decide things by majority vote, if you like, though personally I think that method is dangerously simple. Even if the vote were eight against one, the one dissident might know more about the subject than the other eight."

Rolf's low voice dissipated the last shred of disagreement. "I think we should keep the fire going because *some* of us want to. It doesn't matter to me how many. I'll keep watch tonight. Someone else can do it tomorrow."

Blake blinked rapidly. "Well, of course, the point is, we're hoping we won't have to do it tomorrow night, right? In any case, let's take our turns on the beach. Three-hour watches . . . that would be about right, wouldn't it?"

Looking around the circle, Andrew Held guessed they had all picked up Rolf's implication that they wouldn't be rescued and Blake's assumption that they would be, but no one wanted to dwell on the subject. It was agreed that Rolf, Carlo, and Blake would be on duty tonight. Dr. Held broke a stick into three pieces of varying lengths, and they drew. Blake pulled the shortest and got the ten-to-one shift, Carlo would watch from one to four, and Rolf from four to seven.

They lingered by the bonfire, sharing an unspoken reluctance to leave the warmth and the light. At length Norma broke the silence.

"Was it only this afternoon that you were talking about the energy crisis, Dr. Held?"

Felicia said wearily, "Only this afternoon. It's been a long day."

"The riddle!" Brock chirped. "You were going to tell us the answer to the riddle. Sea water into fuel. How? Or should I say, what?"

As he had that afternoon, Andrew Held gestured toward the open sea. "The *what* is all around us. Deuterium. An almost limitless source of energy."

"Deuterium?" Norma asked.

"Yes. Strange word, isn't it? But it should be as much a part of the layman's everyday vocabulary as words like gasoline or vitamins or apple pie. It's a heavy form of hydrogen. An ideal fuel for thermonuclear fusion. A single cubic meter of sea water, or two hundred and twenty-five gallons, contains enough deuterium to provide four hundred thousand hours of energy."

He paused and rubbed his chin, which was already bristling with a salt-and-pepper stubble of beard. "Think of it! That water, lapping almost at our feet, could supply *billions* of times more energy than all the oil deposits in the world."

"But the waste material? The pollution?" Norma's polite self-control was a poor cover for the anxiety that Andrew Held's statement so obviously aroused. "Radioactive material is deadly, isn't it? Maybe you can convert sea water into deuterium, but wouldn't the conversion process be terribly dangerous?"

"That's just it," Dr. Held responded. "It wouldn't. You're thinking of nuclear power plants as they exist today. They *do* produce radioactive wastes. They use uranium or plutonium and the waste is, indeed, highly dangerous. But the waste from a thermonuclear fusion power plant would be helium, and that's no more dangerous than the stuff we use to blow up balloons for our children. No, I assure you, Mrs. Mansfield. I am as concerned about safety as you are. I am as opposed to pollution as you are. That's precisely my reason for urging an all-out program for utilization of deuterium. It's clean energy, and it's safe. And it could free us once and for all from the ransom we have been paying foreign governments."

Andrew Held paused, and in a much softer voice said, "Forgive me, Mrs. Mansfield. You didn't ask for a lecture." He turned to Felicia. "You're very tired, I know. The watches have been set up. The signal fire will blaze all night. I think everyone but the keeper of the flame should try to get some sleep."

Felicia sighed. "I suppose so. But I don't mind your lectures, Andy. On the contrary, I am pleased to get a glimpse into your mind. You haven't always been so . . . so communicative." She stood up. "But I will be on my way up the hill. No, I don't need a torch. It isn't really dark."

Andrew Held nodded at Blake Mansfield. "You're taking the first shift? Ah, fine. And you've got a wristwatch."

With that he said good night and limped across the beach toward the hill.

In a few minutes they had all followed suit, and Blake Mansfield sat alone by the fire, looking out toward the mainland, awaiting the nocturnal rescuers who must surely be on their way.

It was midnight, and normally the skipper of the Russian trawler would have been enjoying a sound sleep induced by his native vodka and enhanced by visions of the fine catch they would make when they reached a new fishing ground the next day. But he was worried, and therefore disinclined to put his head down on a pillow and lose contact with his situation.

Not that he expected trouble, even though, under the new agreement, he was on the wrong side of the international boundary. The Americans couldn't possibly patrol their entire expanded offshore territory, and so far, his boat had moved through the darkness on a black and empty sea.

He was really more concerned about American fishermen than he was about the American Coast Guard. The latter would take him and his boat into custody. But commercial fishing boats—aha, that was a different matter. Several Russian trawlers had been chased and he had heard bloody details about what happened to one the Americans caught. And to whom could his countrymen complain? They were an embarrassment to their country, not heroes. When they were caught, that is.

The skipper didn't want to be the center of an international incident, even as a hero. The skipper wanted to slip in quietly, fill his boat with fish, and get back to the mother ship. He was risking a cracked head if he ran into an angry American crew and the impoundment of his boat if American officials caught up with him. So he was too tense to sleep. He decided he wouldn't try. Instead he went out on deck.

The skipper's eyes were sharper than the man's on watch. Even before the watch yelled, "Lights off the port bow!" he had seen the tiny point of light on the dark horizon.

Blake thought at first that he might be guilty of wishful thinking. He *wanted* to see lights. Damn his weak eyes! He should have admitted how poor his vision was and let someone else take his shift by the fire—both Donald and Warren had offered to do so—but since it had been his suggestion, he had felt there would be something vaguely dishonorable, or at least irresponsible, about being excused even on legitimate grounds.

But that *was* a light. Or perhaps two or three lights, blurring together on the very edge of the sea. He had already built up a tremendous fire, but he threw driftwood on it recklessly until the flames drove him back and a shower of sparks shot up into the night.

Were the distant lights getting brighter or dimmer? Damn his myopia, he couldn't tell. He ran to the foot of the hill, cupped hands around his mouth, and shouted with all his strength, "Rolf! Carlo! Rolf, Carlo . . ."

When he stopped to catch his breath, their voices were answering from the woods on top of the hill. Seconds later Donald, Rolf, and Carlo ran into the circle of the firelight. The two basset hounds were baying excitedly at their heels as if this midnight chase was something they had thought of themselves.

The men watched in silence broken only by the panting of the hounds and the snapping of dry cedar as it exploded from the heat and ignited.

"It's a boat, all right," Rolf said finally. "A big one. She's pretty far out, but she's coming this way."

"Hurray!" The cheer was from the top of the hill. The others had left their beds, and were moving cautiously down the path. In a few minutes they were all lined up on the beach, all eyes intent on the maddeningly slow approach of the lights.

"Why don't they speed up?" Norma exclaimed. "Why are they taking so long?"

"Never mind," Felicia said gaily. "The point is, they've seen us, they're on the way."

Responding to the excited voices, the hounds thumped their tails on the sand.

It was true, they had been spotted. The trawler's skipper took one long look at the lights off to port and rumbled into the pilothouse like a truculent bull. His orders were short and blunt. Change course. Get out to sea. They would have to move in a lot closer to identify the lights, and closeness was just what he didn't want. The identification would be mutual. Coast Guard, commercial fishing boat—whatever it was, he was going to give it a wide berth. Out, way out, until those cursed lights disappeared.

On the beach they heaped still more wood on the fire, and Rolf lighted the end of a pine bough and swung the torch over his head in frantic signals. As the light at sea grew dimmer and dimmer, they began shouting impotent commands. "Come back!" "Look here, over here!" The desperate voices served only to arouse the basset hounds. Barking frantically, they charged back and forth along the edge of the water.

Andrew Held tried repeatedly to tell them that it was no use, because he was sure their bonfire had been sighted and equally sure that at the moment of sighting the boat had reversed her course and put out to sea. They could not comprehend what he was saying. Someone had seen them and deliberately sailed away? But why? They refused to believe it.

At last the glimmer of light faded and they fell into despairing silence. With a nod at Blake Mansfield, Carlo sat on a log near the fire to take the second watch. The others moved slowly toward the hill, staying close together, helping each other climb the steeply treacherous path.

Chapter Twenty-Two

On the morning of the third day, a west wind blew in off the ocean, whipping the crests of the waves into whitecaps and driving the sea against the island with such force that the gravel floor of the bay tumbled noisily with each rollback of the water. The cold wind suited the mood of the nine weary shivering human beings who were picking at a breakfast of strange new foods. The small hard roots of Queen Anne's lace had been cut into one-inch chunks and boiled until they were soft. Then Diana mashed them and combined the pulp with the purple-black berries of the salal bush and the meat of wild filberts. The result was a bland but pleasantly sweet and nutty mush with all the nutrients of the domestic carrot, a tame descendant of Queen Anne's lace, the vitamins of raw berries, and the high potassium and phosphorus content of nuts. They ate in silence, for failure was in the air like a gray mist.

At midnight, they had gone back to sleep oppressed by the failure of a signal fire that for some troubling reason had driven help away rather than attracting it. A rabbit hunt at dawn had been another failure.

Rolf, Carlo, Donald, and Blake had armed themselves with short, heavy sticks and set out through the woods with the idea of scaring up rabbits and clubbing them. Warren Brock's shrill promise—"If I go along, I'll faint!" —was accepted without comment, but when Andrew Held got up to go with them, they objected.

He swept their objections aside. Mike and Lili would undoubtedly flush rabbits, but at obedience school they had scored twenty points out of a possible hundred, and simply flushing game wouldn't be their idea of where to stop unless he were present to give the order. So Dr. Held struggled through the underbrush in the wake of the hounds and the hunters.

When they returned, they could report one discovery: Rolf had found deer droppings in a small clearing where underbrush formed a natural screen and the weeds had been broken and trampled. It was a deer refuge, a sleeping place, and it meant there were game animals on Phoenix far more important as food sources than the rabbits and chipmunks they had already seen. However, this small hope for the future—how could they hunt for deer when their only weapons were Donald's jackknife and the yellow-handled screwdriver?—did not offset the morning's failure. The hunters had returned without meat.

"Failure is a normal part of all human endeavor," Andrew Held said. "When the Massachusetts Institute of Technology offered a course in failure, I should have enrolled, but I felt too important and too old. Oh, well—here on Phoenix we'll acquire the same knowledge through home study."

Rolf said, "I should have realized we wouldn't catch rabbits in daylight. We've got to do it after dark. You shine light into a rabbit's eyes, and he freezes. Like lighting a deer."

Carlo showed white teeth in a wide and knowing grin. "Hal-lo, my friend the poacher! You talk like you been there before. But where do we get the flashlights?"

"We could make torches . . ."

As they planned, the mood of the group lifted. Only Blake remained gloomy. "I'm awfully sorry. Rolf, Carlo, I'd very much like to go with you, but there's no use pretending to you *or* to myself. I'd be a liability, not an asset. My eyesight. It's bad enough in the daytime. It's worse at night."

Rolf said quietly, "Three's enough, anyway, Mr. Mansfield. Donald and Carlo and I. That's plenty."

"Racing through the woods with torches." Warren Brock lifted one arm and waved it dramatically. "Greek runners carrying the eternal flame. Stay with *us*, Blake. They'll set you on fire."

"There's more to it than that," Norma said solemnly. "Blake, I am very much opposed to your attempting something that might result in breaking your glasses."

"I know." Blake removed his glasses and wiped the lenses on his shirt sleeve. Without them, his eyes looked larger, the color a deeper blue, and yet as they traveled around the circle, their expression was vague and unfocused. "That was on my mind this morning. I've always been fairly fast. Track team in college, and tennis, of course. But this morning, running over rough ground . . ." He shook his head. "I was so afraid of falling that I was the slowest man in the field. I'm awfully sorry. I'm ashamed to make excuses."

Carlo turned to Blake and smiled warmly. "Hey, weren't you born near-sighted? Then why be ashamed? I was born with a dark skin. It's mine, so I like it."

Andrew Held looked into Carlo's peaceful face. "Carlo, you have a truly wonderful gift. I think you'd manage to live inside your skin even if it were green. I'm not nearly as secure, nor," he said, addressing Blake, "as wise in accepting my own limitations. You see this . . ." He tapped his right foot. "Because of this, I *did* fall this morning, Blake. Oh, I wasn't hurt, physically. I got back onto my feet without anyone noticing, which saved my pride. But the point is, I knew I shouldn't have tried to go on the hunt. A man past sixty, whose right foot is a combination of wood, metal, and hard rubber?" He shook his head. "I wouldn't have insisted on going, but you all objected so strenuously that I had to prove you were wrong." He dug into his pocket and pulled out his wristwatch. "You see what happened when I fell. Smashed my watch. We might be able to use the metal wristband, but other than that—the crystal, for instance, which Rolf has recognized as something of value—other than the band, the watch is now useless." His eyes went back to Blake Mansfield. "I am the one who ought to be ashamed of myself."

Blake said quickly, "Oh, no indeed, Dr. Held. I'm sorry you've lost your watch, but I have one, you know. We can still keep track of time."

"But not of the days. Mine was a calendar watch." He gave the shattered instrument a rueful look and stuffed it back into his pocket. "However, man was not born with a gold-plated calendar watch. There are simpler means of keeping track of the days."

Warren Brock pursed his lips. "Why should we? What are we, a little colony of latter-day Robinson Crusoes, fearful lest we forget which are the Sabbath days?"

"I doubt it," Dr. Held responded. "Though we might borrow from the inventive Mr. Crusoe. In fact, making and keeping a calendar would be a good job for me. A daily reminder of *hubris,* the day I insisted on going rabbit hunting. I'll set up a post and every day I'll cut a notch in it. The seventh notch will be twice as long as the previous six, and on the first day of every month, the mark will be longer and deeper than those for the first days of the week."

"What childish games!" Felicia had been bent over the fire with the half blanket from her bed thrown over her shoulders. She stood up, wrapping herself in the sleazy khaki-colored remnant as if she were throwing on a velvet opera cape, and began to pace. "I'm sorry, Andy, but all this desert island make-believe doesn't amuse me. A calendar! It isn't going to bring help any faster, and we're certainly not going to be here long enough to forget the date."

"No, of course not." Norma was wearing a dark gray woolen shirt Blake had discovered among the half-dozen torn and salt-streaked garments in the warehouse. With an immense exertion of self-control, she had suppressed a shudder as the soiled and greasy wool touched her skin. It was keeping her warm, she needed it, but she couldn't help feeling the coarse garment was full of germs. Her eyes followed Felicia's tall figure, white silk swathed in a dirty army blanket and still looking queenly. "Of course not," she repeated. "None of us have ever experienced anything like what we've been through the last few days. How could we forget the date? Today is the seventh of August."

Felicia halted her nervous promenade. "The *seventh*? Norma, dear, don't play Rip Van Winkle. You've lost two days. It's the ninth." The ninth . . . The moment the word sounded, Felicia's amused expression vanished and her face was contorted in anger. Her green eyes blazed, and her chin lifted imperiously. She turned on Andrew Held. "Oh, why did you have to remind me? I promised to be back in Washington on the ninth. I have a meeting of the program committee scheduled for tonight. It's important. It's *very* important . . ." Her voice broke. "Your calendar. Curse your damned calendar! Curse your bloody island!"

Andrew Held looked at her sympathetically. "Felicia, why don't you sit down by the fire. You're shivering."

"I am *not* shivering!"

Held yielded with a lift of eyebrows and a short oblique nod. "I should have said, you would be shivering, if you were the kind of person who shivers." When she sat down, he went on quietly, "It isn't the ninth, Felicia. Norma was right. Today is the seventh of August."

Norma said quickly, "When so much has happened, it's hard to realize what a short time it's taken. But we came to Phoenix on the fourth, and that evening, there was the dinner party . . ." In precise detail, she recited the chronology of their four days and three nights on the island, and ended by saying, "You see, Felicia, it would be possible to get back to Washington by the evening of the ninth."

The earnest statement caught Andrew by surprise. He glanced at her quickly. No, Norma wasn't mocking Felicia. She was totally serious, totally sincere. Felicia's reaction was the greater surprise.

She wasn't grasping the forlorn hope. She didn't even seem interested. With a diffident shrug, she pulled the blanket more tightly around her shoulders and said, "I owe you all an apology. Yesterday I gobbled up berries instead of bringing them back so they could be divided. I nearly killed myself in the process. But that's aside from the point. Today I make a scene over a personal frustration of no interest or importance to any of you." She paused for so long an interval they wondered whether she had finished speaking. Then she continued.

"I suppose I should go back to that first awful night of the tidal wave and also recall that I was the brilliant individual who risked my husband's life by running back to the house when we should have been climbing the hill. On top of that, I rescued a sack of jewelry when in the same amount of time I could have grabbed pots and pans that would have been worth something to all of us." She paused again, uttered a short laugh, and looked down at her hands. "So, I apologize, sincerely. I suppose that in any group of nine, there's bound to be one spoiled, pampered child."

No one spoke. Their faces were thoughtful, as if Felicia had held up a mirror they could not keep from looking into. Andrew Held reflected that he alone was in a position to realize how rarely Felicia apologized for anything, and how difficult it must have been for her to do it today.

On Wolf Island, the shattered structure of the Harbor Inn lay on the beach like a sea monster with a broken back. "Look at that," the manager said to the volunteer fireman. "I've had it. But how was I to figure I needed tidal wave insurance?"

The fireman made a notation in a spiral notebook. "The village was hit harder than you were," he said, wetting the tip of the pencil on his tongue. "After three days, we're still digging in six feet of silt and rock trying to uncover the wreckage. There's boats and cars all tangled up with what's left of the buildings. It's a mess, it's a terrible mess. I don't know when we'll get done with the body count. There were so many people over here from the mainland when it happened. Tourists and like that. We got no way of tracing them."

"Well, I can account for my motel guests and my help. As soon as the deputy came by and warned me, I notified everyone." The manager began enumerating motel units on his fingers. "Twelve guests, and they were all packed and gone in less than an hour. Oh, yes, there were three others. A young couple from New York, name of Mansfield, and a Mrs. Held, but they had checked out before the deputy came by. I think they were all going back to the mainland by the four o'clock ferry. The Mansfields, they came here by rented car from Seattle, I remember that."

"How about your cook and the rest of the help?" The fireman opened his notebook to a page headed "Missing" and ran a blunt finger down the list. "I thought so. Carlo Minatti worked for you, didn't he? And Diana Lindgren?"

The manager shook his head. "Yeah. Terrible. I heard about them. They weren't around here at all that day. Both of them took a week off. The cook, the bartender, and the maids—I sent them home and I've seen them since, so they're okay. But I haven't heard anything from Diana and Carlo. More than likely they were fooling around down at the village and got caught there."

"Did they go around together?"

The manager's curt laugh scoffed at the suggestion. "Diana and Carlo? Hell, no. Carlo was too smooth to play in virgin territory. But they both liked to dig clams and hunt for agates or driftwood, that sort of stuff. They were probably out on the beach somewhere, where they wouldn't have heard any storm warning. What else can you do around here for recreation?"

The fireman said mirthlessly, "I got one idea."

"Huh! So have I, but Diana wouldn't do it."

Once more the fireman dampened his pencil. Beside the names "Diana Lindgren" and "Carlo Minatti" he wrote "Presumed dead."

"It's too bad," he said gruffly. "I suppose you heard we already found the body of Diana's grandmother. So that's the end of the Lindgren farm. We're watering the stock, me and my neighbor, until we find out what's going to be done with the place."

"What about Frank Schmidt, what about our deputy? I'll tell you, when he came by and told me a tidal wave was coming, I damned near asked him what he'd been smoking. I understand he sent his wife and kids to Justin Heights and he kept driving and warning people. Have you found him?"

The fireman's ruddy face was grim. "We found him, all right. Couple hours ago. He was still in his patrol car. The water must have come right up over it. He might have had a chance, if he'd been able to get out. But when the wave hit the village, it was carrying pieces of boats it had smashed up in the bay. The bow of one of them hit Frank's patrol car broadside, damn near sliced it in two. Frank's right arm was gone, and his skull was crushed. The steering wheel was broken off and the boat jammed him so hard on the broken end of the steering column that we had to pull like hell to get the god damn stick out of his chest." The fireman looked down at his notebook. "Funny thing," he said huskily. "He was still wearing his trooper's hat."

When the group gathered, Rolf had been the quiet one, listening to the others, weighing what they said, approving when his dark eyes twinkled and disapproving when his mouth set in a hard line. It was a new, self-assertive Rolf who initiated a plan that would involve them all, not just for the day but for as long as they were isolated on Phoenix Island.

"We've all been looking for food, but we've been living from meal to meal, never thinking beyond what we can find that same day. That would be all right if everything was growing right near our camp, but it isn't. The best spot is the old Furness farm and that's about as far away from the beach as you can get. So we go food hunting, and come back, and go out again, and back, covering the same territory over and over again."

Though his language was plain, the urban sophisticates listened respectfully, and Warren Brock restrained his kittenish patter. Rolf's plan was to organize into teams that any civil servant trained in governmentese would have called task forces. A team of four would go back to the farm, a team of three would comb the shoreline and the beaches. The last man—that's the Old Man, Andrew Held mused, instinctively glancing at his artificial foot—would remain at camp and try to convert the contents of the warehouse into useful objects. Rolf was presenting more than a plan, Dr. Held noted. With beautiful simplicity, he was presenting three concepts from which his plan had sprung.

The first was the economical use of time. Properly organized, their searches for game, seafood, and edible plants would require fewer man-hours to produce a greater amount of food.

Secondly, Dr. Held observed, Rolf was preaching specialization. If the seafood "team" was particularly interested in shore life, it would be more efficient in identifying and gathering it, and he applied the same principle to those who would search the woods and the fields.

A third precept lay behind Rolf's unvarnished statement that everything they had to do could be done faster and better if they had tools. Though he didn't say, "Tools are primarily extensions of a man's hand," Dr. Held felt sure that was only because the vocabulary was foreign to him, not the idea. It amused him that modern industrial society should be based on economic theories so profound that Rolf's Indian forebears were living by them five hundred years ago.

Dr. Held observed that no one in the group listened more closely than Norma Mansfield. He could imagine her in one of his physics classes, frowning nervously as she attempted to transpose every word he uttered into a neat, thick notebook. As if to confirm the image, Norma raised her hand. "I was wondering . . ." She became aware of her schoolgirl arm, flushed, and dropped it to her side. "I just wanted to ask . . . the idea is to gather as much as we can at one time. Won't things spoil? We don't have refrigeration."

"There are other ways to keep food," Rolf said. "Smoking it, drying it. That was always done by the women."

With some difficulty, Dr. Held kept from laughing. The ancient culture recognized the principles of specialization, made its own time-motion studies, and knew man's superiority depended on how cleverly he could invent mechanical devices to do his will. But the ancient culture also rested on the firm foundation of the male's natural right to assign menial tasks to the women.

When Rolf, Diana, and the Mansfields reached the old Furness farm, it was agreed that Blake and Norma would pick apples while the younger couple searched for edible roots they thought might be growing in the damp rich area around the pond.

The wind had changed, and the chilly mists had vanished. The sun shone, bright and yellow. A morning that had been saturated with failure and hostility opened like a flower into a warm, sweet-smelling summer day. Blake Mansfield felt his tension eased. The sun was penetrating his doubt and confusion as if they were sore muscles. As he relaxed, he began to hope that today he could have a real talk with Norma.

He hadn't been trying. From the moment they boarded the plane in New York, every conversation between them had been riddled either with argument or with such obvious attempts on both their parts to avoid argument that it ended in a truce of unhappy silence.

It had been a little different these past three days. Norma had not been responsive but at least she hadn't argued or complained. It was his own sense of guilt whispering, "You got her into this . . ." that had kept him bouncing back and forth between a Pavlovian urge to apologize and the opposing inner voice that shouted down the idea of peace at any price and cried, "Apology be damned!"

If only Norma would act as if they were in this thing together! If only he could open the line of communication without breaking the block with a *mea culpa* he knew he would resent having to offer her. "The trouble is, you're too much alike"—that was the therapist's opinion. They both had perfectionist parents, they had both grown up under a system of negative reinforcement. As a result they were both constantly looking to each other for the approval they had never received from their parents. So now, true to form, he wanted Norma to forgive him for "getting her into this," and he wanted her to applaud him for being admirable and cooperative and . . . well, what? . . . for being a good boy.

The solemn words echoed through his mind and suddenly struck him as funny. In an abandoned orchard, on a remote island, with meadowlarks singing and crickets humming and the sun soaking him to the bone, why couldn't he be happy just picking apples? Why was the child within waiting for Norma to say he was doing a good job picking apples, or better yet, waiting for Norma *not* to say he was doing a good job, so that once more, he would have sought and been denied her approval?

"Norma?"

She was on her knees, searching for windfall apples hidden in the tall grass. She looked up, clearly surprised by his cheerful tone of voice. Obeying an impulse, which was as unusual as this bursting desire to laugh, Blake sat down beside her. "Rest a minute."

Her glance went automatically to the small pile of apples she had collected. "We shouldn't waste time. The more we pick—"

"I said, rest a minute. One minute. For one minute, talking to me is *not* a waste of time."

She opened her mouth, and he knew what sort of defensive replies would spill out in answer to his needlessly defensive statement. He stopped her. "I have a question. Before you answer it, may I remind you, Mrs. Mansfield, that you are under oath. Question: When Dr. Held was talking about making a calendar, why were you so sure that today is August seventh?"

For an instant, her serious dark-blue eyes were clouded by a wary look, but when he smiled, they cleared and brightened, reflecting his mood. "I figured out the date because I knew what day of the week it is. Wednesday."

"Our day for the therapist."

A slow smile began to appear at the corners of her mouth.

Blake dropped backwards onto the grass. "I knew it! Four o'clock on Wednesday, and we're off to Lexington Avenue, where Dr. Gostrand explains that we never grew up. Dr. Gostrand admits that *he* never grew up, either, but the difference is that he knows he didn't. Tell me . . ." Blake put his hand on Norma's bare arm and very gently pulled her down until she was resting against his side. "Do you really mind being here in this old orchard, picking apples and ruining your best dress? Would you rather be in Dr. Gostrand's office?"

"Am I still under oath?"

In genuine astonishment, Blake exclaimed, "Would you lie otherwise? I didn't think you knew how."

"Oh, I'm a good Puritan," she said. "I don't tell lies to other people, only to myself. Back to your question, counselor. No, I would not rather be in Dr. Gostrand's office. I don't know why. I respect him. I have always thought he helped us, just the way I always thought medicine that tastes bitter does you the most good. But right now, I don't feel like swallowing something because it's good for me. For some reason, I'd rather be picking apples."

"If there were a psychiatrist on Phoenix Island, you and I would be sitting in his office right now."

Norma's soft hair brushed his cheek. "But there isn't. Besides there is so much work to do that we don't have time to go to therapists."

Blake laughed. "We don't really have time to be neurotic." For the second time in an hour, he was hit by an impulse and again, he gave into it without the smallest pang of guilt. He raised himself on one arm, placed his free hand on Norma's breast, and with the yielding flesh soft against his palm, kissed her deeply.

The meadow was a black hole in the woods capped by a gray night sky. When Carlo and Rolf walked into it, their bowl of fire glowed in the dark like a fallen star. The camp's one and only metal container rested securely in the center of a board Carlo had scoured out with a piece of shale. Carefully, the two young men lowered board and bowl to the ground.

"We shu-wah get some kine fyah, eh?" Carlo breathed, lapsing into Hawaiian pidgin for the first time since he'd come to Phoenix. "Dis kine fyah shu-wah goin make da rabbits run wild and crazy, wha you think?"

There were four very hungry islanders in the hunting party—for hunger still remained despite all their foraging, a gnawing ever-present problem. Rolf, Carlo, and Donald Campbell were there, and because she had insisted, Diana. "You can't do it with three," she had pointed out. "It will take at least four, and five or six would be better. If I can hunt rabbits on Wolf, I can hunt them on Phoenix."

"This is different," Rolf said. "You've never hunted with a torch."

Diana, knowing that Rolf hadn't either, laughed and said, "You'll show me."

Diana was carrying the nets. They had made two reasonably good copies of an ordinary dip net, using the all-purpose honeysuckle vine in place of circular metal rims and attaching purse-like sacs made from their warehouse supply of damaged gill nets. Donald carried the torches—strips of cedar bark twisted tightly and tied at each end. He dropped his load and peered skeptically across the dark field. "I sure don't see no rabbits."

Rolf pointed toward the thick undergrowth at the edge of the field. "Over there, the ground is covered with droppings. But we'll never scare them out of the bushes. Their holes are under there and they'd just go deeper. If we get any rabbits, it will have to be out in the field, but there are plenty of burrows out there, too. I saw them this morning. Rabbits hole up during the day and run around at night until after dawn. They should be out now, out in the open." He selected a torch and poked it into the bowl of hot coals. When he withdrew it, the burning end was another bright spot to pierce the shadows. He handed it to Diana and picked up a second cedar stick. Briefly, simply, he outlined the technique.

They would work in pairs, one carrying a torch and the other a net. The rabbit would be startled by the flame, momentarily paralyzed, and confused as long as it was caught in the circle of light. When it ran, its course would be erratic. Both netman and torchbearer would have to overtake the rabbit, one keeping it dazed with light and the other scooping it up in the oversized butterfly net.

Donald grumbled, "Jees, I'm strong, but I never said I was fast."

Rolf smiled. "Think of how that roasted meat is going to taste, and you'll pick up speed. Here, Don, you carry the light, and I'll take the net. Diana has done this before and she's fast, so we'll give her the other net, and Carlo, you run with her and hold the torch. Okay?

Let's move out. Slowly, until we scare something up. Then run like hell."

They advanced, a small phalanx in a pool of quivering firelight. They had walked several yards when they spotted their first prey. Three rabbits. Their round eyes stared blindly at the orange blaze as their gray and white bodies crouched in the grass.

"Hal-lo day-yah!" Carlo shouted, leaping ahead with the torch held high.

The pidgin war cry sounded like gunshots on a still night. The rabbits awoke from their paralysis and shot forward in a frenzied attempt to escape the light. The four hunters, almost as startled as the rabbits, bounded after them.

The pursuit was as lunatic as the course the rabbits took. The three animals ran in three different directions, vaulting over hummocks like small kangaroos, racing first to the right, then to the left, hidden one moment by a patch of long grass and then the next, darting across the path of light to circle their pursuers and lose themselves in the dark at the rear of the column.

The disorganized teams plunged ahead blindly, and in the excitement the netmen separated from the torchbearers, so that Rolf and Diana charged into the blackness after rabbits no longer dazed by light and Donald and Carlo had no means of catching rabbits since they were temporarily immobilized by their torches.

"We've got to do better than that," Rolf said when they regrouped in the middle of the field. "This time, stay with me, Don. Carlo, quit yelling in Hawaiian and keep your eye on Diana."

Their second effort was more successful. Flushing two rabbits, the two teams bore down like swooping hawks. Both rabbits leaped sideways, closely followed by Carlo and Diana on the left, Donald and Rolf on the right. As if their pattern had been preset, the two animals completed short arcs and then bounced back toward each other. Both teams wheeled around and in the single-minded pursuit of their own game, tangled with each other.

"Ugh awgh!" Donald groaned, when Diana tripped over his feet and, falling, plunged her elbow into his stomach.

"Hey, you buggah . . ." Carlo sang out as Rolf hurtled past and threw himself and his net to the ground.

Diana wasn't hurt, Donald caught his breath, and under Rolf's net was a rabbit. Carlo secured the animal by the ears and gave it a chopping blow at the base of the skull. "Eh, brada," he said to Rolf. "We do some moah, ah? I goin' try widda net."

Once again, their lights moved across the meadow, catching, and for an instant, holding, the little animals. Once more, they risked bruises, broken bones, and cuts and burns as they attempted to follow the insane leapings and boundings of their prey. This time, Carlo was the only winner. "Hal-lo day-yah!" he kept hollering as he pounded across the field. He returned with a rabbit and dropped the limp form at Rolf's feet.

"You crazy," Rolf said amiably. "Yelling only makes them run faster."

"As aw-right, brada. I wen catch da buggah, anyway."

"Next time save your breath and catch two."

After a short rest, they lighted new torches and started again. For another hour, animals and humans darted back and forth in a wild choreography of circles and zigzags, furious sprints and sudden stops. They threw themselves at rabbits momentarily blinded by the light and, when they missed, jumped up again and set off across the dark field, the hunters and the hunted joining in a wild game like children playing "Follow me!" In the eerie half-light they raced, circled, dived, and leaped to the tune of their own thudding footfalls and labored breathing.

As they were leaving, Donald looked disconsolately at the seven rabbits they had managed to bag. "You guys did all the catching."

Carlo shrugged and said good-naturedly, "No worry, brada. We all goin' eat da same. We goin' share. Anyway, wen you chase-sum and wen we catchum, no make no difference. Dey all da same thing."

"It's more fun to catch."

They ignored the childish complaint and proceeded through the woods toward camp. Donald followed, a petulant frown hidden by the forest shadow. It wasn't only that they hadn't let him use a net. He had another gripe he couldn't express. When Diana ran into him and fell at his feet, he had helped her up. She had gasped "thank you" but she pulled her arm free with a quick jerk, as if she couldn't stand to let him touch her. And he was hungry to touch her. Even in the midst of the rabbit hunt, the feel of her firm smooth flesh excited and distracted him. I'll get her yet, he thought angrily, and that young half-breed, or nobody else, is going to be strong enough to stop me.

Chapter Twenty-Three

Mrs. Eleanor Sutherland was the official chairman of the Harvest Ball, but she was furious at being forced to attend a committee meeting. She was a statuesque, big-breasted woman whose taste in clothes ran to large flowered prints. Mr. Sutherland had made a fortune buying American-made planes from a NATO country and selling them to small Iron Curtain countries, and numerous agencies, foundations, and individuals were eager to help his widow spend his money. But she never spent without buying, nor gave without receiving.

In the case of charity balls, her price was ample newspaper coverage, with touched-up photographs of the general chairman no smaller than a quarter page. It was always understood—and Felicia Held had understood it perfectly—that once the big story had been printed, Mrs. Sutherland was not to be called upon for anything until the night of the ball. Then she would sweep into the grand ballroom on the arm of whatever dignitary had been corralled for the event and seat herself at a table that, alone in the *salle de bal,* stood on a dais illuminated by a rose-colored spotlight.

Tonight Mrs. Sutherland was furious with Felicia Held, whose unexplained absence from Washington had made it necessary for her to take charge and, because of the last-minute nature of the planning, to invite all these women to her home. Finances, contracts, printing and engraving costs—these intricate problems of ball management confused and irritated her.

"Ladies," she said sharply, "can someone tell me when I may expect Mrs. Held to return to Washington and her responsibilities as hostess of the Harvest Ball?"

There was no response. Every woman in the room knew Felicia socially. Most of them had worked with her on other benefit affairs. But Felicia was the friend of many, the intimate of few. Even her marriage to Dr. Andrew Held had been nothing more than a big social event as far as they were concerned, offering them scant glimpse of Felicia's private self. Mrs. Sutherland tapped irritably on the mahogany table and muttered, "Well? Doesn't *somebody* know where she is?"

A small, neat woman with dark eyes and short gray hair rose to her feet.

"Well, Mrs. Hodges?"

"She told me she was flying to Seattle on business and would be back in town late today."

"*Seattle!*" Mrs. Sutherland scoffed. "Why in the world Seattle? And *of course* you haven't heard from her." It was more of a condemnation than a question.

"I didn't expect to. Felicia telephones. She doesn't write."

"She has some kind of a fiancé, doesn't she? Why didn't you think to call him?"

"I did. He knows even less of her whereabouts than we do, and that's strange, don't you think? He had no idea how to telephone her . . ."

"Then why doesn't *she* call *us?*" Mrs. Sutherland asked irritably. "Well, I refuse to take over this committee. I have more important obligations. Here, you, Mrs. Hodges! You're the vice-chairman or assistant hostess or something, aren't you? Here, you come up here and direct this meeting."

The small woman came forward and Eleanor Sutherland swept across the drawing room in a billowing cloud of flowered chiffon. As her exit line, she said, "Somebody here is to keep calling her apartment. The minute she gets back, I want to know about it. I have some things to tell that woman, and if she wants to keep running things in this city, she'd better take my advice." With that, she went through the door and slammed it behind her.

Within their home territories, six of the nine unwilling communalists would have been insensitive or even hostile to one another, but the unremitting need to sustain themselves continued to bind them together. Observing their achievements at the end of two weeks, Andrew Held had to admit that his disillusionment with human beings was challenged by a small but persistent echo of his youthful faith in the goodness of his fellow man.

That there were emotional undercurrents, he could not

deny. Donald lusted after Diana, while Rolf guarded her jealously. Felicia was frequently preoccupied, even sad. The Mansfields seemed to be reconciled to their situation —at least to muddling through until their rescuers arrived—but not really reconciled to each other. Donald was unloved and knew it. And Brock laughed secretly at them all. In spite of these conflicts, two weeks had gone by without open hostilities. Even more important, in the areas of basic human need, such as food and clothing, they had made some remarkable adjustments.

Being hampered by her ankle-length dinner dress, Norma had borrowed Donald's jackknife and, with no apparent regret, sliced off the skirt just above the knee. By splitting the side seam of the bottom portion, she made a shawl. On a cool day, she wrapped it around her body and fastened the ends with a rusty nail. Her lack of self-consciousness was remarkable for someone as studiously conventional as she was, and resulted basically from her lack of vanity. Judging by her plain Jane, neat-as-a-pin appearance when she arrived on Phoenix, Dr. Held guessed that she had always dressed simply and worn little makeup.

But if Norma was remarkable, Dr. Held reflected, Felicia was fantastic. Unlike Norma, clothes and cosmetics had been Felicia's second career. To be handsomely costumed and perfectly groomed—these were prerequisites to her style of living. And yet look at her now!

She had given up her white silk original because the fabric was ideal for filtering pond water. Her panty hose were part of a fish trap Carlo had rigged up in a kelp bed near the mouth of the bay; they had already assisted in catching many small sea bass. Her gold evening slippers had worn through, so Rolf cut the usable uppers into strips and combined them with double soles of rabbit skin to make her a pair of sandals. That left her with one civilized garment—her brassiere—and commandeering its elasticized straps had already been discussed at a meeting.

Her present costume contrasted so comically with Felicia Stowe Held, Washington socialite, that Andrew Held hadn't known whether to joke about it or to sympathize. Above the rabbit skin sandals her long legs were bare. The pink beginnings of a suntan could not conceal the many bruises and scratches she had accumulated in her

stubborn pursuit of food. From knees to waist she was
covered by a pair of men's swimming trunks taken from
the warehouse. Since the trunks were much too large, she
had gathered them at the waist like a dirndl and belted
and secured them with a strip of Norma's yellow linen
gown.

The clownish touch was her blouse. It was a feed
sack, with a hole at the top for her head and openings at
the sides for her arms. Andrew Held speculated about
how far it had traveled and what tsunami may have done
to the cargo vessel that had been carrying it, for the
sack was new, with big red and black letters still broad-
casting the message:

FOR BETTER CHICKS
USE FARMER DICK'S

Felicia made her first appearance in this costume when
the group had gathered for dinner. Almost immediately
she erased Andrew Held's anxiety about what to say or
do. She strode into camp and stared them all down without a tremor of embarrassment. Her face was tanned,
scrubbed, and totally without makeup. Through the
metamorphosis of necessity, her elegant upswept coiffure
had been replaced by one thick braid hanging straight
down her back.

Perfectly poised, she bent forward in a comic version
of a regal bow. "I bring you an important message from
my sponsor, Farmer Dick," she said solemnly, indicating
the bright letters that covered her from armpit to armpit. "Though I can't understand why he printed it upside
down."

Andrew Held's sense of relief deepened into admiration
as he saw what extra touch she had added. Her jewelry.
Most, perhaps all of it, either hung around her neck or
was pinned over her breast. Diamonds, emeralds, topaz,
and sapphire shone against a background saying:

USE FARMER DICK'S
FOR BETTER CHICKS

Dr. Held said huskily, "Bravo, Mrs. Held."
Her smile was supremely gracious. "It's nothing, really. I always dress for dinner."

In two weeks, their clothing had deteriorated but their food supply had improved in quantity, variety, and methods of cooking and preservation.

Their first searches were either for plants Rolf remembered as traditional among Indians, or for the berries and greens Diana's grandmother had always picked. Gradually, through experiments controlled by Norma's six-bite test, they added to their repertoire. Often the food plant served more than one purpose.

They dug the roots of sword and bracken fern, roasted them in hot ashes, peeled them, and ate the mealy center; the foliage went to the dormitory to thicken their "mattresses." The young shoots of the spruce tree they ate raw. The same tree provided a fragrant pitch to be used as chewing gum, and spruce saplings became spring poles for the snares Rolf designed not only for rabbit but, hopefully, for deer. The low-growing holly-like bushes of Oregon grape yielded purple clusters of sour, mouth-puckering berries which became palatable when boiled and combined with the bland fruit of the salal bush. At Rolf's insistence, they took the root as well. His grandmother, a Quinault, had boiled the Oregon grape root and saved the liquid as a sure cure for stomach ache.

Like most seaweeds, the ribbon kelp was a multiple purpose plant. They used the shiny green ribbons, sometimes eight or ten feet long, to line the baking pit. The hollow bulb or bottle end could be cut to make small serving dishes, and they found that any part of the hollow stem was a tough but edible vegetable if it had soaked for a day or two in fresh water. The usefulness of the graceful seaplant did not end there. "Save the long thin end," Rolf told them. "We can use it for fish line. It's no use wet but when it dries it gets as tough as rope and we can use it for lots of things."

At first they had eaten to stay alive. Always half-hungry, their conversation was dominated by nostalgic memories of favorite foods and favorite restaurants. The charming little beer tavern just off Fourth Street in the Village, where roast beef, baked ham, and garlic dills were served on slices of dark rye. The sidewalk café in Portugal where tidbits of barbecued squid were eaten with the fingers. The creamy pastries at Demel's in Vienna and the lobster on Cape Cod, where you chose your entrée by pointing to him in a glass tank of sea water.

As supplies increased both in quantity and variety, they were still obsessed by the subject of food. They all ate twice as much as they ever had, and they talked about it constantly. Even those accustomed to breakfasting on black coffee and one croissant now ate hearty pancakes of mashed roots spread thickly with applesauce or stewed currants and elderberries and argued solemnly about the comparative sweetness of tiger lily versus camas.

Discovery of a previously untried foodstuff was an event calling for thorough evaluation, not only of the taste but, thanks to Norma's encounters with the health food store on Sixty-third Street, of the vitamin and mineral content. Two hundred years before, Norma pointed out, the word "vegetable" hadn't come into existence. The forebears of our produce were "herbs" known primarily for their medicinal properties. So when the group consumed plates of steamed chickweed, which was more tender and a brighter green than spinach, they knew they were swallowing quantities of healthful iron. Dandelion greens, Norma remembered, offer twelve times as much Vitamin A as lettuce. Burdock roots, which taste like white turnips and have a high content of calcium, silicon, and sulphur and miner's lettuce, a type of purslane, would keep them all from getting scurvy.

They found so many foods in or near the pond that Norma referred to the area as "the supermarket," and another Phoenix place name was established along with "dormitory," "warehouse," and "city hall" (where they held their nightly meetings). Besides the skunk cabbage and the plump yellow pond lilies Rolf and Diana had cut during their first day at the pond, they discovered wild onions, tiger lilies, and camas, all with edible bulbs. The onions were too strong to be eaten as a vegetable, but as stuffing for baked rabbit, they were milder and added flavor to the meat. The tiger lily and camas roots were steamed in a pit or boiled with fish. Whatever the food, the surplus was preserved. Berries could be dried, rabbit and fish could be smoked. Roots, in the Indian fashion, were steamed or boiled, mashed, pressed into cakes, and stored after they had dried in the sun.

Rolf's knowledge of Indian horticulture had been diluted by two or three generations, as well as by the Welsh blood that accounted for his height, but it did lead him and Diana to the supermarket's most desirable produce.

They were alone the afternoon Rolf pointed to some white flowers just breaking the surface of the water at the far side of the pond. On close inspection, they found waxy white blossoms with large arrow-shaped leaves growing in several feet of sluggish water.

"Wapatoo," Rolf said with satisfaction. "I'll wade in and dig them out with my toes."

"That looks like a muddy bottom. Can't we pull up the plant?"

"We wouldn't get anything. The stems are so weak they'll break off and leave the roots hidden under four inches of mud."

Like the rest of the group, Rolf's clothing was minimal. Everything but his patched and faded bluejeans had been put to other uses. His nylon windbreaker, for example, was involved in Andrew Held's device for collecting potable water by condensation. He was barefoot because he wanted to save his canvas shoes for a time when he really needed them. He gave Diana a look she couldn't translate, turned his back, and stripped off his jeans.

For an instant, she was transfixed. Even when he turned to face her, his hands hanging easily at his sides, uncovering his lean brown body was so swift and so natural that it seemed perfectly right and perfectly beautiful.

"I don't like to wear wet muddy jeans," he said simply, and walked into the pond.

Rolf waded shoulder-deep among the arrowhead, working his toes into the soft pond bottom until he felt the smooth solid tuber at the base of a stem. Once he had dislodged it, the root rose to the surface, and he scooped it up and tossed it onto the bank. After a few minutes he rested, his arms floating at his sides and water dripping from his long black mustache. "By the way, Diana," he called, "digging wapatoo is woman's work. The men never did it."

Diana hesitated only a moment. In the spot where Rolf was digging, the water would be over her head. But the lovely three-petalled flowers were also growing near the bank. Quickly, trying not to think about it, she pulled off her dress, bra, and panties, and stepped into the muddy water.

"Like potatoes," was the group's term for baked wapa-too tubers roasted in wood ashes. "A little sweeter, a little like chestnuts."

"Very starchy," Norma observed, for she had become the group's chief nutritionist. "I'm sure I could dry them and grind them into flour." A few days later she introduced something new to the dinner menu, a steaming pinkish concoction that tasted like potato soup with delicate overtones of quince. "Rose hip soup," she explained. "I ground the hips, boiled them for about ten minutes, and thickened the liquid with wapatoo flour. We're getting more Vitamin C than we'd ordinarily swallow in a week."

As they talked, Andrew Held realized that whenever they first tasted a wild plant, they quickly catalogued it in terms of a conventional food. Wapatoo, so prized by Pacific Coast Indians that Lewis and Clark spoke of it in their journal, was not itself, it was "like" something else. The seashore plantain Carlo found growing in the crevices of a bare gray cliff was immediately identified as "like green string beans" and not as goose tongue. The thistle root was "like artichokes" and the roots of the sand verbena were "like beets." Roast gooseneck barnacles tasted like tough, strongly flavored scallops. How long will it take, Dr. Held speculated, to accept what is strange and new without measuring it against the old and familiar?

Warren Brock's undiminished yen for his favorite brand of English ovals led to the production of something like tobacco. He and Felicia had joined in a dialogue concerning their dreams. For both of them the most vivid dream scenes were those in which they had finished an elaborate dinner and were searching futilely for a package of cigarettes.

Rolf broke in. "You want to try kinnikinnick?"

Brock pursed his lips. *"Dear boy,* is that something you *smoke?* It sounds like something we used to *do,* when Mother wasn't looking."

Rolf said drily, "It's both. You smoke it, all right, but when I was a kid my father whipped me when he caught me doing it. It can make you drunk."

Brock grimaced in mock dismay. "Oh dear, oh *dear!* Drunk, eh? Where *is* this divine substance, Rolfie boy?"

"Everywhere. Some people think kinnikinnick is just

one plant. A little bush with red bark and bright red berries. It trails along the ground and it grows in the woods where it's dry. But my grandfather called that sacacomis. Kinnikinnick is really a word from back East, and it means several kinds of leaves, dried and powdered and mixed together. Like dogwood leaves, and salal leaves, and you can put in dried needles from the yew. I did, once, and I got a terrible high, like being drugged."

"Quick, quick, with the kinnikinnick . . ." Each staccato syllable popped out of Brock's small round mouth as if he were exploding bubbles. "Point me in the right direction, oh sage of an earlier day, and I shall get on with my self-appointed rounds. If I get a good smoke, I'll bless you. And thrice bless you, dear boy, should I be fortunate enough to become intoxicated."

By the end of the next day, the leaves of dogwood and of kinnikinnick, or bearberry, were drying in the sun. Rolf presented Brock with a small burl as hard as iron and several branches of a salmonberry bush. At the evening campfire, Brock carved, scraped, and cut with the dexterity and patience he would ordinarily be exerting in the composition of a ten-thousand-dollar sculpture. The result was a pipe with graceful lines and an outer surface as smooth as an apple skin. Brock held it lovingly, a violinist getting the feel and heft of his instrument, a master craftsman delighting in the tactile beauty of wood. "Ah," he said softly, and his eyes gleamed.

Next Brock peeled the salmonberry branch, removing the pith, and in this way hollowed out an assortment of pipe stems, each of which fitted perfectly into the bowl he had cut from the burl. "I'll make another pipe for you, dear," he promised Felicia. "Until then, we'll share, but you can have your own stem."

Norma and Blake were resting near a clump of wild plum trees when Norma noticed the bee. The little black and yellow insect was moving industriously through a patch of pink clover, lighting, dipping into the blossoms, sailing up and out to the next stalk. Its concentration was complete. Though Norma pointed and exclaimed, "Watch out for the bee!" the flight pattern didn't change, until after several minutes, it rose and, like a cargo plane that is overdue at the airport, flew straight into the woods.

Squinting against the sun, Blake followed the bee's course. "*Now* I know what's meant by a beeline. When he —or it's she, isn't it?—when she had her load of nectar, she really headed for the barn."

"For the hive," Norma said sleepily. "Oh, Blake! Be careful. There's another. I don't want you to get stung."

"It wouldn't kill me. I mean, I'm not allergic to bee sting, as far as I know."

"I thought everyone was. My mother always said—" She stopped abruptly. This life they were leading was such a strange combination of total isolation and total togetherness, and in different ways both were bringing about a degree of self-examination that their Wednesday afternoon therapist had never achieved. When she was alone, with nothing around her but trees or a meadow or the sea, Norma experienced an all-aloneness that released memories of early childhood, memories long repressed and seemingly forgotten. All of them centered around her mother. Mother's rules and Mother's punishments also came back with painful vividness when they were all together, and the unavoidable intimacy of group life made Norma compare herself with the others. Wasn't she always explaining, "I did this thing, or I feel this way, because my mother . . ."

Bother! she thought. Forget about Mother . . . The heresy was short-lived, for she quickly said out loud, "I hate bumblebees," and sounded just like her mother.

Dim memories of high school biology and a field trip to an apiary were beginning to stir in Blake's mind. "That wasn't a bumblebee. It was smaller, with more black. It was a honeybee. They can only sting you once."

"How many times do you want to be stung?" Norma looked anxiously toward the patch of clover. "Look, now that bee is flying away, too. Thank goodness they aren't coming this way."

"They don't hear well and they don't have much sense of smell. In any case, they aren't interested in us. Isn't it funny, the way this sort of thing comes back to you, after so long?" Blake watched the bee disappear into the woods. "I wonder where the hive is. A hive? But that can't be. The last Furness to live on this farm left before you and I were born. And if they kept bees, they would have built the hives in the orchard, wouldn't they? But we haven't seen a trace of anything of that kind. So these bees must have their hive in a tree. A hollow tree, somewhere in the woods . . ." He jumped to his feet and, walking into the clover, tried to establish the spot where the bees had entered the woods. Luck was with him. A third bee flew out of a clover blossom only inches from his foot. After a short loop to the left and another to the right, the bee leveled off as if it had just sobered up and proceeded with all speed in the same direction the others had taken. This time Blake memorized a landmark. "Come on!" he said, as excited as a small boy following a circus parade. "A honey tree . . . Honey . . . Something to put on the berries and into the rose hip tea. Fantastic!"

It was an exhausting search, on a par, Blake admitted after the first hour, with finding needles in haystacks. There were no paths in the woods, and Blake had been so intent on following the bees' course that he didn't think of marking their own. In a short time they couldn't agree what direction to take to get back to the Furness farm. At the end of an hour they were admittedly lost.

The moment he realized it, Blake began to apologize. They were lost geographically, but emotionally they were back on familiar ground, Blake proposing that they find the honey tree just as he had conceived the idea of coming to these remote islands, Blake aware of his wife's disapproval and trying through apology to exchange it for her approval. But this time, as never before, Norma refused to play her role.

"Oh, stop it!" she burst out. "I wanted to look for honey just as much as you did. I know I acted as if I were coming along against my wishes, but don't you see, Blake? That was to leave the door open so if we failed, I would already have established the fact that I knew we would, and therefore you were wrong. Wrong, wrong, wrong. You weren't wrong! Or if you were, so was I."

Blake was so surprised by her uncharacteristic foot-stamping that he couldn't think of anything to say but "I'm sorry" and that, he realized with a great cleansing flood of relief, was exactly what she was telling him not to say. "What do we do now?" he said at last, looking around curiously. "Look for the gingerbread house?"

Suddenly they were both laughing, and Norma, of her own will, was in his arms.

It took them another hour, but at last they saw an open space beyond the shadowy woods, and moments later the field and brushy growth of wild plum trees came into view. Right there, a hundred feet from where they had entered the woods, they heard the low throbbing hum of the bees.

Moving as carefully as they could, they followed the sound. It led them to the lifeless shell of what must have been a magnificent fir, for the huge snag of the tree was fifty feet tall and ten feet through at the base. Above their heads, beyond the reach of Blake's arm, there was a hole in the trunk big enough to admit a cat. All around it, the surface of the tree was as smooth as if it had been polished and varnished. Bees were flying in and out of the opening with the same sense of high mission shown by the three argonauts Blake had observed in the clover. A wild hive and a big one, for the traffic was so heavy a dozen bees were hovering a foot from the entrance, awaiting their turn to go in.

By tapping the trunk gently, Blake established that the hollow center, and probably the hive itself, began two or three feet above the forest floor. If his recollections of the apiary field trip were accurate, the hive would extend as far above the opening as the rotten core permitted, for wild bees with their incredible building skills do their best work above the entrance where the hive will be warmer and more protected.

"The first step is to cut down the tree," Blake said. "And when you do that, you need bee veils and a smoker, not to mention washtubs to put the honey in. We don't have any of the equipment we need, even back at camp."

"No, but at camp we could get help, and ideas."

Blake grinned. "I agree. When dealing with a swarm of mad bees, caution is a virtue."

Something her mother had always said was on the tip of Norma's tongue. With a pleasant sensation of being naughty and liking it, she decided against reciting it. "Let's put some marks on the trees and then pick up our sack of plums and go tell the others." She could not remember any time in her life when she had possessed so little, and felt so free.

At the meeting that night, they devised substitutes for bee veils and a smoker. The veils could be made by combining the women's nylon underpants with sections of torn gill-net. The cedar bark torches they had used for the rabbit hunt could be modified to serve as smokers. They had already succeeded in making sack-like pails by stitching sections of alder bark together with "string" from cattail rushes. Larger versions of these would do as containers for the honeycomb.

But how were they going to fell the tree?

They had the yellow-handled screwdriver and the jack-knife. They could make stone wedges by prying loose layers of shale from the cracked face of the cliff. In addition, Rolf had fashioned a primitive hammer, a rectangle of granite bound to a short sturdy piece of drift-wood with strips of skin. The depressing reality was that these instruments, ingenious as they might be, would not cut through the trunk of a fir tree.

Rolf was always the hardest to discourage when it came to inventing substitutes. "But we don't need to cut the tree at the base. Blake says that a few feet off the ground, the trunk starts to be hollow."

"Even so, we'd need a saw or an axe." Blake's desire for honey was becoming more and more compelling as the impossibility of obtaining it grew clearer. "Damn it, I wish we hadn't found the bee tree. We were getting along all right without honey."

Rolf pulled thoughtfully on the tip of his mustache. "We didn't always have saws and axes, but we still made canoes. By burning and scraping."

Through his sculpture, Warren Brock had acquired considerable knowledge of Indian crafts. "Of course," he exclaimed, clapping his hands delicately. "Heated rocks, a stone adze, clam shells . . . Bravo, bravo!"

Throughout his career, Dr. Held had left the implementation of his ideas to other, more practical minds. Now every device, every technique had direct bearing on what he ate, what he wore, and how he slept, and practical detail was no longer boring. "Heated stones?" he asked.

Rolf shook his head. "No, not for felling a tree. Canoes were usually made from drift logs, or from trees that were already on the ground. I don't know how we could use heated rocks on a standing tree. But there's another way we might be able to burn through a trunk, at least where it's hollow. Make braids out of dry grass and cedar bark, rub them in pitch, tie them around the tree, and light them, like tinder. After a while the bark would catch fire, and as it burns, you scrape off the charred wood and put more tinder into the groove. It would take a while, but I think it would work."

Blake spoke hesitantly, with a hint of apology in his voice. "That would create a lot of heat, wouldn't it, Rolf? We'd be burning where the tree is hollow, and wherever it's hollow, it is likely that there is honeycomb on the inside."

"Ah . . ." Rolf nodded in understanding. "Sure. We'd melt the honey."

"*All* of it?" Brock was dismayed by the prospect of for-feiting a delicacy that, in less than an hour, had be-come an obsession. "Wouldn't there be a *little* bit left? Couldn't we save enough for one lovely orgiastic meal, all sitting around here, gulping down pots and pots of honey?"

"There could be two or three hundred pounds of honey in that one tree," Blake explained, with a friendly nod for Brock that said, You were joking and I re-cognize it. Blake adjusted his thick glasses thoughtfully. "I think we ought to save all we can." Suddenly his usually serious face wore a boyish grin. "Since the Coast Guard seems to be taking a long time getting to Phoe-nix."

The grin was unusual, but the statement was startling. Andrew Held looked thoughtfully at the young lawyer's clean-cut profile. Somewhere along the line, this polite establishmentarian had given up his belief in prompt, effi-cient rescue. More significantly, he was now able to admit it, and so cheerfully that the only possible conclusion was that he wasn't at all desperate to leave.

"It's not only this one crop of honey," Blake was saying. "Ideally, we would fell this tree so that the hive wouldn't be badly damaged and we could save the queen. That way, the bees would establish a new colony in an-other tree. They still have enough time before cold weather to store up supplies for the winter."

Felicia looked at him curiously. "And where was it you said you attended law school?"

"Oh, this is all high school biology. We had a teacher

who was a fanatic on the subject of bees. Funny thing. I haven't thought about him for years and years . . ." He turned to Rolf. "It wouldn't destroy the colony to take a small section of the comb. As Warren suggests, we could have a *little* honey. Somehow we'd have to climb up to the hole, and reach in . . ."

Within a few minutes, they had agreed on a plan. Three men were required, all wearing the improvised bee veils. One would be the "smoker," creating clouds of smoke to stupefy the bees. The second man would hoist the third on his shoulders. This top man would put his arm through the entrance to the hive and dislodge a piece of honeycomb.

Donald growled, "I'll do any part you say, Mr. Mansfield, but I think I ought to be the one to lift the guy up to the hole. In that spot you need somebody with muscle, and dumb enough to stand still when a bunch of mad bees starts buzzing around."

"Excellent," Blake said approvingly. "I'll be the one to stand on your shoulders."

"I weigh less than you do," Rolf stated, "and bee stings don't bother me much. I'll climb up, Mr. Mansfield."

Donald said gruffly, "Oh, for Chrissakes, what you weigh don't matter to me. I can hold either of you."

Blake nodded. "You could lift both of us, Donald, and you'll probably have to, because the smoker will have to blow smoke right into the hive and I don't believe he can do that standing on the ground." He smiled in Rolf's direction. "You see, even with our bee veils, we're all going to be stung."

"You've all gone crackers," Brock chortled. "Covering your head with girls' underpanties! La! I thought *I* had a problem."

In the Seattle-Tacoma office of the Charge Less Rental Car Company, the manager was having trouble admitting his error about a polite young man named Blake Mansfield.

"It won't hurt to wait a while," he said irritably when his assistant asked, for the third time, if this one shouldn't be reported to the police. "He didn't say exactly how long he was going to keep it."

The assistant tapped the lease form. "Says here, approximately one week."

"Well, what does *that* mean? If you've got plenty of time and plenty of money? I signed out the guy myself. I talked to him. Strictly first-class. Credit cards from here to there."

"It wouldn't be the first time some wealthy customer used one of our cars to drop out of sight with his favorite sex symbol."

"Yeah, but in that situation a man doesn't *steal* a car. That's the last thing he'd do. Besides, I saw the woman with him. That was his wife, all right."

The assistant dropped the lease form into a desk drawer. "Okay. He's had the car now since the third of August. He could be in Mexico City by now."

"Yeah." The manager looked morosely at his desk calendar. "Yeah." He was thinking that he didn't mind reporting to the police half as much as notifying company headquarters. When you lost one, the brass acted as if you'd stolen it yourself.

"Maybe you're right," he said. "Go ahead. Turn him in. But make it routine. No accusations, no fireworks. He might walk in here today yet, or tomorrow. We don't know, he might have connections."

Chapter Twenty-Four

THE Chief U.S. Probation Officer in Seattle was reviewing his file of old parole violation warrants, and he was reasonably pleased. Though he was receiving federal parole board warrants at a rate of fifty or sixty a month, in his district only ten or twelve had been outstanding for as long as two years.

Many years before, when he had been appointed Chief, the work load of the probation officers had been weighted down with the deadwood of fugitive warrants ten years old. It was obvious, the Chief had decided, that anyone who can stay out of sight for ten years with the FBI on his trail is no longer a threat to society. He's dead, or he's in a far place. Or he's made a new life and a new identity for himself and he's going to protect it by staying out of trouble, knowing, as only a fugitive can, that in an age of nationwide police communication and memory bank computers, it wouldn't take more than a traffic ticket to blow his cover. And so the Chief had seen to it that the old warrants were gradually reviewed and withdrawn, to the vast relief of their overworked pursuers.

The Chief reflected that the wanted men might be relieved, too, if they knew the parole board's case against them had been shelved. But you can't notify a man when you don't know where he is. And just as well. Believing a federal warrant was still alive and well in the coat pocket of an FBI agent could keep a tired old offender straight.

He looked critically through the small stack of thin yellow sheets, searching for the oldest warrant application. RILEY, Henry Jackson. The two-year-old document made three charges. First, Riley, when released on parole, had failed to report as directed to his U.S. Probation Officer. Second, he had absconded, for he had been paroled to Seattle but was picked up in California. Third, while being returned to prison as a parole violater, he had escaped from the custody of federal officers, which constituted a new felony. Finally, and the worst allegation for Riley, he had, in the process of making his escape, assaulted a federal officer with intent to kill.

The Chief sighed. There was a quality of sadness, or at least some irony, about this Riley case. The original offense had been a garden variety of auto theft, something for which the guy would have received probation if he hadn't had such a lengthy prior record of small-time check writing that the judge considered him a nuisance. Even as a parole violater, his situation hadn't been too serious, as long as his only violations had been technical, the twin errors of "not reporting" and "absconding his district." But headed back to prison, he had lost control, and it was all downhill after that. By socking a federal officer, he had made his situation a hundred times worse than it had ever been before.

The Chief picked up the telephone, dialed his first deputy, and asked him to come in. "Just looking through the old ones," he said when a big, sandy-haired man in baggy tweeds came into the room. He slipped the Riley warrant across the desk. "Still nothing on this one?"

His assistant shook his head. "I haven't heard anything from the FBI since they thought they had a line on him a year ago. They were looking for him in Seattle. Someone had seen him. But he slipped through the net. He might have gone to Canada."

The Chief chuckled. "Or if he's smart, he might have stayed right here. I've known more than one case who thought he had it made when he got into Canada because he left the FBI behind at the border. When the Canadians got onto him, he learned what cooperation means." He gestured toward the yellow sheet. "What do you think? Shall we ask the parole board to withdraw the warrant?"

"I don't think it would do any good. Not with this assault charge."

The Chief nodded in agreement. "My feelings exactly. We'll keep looking for Henry Jackson Riley."

"Or whatever his name is now," the deputy said with a grin. "He can change his name, but that face of his, with the nose flattened out and that long scar across his cheek? That's going to be recognized, somewhere, sometime."

In the small cove where he had found a plentiful supply of clams, Carlo was digging into the gravel with a sharp stick, and at the same time keeping a watchful eye on the low cliffs extending into the sea like encircling arms.

The water was already lower than he had ever seen it on Phoenix. Equally important, it was still receding. *Now,* he thought. If I'm going to try it, this is the time, when the cliffs are exposed as far down as they're going to be but I still have an hour before the tide turns. Hurriedly, he carried the sack of clams to the slope above the beach where he had deposited his shoes, along with another sack improvised from sections of gill net and the yellow-handled screwdriver. He dropped the clams on the grass, picked up the screwdriver and the sack, and, in a bound, was back on the beach and running into the water.

The shock of cold reminded him he wasn't in Hawaii or California, and that diving without a wet suit was both difficult and chilling. But in a few seconds his body reacted energetically and his arms were cutting the water in long, powerful strokes. With the screwdriver between his teeth and the net sack tied around his waist, he swam along the curving rim of rock toward the mouth of the cove.

He spotted his game where the indented face of the cliff was frosted with a powdery orange-pink fungus and starfish, some in a mottled green-brown, some thick and brilliantly purple, clung to the submerged rock. There they were, two abalone, so drably brown that they seemed to be hiding among their vivid neighbors.

Carlo inflated his lungs and dipped under water. The fingers of his left hand tightened around the flat, oval abalone shell while his right hand grasped the handle of the screwdriver and drove the blade between the cliff and the broad, muscular abalone foot. It clung stubbornly to the cliff, but with two or three determined thrusts, he pried it loose, popped to the surface, opened the sack at his waist and pushed the shellfish into it. With another quick intake of breath, he dived again, and seconds later, dropped the second abalone into his game bag.

Carlo moved along the cliff as rapidly as possible, working feverishly against the inevitable turning of the tide. But he was cautious as well. For one thing, abalone were frequently close associates of both red and green sea urchins, whose spines could make painful punctures. Even more important was the careful use of the screwdriver, the only tool in camp besides the jackknife. If in his struggle to dislodge an abalone he should drop the screwdriver, he would go back to camp ashamed of the loss of a tool rather than proud of finding food. So he worked rapidly but carefully, peering into every inlet and crevasse, diving, grasping, prying, popping up again for more breath. In a period of time he judged to be just under an hour, he had twenty fine, meaty abalone. He also had three wounds where a sea urchin's spikes had bitten into his hand while he was groping along the cliff, but he still had the screwdriver.

He climbed out on the rock and, for the first time, realized just how far he had traveled. The cove where he had been clamming was out of sight, hidden by a headland jutting so far out into the sea that, at low tide, it appeared to be attached to a spine of barren offshore rocks. Until now, Carlo had seen these rocks only at a distance. He looked at them thoughtfully. Seal rocks? If they were, he had made an important discovery.

Seal would mean more than fishy-tasting meat. Seal would provide grease, which they needed, and thick, durable hides. The stomachs could be cleaned, inflated, and used as bottles. Carlo jumped up. Though the tide had turned, the water between the cliff and the rocks was still so shallow he could wade across.

He heard the seal before he saw them. There was a splash and, as he turned his head, a second splash not much louder than the lapping of the waves. A mother and her pup were in the water, gliding away. Two round gray heads, one large, one small, were visible at first and then sank. Long moments later, they reappeared, thirty or forty feet beyond.

Carlo watched with mixed feelings. He had something good to report, but he had an affection for seals that didn't harmonize at all with the idea of hunting them. The group needed meat, he himself was eager for meat, and a quiet inner voice insisted that anything he was willing to eat he ought to be willing to hunt. But a mother, or the cub with big, round black eyes that looked at you as if a harsh word would make him cry? "Dakine baby not foh eat," he said in pidgin, and that seemed to solve the dilemma, at least for this one short beautiful summer afternoon. Humming softly, he climbed the rocky bank, retrieved his sack of abalone and the screwdriver, and started back to the cove.

Felicia was sitting on the grass next to his sack of clams. Dripping sea water, Carlo approached and, after a moment's hesitation, dropped the abalone to the ground and sat down.

With a slight inclination of her head, Felicia indicated the plastic bucket on the grass beside her. It was spilling over with the small gray-green pods of the purple vetch. "The girls have decided that I can be trusted to recognize something that looks exactly like green peas. These vines are growing all along this bank, in and around driftwood logs that the tide doesn't reach." She looked into Carlo's face and said drily, "I just happened to be passing this way. I wasn't following you."

He smiled. "I'm sorry to hear that."

"On the other hand, I didn't *leave* when I stumbled onto your shoes and this bag of clams." She shrugged. "After all, it is a little silly, isn't it, for you and me to continue avoiding each other? We're bound to be alone together sometime, accidentally or otherwise." A small smile curved at the corners of her mouth. "We might as well get it over with."

"I've wanted to talk to you. I've come close to it, a dozen times."

"But you didn't want to embarrass me."

He laughed softly. "In Hawaii, we'd call that *hoomalimali*. Flattery. I couldn't embarrass you. You've got too much poise."

"*Now?*" Felicia exclaimed, fingering her blouse.

"Especially now. It takes real royalty to look elegant in a chicken feed sack. No, I wouldn't know how to embarrass you even if I tried. I don't want to put pressure on you, let's put it that way. That's why I've been giving you room."

She nodded. "Yes, I know. I understand."

"Wait a minute. Don't *mis*understand, beautiful lady. I want you. I've been wanting you. Some other place, some other time . . ." He reached across the space between them and tugged gently on her thick red pigtail. "I had one night with you. I'll never forget it."

Felicia looked directly into his smiling dark eyes. "I won't, either. But things are different now."

"I can see that. And it's right." He shook his head, laughing in a way that mocked his own statement. "Listen to me heah, listen to stupid Carlo. A month ago, this lady would have let me make love to her if we could have managed it without her husband knowing. Today we could make love and no one would find out about it, but the lady doesn't want to. And me, I'm saying, it's right." Though his dark eyes were still bright with laughter, his voice was suddenly intensely serious. "You haven't told Dr. Held why you came to Phoenix?"

She shook her head.

"Don't." Carlo picked up one of her hands and pressed it urgently. "Don't tell him, Felicia. We're going to be here for a while. Let things grow. Let things happen."

For a long thoughtful moment, Felicia looked at him, and then she leaned toward him and kissed him softly on the mouth. "You're a beautiful man, Carlo," she said. "Inside and out. The truth is, I desire you just as much as ever. That isn't what's changed." With that she picked up her bucket of wild peas and quickly left the beach.

Warren Brock was alone when he stumbled over the carcass, and being alone he didn't bother to faint, flee, or cry out at the sight of blood as he would automatically have done for the benefit of witnesses. This was his first venture into the heavily wooded area south of camp. He was hunting for the burls he needed to make pipes and bowls. There were no trails, although he had gradually realized that in taking the easiest way through the underbrush he was following the kind of half-cleared path Rolf described as a deer trail.

Right in the middle of the trail, the remains of an animal lay on blood-soaked leaves and pine needles. "*Nasty!*" Brock murmured, moving in for a closer look. The furry body was gutted and the flesh on both fore- and hindquarters had been shredded. Though it was torn in a way that could be accomplished only by viciously slashing teeth, the head was recognizable. This bloody mutilated thing at his feet was, or had been, a fawn.

Through his many summers on Wolf Island, Brock had

acquired some knowledge of native wildlife. Even now, with this slaughtered creature offering clear evidence that some carnivore might be lurking nearby, he felt secure in his belief that the only Outer Island wildlife that attacks man is the yellowjacket wasp. No wolves, foxes, or coyotes. No bears. Though a fawn would be natural prey for bobcat or cougar, none of the big cats had ever been found in the islands. As far as he knew, there weren't even such unpleasant nuisances as the skunk and the porcupine. What, then, had killed this little deer-child, and then feasted so brutally on its soft belly and delicate legs?

Brock was carrying the jackknife, primarily to cut blazes on tree trunks in order to be able to return directly to any spot where he found a burl. If he located what he wanted, Rolf would follow with stone chisels and the stone hammer. Of course the jackknife was a weapon, the only one the group had. He shuddered as realization dawned that he might have to use it in self-defense. Surely the killer animal wouldn't attack a *man?* He looked around uneasily. Nonsense, he thought. Utter nonsense. Simultaneously, it occurred to him that a sculptor with valor could be a sculptor dead. He made a blaze on the nearest tree, reversed his field, and returned as quickly as he could to camp.

"What did you see besides the dead fawn?" Rolf asked. "Broken twigs, teethmarks, droppings?"

"I *told* you." Brock pursed his lips impatiently. "Just the poor little thing. I wasn't going to crawl around through the underbrush, now was I, dear boy? Come nose-to-nose with some sort of four-legged Dracula?"

Rolf glanced at the sun and made an expert guess as to the time of day. "We've got time before the others get back for dinner. Diana, you stay here, please. Come on, Brock. Show me where you were. And here . . ." he added with a quick smile. "Give me the knife. I'll bring back something for Mike and Lili."

Some distance beyond the dead fawn, Rolf found the first clue. In a small clearing, shadowed by fir and cedar, the tops of two giant slabs of rock broke through the forest floor and leaned against each other at an angle that created a small cave. Kneeling at the opening, Rolf peered into the dim interior. "Bones," he said. "Old bones, well chewed. And the ground is bare and hard. This is where they sleep. I can smell them."

"They?" Brock's voice rose in a tremulous squeak. "I'm not really *loving* this. Just leave our card in the silver salver and let's go."

Rolf drew back. Ignoring Brock, he ran his finger along the edge of the rock at the mouth of the cave. "I thought so," he said softly, studying the wisps of hair caught on the rock's rough surface. "And look here . . ." He pointed to a small dark mound a few feet to the left of the entrance.

Though no woodsman, Brock recognized the feces of a dog. "Dogs?" he exclaimed incredulously. "There isn't a hydrant for miles around."

Rolf's dark eyes were thoughtful. "Wild dogs. The Furness family had sheep. They would have kept a couple of sheepdogs. When they went back to the mainland, they must have left the dogs behind, and they went wild. It's happened on Wolf."

"Feral dogs!" Brock's mind shuffled nervously through half-remembered articles he had read in nature magazines about animals that revert to the wild. "Do they . . . oh, what a perishing thought . . . do they attack human beings?"

Rolf stood up. "You bet they do." With a wry smile, he added, "I think you've got the right idea, Brock. Let's get back to camp."

While Rolf and Warren Brock told their story, Andrew Held studied the attentive faces of the others. It was becoming a habit, this business of silent watching, of weighing reactions, of speculating on what course he, as their appointed leader, should take. He could feel his sensitivity to others growing daily, like a tree whose roots have finally penetrated layers of dry ground to reach the water level.

Obviously they were frightened by the possibility of encountering wild dogs. To pretend they weren't would be senseless bravado and as a group they were already showing a pronounced honesty about their human weaknesses. But how great was the danger?

They could take some comfort from the fact that no traces of feral animals had been seen north of camp. This mid-island beach and harbor area where their primitive settlement was located was a narrow and relatively tree-less strip connecting the great hulking haunch of the heavily forested north end with the lower but equally wooded hills to the south. So far the dogs appeared to consider the hilly south end their territory. As far as Dr. Held knew, they had never wandered onto the saddle of land where his home and outbuildings had presented a degree of civilization that they may have been afraid to challenge. If they had sneaked down the hill during the day, Donald or the boy Jim or Mary the cook would surely have seen them. If they had come at night, wouldn't the keen noses of the basset hounds have picked up their scent?

Not that Mike and Lili were fighters. Their placid peo-ple-loving natures, as well as their full stomachs, had kept them near the house, lying at Dr. Held's feet or literally on top of him when he allowed them on his bed or in his chair. Occasionally a wild rabbit had lured the bassets away from home, and they had loped through the woods, baying like a couple of horns in a Model T. Mike had returned from one such chase with a deep gash in the folds of skin under his jaw. Dr. Held had assumed the hapless hound had tangled with an angry raccoon. But the wound had been in the throat. A wild dog would in-stinctively go for the throat . . . He sighed deeply. No, he could not promise his worried flock that feral dogs on the south end posed no threat. As food gatherers and hunters, they would eventually have to expand their daily foraging to cover the whole island. Besides, the feral dogs had once been domestic animals; they might not be as rigidly territorial as it now appeared. Even if it was frightening, Dr. Held decided, he would have to state the truth. At any time, the dog pack might descend, past the ware-house, past the campfire and the buttery, up the hill to the woods where they slept and the fields and woods where they had been wandering so freely, secure in their belief that the only dangerous creature on Phoenix Island was an angry yellowjacket. In this remote and peaceful place, they would have to be armed.

They had talked of weapons, but as a means of secur-ing food, not of defending themselves. Rolf's snares were weapon substitutes, the first to be made, since they re-quired no materials other than a length of nylon line

from the warehouse. Rolf had placed them in a brushy
spot where droppings and bits of fur indicated a worn
rabbit trail, probably leading into a burrow. A flexible
sapling and a forked stick combined to make the twitch-
up. He bent the sapling into an inverted U and used the
forked stick to pin the top of it into the ground. After
tying one end around the pinioned sapling, he ran the
fishing line along the ground until it reached the rabbit
trail. At this end of the line, he made a lasso about
twice as big around as a rabbit and draped the line from
an overhanging bush so that the big loop hung over the
path at rabbit's eye level. A rabbit headed for the burrow
would stay on the familiar trail and thus attempt to run
through the loop. But its head would catch on the lasso
and automatically tighten it. The animal's struggles to
free itself would jerk the other end of the line, pulling the
forked stick out of the ground and freeing the sapling.
The sudden release of the twitch-up would swing the
rabbit into the air.

This device had produced a small but steady supply of
rabbit meat, but they had begun to talk of making something for larger game. Rolf had seen deer in the woods
at the north end of the island and was dedicated to the
idea of hunting them. Carlo's conviction that there were
seal on some of the rocks offshore emphasized their
need for something more than the jackknife and the yellow-handled screwdriver. And now, the specter of feral
animals, lurking in the woods through which they must
pass every day if they were to gather food and water—
how could they protect themselves against such a vicious
menace?

They had neither guns nor gunpowder. What sort of
substitutes could be made out of the crazy assortment of
odds and ends they called the warehouse? And whatever
they invented—clubs, spears, harpoons, slings—of what
use would such pathetically primitive instruments be
against feral animals that for five or six generations had
learned to exist by killing?

Andrew Held stood up, walked across the beach to
the cedar post "calendar" and cut a short notch, marking
the passing of another day. The voices around the fire
quieted, for this was the recognized manner of calling the
meeting to order. Resuming his place on the log, Andrew
Held began.

"I'm relieved, but not really surprised, to see that no one has panicked at the threat of wild dogs. They're a fact, and at this point we've had some hard lessons in dealing with facts. We can hope the dogs won't bother us. Or more to the point, we can hope we won't bother them." He paused, and a slow reflective smile pulled at the corners of his mouth. "We've been forced to become hunters. Now we may be forced to protect ourselves. For both purposes, we need more weapons." He laughed softly. "It's ironic, you know. We *must* have weapons. We must *invent* weapons. I've been both praised and excoriated for my part in developing the most deadly weapon ever devised by man. But in our present situation, I'm helpless. I don't even know how to begin. I probably know less than any of you about what we should do now. Well? What do you say? Should we start by looking through the warehouse?"

For several minutes, they went through the piles of debris. A thorough inspection of warehouse supplies confirmed the fact that the one material they needed most— metal—was almost totally lacking. A roll of chicken wire, two silver forks, a coffee can, some lengths of pipe. They assembled it all, studying each precious fragment, and fell silent.

Andrew Held looked at the solemn faces and wondered what magic words might have the power to dispel their depression. They had stripped themselves of their belt buckles, shoelaces, hairpins. Blake, the haberdasher's dream, had donated his belt for the leather and was holding up his trousers with a length of rope. Rolf had offered his shoes because their rubber soles could be cut up to make slingshots. They had all given up everything they had . . .

But I haven't, he thought guiltily. I am concealing pieces of metal because I am still concealing myself. He made his decision quickly and acted upon it in frantic haste. He could feel their puzzled stares as he removed his right shoe, lifted the trouser leg, slid off the sock and detached the prosthesis.

"There's metal in this . . ." The imitation foot he was holding seemed to Andrew Held both comical and hideous. He had lived with it, or its earlier counterparts, for many long years, but he regarded it with self-loathing, unable to meet the eyes around the circle. In giving up so much of their clothing, they had all submitted to various degrees of self-exposure. But what they exposed was beautiful, complete, like the firm nipples of the women's breasts, unprotected by brassieres and pressing against a single thin layer of cloth. While to Andrew Held, the prosthesis was ugly and his bare right leg, severed and scarred, ending in a point instead of a foot, was unnatural, and for that reason, repellent. . . . The silence was beginning to press against him. He lifted his head. Not one of them was looking at the bare stump of his right foot, though to him it gleamed white and ugly in the flickering firelight. All eyes were focused on the artificial foot he was holding out to them. Their faces showed curiosity and intense interest, but not a trace of revulsion. Nor of sympathy, which he dreaded almost as much.

"Remarkable!" Blake said enthusiastically, as if he had just been allowed a glimpse of a highly classified nuclear device. "The sole is sponge rubber, isn't it? To act as a cushion. Two springs in the front, one in the back, a rubber toe . . ." He shook his head in open admiration. "I begin to understand why you walk so evenly, Dr. Held."

"Yes, it's fairly complicated. Designed for comfort and for balance, and since very few amputees live near a prosthetist's shop, durability is important, too."

"Well, I don't see no sense in you giving it up so we can get a couple of springs or a steel rod." Donald's voice was gruff. Ordinarily he sat through meetings without asserting himself beyond a few surly objections, which he expressed vaguely and quickly withdrew at the first sign of disagreement. Now he was moved by a feeling that had been developing ever since the tsunami—loyalty to the Boss. He looked around belligerently. "We ain't even begun to see what we can make with what we've got. Like, I'm going to make a slingshot. That would do a lot more to chase off a pack of dogs than some kind of dagger we might make out of the metal in Dr. Held's foot. I'm for trying everything else before we break up that foot."

"Mr. Campbell is right," Norma said firmly.

"Of course he is. Absolutely!"—this from Blake, while Warren Brock studied the prosthesis with a professional eye and murmured, "Beautiful job, *beautiful.*"

For once Donald Campbell had the unqualified approval of people to whom he felt inferior. His scarred and weathered face shone with simple delight, the face of a child winning first prize.

Andrew Held said unsteadily, "Well, I can walk without it. I thought it might be made into something useful." He withdrew into silence, shaken by two strong but conflicting emotions. He was grateful for Donald's loyalty, and pleased as a concerned parent that the big man had managed to express himself. But when he offered his prosthesis he had assumed it would be accepted, and the thought of casting it off forever had awakened a tingling sense of relief. But it was still his. Because they were kind, he was still chained to it. Slowly, thoughtfully, he leaned forward and fitted the device to the tapered stump of his leg.

The meeting was over. They had discussed a half-dozen primitive weapons and agreed to hunt for natural materials that could be combined with the manufactured bits and pieces in the warehouse.

Yew, because it was strong enough and tough enough for harpoon shafts and for bows and arrows. Sitka spruce because the roots could be used for tying the tines of a spear and a sapling would do as the spring pole for a snare large enough to catch deer. Willow because the bark could be made into a heavy rope to serve as harpoon line. Hemlock for the stanchions of a fish trap, fir for the handles of dip nets, ironwood or spirea for prongs of a duck spear. Hereafter, the meeting was to be a work session for the design and construction of housekeeping necessities—bowls, baskets, pails, spoons—as well as weapons.

Andrew Held had insisted on taking a shift as fire-watcher, and so he remained on the beach when the others climbed the hill to the dormitory. Felicia, the last to leave, turned back at the foot of the hill and sat down next to him. Looking into the fire, she said, "Andy, you were magnificent."

He understood her, but even before he replied, Felicia knew he would feel compelled to pretend he hadn't. In relation to his injured leg, concealment was too old a habit to be broken in an evening.

"Magnificent? Tell me how, so I can try it again sometime."

To Felicia's ear, his effort to sound amused was not convincing. "Don't hide, Andy. At least, not from me." She leaned forward and in a firm, uncompromising manner, raised his right trouser leg so that the artificial limb was exposed. Smiling, she patted it affectionately. "It's part of you. Accept it. I always did." She let the trouser leg fall back and straightened up. "As I said, magnificent. I know what it cost you to remove that wonderful device and show us the shocking, ugly thing you had been so careful to cover up. But did you notice? No one stared, no one ran from the scene screaming in terror. Therefore no one knew what a terrible moment it was for you. Except me."

Her voice softened. "Do you realize, dear Andy, that your right foot is your only sacred cow, the one and only subject you cannot laugh about? Once you did, only once, and I'll never forget it. We were dancing. There was a waxy spot on the dance floor. I began to slip and in catching my balance I gave your right foot a good hard kick. I said 'Oh, sorry!' and you grinned and said, 'Ouch!' It took me a second to realize it was your 'good foot,' as you called it, and that you had actually joked about it. Oh, I loved you a lot, Andy, but never more than then. I felt as if my heart turned over."

He looked intently into her sparkling green eyes. "Thank you."

"What for?" She thought, Now it's my turn to panic.

"For being so . . . so very tender."

"Tender?" she repeated defensively. "That's hardly my style, is it?" She stood up to go.

"Wait. Please. Sit here for a minute."

She sat down on the sand, arms wrapped around her legs, her chin resting on her knees. "I know, Andy. There's something you want to ask me."

"You're perceptive, as usual. You probably know what I want to ask."

She nodded, eyes fixed on the fire. "Why did I come to Phoenix."

"Exactly. You had hardly stepped out of the *Trident* when you announced you had a mission and that I wasn't going to like it."

"But I've said nothing since, and you're curious."

"Do you blame me?"

"Of course not." Carlo's advice rang in her mind like a

warning bell. Don't tell him. Let things grow. Let things happen . . . It was impossible. She could not be dishonest with Andrew Held. It was the base on which her respect for him was built. And for herself. She had been honest even about her infidelity.

"Andy, I came to Phoenix to tell you that I planned to remarry. Which meant, of course, obtaining a divorce."

He did not speak. What price "honesty," she thought, staring into the fire. Why had she felt compelled to cleanse herself at his expense? Was she afraid he would be indifferent to her announcement? Had she been "honest" because she wanted to know whether she could still hurt him? She looked up. His eyes were hidden, covered by his hand, but his mouth was moving in silent pain. "That's only half the truth," she said, fighting to control her voice. "If I tell you part of the truth, I should tell it all. I've changed my mind. I'm not going to marry the man in Washington. I haven't thought about him twice in a day. Give me another week on Phoenix and I'll forget what he looks like."

Andrew Held's hand dropped away from his face. In the rippling shadow his blue eyes were almost black. "You've changed your mind about him. Does that mean you will stay here with me?"

The irony of the question occurred to neither of them. "I don't know," she said unhappily. "Andy, it wasn't that simple, was it? The trouble between us. It was never really another man."

"I know that." He smiled. "Don't be sad, Felicia." He stood up and held out his hands. She grasped them and he lifted her to her feet. "All right," he said, closing his eyes. "Tell me the color of my eyes."

"You tell me first . . ."

Laughing, they clung to each other, and Felicia felt his cheek wet against her own.

In a small hospital in southeast Alaska, Andrew Held's cook, Mary, was known as 16A, indicating Bed A of Room 16. On the clipboard at the foot of her bed, brief periods of semi-consciousness were recorded but she had never fully awakened nor made sounds other than an occasional rasping moan.

In the admissions office, she was described as a survivor, probably of the August fourth tsunami, rescued at sea and transported to the mainland by the Coast Guard. Name, unknown. Sex, female. Age, approximately sixty. Permanent address, "undetermined," to which someone had added in pencil, "Best guess, some town on the coast between Coos Bay, Oregon, and Wrangell, Alaska."

Though an unconscious old woman was a mystery to hospital administrators (who wanted above all to determine what health insurance program her bills should be charged to), the medical staff had a body whose secrets could be probed. "Cerebral angiography indicates severe edema. No overt skull fracture . . ."

Nurse Watkins, coming on duty, asked the nurse she was replacing, "Anything new with Sixteen-A?"

"No change. It's been three weeks, hasn't it? Or four?"

"At least. Poor old soul. I wonder who she is? It could be weeks, even months, before she can tell us."

"Report came back from the FBI," the younger nurse said matter-of-factly. "Zilch on the fingerprints."

Nurse Watkins sighed. "Too bad. It would help if she had a criminal record."

Chapter Twenty-Five

At the meeting the night before, it had been agreed that Norma and Blake would pick the blackberries ripening near the site of the old Furness farmhouse. The only evidence of wild dogs had been found on the southern end of the island. During excursions to the north end, where the farm was located, they had never encountered any sign of the pack. They concluded that the dogs stayed within their territory, and that the area north of the beach was "safe." Besides, the species of tiny wild berry that grew on trailing vines was a far greater delicacy than the larger evergreens and Himalayas that would ripen later on.

The berries were especially plentiful wherever the ground had been burned over. Evidently, years before, in an abortive attempt to rid himself of stumps or brush, some unlucky Furness had let a fire get out of control. Though he had saved the house—the logs and rough-cut timbers where the house had collapsed were partially rotted but not charred—the big cedar stumps at the west end of the meadow were scoured by fire, and a small outbuilding only thirty or forty feet from the farmhouse had apparently burned to the ground. Blackened boards were still visible underneath a matted covering of blackberry vines.

Norma and Blake started picking at the west end of the field and had filled their coffee cans by the time they reached the farmyard area. Blake parted the tangle of vines that partially concealed the remains of the shed. "I can see some boards," he reported, "but they're so badly burned I doubt we could use them for anything. Wait a minute. There are some nails, too."

Vines smothered the half-burned walls of a shed, but under these there was a low mound, some ten or twelve feet in diameter and raised a foot or two above the ground.

"We know there was a bad fire," Blake mused, peering

into the thicket. "It must have burned one outbuilding, perhaps two. It seems to me that a farmer would be so busy saving his house he wouldn't be able to rescue the contents of a woodshed or a barn. I wonder . . . When it was all over and he tried to clean things up, wouldn't he pile all the rubbish in one place? Into a heap, like this?"

Norma's answer was an excited nod. Even rusty nails were a valuable find. Their arms and legs were badly scratched by blackberry thorns but the possibility of discovering metal was strong incentive. With sticks and bare hands, they tore at the brush, buccaneers digging for buried gold.

After a few minutes Blake sat back on his haunches to catch his breath. His face was streaked with dirt, hayseed was sticking to his perspiring neck, and rivulets of blood marked the spots blackberry thorns had torn in his skin. But look at his neat, city-bred wife! She was on her hands and knees, scratching the dirt with broken fingernails. Her lips were parted in a happy, anticipatory smile.

"My dear Mrs. Mansfield," Blake said, "if your fairy godmother appeared right now and offered you one thing and one thing only, what would you ask for?"

"A shovel."

"Not a plane ticket to New York?"

Norma stopped digging, turned her head, and looked thoughtfully into her husband's dirty, sweaty face. "Some other time. Right now, I'd take the shovel."

Diana and Rolf had been exploring the woods beyond the orchard. They had never been this far beyond the old farm, and they had already discovered something more important to them than gold. It was a spring, a small pool of icy clear water rising to the surface from some hidden underground source. It ran a short and quiet course between lush green banks two or three feet high and then disappeared under a bed of moss. Even after it had submerged, its course was marked by rushes, marsh grass, and buttercups, signs as clear as a blaze on a tree that water was close to the surface. They followed the hidden stream and were soon back out of the woods standing at the edge of the pond.

"I should have figured something was feeding into the pond," Rolf said. "Or at least I should have come around to this side before now. I did wonder if the old farm didn't have some source of water beside the pond, but I thought it would be a well, somewhere close to the house."

Diana dropped to her knees and poked her fingers into the mossy turf. "The spring isn't far from here and it's probably running close to the surface. We could dig it out. Brook water. Lovely, clean brook water."

Rolf looked down into her face and thought, She glows, as if there was light coming from the inside. He sat down beside her. The soft green bank was cool against his legs. He touched her arm, and it was warm. Smiling, he lifted it to his nose and the skin smelled sweet, like dried hay. He kissed the hand and pressed it against his chest. "That's my heart," he said. "When you're around, it goes crazy."

Diana's hand lingered on the warmth of his skin and the beat of his heart. It seemed natural to be touching the body she had seen and slept so near and glided against when they swam together in the pond. She moved her hand across the smooth dark skin, and her fingers caressed the nipple. Her hand drew back like a startled animal, but Rolf caught it. One arm drew her back while the other gently lifted her chin so that she was looking directly into his eyes. Dark eyes, bright, but as gentle as his hand. Instead of pulling away, she rested against him, longing to be kissed.

At first his lips touched her lightly, but then the pressure of his mouth unleashed such a flood of yearning that her own lips parted and hungrily accepted the gentle probing of his tongue. Very slowly, Rolf lowered her onto the satiny bank. His body pressed against her side and the kiss continued, open-mouthed, binding them together.

When he lifted his head, she could not speak. When he opened her dress and softly fingered her bare breasts, she could not move. She felt the nipples harden and instinctively arched her back as he lowered his head and licked the sensitive tips. Deep in her body, she was aware of him. His thighs, pressing against her, awakened a hot throbbing sensation between her legs. As never before in her life, she was conscious of every surface, every opening, in her body.

His hand was moving now toward the awful secrets of that dark, rainy Saturday night, down her belly and into the dark hidden place that in spite of her fear, was crying out to be entered. But now the hand that searched her body was gentle. The fingers were loving her, not thrusting or hurting. She whispered, "Rolf . . . I wasn't going to, until I could tell you what happened."

With his mouth against her ear, he said, "Does it really matter?"

"I don't know. I'm so afraid . . ."

"Are you afraid of me?"

"No. Oh, no . . ."

"We've both been wanting this. It's been piling up. We've waited long enough, Diana. Let loose, let the feeling go."

Once again his lips were on hers, tasting her, gently sucking until her tongue responded and moved feverishly along the roof of his mouth. When the kiss ended, she murmured, "I do want you, Rolf . . ."

He pulled her dress down over her feet, threw it aside, and as quickly removed and discarded his jeans. Sunshine dropped through the overhanging branches and fell on his naked body in pools of golden light. Trembling, she let him part her thighs and caress the damp valley. Then he was above her, resting on his arms and kissing her forehead, her cheeks, her ears, her neck. Down below, where fear had been driven out by longing, slow thrusts of his pelvis were driving him into her body. The strokes speeded, and were deeper. Frantic with need for him, she opened wider, and her hips responded in a rhythmic movement beyond her control. The anguish mounted. Even the warm ground under her seemed to be throbbing with it. She clung to him and rocked with him and the incredible sweetness swept through her until it was unbearable, uncontainable, and her body exploded with it. Strange joyful loving words burst from her mouth in the last spasm of desire.

Rolf raised himself on one elbow and looked down at the face of the beautiful sleeping girl. Her lashes were dark against her cheek and her lips were slightly parted, as if she had been about to say something when she fell asleep. Carefully so as not to wake her, he stood up, stepped into his bluejeans and knotted the ends of the rope that served as his belt. With several backward glances to assure himself that he hadn't disturbed her, he

walked stealthily to the edge of the woods where he had
seen honeysuckle blooming.

When he came back, he was carrying several kinds of
wild flowers and long grasses. Flame-colored orange
honeysuckle on a long vine as tough and flexible as a
rope. Wild ginger, with its lily-pad leaves and spherical
dark red petals. Long, densely flowered spikes of the
hooded ladies tresses. Leaves of the rattlesnake plantain,
dark green and veined in white.

Diana was still sleeping. He sat down and went to
work quickly, braiding the grass and the long slender
stems of honeysuckle vine. Once the braid was the right
length, he wrapped and tied the ends together and into
this plaited ring inserted the stems of the flowers and
the plantain leaves. When Diana opened her eyes, he
was holding the crown of blossoms in both hands and
smiling.

"Oh, beautiful!" she exclaimed, sitting up.

He knelt beside her, holding the ring of flowers as
carefully as if it were truly a jeweled crown on a velvet
pillow. *"You* are beautiful." His voice was very quiet, very
low. "Diana, do you love me?"

Her wide eyes were gray-blue like a stormy sky and
deep as the forest shadows. "I love you, Rolf."

"Then we are together. You're mine. But I promise
you, I'm yours, too." He placed the wreath on her head.
"All the way," he said softly. "All the way."

For a long moment, he looked at her and neither of
them spoke. The brilliant colors of the flowers flamed
above her silky head. She sat perfectly still, with her long
dark hair falling over her breasts, her hands resting at her
sides. Looking into his face, she repeated the vow. "Yes,
Rolf. All the way."

Rolf was about to kiss her when they heard a woman
scream.

Norma was so preoccupied by the treasures buried in
the refuse pile that Blake's absence did not disturb her.
Their first discovery had been a jewel beyond price—an
ax head. Dull, rusted, and lacking a handle, but still that
one basic tool with which they could hew, hack, cut and
shape their way out of the latter-day Stone Age in
which they had been living. So far nothing hidden in the
layers of dirt, ash, and rotting board had been as exciting

as the ax, but measured by their present standards, even lesser finds—a pair of pliers, a large hook, a few links of chain—were also of inestimable value. And the secrets of the mound were by no means exhausted. So when Blake said, "I'm going to look around in the rubble where the house used to be," Norma murmured, "Yes, good idea . . ." and didn't even look up.

Fifteen minutes later—or ten, or twenty? Her interest in the mound was so intense that she had lost all sense of time—she thought she heard Blake's voice. It sounded very near. She looked over her shoulder, expecting to see him standing directly above her. He wasn't there.

She stood up, eyes searching the fields, the farmyard, the area around the farmhouse. Crickets were chattering, bees hummed. A bird with an orange breast surveyed her from the top of a charred stump, but there was no other human being in the entire sun-drenched expanse of meadow. Wherever he was, Blake couldn't have called her. She had imagined it. A curious chill went through her. Where could he have gone?

Slowly at first, she began to walk in the direction he must have taken. The old farmhouse was nothing more than logs and timbers lying on the ground wherever they had fallen. No standing wall, no hedge or fence existed to conceal Blake's figure. Unless, of course, he was down on his hands and knees, as she had been, scratching in the ruins. She called his name, and stopped to listen. There was no answer. Then she began to run.

It was stumbling that saved her life. Her toe caught on the edge of a rotting board imbedded in the ground and overgrown with weeds and blackberry vines. She fell and, gasping for breath, saw that the board was one of several nailed together into a rough cover or lid. At the center was a jagged hole two or three feet across. She knew even before she crawled to the edge of it that the rotting boards had disintegrated under the weight of a man's body, and that whatever lay under the wooden cover, she had found Blake.

Lying flat on her stomach, she reached the hole and looked down. Cold damp air laden with the smell of mud rose from the blackness. Her eyes, accustomed to bright sunshine, refused at first to penetrate the shadows. But she heard him. "Norma!" His voice was weak and hollow, a lost sound echoing up through the dark shaft. "Go back! You'll fall!"

"It's a well," she said, with strange matter-of-factness. Her pulse was pounding but her head was clear. She felt as if some second Norma Mansfield, a practical, cool-headed, and ingenious Norma Mansfield, had stepped into her body and was now in charge. This emergency Norma commanded that her eyes adjust and bring shapes out of the empty black.

A round hole in the ground, about six feet in diameter. A shaft with slippery vertical walls and at the bottom of it, some thirty feet below, Blake struggling to keep his head above water.

He could not climb out, and she had no rope to throw him. She had to save him from drowning, but if she moved impetuously, the board under her would give way and she would die with him. This possibility did not frighten her. If Blake drowned, it didn't seem very important. But she was his only hope. It wouldn't be fair, the sensible Norma admonished her, to be foolhardy or careless and throw away his only chance.

"Hold on, Blake. Just hold on . . ."

Still flat on her stomach, Norma inched her way back to solid ground. Gripping the board with both hands, she pulled. The well cover resisted. She took a deep breath and pulled again. At her third desperate try, it broke free of the tangle of vines and weeds and she was able to drag it away from the opening.

Light shone down the shaft onto Blake's upturned face, ghostly white and floating on top of the dark water. "I'll be right back," she said calmly to that disembodied head, as the self-possessed Norma-in-charge noted that he wasn't wearing his glasses.

She ran to the ruins of the farmhouse. A rope, a ladder . . . Her frightened, desperate self mumbled "Please, God . . ." while her icy calm stand-in searched efficiently and swiftly for anything long enough to reach the bottom of the well. There was nothing. The boards were too short, the smallest log was too heavy, and there wasn't a ladder, a rope, or a coil of wire.

Perhaps something still buried in the mound . . . As she turned to go back, a shape at the edge of the woods caught her eye. It was a tall skinny pine, bare of all but a few branches at the very top. It stood out from the straight healthy trunks around it because it was no bigger around than her fist and it was leaning at a forty-five-degree angle. After a month on Phoenix, Norma automatically identified a dead tree, probably rotted at the roots so that her body weight would crack it off at the ground. Being dead, the tree would be dry and light so that she would be able to drag it across the field to the well.

Norma was back at the well when she remembered that Rolf and Diana were exploring the woods near the pond. They would not hear her call unless they were on their way back, but this late in the day, that was a possibility. Should she try to find them? No. Blake could drown while she was gone. Instinct told her that above all, she must stay with Blake.

Peering into the dim light, she lowered the small end of the long, thin pine, guiding it carefully down the wall of the shaft. Sensible Norma-in-charge was keeping hysteria at bay. Her husband might have slipped underwater, he might not be able to hold onto the pole, he might die—and still her mind was spinning with idiot thoughts like, Why isn't he wearing his glasses?

"Can you reach it, Blake?"

His voice was a hollow echo. "Not . . . not . . . not . . . quite . . . quite . . ."

She slid forward until her head and shoulders were over the cavity. Now, with her arms hanging inside the well, the pole extended another foot or two.

"Almost . . . almost . . . almost . . ."

"Try," she urged him.

"It's . . . so . . . cold . . ."

"Try!" she commanded. "Reach for it! Now!"

The water splashed. His voice seemed weaker, coming from a distance. "I missed . . . go back, Norma . . ."

"Blake! Listen to me. You'll get it this time . . ." (What did he do with his glasses?) "Blake, this time you'll reach it. Ready, get set, go . . ."

The sudden jerk nearly pulled the pole out of her hands but told her that Blake had caught the end. She renewed her grip, observing as if her hands didn't belong to her that the rough bark had torn the skin on her palms and bits of crumbly wood fiber were stuck in the open wounds. "Now hold on, Blake. Just hold on. I'm going to start screaming. I don't want you to be worried. It's just that Rolf and Diana might be down at the other end of the farm."

She spoke as if it were as easy as a fourth-grade problem in arithmetic. The truth was that, even if Blake could hold on, she wasn't strong enough to pull him up. Furthermore, any strain on the half-rotted pine tree might break the lifeline. Her hands were bleeding now and the weight of Blake's body and the pole brought a wrenching pain to her arms and shoulders. Slowly, deliberately, she inflated her lungs, lifted her head, and with all the strength her body could muster, she began to scream.

Panting, Rolf threw himself on the ground and took the pole from Norma's hands. "How long has he been down there?"

Norma shook her head. "I don't know." It was a hot day, but her body was shaking as if it were resisting a cold wind.

"This pole wouldn't hold me if I tried to climb down. Even if it did, it wouldn't take our weight when I tried to bring him up." Rolf looked up at Norma. "You said you found a hook. A baling hook?"

"I don't know what a baling hook looks like."

"Heavy metal, about six inches across, with a handle at right angles."

"I'll go see." Diana was already running toward the mound Norma had been excavating. She returned with a baling hook, the chain, and the ax head. "No rope," she said quietly.

"Buried like that, it would be rotten anyway. If we had time, we could braid a rope out of honeysuckle." He shook his head, and the gesture said plainly that they didn't. "We'll have to use our clothes."

No one spoke. Diana unbuttoned her dress and stepped out of it. Norma hesitated, but the sight of Diana, holding her dress in her hand, broke the moment of paralysis and she quickly opened her own dress and pulled it over her head. Naked, Diana knelt beside Rolf and he lifted his hips so that she could pull his jeans down over his feet.

"About four-inch strips," Rolf said. "You could use the ax to start the tear."

In minutes all their clothing had been reduced to sturdy

lengths of denim, linen, and muslin, and Diana and Norma were tying the ends together.

"One of you take the pole," Rolf said. "The other will have to hold one end of the rope."

Their naked bodies might have been moving in a well-rehearsed drill. Norma dropped to the ground and took her former position with the pine pole in both hands. Rolf tested the rope, giving each knot a vicious jerk and then handed one end to Diana. "You'd better wrap it around your wrist. That will keep it from slipping." He stood at the lip of the well, with the improvised rope in his hands and the baling hook held firmly between thumb and forefinger. Methodically he played out the rope, two feet at a time until the line from Diana hung straight down the shaft and disappeared in the shadow.

"Is it long enough?" Norma asked. "Can you reach him?"

"I can't see yet. But we'll get him, Norma. Just hold on." Rolf turned to Diana and smiled. "You hold on, too. All the way."

Blake was beyond helping himself. His hands clutched the pole convulsively but Rolf could see even in the half-light that his face was the blank mask of a man fighting to retain consciousness. It was bitterly cold. Blake's body felt stiff and there was no responding movement when Rolf grabbed him under the arms and tried to lift him out of the water.

Rolf had had small hope that Blake would be in condition to pull himself out of the well, hand over hand on the rope. Now he knew for sure that Blake would have to be carried. The question was whether he had the strength to do it, and whether Diana would be able to hold fast while he made the effort. And how much use could he make of the baling hook? His idea had been to thrust the sharp point into the wall of the well, as a mountaineer uses a piton, and thus make handholds for himself that would greatly reduce the weight on the line. He tried it, pushing the point of the baling hook into the slippery clay. It stuck, but when he tested it with his full weight, the hook cut a groove and was loose in his hand. So the hook could not be trusted. His reassuring "We'll get him, Norma" had been a cruel boast, an empty promise. In the sunlight, anything had seemed possible. At the bottom of the well, death grinned at him grotesquely from a pool of black water.

Desperate, he decided what to do, knowing fully that unless he was blessed with supreme luck he would lose everything.

Rolf had looped the end of the rope around Blake's waist, and fastened it with the baling hook as a diaper is secured with a safety pin. He untied the manila rope Blake had been using as a belt, wound it tightly around Blake's wrists and tied them to the cloth rope at a spot above Blake's head. Now Blake was attached to the rescue line in two places; his body sagged, suspended by the wrists and straining at the waist, but the rigging held. Only half-conscious, the body twirled slowly, as if the baling hook were holding him up by the navel.

Though Blake had released his grip on the pine pole, Norma was still holding her end. For several minutes, Rolf had had nothing to hang onto as he attached Blake's limp form to the rescue line. He grabbed the end of the pine pole and gave himself a minute to catch his breath. Diana alone could not raise Blake. She and Norma could do it together. That meant Norma would have to drop the pole and, until they had lifted Blake to the surface, then freed the rescue line and lowered it, he would have to tread water.

He called out, "Norma, let go of the pole. Put both hands on the line, like Diana. Then pull together, slowly, a little at a time. Careful, because he's going to be scraping against the side . . ."

The pine pole fell into the water with a gentle splash. Slowly, just as he had instructed them, Diana and Norma raised the inert form of Blake Mansfield, while Rolf treaded water, paddled with his hands, and counted. And counted, and counted, and in the desperate cold, lost count.

A curious peaceful feeling was beginning to invade his body, a feeling like falling asleep, when the end of the rescue line brushed against his face and he heard Diana calling from some far, far place. "Wrap it around your wrist. Hold on with both hands. Rolf, do you hear me? Rolf! Do as I say!"

Her voice dispelled apathy. Clutching the end of the lifeline, he thought, I'll be goddamned if I'm going to die at the bottom of someone's old well . . . The line grew taut, he was being lifted, there was light over his head, and Diana's voice, calling "All the way, Rolf, all the way!" They were slowly pulling him back to life.

When Blake regained consciousness, naked figures were hovering over him. He looked at them unbelievingly. Then slowly he raised himself to a sitting position.

His expression was so puzzled that Norma said, reassuringly, "We're real, Blake. You're safe. Everything's all right . . . ." Then the truth hit her. The vagueness in his dark blue eyes was not confusion, it was the groping gaze of the extremely near-sighted. His glasses were buried in mud at the bottom of the well. Blake was alive, thank God, but Blake was almost blind.

Chapter Twenty-Six

THE ritual of the nightly meeting opened with the marking of Andrew Held's "Crusoe Calendar." A short notch for each of the first six days of the week, a longer notch for the seventh day, which, after some discussion, they agreed was Sunday.

Their first Sunday was indistinguishable from other days, for there was so much to be done no one thought of interrupting the weekday work routine. But on the evening of their second Saturday, Andrew Held sensed a general weariness of spirit as well as of body.

"Tomorrow is Sunday," he said as he inscribed a short notch on the calendar pole and resumed his place in the circle. Someone nodded, someone else murmured in agreement, but they were too tired to react further. Looking at passive faces and dull eyes, Andrew Held realized that his responsibility as leader went beyond keeping them fed, watered, and sheltered; he was more than a herdsman protecting prize cattle. If they were to survive, then their inner selves, disparate as they were, would also have to be nurtured, or physical fatigue would sink too deep to be erased by a good night's sleep.

And there was another factor that he, as leader, could not afford to ignore. This little colony included three single males whose sexual appetites were not going to subside simply because they had no partners. Nor was the physical beauty of the three females going to be less disturbing, at least to Carlo and Donald, because they were already spoken for. Of course the arrival of a search party would solve everything. But an acceptable alternative, Dr. Held mused with a wry smile, would be the magical appearance of two pretty girls and one pretty boy. Rescue, in that case, might lose some of its charm . . .

He cleared his throat. They *could* do something about physical fatigue. "We need a change of pace," he said. "What would you think of making Sunday different in some way from the other days of the week? I'm not sure how. That's up to you. But shouldn't we mark Sunday in some special way?"

"On Sunday, we always had roast chicken," Norma mused, looking dreamily into the fire.

"On Sunday," Warren Brock said brightly, "dear *maman* broke out her best sherry and wore her black velvet. She was at home from three till five."

"Are you thinking of some sort of religious observance, Dr. Held?" Blake's voice was deferential in spite of an overtone of doubt.

"Religion," Felicia echoed sleepily. "When I was fifteen I got interested in the Young Peoples' Prayer Meeting that met on Sunday evening because my girlfriend assured me a boy always walks you home. I went, no one asked to take me home, and that was the last time I attended Young Peoples' Prayer Meeting."

"I can't understand it," Andrew Held said with a smile. "A beautiful red-headed girl?"

Felicia shrugged. "I had braces on my teeth and my mother wouldn't let me wear high heels."

Andrew Held chuckled and returned to the issue.

"Something religious, if that's what you want, though that sounds more formal, or perhaps more restrictive, than what I had in mind. An hour, or even a half-hour of meditation, right after breakfast Sunday morning? When we could think our own thoughts, or, if we wish, pray our own prayers? Carlo might sing, someone else might recite, though I feel . . ." He paused and turned toward Warren Brock. Smiling, he said, ". . . though I think your particular genius for poetry would be better expressed on Saturday nights."

"There was a young lady from Phoenix . . ." Brock began cheerily.

Andrew Held broke in. "That's what I mean. All right, shall we try it tomorrow morning? One hour of quiet contemplation, to be followed by a day of rest in which each of us decides how he wishes to spend his time?"

It was agreed, and one of civilization's oldest concepts became a keystone of Phoenix Island's lifestyle.

On the first of September, the group had looked on silently as Andrew Held cut two parallel horizontal lines into the cedar post to record the beginning of their second month. Almost a month on Phoenix, and help had not come. The solemnity of the moment had bordered on despair. But on the first of October, the sober act of marking a new month didn't depress them. They watched thoughtfully while Dr. Held carved the double line, but when they began to talk, it was not about rescue but about their accomplishments.

The physical appearance of the calendar reflected how, with each new achievement, the group's spirits rose. Early in September, Warren Brock had begun to carve tiny symbols and figures to embellish the slashes on particularly memorable days. A bee, on the day they first had honey. A candle with a tiny flame to commemorate Norma's success in making a candle out of wax from the wild hive. A shower of slanting raindrops for the storm that brought a harvest of big, sea-green Japanese glass balls, floats that had broken loose from some fisherman's net on the far side of the Pacific. So when Dr. Held sharpened the jackknife on a stone and cut parallel lines to herald the new month, a pictorial history of their successes was engraved on the calendar, just as Indian folklore is told on totems and house poles. The plain day-by-day marks might remind them that they had been lost for two months, but the delicate pictographs spoke more loudly of exciting discoveries and clever inventions. Reviewing their progress, they were pleased with themselves, and when Andrew Held, as town crier, declared, "It is now October the first!" a spontaneous cheer rose around the campfire.

By now they knew every inlet, cliff, stream, meadow, woods, and hill on the north end of the island. "Island combing" was the name they gave to their daily searches, for, like beachcombing, its purpose was the discovery and collection of any substances or objects that might be useful in their daily lives. There was nothing haphazard about their approach to it. Though the only evidence of wild dogs had been found on the southern end of the island, they decided not to wander far from camp except in twos or threes. Working in teams was safer as well as more thorough. At the nightly meeting, each team reported its finds, discussed the possible uses of each one, and agreed on team assignments for the next day.

As had been established early in their exile, Andrew Held was not expected to range very far from camp, and as the others discovered places he'd never imagined existed, such as a tiny bay where a stream of clear sweet water cut across a grassy tideflat to meet and blend with the sea, he began to realize how provincial he had been. He had remained in his house and in his harbor, attached to his conveniences and his books. The evening when Norma referred to the "ecosystem," he reflected that he had lived in the heart of a perfectly balanced natural environment but had never become a part of it. He had simply retreated from one environment without actually joining the one to which he had escaped. Like the menu at the dinner party the night of the tsunami, his life on Phoenix had been imported.

The circle of exploration had widened slowly, guided by the gospels of survival. Move slowly. Stop frequently to look and listen. At every distinct bend in the trail, turn around to memorize landmarks so that you will recognize the way back to the beach when you are coming from the other direction. Move cautiously so that you won't be hurt. Keep eyes and ears alert to signs of danger whether from a patch of quicksand, a tricky rockslide, or more evidence of the lurking presence of feral dogs. Advancing slowly and methodically was necessary not only to self-preservation but to reaping the island's natural bounty. Don't overlook anything, the survival scripture said, and when you find something you can't bring back to camp—a grove of a certain kind of tree, for example, or a new fishing hole, or fresh deer sign—observe landmarks accurately so that you can find your way back.

Initially, food had been their first concern. Nothing was more important than knowing where the big hard-shelled Dungeness crab hid in a bed of eel grass, where kelp sheltered cod and bass, where oysters could be picked off the rocks, and where, at low tide, you could dig shrimp as small as your little finger and clams as big as the palm of your hand.

As food supplies increased, there was a subtle shift of interest. They were no longer hungry nor even in danger of going hungry, since the buttery, as Felicia dubbed their stores of dried and smoked foods, was well stocked and constantly growing. The immediacy of staying alive gave way to a new, more sophisticated purpose of making life more comfortable. Now the way to gain applause at the meeting was to find a grove of maples, for that wood was particularly desirable for carving bowls,

spoons, and platters, as well as parts for various primitive weapons. Vine maples were another exciting discovery—they could be woven into baskets for carrying
clams and fish, and their long straight shoots were ideal
for the wattleworks of fish traps. Crabapple wood for
the prongs of a seal spear, yew for bow and arrows—
every wood had its own character. Whether especially
tough or especially flexible, extra soft and light like the
cedar, hard as metal like ironwood, or dense and heavy
as madrona, there was some purpose to which each
species of wood could be put if they, as a group, had the
collective imagination to figure out what it might be.

When Warren Brock discovered a bank of pure blue
clay, a whole new range of possibilities opened up.

"Dishes?" Brock exclaimed at the meeting. "I'm a
sculptor, not a potter. I could use that clay in the creation
of a beautiful work of art, something you would feast
your souls on, and you want a tureen for the codfish
stew. *Merde.* Is this what happens to genius in a primitive
society?"

Felicia patted the top of his head. "Genius," she said
affectionately, "will find a way to make it a *beautiful*
tureen."

Despite his protests, Brock modeled a variety of utensils, and since these had to be baked to be permanent,
he designed an oven, mixing sand and clay and applying
it like cement to a domed armature of green alder twigs.
This kiln led to the idea of building a smaller cooking
oven which in turn gave them their first loaf of bread.

It was coarse, because the wild grains had been ground
with a stone mortar and pestle. It was hard, for Norma's
first effort to make yeast out of wapatoo and honey was
only partially successful, but it was bread. They cut thick
slices, spread them with wild honey, and ate them with
rose hip tea drunk from Brock's gracefully sculptured
mugs.

"I love bread," Felicia said moodily. "God, I had almost forgotten how I love bread."

With some difficulty, Andrew Held repressed a smile.
Felicia's ardent praise for a slice of coarse unleavened
bread brought back memories of Felicia in some of the
finest restaurants in New York and Washington, haughtily
instructing the waiter to take some slightly deficient delicacy back to the kitchen.

How their values had changed! Once Felicia would
refuse a dish because it was seasoned with black pepper
when she believed white pepper was preferred, but no
one had been more excited than she over Norma's recently invented condiment. One of the many varieties of
mushrooms Norma had picked proved, through her six-
bite test, to be nonpoisonous, but it was as hot as a chile.
She dried it, ground it in the stone mortar, and now
their meals were seasoned with "pepper," to Felicia's unqualified delight.

Andrew Held could smile at Felicia's new concepts of
gourmet cuisine, but in the area of cosmetics, her childlike appreciation of the simplest refinements touched him
too deeply to amuse him. The collection of creams and
ointments on her dressing table in Washington had always mystified him. Once, early in their marriage, he had
blundered so badly as to buy her a box of soap, assuming,
because it was scented and ridiculously expensive, that it
would please her. She had thanked him graciously but
the next morning he saw her giving it to the maid. Here
on Phoenix, Felicia made "soap" from the pure white
globes of snowberry. He watched with amazement as she
demonstrated to Norma and Diana how to crush the berries between the palms and rub them vigorously into the
skin. "It's a good cleanser, and an astringent. See? It
cuts right through grease, and try it when you've been
handling fish or wild onion. It seems to kill the odors and
leaves a lovely, fresh smell."

Her second beauty product was one they all shared,
even Donald Campbell. Recalling that some kinds of seaweed were used in the cosmetics industry, Felicia had
conducted several blind experiments with kelp, drying it,
soaking it, squeezing it, but without results until her
numerous laboratory specimens were exposed to a day of
rain. Afterwards, the bulbs were swollen, and small sacs
formed on the inside as if rainwater had been drawn
through the membrane. She opened these sacs, and a
colorless fluid dropped onto her hands. "Like glycerine!"
she exclaimed, rubbing her hands together. "There's no
odor, good or bad, but it isn't sticky and it makes my
skin soft. Hand cream, face cream . . . hurray! We can use
it as sunburn lotion, too."

Andrew Held could not hide a smile, for as sunburn
lotion, Felicia's kelp product was certainly a little late.

Her skin had been burned, peeled, burned again, and tanned, until every visible part of her—arms, thighs, neck, face—was as brown as cedar.

Testing some of the fluid on her own skin, Norma said, "I should think it would also be good for chapped skin."

Norma, Andrew Held reflected, is looking ahead to cold weather, not in an overheated New York apartment but here on Phoenix. Yes, on Phoenix, where mushrooms make pepper and seaweed makes hand lotion and no one, not even Felicia, has spoken of rescue for the last two weeks.

When Felicia charged him with preaching, Andrew Held had defended himself by saying he was only trying to remember things he may never have known. This quip during the first few days after the tsunami had matured into the group philosophy: Remember everything you've forgotten you knew.

When Warren Brock sighed over the lack of sandpaper for finishing his wooden bowls, some long-forgotten memory of Indian custom came awake in Rolf's mind. Dogfish skin. The Indians, especially to the north, had used this small shark in the final polishing and decoration of paddles and dugout canoes. One of Rolf's recent finds was a spot where a low cliff dropped down so sharply that a deep fishing hole lay within reach of a fisherman on shore. It was a natural spot for dogfish, and that night he brought three of the small creatures into camp, where he skinned them, stretched the tough hides over boards, fastened them with lacings of split cedar root, and in a few days presented Warren Brock with a set of sandpaper blocks that were both durable and abrasive.

Donald Campbell's memory of early boyhood in West Virginia led to development of one of the first weapons in the arsenal. A boy in the Campbell family had to earn the money for his first .22, but he could hunt with a slingshot as soon as he was enterprising enough to make one. Careful combing of all the island's inlets and coves had produced many articles for the warehouse, and the day Donald found an inner tube he recognized it as the most important component of his childhood weapon.

Next was a suitable crotch stick, which he selected from one of the farm's apple trees. He cut the stick carefully, each fork almost an inch in diameter and four inches long, with the V between them perfectly symmetrical so that the stick forked evenly in the middle. Finally, he sliced two strips from the inner tube some eight or nine inches long, and pulled the leather tongue out of his shoes to serve as the pocket. With these pieces assembled—one end of each strip of rubber was fastened to a slit cut into the pocket, and the opposite end to an arm of the crotch stick—all he needed was ammunition. That, being round pebbles the size of marbles, could be picked up on almost any beach.

He finished the slingshot on a Saturday night and displayed it boastfully at the meeting. "I used to bring home a sackful of squirrels every time I went out. I might be a little rusty, but anyone want to bet I won't show up with meat the first time out?"

"Meat, yes," Rolf said quietly. "Squirrels, no. There aren't any."

"Yeah. Yeah, I know that." Donald's voice was surly, for he hadn't known it at all. As usual when he felt that in some indefinite way he had "lost," Donald lapsed into angry silence. But he swore that the next day, being a free day, he was going hunting, and never mind the rule about staying in pairs. Wild dogs on Phoenix? He'd believe that when he saw it. Never mind, either, about sticking around until after Sunday "meditation."

In the morning, Donald left the dormitory while the others were still sleeping. With jackknife and slingshot, he headed south. This area was off limits because of the menace of feral dogs. Dr. Held's orders were to stay north of the beach until they had made more weapons so that a party of three or four armed men could go out on a deliberate search. Damn it, he wasn't going to wait. He was a little tired of Dr. Held's orders anyway. Rolf said there were no squirrels. What did he know about the south end?

Pushing through the underbrush, Donald clutched his pouch of pebbles. On the beach, he could replace ammunition as fast as he used it. Now he had to be careful, for once his pouch was empty, he had no weapon other than his jackknife. He knew one thing for sure. He wasn't going to spend his ammunition on rabbits. Rabbits could be snared, as Rolf had already proved. Donald wanted to bag something they hadn't eaten before, something that would make them all open their eyes. He

higher and higher above the ground. Donald could not control his thudding pulse, but his old sureness with the slingshot steadied his hand and sharpened his eye. He drew back, squinting against the bright sky. Sighting the center of the flock over the fork of the stick, he let go. A few seconds later, he was bounding triumphantly across the field.

Two birds had dropped. The first was dead. He scooped it up and ran to the second. It was flopping helplessly in an effort to fly with a broken wing. With a quick twist, he wrung its neck. Six birds. Not bad, not bad at all. Even Mrs. Held would have to admit he had done well.

But he might do even better. He hurried back to the spot where he had left his string of grouse and tied the pigeons up with the others. He was looking out across the tall grass, trying to decide which direction to take, when a sound in the woods made him stiffen.

He whirled around. Though he did not immediately identify the noise, all his senses screamed that he was in danger. Somewhere in the shadows, the rustling underbrush was being parted by the advance of an animal. Seconds ticked by. The whispering movement grew louder. He heard a low growl . . .

Clutching his slingshot, his precious string of birds securely fastened around his waist, Donald ran wildly for the nearest tree. His size and weight were against him, but fear gave him a moment of superhuman strength and daring. When the pack of wild dogs broke through the bushes, he was seven feet off the ground, his feet braced precariously on the lowest limb of the tree, his arms flung desperately around the tree trunk. Below him, four wolfish dogs with shaggy coats and lean hindquarters snarled at each other as they sniffed at the spot where his string of birds had been placed, leaving a small patch of bloody ground.

Andrew Held was deeply troubled, and not by Donald's absence from the evening meeting. The man had obviously gone hunting, and dogged as he was about making a showing with his slingshot, he wouldn't return until it was too dark to take aim. Dr. Held was far more concerned about Blake, who was safe in camp but sitting on a log staring sightlessly across the bay.

Since the loss of his glasses, Blake Mansfield had become more helpless with every passing day. Having suffered another kind of crippling, Andrew Held was particularly sensitive to the younger man's frustration. Blake blamed himself for falling into the well, just as, many years before, the young Andrew Held had cursed his youthful foolishness in leaping onto a fast-moving streetcar. The pity was that before Blake's accident, a new relationship had been developing between the Mansfields, visible to the others in small ways; Norma had begun to laugh easily and naturally, and Blake had ceased his often tiresome politeness. But without his glasses, he was suddenly dependent, on all of them to some extent but on his wife in particular, and his conversation was again punctuated with apologies.

The tragedy was that just as Blake was beginning to get in tune with this wild place, he had been virtually separated from it. He could not see it, he could not go out into it. During the daily trips of discovery, he stayed at camp with Andrew Held and tried to weave baskets of cedar bark and heated twigs. He called his work area the broom factory, a reference to the traditional handicraft for the blind that failed as a joke and brought tears to Norma's eyes.

The only antidote, Dr. Held decided, was to expose the psychic wound and treat it with the realism and humor which these oddly assorted individuals sometimes projected when they got together as a group. For the nightly meeting had been changing. From its original form as a period set aside for recitation of the day's activities and assignment of tomorrow's chores, it was gradually evolving into a forum. "My encounter group," Andrew Held mused when the discussion went beyond practical routine into the sensitive area of feelings and reactions and troublesome memories. But how was he to bring up Blake's problem?

When all but Donald had gathered around the fire, Andrew Held completed the ceremonial marking of the calendar and turned to the group. "I don't know what's keeping Donald. My guess is that he kept hunting until dark."

"He wasn't supposed to go out alone." Blake's voice was peevish, like that of a sick child.

"That may be why he went." Andrew Held looked around the circle, noting the concentration with which they were working. Weaving and plaiting and carving, and the long day had begun shortly after dawn, though it was Sunday, their "free" day.

He tried to keep his own mind on the cedar fibers he was braiding into rope. Blake was doing the same thing, and Dr. Held's attention kept wandering to the other man. Something about the way Blake was squinting seemed familiar. Memory stirred, and he was engulfed by a sense of *déjà vu*. Suddenly a sharp, perfectly focused mental picture flashed onto the screen of his mind. It was of himself, Andrew Held, seated in the oculist's office, squinting through a tiny pinprick in a piece of paper.

"If you ever find yourself in a situation where you don't have your glasses," the doctor had explained, "punch a small hole into a piece of paper and look through it." He had experimented that day, found that it worked, and then forgot about it, until the day he and Felicia had attended an exhibit . . .

"Felicia," he said, breaking into the silence. "Felicia, do you remember that Alaska exhibit we saw in Washington? The section with Eskimo artifacts?"

"Yes, vaguely."

"There was a strange little gadget, entirely of wood. I told you it reminded me of something my oculist had said years before. Something for near-sighted people."

"Ah . . ." Felicia's head lifted and her eyes brightened with understanding. Casting a meaningful look in the direction of Blake Mansfield, she said, "I remember."

"Yes, yes." Conscious that Blake had tuned in and was watching him intently, Andrew Held said carefully, "Eskimo sunglasses. Very thin pieces of wood where the lenses would normally be. Solid wood except for the small holes, one for each eye, like the pinpricks in the piece of paper."

"You were very naughty," Felicia said with a smile. "You plucked them right off the open display shelf and you tried them on. And they worked. They weren't fancy, but they worked."

"Remarkably well."

Blake's depression had touched them all, and the dialogue between Felicia and Andrew excited a round of encouraging comment.

"Hey, Blake, bradda, wakine glasses you like?" Carlo turned to Warren Brock, dropped the light-hearted pidgin and said seriously, "You tell me what to get. Cedar? Maple?"

Blake murmured, "Right now? Tonight?"

Warren Brock shrugged and pursed his lips. "Since I seem to have been chosen to perform a miracle, why keep you all in suspense? Make it cedar, Carlo mio. And bring the screwdriver and some of those pieces of broken glass from the warehouse. This is going to be a real *tour de force* since the missing Donald seems to have absconded with his jackknife."

As Brock worked, they abandoned their own projects and watched the sure, deft movements of the sculptor's hands. He split and trimmed the soft wood until he had two sliver-thin squares. Cutting off the corners to make two hexagons, he smoothed the edges with dogfish sandpaper. After careful measurements, he cut temples and a half-frame; these were also of wood but thicker than the lenses so that they could be grooved. The lenses were then fitted into the half-frame and temples and the frame hinged together with little pegs of wood. The tiny holes in the lenses were made by heating one of Felicia's hairpins and burning as well as boring through the soft cedar.

It was late when Brock finished, for he worked with painstaking care and the creative artist's total unawareness of the passage of time. At intervals, he tried out his work, commandeering Blake's head as imperiously as a *couturier* directing a model. At the last fitting, he adjusted the temples over Blake's ears, studied the effect from the front, and lifted Norma's arm so that the wristwatch was at a normal reading distance from Blake's eyes.

"What time is it?" he asked quietly.

The circle waited expectantly. The moment of tension lengthened as Blake moved his wife's arm a little forward and a little back, until the face of his watch was clearly illuminated by firelight. "Half past ten," he said. "Half past ten!" he repeated, and broke into jubilant laughter. While the others cheered, Andrew and Felicia exchanged looks of relief, gratitude, and mututal understanding.

"How do I look, Norma?" Blake said happily.

Norma was laughing as she hadn't for many days. "Like Dr. Caligari," she said. "But very handsome—and very distinguished."

They had been so intent on the fitting of the glasses

that no one noticed Donald Campbell stumble across the beach with a string of game birds dangling from his hand.

"Donald!" Dr. Held exclaimed as the big man emerged into the firelight.

In a hoarse voice, Donald spilled out his story. Of four dogs, snarling at the base of the tree. Of endless time—one hour, two hours?—gripping the rough tree trunk, fearful that the limb he was standing on would crack under his weight. Of shooting at the dogs and missing, time after time, until his pebbles were gone. Of deciding, as night fell, that his only escape would be to sacrifice some of his birds. Of the fight between the dogs when he threw down three grouse and their vicious yelping as he leaped to the ground and ran blindly through the woods, running and falling, picking himself up and running again, until the ugly sounds were lost in the night.

"You're not bitten?" Norma asked. "You're all right?"

Ignoring the question, Donald flung the remainder of his prize at Norma's feet. "There. That's three birds, anyway. We ain't had nothing like *that* to eat before."

His entrance wasn't turning out right. No one was admiring the game, and when Dr. Held asked, "You went *south,* Donald?" they frowned with disapproval instead of patting him on the back for being brave. All they could talk about was the pack of wild dogs. "How many? How far south had you gone? Were they big dogs? Did they follow you?" He had their attention, all right, as long as he was answering their questions about the dog pack. He had been plenty scared. He could understand that they were, too. But that wasn't the whole story. He wanted their applause for his skill with a slingshot. He waited hopefully for the voice that said how fine the birds were and how clever he had been to bring down two at a time. He looked around the campfire, searching for a sympathetic face, and for the first time noticed the crazy wood mask Blake Mansfield was wearing.

His startled "huh?" and his stare dealt the lethal blow to his sickly hope that, for once, Donald Campbell would be the center of the show. Donald, the grouse, the slingshot, even their skittery questions about the dogs were suddenly pushed into the background as the group's attention refocused on Blake's eyeglasses. They all gathered around Blake, testing his vision by holding up different objects, clapping as one by one he proved he could identify them. Diana's expression had brightened when she looked at the pigeons, but now even she seemed to have forgotten them. Angry and disappointed, Donald walked to the far end of the beach and sat there alone until the chilling night wind seeped through his clothing and sent him back to the heat of the campfire.

With his keen blue eyes masked by hexagonals of wood, Blake looked sightless as he hadn't before, and that made his agility seem like a miracle. The wooden lenses were far less effective than their civilized ground-glass counterparts, but they gave Blake a greater sense of freedom for he was relieved of his obsessive fear of breaking his glasses. If he did, Warren could make another pair in an evening.

Within a week, he had become so accustomed to his primitive spectacles that once more he was part of a discovery team, foraging, hunting, collecting all over Phoenix Island. He moved more slowly than the others, but they were repeatedly astonished by his ability to spot small objects the rest of them had missed. The pinpoint holes through which he saw the world narrowed the area of his vision, but at the same time seemed to sharpen the focus, like tiny magnifying glasses. His confidence grew as his skill increased and he was no longer shackled to the broom factory. No one was surprised when he proposed they return to the bee tree, and he volunteered to take charge of obtaining the rest of the honey and relocating the colony.

"Now that we have an ax we can fell the tree. We should do it immediately so that the bees will have time to build up stores in a new location before the cold weather sets in. It's already late for this and some of the colony may starve over the winter, but we can leave them some supplies. Dr. Held tells me that even in January the temperature seldom goes down to freezing, so they're not likely to suffer from cold. If I can locate the queen, I think we can have our honey and eat it, too."

This time the bee-tree team was equipped with an ax, for which Brock had lovingly carved a graceful handle. He had also carved a wooden trough like a small dugout canoe, and a larger version of the alder bark "pails" that

had been their first and simplest Phoenix-made containers. Once more, their heads were protected by the comical
combinations of the girls' underpants and torn gill net
they called bee veils, and they carried cedar bark torches
and damp seaweed as the "smoker."

When they reached the bee tree, the bees were earnestly at work storing up for winter. The three men, Blake,
Rolf, and Donald, walked to the foot of the snag, set
down their equipment and discussed their first move,
while the workers still flew in and out of the tree without a single detour to inspect what was going on below.

"Amazing!" Blake breathed through the protective
mask of his wife's nylon underpants. "It's just what they
told us at the apiary. Honeybees are such dedicated
workers, they don't bother to protect themselves. If they
knew we were about to destroy their home, they'd be
attacking us or moving their colony to another tree."

"They'll know soon enough," Rolf said drily. "And
they'll let us know they know, too."

With an experienced eye, Rolf calculated the direction
in which the tree should fall, and on that side cut a pie-
shaped slice out of the trunk. While Blake combined
wet seaweed with dry cedar bark, creating a cloud of
white smoke, Rolf and Donald took turns with the ax.

"Keep up the smoke," Rolf urged, for the bees, though
confused, were flying around drunkenly at the mouth of
the hive and hovering a foot or two over their heads. As
the blows of the ax continued, the peaceful hum became
an angry buzz. "Smoke!" Rolf gasped, swinging the ax
with a wide lateral stroke. There was a cracking sound
as the old snag leaned, a rending and tearing as it caught
and ripped the limbs of nearby trees, and a violent splintering as the trunk hit the forest floor and, like a fallen
beast, shuddered and lay still.

They were lucky, they decided that evening at the
meeting. The old tree had dropped as Rolf planned it,
onto the side where most of its limbs grew so that they
cushioned its fall. They were also lucky because the bees
were at least temporarily stunned by the crash.

The moment the tree hit the ground, Blake dropped to
his knees and blew smoke into the gaping entrance of
the hive. Though pacified by smoke and shocked by the
fall, the bees were already at work. Like troops during an
orderly evacuation, they began leaving the tree.

They had been filling their honey stomachs, Blake explained, preparatory to moving operations to another tree. A few undisciplined workers broke ranks and stung him in three places, but the main swarm hovered in the air where the entrance to the tree had been and, in a short time, flew away.

Their next stroke of luck was that the hollow tree split open so easily. With his stone hammer, Rolf drove six or eight stone wedges into the weakened trunk and then worked up and down the line, pounding each wedge a little deeper every time. Finally he inserted the screwdriver into the crack, withdrew it, and tested the tip of it on his tongue. "Honey," he announced. "I'm through on this side."

They rolled the log over, and this time Donald drove in the wedges. They were arm-weary, glistening with sweat, their eyes stung from the smoke, and Blake's bee stings had swollen into painful lumps, but at last the two sides of the tree lay side by side.

"Fantastic!" Blake's tone was worshipful. "I've read about it. I never thought I'd see it."

The comb was six feet long, firmly anchored at the top and at intervals along the sides of the cavity. Except for oddly shaped cells where the irregularity of the hollow did not permit perfect symmetry, the comb was made up of hexagonal cells, all but a few exactly the same size.

Through the tiny holes in his wooden lenses, Blake's eyes peered anxiously at a group of large cells near the entrance to the hive. As his focus sharpened, he felt a surge of excitement. His glasses met their first important test as they picked out a bee larger, longer, and slimmer than the others. "I think this is the queen," he said eagerly, and got to his feet.

Ignoring the bees still circling above the fallen honeycomb, Blake picked up the outsize alder pail and wedged it securely into an angular space between limb and trunk of a nearby tree. On its side, like a cylinder of bark closed at one end, the primitive pail was to be the new hive. Blake returned to the honey tree, dug his thumb and forefinger into the comb, pulled out a large glob of honey, and smeared it on the inside of the pail.

A dozen bees began humming around the mouth of the pail. A dozen more were hovering over the queen. Blake

said, "I'll borrow the jackknife . . ." With utmost care, he
lifted the queen and gently clipped the end of one of her
wings. Pursued by a cluster of bees, he carried her to
the nearest tree and set her down tenderly on a branch
opposite the alder pail hive. The smaller bees followed
their queen and immediately began collecting around her.

"We'll hope for the best," Blake said prayerfully. A
few minutes later the team of bee hunters was on its way
back to camp with two or three hundred pounds of
honey. By the time they left the woods, the air was full
of bees.

Rolf called, "Hey, Blake, your glasses really worked.
I couldn't spot the queen and I'm supposed to have
twenty-twenty."

"I'm glad it worked out," Blake answered absent-
mindedly, for he was already planning how to construct
more and better alder cylinders in order to enlarge the
hive.

Though they had quarreled, Warren Brock's young man,
Kirk Aspinwall II, had left Wolf Island with the understanding that his lover had not withdrawn his patronage
entirely and would, within a week or two, drop down to
San Francisco for a few days. Local newspaper reports of
the August fourth tsunami did not mention Wolf, so when
his mother was out of the house he cloistered himself in
her bedroom beyond the hearing of the servants and put
through a collect call to Brock's home on Wolf. No one
answered.

During the next few days, he tried repeatedly to telephone. He also wrote Brock several letters, each more
frantic and pleading than the last. On the pretext of doing some advance study for fall quarter at the U, he spent
hours at the public library, combing through Seattle newspapers for references to tsunami damage in the Outer
Islands. "Fifteen known dead. Volunteers compile list of
the missing . . ." was the extent of the "news" about
Wolf, and by the end of the week Kirk gave up hope
that names would be furnished. There was ample coverage in San Francisco as well as in Seattle newspapers of
the fate of Dr. Andrew Held, world-famous physicist.
Large black headlines gave various versions of "Coast
Guard search reveals total destruction of scientist's island
home." Editorials commented on the irony of the "Fa-

ther of the H-Bomb" going to his death as a result of a
tidal wave triggered by a hydrogen bomb test. But Kirk
had no reason to associate Warren Brock with Dr. Held
or with Phoenix Island. The more he thought about it,
the more he was convinced that Brock had left Wolf
before the disastrous storm. He hadn't answered the telephone because he had already departed for California.
Why, then, hadn't Brock called? Was he being punished?

Kirk dialed Brock's studio in Marin County. A tape
recording advised him that the telephone had been disconnected. That was as usual. Though lavish in some ways
—Brock had once given him *two* wristwatches, one to
harmonize with blues and grays, the other for brown,
red, and orange tones—he had pet economies, such as
having his California telephone disconnected while he was
in Washington. But maybe Brock *was* in his studio, and
teasing him, making him wait for a call. Maybe Brock was
in one of his working moods and had cut himself off from
the world in every way possible, pulling out the telephone
jack, refusing to pick up his mail, sending someone else
out for groceries.

Kirk's pulse raced at the thought, for *he* had been that
someone else. In a creative fit, Brock wanted his loving
—wild, intense loving—several times a day. If he was in
seclusion now, holed up in his studio during a working
binge, there was someone with him. Someone else.

Hurt and suspicious, Kirk violated one of Brock's absolute rules: He called on Brock's mother.

She was a tiny woman with a dainty, Valentine face
marked by a hundred fine wrinkles. Her shrewd blue
eyes rested on him sympathetically as he stammered out
his mission. He was a friend, he had done some modeling
for Brock, he had expected to hear from him about pos-
ing the first week in September . . .

Brock's little-bird mother perched on an elegantly
gilded chair and nodded as he stumbled to the end of his
recitation. "I'm sorry to bother you. I shouldn't have
come."

"Nonsense!" she said pertly. "I know. Warren told you
not to. Silly boy. He doesn't want me to know of his
preference for beautiful young men." She sprang off her
chair, hopped to a French antique sideboard, and filled
two stemmed glasses with a dark amber liquid. "Here,"
she said, thrusting one of them into Kirk's hand. "We'll

have some sherry. We both need it. Because I don't have the faintest idea where Warren is, and that's very unusual. As a person he is a complete eccentric. As a lover, I presume he takes more than he gives. But as a son, he is the soul of filial piety, and he has never given me a moment's concern, as to his whereabouts, that is, and his state of health. Until now." She sipped her sherry, her bright little eyes appraising Kirk over the rim of the glass. "I think we should make some inquiries, don't you, Mr. Aspinwall? You and I are really all he has. Where shall we start?"

Chapter Twenty-Seven

In a village on the coast of Maine, Norma Mansfield's uncle, Cabot Sterling, was biting his thin lower lip in a combination of anxiety and displeasure. He was a spare man with fine bones, narrow shoulders, a severe profile, and a wise gleam in his deep-set eyes. For several weeks thoughts of his niece had intruded into the serene little world of his retirement, a world he had taken some pains to insulate against disturbing emotions.

At first he had been puzzled. Norma was always very good about writing. She was particularly faithful whenever she traveled. A typed itinerary, mailed before she and Blake left New York, was always followed by a steady flow of postcards with appropriate comments in a careful script, reporting the high points of their trip. But this summer he had received only one brief note on the letterhead of the Olympic Hotel in Seattle, Washington.

Perplexity had given way to irritation as her silence lengthened. Though she was his heir, he had never made demands. Norma had always written him because she *wanted* to write to him. Therefore it was incredible that she had left on vacation without sending her itinerary. It was inexcusable to be gone for so long without offering some explanation for her most unusual behavior. Cabot Sterling was too much of a gentleman to consider revising his will, but he was certainly going to express his disappointment when she got back to New York.

The newsmagazine resting on his knees supplied the reason that today he was more worried than vexed. In the obituary column he read, "HELD, Dr. Andrew. Victim of tidal wave at age of 62. See *Science*." Turning quickly to the full article, he read on with increasing nervousness.

His old friend had died as a result of the August fourth tsunami, either at sea in his cruiser *Trident* or when his remote private island was struck by a series of monstrous waves that crushed and carried out to sea every vestige of the estate he had built on its shores, except the pilings on which the pier had rested. As he followed the science editor's eloquent review of Dr. Held's career in nuclear physics and his sensational conversion to the philosophy of disarmament, Cabot Sterling's mind kept sorting out facts and dates. Computer-like, it presented him with a print-out that said Norma may have been in the Seattle area at the time of the tsunami.

He rose briskly from his comfortable reading chair and crossed the room to a large oak roll-top desk. Because he never lost or misfiled anything, he was able to put his hand on Norma's note immediately. The postmark was blurred. He opened one of several small shallow drawers, picked up a round magnifying glass with a brass handle, and adjusted it at a proper level above the envelope. August first. Three days before the disastrous storm. And she was carrying a letter of introduction to Andrew Held.

Cabot Sterling sat down at the desk and selected one of the sharply pointed pencils he always kept in a row beside a pad of lined white paper. He must get his thoughts in order. At eighty-one years of age, he was finding this was more easily achieved by writing things down. In a few minutes, he had completed his list.

1. Telephone New York apartment. If no answer, then:
2. Telephone Blake's law office. If no definite news, then:
3. Write to Seattle
   a. Manager of Olympic Hotel
   b. Police Department
   c. Coast Guard headquarters

This done, he left his desk and proceeded to the telephone in the front hall. With orderly procedure determined, the wraithlike sense of foreboding faded. Only a whisper persisted, a tendril of fear rising from the page of neatly-penciled notes to ask him, And if you've learned nothing when you get to the end of the list, what then?

Rolf's desire to bag a deer was becoming an obsession. He had identified their trails and their sleeping places. He had seen fresh prints cut into soft ground near the pond and had come upon places they had passed so recently that their droppings were still warm. Deer meant more than venison. It meant bone for tools and implements. Leather for clothing and bedding. Rawhide thongs for the drill for starting a fire and for various primitive weapons. Above all, it was big game, the largest on Phoenix Island, an animal that challenged the hunter with its acute senses and awed him with its speed and uncanny elusiveness. But there was nothing in the arsenal with which to kill it.

Their collection of ingenious weapons-without-gunpowder was providing a regular supply of rabbit, ptarmigan, wild doves, chipmunks, and raccoon. Besides Rolf's twitch-up snares and Donald's slingshot, the arsenal offered a variety of spears with fire-hardened shafts and tips of razor-sharp shale or carved madrona. There were short, sturdy sticks which could be bound to the jackknife or the yellow-handled screwdriver to create a potentially lethal dagger. And finally, there were three hunting slings similar to the one David used to slay Goliath.

These were diamond-shaped pieces of leather five inches long and three inches wide, with two-foot thongs looped and tied through slits at each corner of the longer dimension. In the center of these leather pockets, tiny diamond-shaped holes were cut so that the projectile, a smooth round stone, would nestle there securely until the hunter wanted to release it.

Donald, Rolf, and Diana practiced daily, for the hunter's sling, though far more powerful than the slingshot, was also less accurate in inexperienced hands. The end of one thong was tied into a loop which fitted over the middle finger of the right hand. The same hand grasped the other thong between thumb and index finger. After lowering the pocket until the stone rested against his leg, the hunter raised his right arm and whirled the sling around his head, gaining speed and power with every circular sweep. As the rock came from behind for the fourth or fifth time, his right hand released the loose thong, and the stone shot forward with great force.

Andrew Held often watched their practice sessions and observed a lively competition develop between the three of them. Donald, the biggest and strongest, was clumsy at first, while Diana, whose slender body weighed less than half as much as Donald's, was naturally coordinated and graceful. From the first she went through the ritual of lifting, whirling, and releasing as if it were a dance. Dr. Held set up targets, and gradually they all developed a remarkable degree of accuracy. But when Carlo suggested that Rolf was now ready to get his deer, Rolf shook his head. "This is no way to hunt deer. You'd have to hit him in the head, and even then you'd only stun him."

"How about a trap?"

"No good," Rolf said stubbornly. "You have to bait a trap, and there's no such thing as bait a deer will take."

Carlo smiled broadly. "Eh, bradda, whatsa matta? I think you no feel like catching deah. Maybe it's moah betta we use a beeg snare, or sumteen? I dunno."

"Snare?" Rolf scoffed. "Not for deer. Slings, traps, snares, that's for little stuff. I'm going to make a bow and arrow."

"Hal-lo dayah!" Carlo said approvingly. "Okay. Go make da bow and arrow for da deah. I going make harpoon so I can get my seal. We going see who can bag his game first, okay?"

From then on, evening work sessions were enlivened by the rivalry between Rolf and Carlo. During the day, Diana helped both men collect and cure their materials. Yew for the bow and the harpoon shaft. Cedar for arrow shafts, and Douglas fir for the harpoon. Rabbit skin for the bow hunter's wrist guard and feathers for the fletching of his arrows. Willow bark to be pounded and twisted into a harpoon line as well as a tumpline for the sling Rolf would need to haul game. Beach agates from which arrowheads could be chipped, and a softer stone to be chiseled and ground into doughnut-shaped tools for straightening the cedar arrow shafts.

Night after night they worked, peeling, rubbing, chipping, gouging, and warming wood to make it soft or firing it to make it hard. They experimented, and failed. They finished an arrow or a harpoon point, and it broke. But they persisted, Carlo good-naturedly shrugging off every reverse, Rolf growing more determined every time he was disappointed.

"What patience!" Felicia commented one evening when Rolf was laboring over a stone with the intense concentration of a diamond cutter entrusted with the Hope Diamond. "And everything takes so much *time,* because we can't make something until we've made the tools to make it with, and before that we have to search for the raw materials to make the tools to make it with . . . Look," she said, holding up the crude loom on which she was weaving a mat of cedar bark. "Think of how long it took you to put this loom together, Andy. And I was days and days rustling through the woods looking for cedar, and peeling the bark, and shredding it."

"Never mind, dear," Warren Brock said brightly. "I was a world-famous sculptor and now I spend two days making a potty. But we're not getting union scale."

Andrew Held smiled. "We're certainly learning a different attitude toward the value of time. Industrial society calculates the laborer's worth not by what he produces but by how much he can produce and how fast he can do it. 'Time is money'—we've heard that so often that we believe it. But on Phoenix, this great twentieth-century truth is a lie. We have nothing *but* time."

"If I were getting minimum wages," Norma mused, "the flour I ground for the bread would cost fifteen dollars a pound."

Dr. Held nodded in agreement. "Of course. But did you make the bread in order to earn money?"

"No. I made it so we wouldn't be hungry."

"Ah . . ." Dr. Held smiled at her. "That's the heart of it. Survival."

On the same day, Carlo set out with his harpoon and Rolf with his bow and arrow.

"See you tonight, bradda," Carlo sang when they separated at the top of the hill.

Rolf's dark eyes were bright with excitement. The bow was smooth in his hand, and the quiver of arrows rested lightly across his back. "Good luck," he said, smiling. "If you get back to camp before I do, get a good fire going. We're having venison steak tonight."

Rolf moved through the woods swiftly until he was approaching an area where he had seen a deer trail. The woods at the edge of the pond was the likeliest spot, especially at dusk when the animals would leave cover to drink at the waterhole and might venture farther to graze in the meadow or nibble windfall apples in the orchard. But Rolf had seen signs of deer in many other places, and today he spotted them long before he reached the old farm or the pond.

In a brushy pocket in the woods, the bushes were trampled, the trunks of the trees were skinned, and undergrowth and small lower limbs were broken. It looked as if an infuriated beast had deliberately attacked everything in sight. And the damage was recent, for the wounds in the tree trunks were still sticky with sap. A buck. A buck in the rutting season, expressing his pugnacious instincts by ripping up the bushes with his antlers.

Rolf dropped to his knees and studied the forest floor. Although the carpet of dead leaves and pine needles had been disturbed, he couldn't find marks to indicate how big the animal might be nor which way he had gone. But this was definitely buck territory. He chose the direction in which a few crushed leaves and broken twigs hinted at a trail.

He walked stealthily, keeping his eyes on the ground. If he stepped on a dry twig, the snap would shock the silence like the crack of a gun. If he bent a low-growing limb, it would spring back when he released it, and even this soft twang would be warning to the buck if he was close by.

As Rolf proceeded, the signs improved. The faint trail became wider, more distinct. He found an occasional tuft of hair and scattered droppings. And finally, a print. It told him that, so far, he hadn't frightened his prey. The hind foot was almost on top of the heart-shaped indentation made by the forefoot. The animal was walking, not running. Furthermore, the prints toed out a little. This buck was a big one.

Rolf saw him first on the edge of the meadow. He was a magnificent animal, a three-pointer, with beautiful haunches, a noble head, and an arrogant upstanding white tail that kept switching as he grazed contentedly, secure in his isolation.

Rolf stole forward. He had hunted deer since he was ten years old and had never gone through a season without getting his buck. It was a different story now. His experience in tracking still applied, but his skill with a rifle was useless. What was the range of his bow and arrow as compared with a 30.30? He could only guess. How deeply would his stone arrow penetrate? And if he only wounded the animal, what were his chances of getting a second shot?

When he stepped into the open field, he was so tense that his chest tightened, repressing the rise and fall of his breathing. He had an arrow in place, left hand clamped on the bow, three fingers of the right circling the bowstring and small end of the shaft. He was in luck—the deer was to the north of him and the tall trees to the east cast long protective shadows. He had advanced twenty or thirty feet before the buck lifted his head and slowly, majestically, turned to inquire.

Rolf froze. Again he was lucky. The light afternoon breeze was coming from the northeast; the deer had not caught his scent. If he came up behind the deer, he increased his chances of not being seen, but to get a good straight shot, he would have to approach from the side. With a high-powered rifle, he would have aimed at the head, and at a distance of a hundred and fifty yards. With bow and arrow, it would be foolish to shoot at anything more than forty yards away, and he needed the largest possible target. Not the head, nor the soft vulnerable neck and throat, but the body, just behind the foreleg.

He continued straight ahead, still behind the buck, and then began to circle to the right. He was supremely patient, he was light on his feet, he was stealthy, and he never took his eyes from the target. These attributes of the hunter, learned in boyhood, brought him closer to the deer than he had dared hope he could come. Judging by what he had learned in target practice during the last few days, he was well within range. This was the moment to shoot.

Keeping his eyes on the buck, Rolf lowered his bow until the arrowhead pointed to the ground. In that position, he pushed forward on the bow and pulled back on the bowstring, until the tension on the curving bow reached an explosive maximum and his upper arms and shoulders were as taut as his weapon. At that point he swung the bow upward and through narrowed eyes lined up the tip of the arrowhead with the buck's forequarter. In the same instant, the great deer raised his head and Rolf released the arrow.

Startled, the animal leaped forward. The afternoon quiet was shattered by his loud whistling snort. But his leap was delayed by a split second. As his large brown eyes identified the enemy, he hesitated, and that would have been enough had Rolf's arrow gone straight to the target. But the shaft was imperfect, and the crude agate arrowhead was not balanced. The deadly projectile flew in a slight arc, missed the target by an almost invisible margin, and dropped to the ground fifty feet beyond the startled deer. Rolf raced forward, fitting another arrow as he ran, but he was too late. The buck, still snorting, bounded out of range and disappeared into the shadow of the woods.

"Don't feel too bad, bradda. I didn't get my seal, either." Laughing, Carlo pointed to the carvings on the totem calendar. "But we try again tomorrow, eh? Tomorrow night Brock goan cut two little pictures, a deer right here on this side, a seal over here on the other. Tomorrow, that's the day."

Tomorrow brought another double failure, and so did the day after that. On the third day, Rolf spotted a spike deer, but again, his arrow missed and he returned to camp empty-handed. Carlo was already there, and he had bagged a seal.

He had also injured himself. The flesh along his right hip and thigh was gouged and bleeding. There were deep jagged cuts in his right forearm and bruises all over his body. He explained, with a wide white smile, that it was a good thing he hadn't knocked out his teeth, because when his harpoon broke, he threw himself on top of the seal and bit him to death.

"Tell us the rest of the story," Warren Brock exclaimed, clapping his hands like a happy child. "But be quick about it, because I think you're bleeding to death."

"What was it, barnacles?" Rolf asked.

Carlo nodded. "Yeah, bradda. I wen rassle da bugga. I had to. He was shu-ah strong. He wen try to drag me off the rock. I wen hold on and I had the knife but we was thrashing around and struggling and all kine stuff and asswen I wen get it. And I wen get it good!"

In two months they had all been bruised and cut, but no one as seriously as Carlo. Norma looked with concern at the worst of the wounds. "We really ought to do something to dress this."

"Rolf, Diana . . ." Warren Brock, after a hasty glimpse of Carlo's bloody thigh, had been studiously avoiding the

sight. "Your grandmothers told you all manner of marvelous things. Veritable *founts* of folk wisdom, judging
by all the ideas you two have come up with. Wouldn't
they have had some nostrums for our suffering seal-stab-
ber?"

Rolf signaled to Diana. "Have we got some of the
stuff I was using for the bows?"

"Yes."

"Any spruce?"

"I think so." Diana ran to the warehouse and returned
with limbs of spruce and yew. While the others looked
on curiously, Rolf stripped off a handful of yew needles.
"Lie down, Carlo," he said, and stuffed the needles into
his mouth. He chewed energetically for several minutes,
and then pushed the pulp into his cheek and leaned over
Carlo's leg.

"Gracious *Maude!*" Brock exclaimed. "I thought so! He's
going to spit!"

As Rolf's saliva filled the open wound, Carlo winced.
"Hey brudda, that wen hurt!"

Rolf scooped out his cheek with his forefinger and
wiped his mouth on his hand. "It's supposed to. But it
helps healing."

"Hey, now what you goan do wid that?" Carlo asked
as Rolf picked up the spruce and pinched off a small
sac of gum.

"My grandmother was Quinault," Rolf answered, as
if that explained everything, and applied the sticky substance to the wound. He stood up. "Next thing is to boil
some pine bark. Lots of bark, not much water. Then you
wash all your cuts with it, two or three times a day."

Carlo raised himself on one elbow. "Okay, Doc. How
long have I got?"

"Another fifty years." Smiling, Rolf extended his hand
and helped Carlo to his feet. "Unless you keep wrestling
bull seals."

"Not me, bradda. I'm goin' make me a better harpoon."

Andrew Held looked intently into the Hawaiian's
dark expressive face. "You spent three days on the one
that broke."

"I was in a hurry," Carlo said genially, dropping the
pidgin as he usually did when he spoke to Andrew Held.
"I had to beat out Rolf. This time, I'll spend six days.
Or eight or ten. If it takes a month, I'll get another seal."

"A month?" Blake had removed his cedar glasses and his eyes squinted in the general direction of Carlo's voice. "Another *month,* here on Phoenix?"

"When are you going to quit thinking about being rescued?" Donald Campbell's voice was as close to expressing hostility toward Blake Mansfield as he had come since the day he had been invited to use his first name. "Maybe some of us don't want to leave. Did you ever think of that?"

No one replied. In silence, they began preparations for the evening meal.

While they skinned the seal, stripped it of its blubber, and stuffed it with wild onions, wapatoo roots, wild thyme, and grated wild horseradish, Andrew Held speculated as to the reason the word "rescue" had silenced them so completely. Which of the nine might be included in the "some of us" Donald felt might not want to leave? Felicia . . . How about Felicia? Andrew Held could venture some guesses about the others and had some confidence in his accuracy. But Felicia, for whom he cared more than any other living human being, remained an utter mystery—as usual.

By the end of the evening they had agreed to establish "the apothecary," where they would keep herbs, leaves, barks, seeds, infusions—anything they had found to be healing or curative. And Rolf had decided to hunt deer by some means other than bow and arrow.

"I haven't given up," he said quietly. "But I need more practice. Just being an Indian doesn't make me a good shot with a bow and arrow. That big buck is up there some place, and I'm not going to wait until I'm sharp enough with the bow to get him. I'll try another way."

"What way?" Donald asked. "A snare?"

Rolf's low voice was hard as ironwood. "Not me. I said before, a snare is for small game. But I will try a trap. Something like a fall-log trap."

Rolf set out the next morning with the ax. All that day and the next, he worked to perfect a trap clever enough to attract a deer and strong enough to hold him. It was a stockade eight feet tall, with an opening framed on two sides by grooved boards. A door was inserted into these grooves and suspended above the entrance by a rope

looped over an overhanging limb. The opposite end of
the rope hung inside the stockade and was tied to a sharp
stick on which the bait, an apple, was impaled. Using
rocks, sticks, vines and cedar bark rope, Rolf devised
a weighted triggering mechanism so that a pull on the
apple would release the door, dropping it between guide-
poles to close the entrance.

A week earlier he had stated emphatically that a deer
would never take bait, but at the meeting he reported he
had baited his stockade trap with an apple, admitting
that he might have been wrong. He was up early, racing
through the woods with the knife for skinning deer and
the carrying sling for hauling it back.

His stockade was in a shambles. The entrance was
closed, so his system of weights and forked sticks had
worked. The bait had been taken. Half the apple was gone
and on the remaining half the teethmarks of a deer were
very clear. But the animal, though the door had closed,
was gone. Its escape route was obvious. A large section
of the stockade was broken down. The buck had charged
the wall, kicking and splintering it as he leaped for freedom.

While he was rebuilding the trap, making if far more
sturdy than before, Rolf hardly spoke, even to Diana. His
dark eyes looked inward, focused on an adversary he
could see with his eyes closed. After the trap was repaired, he baited it as before. For two days the apple
was untouched, and the trap door hung harmlessly over
the entrance.

On the third morning, Rolf saw even at a distance
that the door was closed. He ran, triumph and excitement surging through his body. Grasping his knife like a
dagger, he peered through a gap in the stockade.

His game had taken the bait and was still enjoying it.
Standing on his hind feet, a big raccoon held the apple
between his forepaws and was energetically demolishing the fruit. Rolf leaped to the door, lifted it, and charged
through with his knife hand in the air. But the raccoon
was too quick. He scrambled up the tree, settled himself in a crotch well beyond Rolf's reach, and looked
down owlishly, a piece of apple clasped between his paws.

Chapter Twenty-Eight

ANDREW Held listened to Rolf's account with growing admiration for the young man. He told his story simply, without self-justification, and with a good deal of humor as he described the raccoon's black-masked face and impertinent expression. Rolf had been humbled, but he was not a whit less determined to get his deer, and by now, "his deer" meant the big buck. No spike, no two-pointer. In the morning, he said, he'd build a snare.

Andrew Held looked quickly at Donald Campbell, who had repeatedly suggested a snare and had as often been ignored. This could be Donald's moment of triumph, the rare and wonderful occasion when he, the black sheep of the family, could inflate his unhappy ego with a thoroughly justified I-told-you-so. But Donald did not speak. He was looking directly at Rolf, his scarred face split by a grin so broad it looped between his ears. And Rolf was smiling back. "Yeah, buddy," Rolf said, laughing. "Just like you tried to tell me. A snare. That's what I've got to. I just had to get there my way."

Rolf chose the site carefully. It should be on a well-marked deer trail, preferably one leading to the watering hole. There would be no way to select one particular animal. This bothered him because he was more intent than ever on bagging the big buck. However a snare would not kill a deer, only catch and hold it, like a lasso. The killing would have to be done with a spear or knife.

At a spot in the woods just north of the pond, Rolf set up the snare. It was a larger and heavier version of his rabbit twitch-up. He suspended a lasso-like loop from the limb of a tree as the same height aboveground as the head of a deer. Some distance from the deer trail he bent an older sapling into an inverted U and secured the top with a forked stick driven into the ground. The far end of the lasso was tied to the twitch-up. If all went well, the deer in the course of following his habitual trail would try to walk or leap through the loop. The pull on the rope would release the twitch-up, and as the sapling sprang back, the lasso at the other end of the rope would tighten around the deer's body. At that point, a successful kill would depend on how quickly the hunter reached the snared animal and how skillful he was with a knife. The snare would not restrain a two-hundred-pound buck for very long.

The morning he left camp to build the snare, Rolf told Diana that the only way he would get his deer would be to stay hidden as near the deer trail as he could get without being scented.

"All day?" she asked. "And all night?"

"However long it takes," he replied. "Until I get my deer."

At dusk on the first day, a fawn walked into the snare and hung choking with his hind hooves pawing frantically until Rolf loosened the knot and released him. He reset the snare and went back to his hiding place in a thicket ten or twelve feet off the trail.

He slept fitfully, awakening at every night sound. The darkness was alive with invisible, rustling creatures, but he held himself still, tensed for the moment when the first pale beginnings of the new day would filter through the trees and the deer would leave their sleeping places and come to drink at the pond.

The sky was silver-gray and streaked with pink when Rolf heard the sound—a soft snort, the crackling of a broken twig, the whispering movement of underbrush. Though he wanted to leap to his feet, Rolf forced himself to stay down, keep hidden, and wait. With his knife gripped tightly, he peered through the bushes, almost holding his breath as the sounds grew sharper and nearer.

At last the deer appeared. A buck. Smaller than the magnificent animal he wanted, but a fine big deer with two points on his furry antlers. He was following the trail faithfully, complacent in his solitude, wary of no creature except another buck big enough to challenge him. He was so near the noose that Rolf's muscles tensed in anticipation, as if it were his own head about to go through the loop. And then suddenly the deer stiffened. After a moment so brief Rolf didn't have time to realize what was happening, the buck leaped sideways off the path, thundering through the brush and back into the deep woods.

Rolf groaned and beat the forest floor with an impotent fist. He had been spotted, perhaps scented. For several minutes he thought of giving up. He had to post himself near the trail, and that very necessity had defeated him. His hiding place was no good.

His eyes stung with fatigue and his body ached from being held so long in cramped positions. He had been here for twenty-four hours and the food and water he carried with him were exhausted. But the stream wasn't far, and there were still apples in the orchard and blackberries in the field . . . He stood up. His mother's people were better hunters than he, but his father's people, the Welsh, often succeeded through their trait of sheer endurance. What he lacked in skill he might still make up through stubbornness.

An hour later he was back at the snare, refreshed by cool brook water and several small red apples. Looking over his ambush, he realized his error. He had been hiding at ground level, where he could be seen and scented. But deer don't look up. If he was above the trail, and if he figured the direction of the wind . . .

He studied the nearest trees, looking for one with sturdy limbs and some concealing foliage. Ten minutes later he was sitting in the crotch of a fir, with the rough bark biting into his buttocks, and pitch and bark fragments sticking to scratches on his hands and arms.

The long day went by, and then the night. He fought sleep for fear of falling from his perch, and he fought the numbness that his tortured body marshaled to screen out pain. At dawn on the third day he saw his deer.

He came down the trail with delicate, dancy steps, wearing his antlers like a crown. He stopped every few feet, turning his elegant head slowly from side to side, and, seeing nothing amiss, proceeded toward the pond. He did not hesitate when he reached the big loop. As if it were some lesser creature that would automatically get out of his way, he continued, preferring to keep to the easiest route.

As his head went through the lasso, his antlers grazed the rope. He leaped straight up. Simultaneously there was a loud ping and a spanking sound as the twitch-up pulled free of its anchorage and jerked on the line. The buck, momentarily dazed, was caught just above the haunches, with his hindquarters several inches off the ground.

Rolf was unaware of skinning his legs or bloodying his hands as he slid down the rough trunk. He did not waste a second. He took careful aim and struck at the neck. The buck struggled, throwing his full weight against the snare. Rolf stabbed again, less accurately this time because warm blood spurting from the first wound covered and blinded one eye. The lasso broke, dropping the deer's hindquarters to the ground. Rolf lunged, grasping the antlers with one hand and thrusting the knife with the other.

Wounded and furious, the buck leaped ahead, crashing through the underbrush in a desperate attempt to throw off his tormenter. Rolf held on, numb to pain, almost completely blinded, still doggedly striking with his knife. How far he would be carried, how long the buck would keep running, he did not know. All that mattered was that he held on.

At some dim spot in the forest, the light went out altogether, and Rolf sank into a warm, enveloping blackness. When he came to, the sun was high. Streaks of light pierced the shadows and one golden beam fell like a spotlight on the kingly buck, who had fallen not ten feet away.

Though he was bruised, groggy, and smeared with the deer's blood as well as his own, Rolf proceeded systematically with the all-important business of dressing out his deer. He had anticipated his needs and, in spite of the wild chase through the woods, he was able to gather up the equipment he had brought with him. The jackknife, which had never left his hand. A length of rope. A dry cloth. And a large, loosely woven basket sling Diana had optimistically made for carrying the meat back to camp.

It was a familiar routine. Even as a small boy, Rolf had been taught how to clean and preserve game. When he was old enough to shoot a deer he was assumed to be old enough to dress it out. Each step in the process had to be completed as quickly as possible, for yellowjacket hornets were dedicated carnivores and would materialize in a vicious swarm the moment raw meat and blood were exposed. And each step had to be carried out with meticulous care, for a careless cut of the knife or awkward handling of the organs would contaminate the meat and ruin the flavor.

His first step was to drain the carcass of as much blood as possible. With one sure thrust of the knife, Rolf cut the deer's jugular vein. Then he tied the rope around the buck's hind feet, threw the free end of the rope over the limb of a tree, and hoisted the animal by its hindquarters. Because of the repeated stabbings the buck was already partially drained, but Rolf guessed the chest cavity was still full of blood. The dark pool spreading thickly on the forest floor proved him right.

While the blood was running out, he searched the underbrush for a sturdy stick about two inches in diameter. Cutting a two-foot length, he sharpened both ends. The purpose of this stick was to spread the hindquarters and thus facilitate the gutting process. On each hind leg, Rolf made a cut between the hamstring and the bone and inserted the pointed ends of the stick into these slots. With the back legs held firmly apart, he could proceed on the underbelly.

As he castrated the buck, he was careful not to disturb the musk glands that lay like powder puffs on the inside of each hind leg. During rutting season, the buck rubbed these furry protuberances together, leaving a powdery trail meant to telegraph his presence to local does. With rough handling, the strongly scented powder would drop onto the flesh and leave a taste no amount of cooking would eradicate.

Equal care was necessary when he made a ventral cut, slashing straight down the lower belly to a point below the stomach. The next step—cutting around the anus and the bladder—was a particularly delicate operation, for a damaged bladder would bathe the meat in bitterly pungent urine. Having thus opened a hole, Rolf thrust his hand inside the carcass and felt for the opening of the bladder. Pinching it firmly between thumb and forefinger, he pulled the lower entrails back through the hole and cut them off. Now he was ready to work on the forequarters.

Using the heaviest blade Donald's knife had to offer, Rolf split the chest cavity. As he removed the paunch and intestines, he took special care to retrieve the greatest delicacy of all, the liver. With the sternum split and spread apart, he cut around the lining of the chest and pulled out the heart and lungs. He considered cutting off the head and decided it would be easier to postpone that until he got back to camp, where his collection of razor-sharp stone wedges and his stone hammer would simplify the job.

The deer was completely gutted. Flies and yellow-jackets, always attracted to moisture, would start gathering if he didn't dry it thoroughly. He reached for the cloth, and with painstaking care blotted every inch of the body cavity. The butchering was complete except for the skinning.

Rolf straightened up. His head throbbed, his back ached, and the long walk back to camp was going to be an ordeal, since he would be half carrying, half dragging at least one hundred and fifty pounds of meat. He decided to skin the buck after he got back to camp. Leaving the hide on would keep the carcass clean. The skinning process would be simple, anyway. A cut around each hind leg, two more cuts around the forelegs just above the knees, and the hide could be peeled off in one piece with little more effort than a man puts into pulling off a tight sweater. Of course there were other chores to follow. The leg tendons would make lacings tougher than rawhide thongs. Once they were thoroughly cleaned, the paunch and the intestines had their special uses, too— the paunch as a bottle similar to an old-country wine gourd, and the intestines as sausage casing.

He had a prize, all right, and the thought elated him despite his fatigue. He said he would get his buck and he had stayed with it until he did, though he hoped fervently that he wouldn't have to do it again in the same way. Dragged through the underbrush by an enraged and wounded buck . . . Rolf shivered involuntarily. It was a miracle that the buck's hooves hadn't killed him, for as weapons they were even more dangerous than his antlers.

Suddenly he wanted to get back to camp as quickly as possible. Moving quickly but efficiently, Rolf cleaned the jackknife and slid it into his hip pocket, dug a hole with a pointed stick and buried the entrails, rolled the deer onto the basket sling, looped the rope through the basket's handles and slung it over his shoulder. He would haul basket and buck as a horse would drag an

Indian travois. Bone-weary but triumphant, he set out for camp, carrying in his head a vivid picture of Diana's face when she saw what he had brought.

Rolf's numerous cuts had been treated with the apothecary's best cures. The buck had been skinned and the hide scraped with clam shells and sharp stones and buried flat, hair side up, about ten inches underground. These things accomplished, their interest turned to preparation of the most elaborate meal they had planned since the beginning of their exile.

Prattling cheerily about the way his Greek friends had roasted a lamb over an outdoor firepit, Warren Brock took charge of the entrée. A hindquarter was spitted on a stick long enough to extend across the pit. Sturdy forked sticks were stuck into the ground at opposite sides of the pit fire. When the flames had retreated into a bed of glowing red coals, the men suspended the meat over the pit and took turns cranking the spit so that the meat would roast evenly on all sides. Meanwhile the women prepared the side dishes.

"A course dinner!" Warren Brock exclaimed when Norma went the rounds offering bowls filled with two *hors d'oeuvres* they had never seen before. One dish appeared to contain bite-size cubes of watermelon rind pickle. Brock sampled it daintily. "It *is* melon pickle—I think. Very lemony, not very pickly."

Laughing, Diana shook her head so vigorously that her soft thick hair lifted as if caught by a sudden breeze. "No, it's kelp. Tubes of giant kelp." She had peeled it, cut it into one-inch rings, and soaked it overnight. In the morning she had boiled it in a syrup of wild honey from the bee tree and cider from apples in the old Furness orchard. "It's not as pickled as it should be because we don't have vinegar. I'm making it, but it takes almost six months for cider to reach the vinegar stage. It will be ready in the spring."

"Diana, lovely," Brock said thoughtfully, licking his lips. "Do my taste buds deceive me, or is your cider already a leetle bit hard?"

Diana's wide eyes twinkled impishly and her soft lips pressed together in mock dismay. "Oh, my, *no*. That would be alcoholic, wouldn't it?"

"Exactly, my gentle wood nymph. I see your grandmother taught you well. If you want vinegar in the spring, you'd better hide your still."

Diana was pointing to the second bowl. "Rolf thought of that. *Wokas*—Indian popcorn. We roasted the seeds of the yellow lilies that grow in the pond."

Their second course was a green salad of chickweed and wintercress spiced with wild mustard seeds and aromatic with the addition of wild mint. In place of salad dressing, and with another apology for the slowness of vinegar making, Diana sprinkled it with more of the cider.

As they consumed the appetizers and the salad, their senses were tantalized by the rich fragrance of roasting meat. Now the entrée was ready and, in spite of the preliminaries, they ate it ravenously, with their fingers. In between bites of venison they stuffed their mouths with the tubers of Jerusalem artichoke baked in the coals, a starchy sweetish vegetable with flavor that might result from crossing celery root and sweet potato. On this great occasion, they even had dessert: winter pears from the orchard, split, cored, and baked in honey.

"*Olé!*" Warren Brock set his wooden dish onto the ground and patted his lips with the end of his shirttail. "The hungry body has been appeased. Now for the trembling psyche." He drew pipe and pouch from his pocket, filled the bowl with his euphoric blend of kinnikinnick, dogwood leaves, and yew needles and, lighting a wood splinter in the cooking fire, cupped his hand over the flame as he held it to the tobacco.

The mood at the meeting was jubilant. It was the first time, Andrew Held noted, that they were united by a feeling of celebration. Work had always brought them together, and work had dominated their waking hours, even their evenings by the fire. We have advanced, he mused. We now have leisure time.

Warren Brock had been smoking his pipe even before dinner, and his pretty old-Apollo face had the gentle expression of the pleasantly tipsy. "How do you call it?" he asked the group in general. "Kinnikinnick . . . Kinny . . . Kinnick . . . Oh my blessed aunt, what a fine thing you have done this day, Rolfie lad. We've missed you, you know. Knew you were up there on the hill someplace, day after day after day. Proving your manhood and all that. Here, Blake, have a puff. Won't hurt

you, counselor. Just a marvelous combination of perfectly legal substances. It would put them out of business
at Haight and Ashbury. That's it, take a long pull on it.
A real drag. It will do *wonders* for the reluctant Id.
Simply *erases* the uglies. Honey, sweet . . ." he continued, beaming at Felicia, "pass yours around, too." He
giggled, raised his eyes to the sky, and said, "I have just
composed a poem. Attention, *mes vieux*. Here it is: I'm
glad . . . To be bad . . . And I would be gladder . . . If
I could be badder."

The two pipes made the rounds. Donald inhaled greedily. Norma hesitated but finally, with a small shrug, put
the pipestem to her lips and pulled long and deeply. No
one refused.

As he took his turn with the kinnikinnick, Andrew
Held reflected that the discipline of survival might be
producing a colony of dull Jacks. He had instituted Sunday as a "free day," the only proviso being that before
they set out to do whatever they wanted, they join in an
hour of meditation. Except for Donald's lapse, they had
been faithful to these Sabbath sessions and had even
prolonged them voluntarily when one of them, in the
spirit of a Quaker meeting, was in a mood to speak out.
But was one free day enough, since they had rarely
used it as if it were truly leisure time?

"There is so much to *do*," Norma had explained when
Andrew Held asked why she spent Sunday harvesting the
wild wheat that grew in several areas near the old farm.
"And in my case . . ." She had paused, giving him a
wistful smile. "Remember the Puritan work ethic." She
had gone on to describe her memory of her seventh
birthday. Her mother had asked if there was something
special she wanted to do, something "within reason."
Norma had responded eagerly. Yes, indeed there was.
Since this was her birthday, she would like to do only
those things she wanted to do, all day long. Her mother
agreed and the lovely free day began. Seven-year-old
Norma did not make her bed, nor dust her room, nor
take her afternoon nap. She played, and read a book,
and sat in the sun with her new puppy. Until midafter-
noon, when her mother reminded her severely that she
had neglected her daily chores.

"But you said that all day I could do whatever I
wanted to do!" the little girl protested, and her mother

replied, "Certainly. But I assumed you would *want* to do what you are *supposed* to do."

No, Sunday wasn't enough, Andrew Held decided, pulling deeply on the kinnikinnick pipe. "I would like to introduce an idea," he said, passing the pipe along to Felicia. "The idea of recreation. Fun for fun's sake. We've been so involved in staying alive that we've nearly killed ourselves with staying alive. Carlo with his seal, Rolf with his buck, all in the name of providing food. At this point, we are well-fed. We are even semi-comfortable, since we put up shelters in the dormitory and over the cooking area. But for a few hours each day, let's gloat over the fact that, for a few hours, we don't *have* to work. You, Norma, should have the most fun of all. With that work compulsion of yours, you can double your pleasure in doing nothing by thinking of all the things you ought to be doing."

Norma laughed outright and snatched the pipe from Blake's hand. "Hurrah! It's a birthday, everybody's seventh birthday."

Felicia was preoccupied by the serious business of blowing smoke rings and trying to stick her forefinger through the center before the ring broke up. "Let's cut loose. I'm a confirmed hedonist and I don't want to get out of training. But how?"

Brock twinkled at Felicia. "Rover red Rover, let Johnny come over . . . Fill the pipes, dear, that's a sweetie. Now . . ." He addressed the others with a hand movement like a ballet position. "You've heard our leader. We are going to *play*. Games, anyone? Anyone who can suggest a game?"

Diana turned to Rolf. "Do you think they'd like the bone game?"

Rolf puffed on the pipe and passed it along to Blake. "I don't know. Dr. Held, do you like to gamble?"

Andrew Held said quietly, "I've never done anything else."

"Why Andy!" Felicia exclaimed. "What secret vices are you confessing? Poker? Roulette? Blackjack?"

Andrew shook his head. "I never played any of them."

"But you've always gambled?"

"On people. On myself." Softly, so that only Felicia could hear it, he added, "And on love."

The bone game, which Rolf knew as "slahal," had been standard entertainment for Pacific Northwest Indians and was still played on reservations during annual meetings or potlatches. In preparation for it, Rolf cut fifty slivers out of cedar, sharpened them at one end and stuck them into the ground. "These are the tally sticks," he explained. "They represent the stakes. The game goes on until one of two teams has taken them all. The number of tallies was always set before the game started. Sometimes they would use as many as a hundred."

He left the circle, sifted through the gravelly rim of the beach, and returned with four stones, two of them white, two black. "We should have bones, like the large bones of duck wings. Two were painted white, and they represented men. Two were plainted black, and they were the women. These rocks will do instead of bones. There was always more than one way to play the game, anyway. It was different in different villages. Now all we need is music." He turned to the pile of driftwood and quickly selected eighteen sticks and distributed them, two to a player. "Okay. We need two teams, line up on the logs so that we're facing each other. Diana and I know how to play, so I'll be first leader and she'll be second. We should have an even number of players but it won't make that much difference."

They regrouped themselves quickly, Diana and four teammates seated on one log and Rolf with his team on the opposite side of the fire.

"One pipe per team!" Brock trilled. "Hand it back, Carlo."

Once they were settled, Rolf explained the ritual. Each team started with a white and a black stone. Beginning with the first leader, one player would conceal these "bones" while a member of the opposing team would guess the location of the white one. Good guesses earned tallies, bad guesses gave tallies to the other side. The game continued until all the little cedar sticks were on one side of the bonfire.

The "music," as Rolf called it jokingly, was an all-important part of the game. Everyone, except the player whose turn it was to gamble on the whereabouts of the white stones, was to shout or chant at the top of his lungs. This diverting outcry was to be accompanied by a slow but steady rhythm of stick beaten against stick or against the log on which they were sitting. "Not fast, but loud, and in time with each other."

"Play on, oh noble savage!" Brock was holding two pieces of driftwood aloft like a cymbalist waiting for his one big crashing note in a long symphony.

Rolf nodded, cupped his hand around the stones and shook them so vigorously they rattled.

"Ayeeow!" Brock's voice rose in a musical wail. Carlo echoed him in a dramatic baritone. One by one the others joined in a wordless chant accompanied by the hollow thump of wood against wood.

Now Rolf's hands rested on his knees, closed tightly around the stones. Diana, her eyes brimming with amusement, observed the traditional manner of pointing to the white stone. With great ceremony, she slapped her left breast with her left palm, and pointed with her right forefinger. The cacophonous din increased as Rolf opened his hands. Diana had guessed right.

"She gets all four stones and one of the tally sticks," Rolf called over the woozy uproar. "Now she rattles them, the way I did, and without showing the color, she passes one pair to the person on her left, the other to the right. I've got to guess where both white bones are . . ."

As the pipes went around, the clamor and the laughter rose dizzily above the offbeat thunder of the opposing percussion sections. When a leader guessed the location of one white stone and missed on the second, he received one tally and regained possession of one set of stones. If he lost both guesses, he gave up two of his tallies and the opposing leader retained the bones and passed them to two different teammates. Each time the stones changed hands, the winning leader rattled them and passed them along, while the chanting and beating rose in a deafening crescendo.

They had been at it for almost an hour when Donald waved both arms to halt the game. "Hey, wait a minute. Wasn't this supposed to be a gambling game? I see tallies but I don't see no stakes."

Rolf nodded. "That's true. The tallies only represent stakes, like poker chips."

By now they were high on kinnikinnick and drunk with the beat of their crude percussion instruments. Andrew Held, who had never achieved more than mo-

mentary relaxation from the use of alcohol, was enjoying such euphoria that he wanted to sing. "That's
right, Donald. But without any money, how can we cash
in the tallies?"

"We got Mrs. Held's jewelry," Donald retorted with a
shrewd glance in Felicia's direction.

Felicia threw back her head and laughed gaily.
Normally she would have ignored Donald or simply regarded him icily, without speaking, but the kinnikinnick
had softened her. "Oh, no, *we* don't, Donald. *I* do. I'll
put my jewels into the pot when everyone else antes up
the same amount."

Brock said brightly, "Well, I've read about the bone
game and the stick game and, careful scholar that I am,
I recall that the Indians used to ante up their wives.
However, dear friends, I am opposed to such stakes because I would obviously be left out of the game. So . . ."
He bathed them all in delicately drunken approval. "So
. . . I suggest strip poker. A nice clean game. We used to
play it in kindergarten whenever we got tired of spin the
bottle."

Blake, the pillar of convention, was overcome by what
seemed, at the moment, hysterically funny. "Strip poker?
After the way Norma and Rolf and Diana came back
from the farm the day they pulled me out of the well?"
He was swamped with an uncontrollable wave of laughter. "I'll never forget it! Rolf with a big maple leaf hanging from his belt and the girls wearing sword ferns and
strips of cloth around their breasts, and damn it all, I
could hardly *see*." His laughter subsided into gentle hic-
cups. "I don't know, but at this point, uncovering our
bodies isn't much of a gamble, is it?"

Donald's eyes fastened on Felicia's full breasts. "Oh, I
dunno," he said thickly. "I'd like stakes like that."

Andrew Held studied the big man's face. "No, Donald." His voice, though very low, quivered with warning. "Don't spoil the game."

Donald dropped his gaze and muttered, "I didn't mean
nothing."

Smoking had given Norma a joyousness that erased
the last prim line in her face. "We don't have anything,"
she said light-heartedly. "So we have nothing to lose and
nothing to gain. But we could bet on wishes. Everyone
make a wish, and the winner gets his wish fulfilled."

In the same spirit, they made their wishes, with a round of applause when someone reached a new height of ridiculousness. Felicia wanted six pairs of false eye-lashes from Pierre's Salon on Fifth Avenue, to be shipped air freight. Blake asked for a set of wood-carving tools so he could make his own glasses, forgetting entirely that while he was "wishing," he might as well wish for prescription lenses from his oculist. And so it went, all nonsense and laughter, until the last to make a wish, and that was Donald. Lacking the humor and the imagination of the others, Donald blurted out the truth. "I want a woman. I want a woman, and bad."

Silence settled over the group like a damp fog. Donald looked at them defiantly. "I mean it. You guys got yours, except for Carlo." His glance traveled suggestively from Carlo to Felicia and back again to Carlo. "And maybe I don't need to worry too much about Carlo. But me, I need a woman. I don't miss nothing else."

Warren Brock said cheerily, "Donald, old fellow, don't feel sorry for yourself. Here, have a pull on the pipe. And think of it this way: you're no worse off than I am."

In spite of himself, Andrew Held guffawed at the sculptor's frankness. The jubilant mood was restored, and though Donald sat a little apart and brooded over his pipe, the others went back to playing the bone game. The shouting, the laughter, the beating of sticks went on until Blake peered at his watch and announced that it was midnight.

Andrew Held was the last to climb the hill. Felicia was waiting for him at the top. In the flickering light of their cedar torches, her face looked drawn.

She put her arm through his. "Andy," she whispered, "may I move my bed next to yours? I'm frightened."

The question excited hope, but the explanation dashed it. "Frightened?" he repeated.

"That man, Campbell."

"Oh, yes." Though the impression had been vivid at the time, Andrew Held had almost forgotten Donald's bold stare and his own admonition. "Of course, Felicia. You don't need to offer a reason. It's what I want. We'll move the beds. But are you serious? Does Donald really frighten you? He's all talk, it seems to me."

Felicia said thinly, "He's all animal."

He pressed her arm. "I would be pleased to be your protector, though we both know, don't we, that if I ever had to fight Donald, I would have to kill him with the first blow. I'd never get a second."

"Don't joke, Andy, please . . ." Her hand holding the torch trembled so badly that Andrew took the flaming stick away from her, dropped it on the ground and crushed out the flame.

"Come along," he said, putting his arm around her. "One light is enough." Slowly, in silence, they walked along the path to the dormitory.

Jean Charles Brouillet considered jealousy an impractical emotion. On the rare occasion when a tiny flame licked around the edges of his incombustible *savoir faire*, he doused it quickly by adding a new face to his cast of sexually appreciative women. But the existence of Andrew Held had always bothered him, even after he and Felicia were firmly affianced.

He had never met the man. When he left Paris (*Dieu*, that was a sad moment!) on assignment as cultural attaché to the embassy in Washington, D.C., the famous physicist had already folded his tent and quietly stolen away to some barbaric shore on the opposite side of the continent. His name, however, was spoken so often and with such partisanship, both for and against him, that when Monsieur Brouillet finally saw a photograph, the intense blue eyes, the dark bushy eyebrows, and the narrow, aristocratic nose were features of a man he seemed to have known for a long time. An older man, he had noted with some satisfaction, charming in the drawing room but probably less impressive in the bedchamber, especially to a woman as young as Felicia.

Felicia herself had assured him that they were totally incompatible but had never enlarged on that statement. In fact, she never discussed her marriage to Andrew Held at all until circumstances forced her to admit that, even after two years' separation, she had never dissolved it.

"Yes, of course, he did 'desert' me, in that he left Washington and never came back. On the other hand, I refused to follow him to that island of his, and so, according to the codes which require that the wife remain with her husband wherever he goes unless the move is a threat to her health or sanity, it is *I* who deserted him."

"But it was true, was it not? Following him to that island would have endangered your sanity, if not your health?"

Felicia had smiled in a way that was vaguely disturbing. "I never found out, Jean. I never tried it."

The curious blend of resentment and admiration that stung Jean whenever he thought of Felicia's husband exploded into that most useless and impractical emotion, jealousy, when Felicia insisted on talking to Dr. Held personally before filing for divorce. It wasn't necessary, Jean Charles Brouillet had contended angrily. It could all be done through her attorney. Discussing it *vis à vis* could only lead to unpleasantness. And he did not want her to be away from Washington just then. There were several events of importance, among them the Ambassador's reception in celebration of the *Victoire* test on Pater Island.

But Felicia had departed on schedule—*her* schedule, he thought irritably, which also dictated that he meet her return flight the evening of ¯August ninth. He was not surprised that she neither wrote nor telephoned. Felicia was never late for an appointment and never cancelled one. When Flight 181 arrived from Seattle, Felicia would be among the disembarking passengers.

He had argued against her visiting Dr. Held on the grounds that he wanted her by his side, but as it turned out, he scarcely noticed her absence. At such a terrible hour, how could he? The test of the *Victoire* was an international disaster, the embassy was in an uproar, the reception was cancelled, and black crepe festooned the chancellory. Only by exercise of an extraordinary respect for protocol did Monsieur Brouillet remember to have fresh flowers sent to Felicia's apartment before he went to meet her at the airport.

"Incredible!" he thought when she didn't appear. He checked with the airline. There was no Mrs. Held on the manifest. He rang Felicia's travel agent, and a musical voice expressed sincere regret that, because of office policy, Mrs. Held's travel arrangements could not be divulged without Mrs. Held's express permission.

After two days without any word from Felicia, Jean Charles began to realize what had happened. She had never ceased to care for Dr. Held. Seeing him again, her true feelings had been reborn. It was inconsiderate of her not to let him know, but he was charitable; she had not meant to deceive him, she had truly loved him but, with respect to old ties, she had deceived herself. Hadn't he known, really, all along? Hadn't those silly whispers of jealousy come from a sensitive inner voice that had tried to tell him why she was so taciturn about her marriage, so quick to repel his tactful inquiries into her personal affairs?

At the end of the week, Monsieur Brouillet was dead sure his fiancée had deserted him for her husband. But now his emotions underwent a change. Charity gave way to anger, and anger cried out for retaliation. One of Felicia's friends had been frank in saying that his engagement to her long-time friend was a cruel disappointment. He took her to dinner, and then to bed, where slowly and carefully, with passionate attention to the finest detail, he proved that Felicia's loss was her gain. When he left her, a languid body on a disheveled bed, he promised to be back the next evening and, on the way out, he noted the color scheme of the living room so as to make an appropriate selection at the florist's in the morning.

Chapter Twenty-Nine

THOUGH Andrew's nearness was comforting, Felicia slept badly. Andrew was in her dreams, in jumbled juxtaposition to her fiancé Jean Charles. Sometimes they were distinct from each other, sometimes blended, one figure superimposed on the other. It was getting dark. Andrew was going away from her. She followed, and he pushed her back. She cried out to him, but her voice made no sound and he grew smaller and smaller as he drifted father and farther away.

Someone was calling. It was Jean Charles. She turned toward him, but he had no face. She tried to explain that she had to find Andrew. He laughed. Suddenly frightened, she looked at him closely. He was Donald Campbell, naked . . .

She screamed, and the dream sound came out of her mouth in a soft moan. As she grasped the edge of wakefulness, her body tensed, her heart beat rapidly, and dream shapes crowded the darkness around her. "Only a dream," she told herself, pushing back scenes still throbbing with reality.

Fully awake, she lay very still. For weeks, awareness of her body had been growing, and her sleep, even her daytime thoughts, had been obsessed by sexual need. Proximity to Andrew was not helping. She had yearned for him at a distance. With her bed next to his, desire was so strong she could not black out erotic images of Andrew touching her, Andrew gently caressing her breasts, Andrew's body covering her and pressing her against the ground.

The others, having seen Andrew move their beds together, undoubtedly assumed they meant to make love. There had certainly been some wise looks and a show of exceeding tact in the way the mated pairs, Norma and Blake, Diana and Rolf, had hastened to their individual pine bowers and the singles, Warren, Carlo, and Donald, had dragged their beds to the dormitory's farthest corners.

It was ironic, cruelly ironic. Andrew had not touched her, except for a good-night kiss.

She had not expected that he would. She knew the pattern well. Andrew was afraid of being impotent, and hid behind the pretense that he had no desire. If she were the aggressor, as he had liked her to be during the first years of their marriage, she risked his rejection, which would hurt her, or she risked exposing his impotence, which would hurt them both. And so she was as careful not to touch him as he was to avoid her, and the old familiar sexual pressure was building as it had before. Fatigue, pride, secret fears—they had combined in Andrew to repress his desire and strip him of his strength, until finally she had allowed another man to satisfy her.

Felicia closed her eyes and wished fervently for peaceful, dreamless sleep. God, she had called Donald an animal, but was she any different? If she could manage it, wouldn't she be with a man right now? Carlo would need nothing more than a gesture, a look . . . She turned her body away from Andrew's sleeping form, away from his body warmth and the intimate sound of his breathing. Her hands were clenched into fists. She opened them, forcing herself to relax, to breathe deeply, to let her aching body and her whirling mind sink into a nothingness where there was no desire.

Blake Mansfield's cedar eyeglasses had been their cleverest invention, and the ax their most valuable find. The value of the glasses could be seen in the restoration of Blake's usefulness and self-esteem. The ax's value, from its inaugural use in felling the bee tree, was more visible, for with the ax, the Phoenix colony entered an era of construction.

They immediately recognized Andrew Held as the designer, not because he was already their administrative officer and judge advocate, but simply because he thought of things before anyone else did, and the greater the difficulties the keener his interest. He was, as always, the master planner. He was not physically able to implement his plans. Others cut the trees, peeled the trunks, notched the logs, and carried the clay. As it had been throughout his career, he was the idea man, not the mechanic, and this was just as pronounced when the project was a log shed as it had been when he discovered the basic principle of the hydrogen bomb.

The first significant building project was a smokehouse, and Andrew addressed himself to the problem as if he were designing a nuclear fission plant. If the meat, fish, or game birds to be cured were exposed to direct heat or if the heat was too intense, it would be cooked rather than smoked, and smoking was essential to preserving it. If the firebox was on the ground below the food, the proper ratio of heat to smoke would be hard to control, for every time new alderwood was laid on too much heat might be kindled. In addition, the smokehouse had to be properly vented or the fire would go out, but if there were too many openings the smoke would escape without doing its job. Andrew Held analyzed the problems and conceived the solutions. The others put up the building.

The end product was a narrow structure roughly the size of a telephone booth, a skinny log cabin except that the logs were set vertically rather than horizontally. Since the rusty nails they had salvaged from the wreckage of the old farm buildings were too precious to use if any substitute could be devised, the logs—tree trunks about six inches in diameter—were tied together with slender roots of spruce trees and the resultant walls were fastened to four cornerposts driven into the ground. The women chinked the cracks with moss, spruce pitch, and seaweed, and wove coarse mats to be suspended, like racks, at different levels.

The real *coup,* and Andrew Held's pride, was his design for obtaining the greatest amount of smoke with the smallest amount of heat. The firebox, he decided, should be separate from the smokehouse but connected to it by a passage or culvert through which smoke, but very little heat, would travel. Warren Brock went to his precious clay bank for material and, following the blueprint Andrew scratched into the sand, he modeled a domed firechamber and an arched conduit leading from it to the smokehouse.

"And on the seventh day, they rested," Andrew Held observed with satisfaction when the first food to be smoked was loaded onto the racks and Brock was decorating the cedar post calendar with a tiny bas relief of a smokehouse. "Is it too soon to admit that I've got a plan for something else?"

His next invention, which they named "the spa" even before they built it, testified to the fact that Dr. Held had bathed in a good many different countries. It was a far more ambitious structure than the smokehouse, for there was room inside for a bench, a large wooden tub, a hearth, two large vessels for fresh and sea water, and a small bowl for dipping and pouring. As in India, the bather would achieve maximum cleanliness with a minimum amount of water. One small bowl of seawater poured over the body, then a thorough soaping and a second small bowl (of fresh water, this time) for rinsing—this they called the Hindu bath. As in Japan, the bather, already soaped, scrubbed, and rinsed clean, could climb into the wooden tub for a leisurely and relaxing soak. By heating stones on the hearth and dropping them in one of the large containers, the bather approximated the Scandinavian technique of stimulating circulation by sudden transfer from hot to cold. If he laid wet seaweed on the hearth, he created a steam bath. Since the spa was on the beach, the hardy bather could risk the Pacific Coast Indian's cure-all—a steam bath for as long as his body could tolerate the heat, followed by plunging naked into the icy sea.

They were so long finishing the project that Andrew became restless with new ideas. At the meeting one night, when cold air and rising wind reminded them they were now well into October, Dr. Held spoke out. "What next? Who has plans for the future?"

To everyone's surprise, Rolf spoke up. "I do. I'm going to build a canoe."

They all looked startled. Andrew Held noted that even Diana turned to Rolf questioningly. "That would be a challenge, Rolf. A dugout, like the Nootka Sound canoes?"

"Nothing as big as their war canoes. More like a whaler. Around twenty feet."

"Have we got the tools?"

"Besides the ax, all I need is an adze. I think I can make one out of polished stone, or maybe I'll try with bone. Half the job is hollowing out the log, and that's done by burning."

"I have a question." Felicia's green eyes mirrored the

flickering light of the fire. "What gave you the idea, Rolf? What are you going to do with a canoe?"

Rolf said quietly, "I'm going to go get help."

"Oh my sweet aunt!" Warren Brock exclaimed. "I don't doubt your cleverness, dear boy. For all the marvelous things you've made, you have my *boundless* admiration. But a *canoe?* Rub-a-dub-dub, Rolfie. You might as well set out across the Pacific in one of our cooking bowls."

Diana grasped one of Rolf's hands and leaned forward to look directly into his face. "It's not necessary," she said softly. "I'll be all right."

Felicia's head turned, her eyes bright with understanding. "Ah," she said, "now it comes clear. Diana, you're going to have a baby."

Diana's lips parted in a soft smile. "Yes. But I can have it here."

"Lawsey *me*." Brock's blue eyes had never looked so round or so big. "Now we're having a baby. *Merde*. What will we think of next?"

"Your concern is touching," Felicia said crisply. "But to be candid, Warren, this baby has nothing to do with you."

Brock's rosebud mouth formed a reproving *moué*. "Don't be cutting, Felicia. I *have* sired a child." He darted a sharp look at Felicia. "Aha!" he chortled, wagging a finger under her nose. "That surprised you, didn't it, love? I'll tell you all about it sometime, but for being so sniffy, you'll have to wait. Meanwhile, let me assure you that short of taking the babe to breast, I have considerable expertise in the care of the human infant."

Andrew Held stopped the dialogue with a commanding wave of his hand. "When the time comes, Brock, I'd like to hear your story, too. At the moment, let's get back to the canoe. Rolf, I am deeply concerned. A canoe for fishing purposes, for setting out a crab trap, for moving more easily from one beach to another—that's one thing. But to try to paddle to Wolf—and that would be the closest inhabited island—that's something else."

"I might run into a fishing boat somewhere between here and Wolf."

"And you might run into a storm. You know better than I how suddenly they come up."

Donald Campbell's gruff voice broke out angrily. "It'd be god damn stupid to try crossing in a god damn dugout canoe, I don't cáre how good it's built. You got the tide going against you no matter when you start out. Either you fight it when you leave Phoenix or it turns on you when you're somewhere out in the middle. You might as well commit suicide. Christ, there's no use trying to get off this island. We're doing all right anyway, aren't we?"

Brock's eyes twinkled. "What are we hearing from the great stud? I thought you wanted a woman."

"I do," Donald growled. "But I don't want to leave Phoenix."

"Obviously," Brock purred.

"Don't do it, Rolf." Norma had been listening attentively, her forehead creased with a frown. Now the frown was gone and she spoke with the calm voice of a person who has weighed all the factors. "We've taken enough risks. Carlo has been injured, and so have you, Rolf. We nearly lost Blake, though that was an accident. Donald and Rolf and Blake took serious chances when they cut the bee tree. All of us have been cut and burned and scratched and bruised, and that can't be helped. There are wild dogs on this island so that every time we leave camp, we're taking a chance on being attacked, and that can't be helped either, because we have to keep hunting to stay alive. But I *do* believe we can choose between risks that are necessary and those that are not. It is *not* necessary to try to paddle a canoe from Phoenix to Wolf. You want to do it for Diana's sake, I know that, Rolf. We all know that. But if you drowned? Would it comfort Diana to know it had happened for her sake?"

It was Norma's longest and most eloquent statement, and they honored it with a moment of silence.

"I think," Andrew Held said at last, "that Norma has spoken for all of us, and very well. Certainly I can't think of anything to add."

Blake Mansfield cleared his throat. "I do have a question or two." His tone was thoughtful. "First, Diana, my sincere congratulations. Norma and I have always wanted children, but we haven't been fortunate. So we are delighted that . . . that *we* are going to have a baby . . ." this with a quick smile for Brock. "But that will be some months from now, right?"

"Yes. I wasn't even sure about it until this week."

"Oh gracious!" Brock rolled his eyes. "My least favorite subject. Menstruation."

"Tais-toi." Felicia snapped. "Blake, I think I've caught your drift but please go on. Ignore our local comedian."

Blake said soberly, "My second question is about the canoe. Can you estimate, Rolf, how long it will take to build it? I'm certain we would all help in any way we can. But there's a good deal to it, isn't there? I've done a little reading about the coastal tribes."

Rolf uttered a short, self-deprecating laugh. "I'm not even sure that I *can.* They were specialists, the canoe-makers. If a chief was rich enough, he hired one to make and repair all his canoes. And when it came to the big canoes—some of them were the size of a schooner—the head canoe-maker had a couple of assistants. So I don't know. Even with your help, I'll be slow. But from now on the weather will be right. They made canoes over the winter because in summer the heat tends to crack the wood. And I've already spotted the hull log. So, I'd guess six weeks to two months."

"Well . . ." Blake said uneasily. "The point is, we've been discussing the completion of a canoe and the birth of a baby as if they were to take place right here. Should we assume that seven or eight months from now, even *two* months from now, we will still be on Phoenix Island?"

"We shouldn't assume anything," Dr. Held said emphatically. "Nine people cannot drop out of sight without someone deciding to investigate. The fact that a search was made and the helicopter saw nothing here but total devastation, and unquestionably reported just that, suggests that some very definite proof of our existence will have to surface before the authorities will take another look at Phoenix. However, rescue may come at any time. Six months from now, or tomorrow."

"We seem indifferrent," Blake mused. "We don't always bother to keep the signal fire smoking."

"I know. And it's been at least six weeks since Warren told us how exquisite the pastries are at Demel's." Andrew Held picked up Felicia's hand, studied the scratches on the back, touched the broken fingernails. The skin was stained red-brown all the way to the wrist. "Who would have guessed that the most elegant hostess in the nation's capital would become so interested in weaving baskets that she's now making dye out of hemlock bark so as to decorate her handwork?" He laughed softly. "I think what's happened, Blake, is a natural shifting of our interest from rescue to survival. Rescue is something that must be done *to* us, survival is something we can do for ourselves. It's human nature to be more interested in what we can do than in what is done to us. We are not passive people, thank God, and as soon as we recovered from our shock and self-pity we became absorbed by the serious business of saving our skins. Now we've advanced beyond bare existence. At this point, we can embellish existence, as Felicia is doing when she goes from a plain basket to one with designs. We can afford leisure time, as we proved the first night we devoted the meeting to playing games instead of to working. No indeed, we are not at all indifferent to what is real and vital." He paused, rubbing his beard. "End of lecture, eh, Felicia?"

"I should think so," she replied with a smile. "Though I must say, it was one of your better ones."

"Okay, bradda Rolf," Carlo sang out in pidgin. "We go make some fine kine canoe, okay? And then, I tell you, you goan help me."

Rolf nodded. "Sure. Making what?"

Carlo hummed a few notes and gestured with both hands. As if the instrument were already cradled against his chest, he murmured, "I'm goan make a fine, fine guitar. Da best kine."

A cheer went around the circle.

"Could you make some other instruments, too? Or show us how?" Diana asked. Her lovely child-woman face was glowing with interest. "Like recorders, or a drum? I agree with Dr. Held. We're happy when there is something we can *do*. Even if we can't do more than beat sticks together in time to the music, we could all play, couldn't we?"

"Shu-ah," Carlo responded. "Play *and* sing. Hey, Warren bradda, you ever seen a wood xylophone? They make good kine music. You real genius at carving. I think you can make one fine xylophone."

Brock nodded excitedly. "*Divine!* Today a xylophone, tomorrow a Wurlitzer."

The conversation galloped merrily from idea to idea for the combo Brock wanted to name "the Phoenix Phiddlers." For the rest of the evening the only deviation from the subject of music was a comment Andrew Held dropped in suddenly and completely out of context. "I wish I had paper and pencils."

The rollicking chatter ceased abruptly.

"So that you could write?" Felicia nodded sympathetically. "I've thought many times that destroying all your manuscripts, especially your new book, was probably the worst thing the tsunami did to you."

Andrew Held smiled. "I thought about it at first. I haven't, though, for weeks. No, I'd like paper so that I could draw plans. I've got an idea for a project, but it's too big to blueprint by scratching in the dirt with a stick."

Several voices in unison asked what he planned to build, but Andrew shook his head. "I want to work it out first. I want to be able to give you enough detail so that you can visualize it clearly before you decide whether to undertake it. Because it would require hard work on the part of all of us, and a kind of . . ." he hesitated, his bushy eyebrows drawn together in concentration " . . . a kind of change in our philosophy."

Brock's round eyes were quizzical. "I don't know what you are scheming, Andrew. Obviously it is not ours to know at this time. But I can make you a clay tablet, as large as it need be, and I can carve sticks with fine points or with broad points, or both. As long as you keep the tablet damp, you will be able to draw on it. And think how easily you can make erasures!"

"Very good. Excellent! Thank you, Warren. That's just what I need."

For a few minutes they waited expectantly for a hint as to the nature of the project, but Andrew Held's eyes were focused on the bonfire as if the leaping flames contained images he alone could see. Mike, the big male basset, made a bid for attention by resting his chin on his master's knee and looking up with imploring eyes. Dr. Held patted his satiny head absent-mindedly, only half aware of the hound's silent appeal. He was truly lost in his private world of ideas. If any of the others had withheld information of such vital interest, he would have been pelted with questions and pinpricked by Brock's sadistic whimsy. But Dr. Held's retreat into concentration was so complete that he was out of their reach. And he was the leader, a modest and kindly leader, but a leader they had never questioned.

In Blake Mansfield's law office in New York City, Gloria Tucker was sorting her employer's mail. Her instructions were to open all business correspondence, write brief acknowledgments, and refer urgent matters to Mansfield's partner, Simon Boyd. On Fridays she was to pick up whatever personal mail had collected at his apartment and, as soon as he and Mrs. Mansfield had worked out a definite itinerary, he would send her forwarding addresses, probably from Seattle. But a month had passed since the Mansfields left New York, and still no word from either of them.

Ms. Tucker was more irritated than surprised. Through the sensitive radar system peculiar to really good private secretaries, she had been picking up messages for weeks before her employer went off on vacation. Mr. Mansfield wanted to go out West and just wander around. Mrs. Mansfield was upset because she didn't like to go on a trip unless all hotel reservations had been confirmed in advance. She also prepared for every vacation by reading Fodor and, having carefully underlined her selections of the best restaurants, the most interesting shops, and the most important historical monuments, she carried the annotated volume in her travel handbag wherever she went. But there was no Fodor's *Guide to the Pacific Northwest*, a fact which seemed to delight and relieve Mr. Mansfield, to Mrs. Mansfield's obvious irritation. So Ms. Tucker wasn't surprised she hadn't received an itinerary. She *was* a little annoyed, however. She would have enjoyed telling people she wasn't at liberty to reveal her employer's vacation plans, but she hated to reply that she hadn't the least idea what they were.

She was systematically slitting the envelopes with the letter opener Mr. Mansfield brought her from Florence when a Seattle postmark caught her eye. The return address sprang at her from the left-hand corner of the long business envelope. Seattle Police Department! She opened it quickly, unfolded the single sheet, and to her utter amazement read that Blake R. Mansfield was wanted for stealing an automobile.

"Ridiculous!" she exclaimed out loud, and over the puzzled protest of Boyd's secretary, Chrissy, she charged into the office of Mr. Mansfield's partner.

Simon Boyd, a portly white-haired gentleman with a slow, calm voice and beaming blue eyes, agreed with her but assured her a mistake had been made that could easily be rectified. He would simply call a former colleague now in practice in Seattle and ask him to look into it.

"But I don't know where they are!" Gloria Tucker blurted out, abandoning completely the preferred image of the secretary who is privy to everything. "I haven't heard a *word!*"

"You say they flew to Seattle, and that's all you know?" She nodded unhappily.

"No idea as to specific places they were going to see, or friends they were to visit? Were they going on to Alaska, perhaps?"

Again she nodded. "Mr. Mansfield did talk about Alaska, but nothing definite. And he spoke of some islands, somewhere off the coast of Washington, I think they were. Mrs. Mansfield's uncle in Maine had a friend who lived on one of the islands. I heard her say something about calling on him, if they were passing by."

"Do you know the name of the uncle?"

Ms. Tucker frowned thoughtfully. "I've heard it. Mrs. Mansfield's parents have been gone for years. He is her closest relative. But I don't handle her correspondence, of course, and all I can remember is Mr. Mansfield's reference to an uncle in Maine."

"But you don't recall the name of the island where the uncle's friend is living?"

"I can't, because I never heard it," Ms. Tucker retorted defensively. "It was just . . . well . . . way off someplace. That's why Mrs. Mansfield was so disturbed."

"Mmm . . . Well, it will all come clear." Simon Boyd's eyes were kind and his voice reassuring. "Send Chrissy in, will you? And then take a cab over to the Mansfields' apartment and bring back the mail."

"But it isn't Friday . . ." The automatic protest was never spoken. She said, "I'd be glad to, Mr. Boyd," and left the room. When she was gone, Simon Boyd pulled an atlas down from a shelf of miscellaneous reference books, opened it to a regional map, and thoughtfully studied the hundreds of tiny islands strewn along the coasts of British Columbia and Washington.

Chapter Thirty

THE spa was finished. Besides the wooden tub, the bench for reclining, the hearth, and the various vessels for carrying and dipping water, it offered several refinements, the work of Felicia, Norma, and Diana.

"I feel like a throwback to the days we didn't have opposing thumbs," Felicia commented when she first tried to carve a comb out of syringa or mock orange, but she persisted until she had completed nine of them, for the long-haired, heavily bearded men now needed combs even more than the women. In addition, she and Norma improvised bath brushes and sponges, using the coarse white moss that grew prolifically in the cracks of out-cropping rocks.

They now had three kinds of soap. The snowberries they had all been using since Felicia discovered their cleansing and astringent effect, as well as the liquid cleans-er made by boiling the bark of the thimbleberry bush, were borrowed from the household lore of coastal In-dians. The soft soap they used for laundry and for bath-ing was an old-fashioned staple Diana had often seen her grandmother make on the farm. The ingredients were tallow from Rolf's first deer, pine needles, and wood ashes from the cooking fire. She stored all ashes in a wooden barrel, and repeatedly poured scalding water over them. This liquid draining through a hole at the bottom of the barrel was the cleansing agent, com-parable to the lye found in cans on the shelf of a super-market. The pine needles provided perfume. Diana boiled them in a small amount of fresh water and added the fragrant liquid to the lye solution. After this mixture set overnight, she skimmed off the froth and added melted deer tallow. She boiled this slowly, and again set it out to cool overnight. By morning, the soap had risen to the surface and Diana skimmed it off with a wooden paddle.

Their most sophisticated toiletry, Felicia felt, was shampoo. They had developed two kinds—one made by soaking willow roots, the other by boiling stalks of the horsetail rush. "For dry hair, and for normal hair," Felicia explained, when her latest products were presented to the group. There was no need, she decided, to add that, according to Rolf, the latter decoction was standard Indian treatment for scalp vermin.

On an afternoon more like mid-August than late October, Felicia returned from picking the last evergreen blackberries, set her pails down near the cooking area, and looked around. It was still early. The others were away on their various assignments. Camp was deserted.

She had been thinking about a bath, and longing for it. Visiting the spa was too involved a procedure to be a commonplace activity, like stepping in and out of a glass-enclosed apartment house shower. Now was the time, while the others were gone and she could go through the ritual as devotedly as she wished. With a fresh, sun-dried undergarment from the warehouse thrown over her shoulder, she proceeded along the curving beach to the spa. They should have named it "the temple," Felicia thought, smiling at the faintly blasphemous parallel. Filling the reservoir bowls, starting the fire to heat water, soaking and scrubbing and shampooing—these were sacred rites. The mass of purification. Along with the shampoos and the soaps and the bath brushes, they should have furnished it with a collection plate.

Walking softly on moccasined feet, Felicia was in clear view of the spa's open door when she realized the cabin was occupied. Donald Campbell, naked as in her dream, was just inside the door.

He was bent over, drying his legs and thighs by rubbing the skin briskly with the palms of his hands. It was obvious that he had neither seen nor heard her.

She hesitated, gripped by the sight of this very real male body. Deeply tanned except for the stomach and buttocks, heavily muscled, a powerful being whose entire anatomy seemed to her, in the brief moment of unexpected and unseen observation, to exist to carry and protect the proud member emerging from its dark bed of pubic hair. She took a step backward . . .

The massive body straightened up, and his small eyes caught and held hers. He stood erect, making no effort to step into the shadow nor to close the door. She tried to speak, and no sound came out. She tried to run, but her body did not respond. It was like her nightmare, when a faceless Jean Charles had been transposed into a naked Donald Campbell and she and he had been bound together by the misty paralysis of the dream. Except that in the dream Donald had been grinning. The real Donald had longing and hope in his eyes.

"It's you."

"I'm sorry. I thought . . . I assumed no one was here."

"Only you and me."

"Put something on." She meant to scold, to dictate, but her voice shook.

"I don't want to," he said thickly, and walked toward her.

Her heart was pounding and an inner voice screamed "Run!" But her feet, knees, and thighs were immobilized by an overpowering weakness.

"I ain't been too bad to you, have I?"

She gasped, "The devil's clubs! That day in the woods. You stood by and watched, knowing what would happen when I touched them. You were going to let me . . ."

"I felt sorry about that. Forget it. I ain't done nothing since. I'm talking about something else. A way I been good to you."

She nodded helplessly. "You mean you haven't told Dr. Held . . ." Her words came out unevenly, jerked out of her mouth by her furious pulse. ". . . That you haven't told him about Carlo."

Donald's big head moved up and down in slow assent. He took a few more steps, as slow and inexorable as a figure in a dream. "I ain't going to tell him," he said, looming over her. "I *was* going to. I don't want to no more."

"Go away." It was an anguished whisper. "Go back."

"You don't mean that. I'm big and dumb. You called me an animal. Maybe I am. But I got eyes. You can call me anything you want to, but that don't change what I know, and I know you're hurting just as bad as I am."

She stared up at him, trembling with awareness of a body her mind commanded her to flee from. Transfixed, the mute and helpless Felicia stood perfectly still even when she saw what he was going to do, while another Felicia, standing outside the circle of the dream, watched him open her shirt, pull it off her shoulders, and drop it to the ground.

"Oh sweet Jesus . . ." he said hoarsely, his eyes fixed on her full breasts. He licked his lips and slowly, worshipfully, bent his head. When he touched her, the nightmare dissolved. The rasp of his breathing, the hot searching tip of his tongue, released her. "No!" she screamed, and unlike the dream, the full sound of terror burst from her throat.

She leaped to the side, retrieving her shirt with a lightning-fast sweep of her arm, and holding it over her breasts, she turned to run. A powerful hand grabbed her shoulder, jerked her backwards, and threw her to the ground.

She struggled even when his great strength held her easily. She cried out again and again, even knowing there was no one around to hear her. Her shirt lay to one side. Pinning her arms to the ground, he buried his face between her bare breasts, and resting on one knee, slid the other knee up and down her thigh in a frantic effort to lift her skirt.

She was bare now, her legs and lower trunk twisting and turning to escape him. Her skirt was a wrinkled ribbon across her belly. The harder she fought, the louder she shrieked, the more desperately his pelvis pressed against her resisting thighs.

"Don't fight," he pleaded. "Baby, don't fight . . ."

Locked like animals in mortal combat, they rolled onto their sides, and his legs were a vise she could not break. Panting, he forced her onto her back, and with an angry lateral jerk of his hips he spread her thighs. "Now baby, now baby," he crooned, almost weeping as he thrust himself into the warm valley and the hard bursting member probed furiously for entrance. Her strength was waning. Her legs trembled with exhaustion and an all-pervasive lethargy was seeping through her like a drug. Over and over her reeling mind kept protesting, But this isn't what I want!

She closed her eyes, marshaling the last of her strength to prevent the final insulting invasion of her body. In the dark, she felt him suddenly pull back. His hands released her arms. He jumped to his feet. The crisp autumn air was playing against her body, and she was still screaming . . . She heard a loud grunt, and the thud of a falling body.

She opened her eyes. Donald lay on the ground, Carlo

standing over him. Donald, stunned by the fact that a man he could so easily crush would have dared attack him, rested on his elbows and squinted up at Carlo. His thick lips were locked into an incredulous grin.

Felicia sprang to her feet and pulled down her skirt. Carlo picked up her shirt and handed it to her. The laughing friend-to-all was gone. In his place was a man whose dark eyes blazed and whose mouth was set in an expression of cold fury.

"Get out of here!" he said evenly. "Fast!"

Donald, grunting, was up on one knee.

Felicia gasped, "Carlo, run! He'll hurt you."

Carlo shook his head, pointed toward camp, and repeated his order. "I said, leave. Right now."

"My God, Carlo! He'll kill you!"

Donald, still kneeling, nodded agreement. "You said it, baby," he muttered hoarsely. "But you better stick around. This is going to be something to see. It won't take long."

Felicia's voice rose in desperate protest. "He's so much smaller than you are! He hasn't got a chance . . ." Donald was rising, fists clenched and a brutish grin of anticipation clamped on his face. She cried, "Stop it, Donald! Stop it!"

Carlo's right arm shot out, a piston-like punch straight from the shoulder.

Donald staggered, catching his balance after two or three lurching steps. He stared at Carlo. Donald's grin was gone now. One big square hand went to his face and awkwardly caressed the fresh cut at the corner of his mouth. "Well god damn you, you dirty little Dago!" Donald growled. "You don't let a guy get to his feet. I was going to take it easy, but I ain't now. I'll break you in two . . ."

Carlo's right fist cut off the rest of the sentence. Bawling wordlessly, Donald lunged, his powerful arms extended in a murderous vise.

Carlo jumped to the side. Two or three quick, light steps, and he was out of reach.

"Stand up and fight!" Donald bellowed, arms and fists poised in front of his chest.

Without taking his eyes from Donald's flushed and angry face, Carlo danced backwards. He had no illusions. He weighed 135 pounds to Donald's 240. One solid blow from Donald's fist and the fight would be over. Or worse. For Donald there was no "law" on Phoenix, since there was no one strong enough to enforce it. He was already in some kind of trouble, probably serious trouble, for he had made it clear to Carlo that, for him, Phoenix was a hideout. So he had little or nothing to lose, and that made him doubly dangerous.

My only hope, Carlo thought, is to remember what Joe Kaalehone taught me in the high school gym in Hilo. "You're a peaceful enough kid," the old pug had observed, "but before you're an old man you're going to get into some real fights, and in some of them you're going to be up against a much bigger and stronger guy. He'll have the weight and the reach on his side, you'll have the speed. He'll tend to be a swinger. You gotta learn to punch. But the real big advantage you'll have, if you use it right, is that he'll *expect* to win. The first time you tag him, he's going to be all shook up even if he isn't hurt. So practice that short, hard punch. Practice your footwork, especially sideways and backwards. Practice, practice, practice. When you're in a fight, you don't think, you react, and reacting comes from practice." With a prayer for the soul of his old boxing instructor, Carlo thought, If I can keep cool while Donald gets mad . . .

Donald charged, fists clenched, teeth bared in an ugly smile. His left arm swung forward in a deadly roundhouse. Carlo ducked, and the long arm whistled over his head.

For a second, Donald's equilibrium was lost as the momentum of the misdirected blow pulled him forward. That was time enough. A brutish grunt broke from his open mouth as Carlo put all his strength into two quick punches to the stomach.

Enraged, Donald charged again. His right fist grazed Carlo's cheek but his left swung harmlessly, for Carlo dodged to the right and ran behind him. A string of obscenities poured from Donald's swollen mouth as he wheeled around, swinging blindly at an opponent who wouldn't stand still.

Donald advanced, and Carlo backed away. Donald swung, and Carlo leaped nimbly to the side. Maddened and frustrated, Donald forgot everything but his need to catch and to crush. After every murderous blow that didn't land, every charge that left him facing in the wrong direction, there was that split second in which Donald was off balance, both physically and mentally. Each time, Carlo, his mind cold as ice, smashed his fist into the big man's face.

At the first blow, Felicia had retreated to the shelter of the spa. There was no use running to get help. If any of the others had returned to camp, they would have heard her screams and would have come with Carlo. Her first impulse was to pick up the biggest stick she could find and rush to Carlo's assistance, but as the two men fought, the insanity of this idea was obvious. Carlo moved too quickly to be "helped" by a woman wielding a piece of driftwood. But he did need help. So far he had protected himself, but he was only holding Donald at bay. At any moment, the terrible force of Donald's fists would catch him.

Her gaze swept the interior of the bathhouse, seeking a weapon better than a driftwood club. A bowl, a burning stick from the hearth. Donald's jackknife . . .

It lay on the bench next to his clothes. She stared at it, desperation eroding her instinctive reluctance to touch it, while the curses and grunts of the killer animal outside battered her senses. In dreamy slow motion, she approached the bench and her hand, seemingly independent of her, reached out toward the knife. She picked it up. Thumb and forefinger carefully pulled out the heaviest blade.

The dream sequence continued jerkily, like a hand-cranked motion picture. With the butt of the knife firmly grasped in her right hand, the wide blade extended like a dagger, she walked out of the spa and proceeded slowly toward the men.

Donald and Carlo were facing each other, both crouched and watchful. Donald's puffy face was smeared with blood from a bad cut over his mouth. His small pale eyes had lost their habitual look of shrewd suspicion; they were vacant and unfocused. His big chest heaved with the rhythm of his heavy breathing.

Carlo, too, had been hurt. A gash over one eyebrow was sticky with blood, and his cheek was raw from one of Donald's grazing blows. The difference between the two men was not the extent of their injuries, but their frame of mind.

Donald had begun the fight with supreme confidence that in one blow, maybe two to make sure, Carlo would be lying at his feet. Carlo had gone into it expecting to be smashed senseless, perhaps killed. At this point, Donald knew he had thrown everything he could, and crazy as it seemed, the smaller, weaker man was still on his feet. His futile plunging and swinging were wearing him out, and even his righteous rage at Carlo's dodging tactics had become a burden rather than a help.

As Donald's confidence ebbed, Carlo's mounted. He hadn't won the fight, but by some miracle, he hadn't lost it. He had Donald off balance. Anyone would bet he couldn't defeat Donald, but hope whispered that with his present tactics, he could get Donald to defeat himself.

He waited, tensed and wary, for Donald's next move. Suddenly his peripheral vision picked up the figure of Felicia moving toward Donald with a knife in her hand. As Donald's big head swiveled toward Felicia, Carlo shouted, "No! Felicia, stop! Go back!"

She obeyed mechanically, turned around, and hesitated, her back to Donald.

Carlo and Donald lunged at the same time. Donald aimed at Felicia's back. One long arm reached for the knife. Carlo threw himself at Donald, bringing his full weight against the back of the big man's knees like a football player clipping an opponent. Donald's body dropped with a thud, dragging Felicia with him. Even then his attention remained focused on the knife. On his knees, he groped for it, panting and straining against the obstacle of Felicia's body. He didn't see Carlo at all before his head was rocked forward by a fierce blow— a "rabbit punch" behind the ear—and then a second, and a third. The third time Carlo's fist crashed home, Donald exhaled deeply, and grinning stupidly, slumped unconscious to the ground.

Andrew Held's fury was intensified by his sense of helplessness. When he had returned to camp he found Carlo standing guard over a mute and sullen Donald, while Felicia nervously collected more firewood than they needed. In a glance he knew there had been a fight. Felicia's tense, tear-streaked face told him she had been involved.

It was Carlo who explained what had happened.

Felicia was as mute as Donald, though her whole body responded in a series of visible but apparently uncontrollable shudders when Carlo began to describe the scene at the spa. Suddenly she left them, returning to the beach almost at a run.

"What you want to do with him, Dr. Held?" Carlo asked when he had finished.

Andrew could only shake his head. In all their earlier disputes, he had functioned with judicious calm, nonjudgmental as he listened to the evidence, objective in rendering a verdict. The attempted rape of Felicia brought him down from Olympus and dropped him into the human jungle. He shook with raw emotion: anger at Donald, outrage that the man he had befriended would repay in such coin. Plus a deep, throbbing fear of what the experience might have done to Felicia.

Carlo asked what he wanted to do with Donald. That was simple. He wanted to kill him. Not by decree, letting some substitute firing squad do the job for him, and not with a gun or any other weapon that would separate him physically from the act of killing. He wanted to hurt, to mutilate, to destroy this human animal with his own animal body. But he wasn't physically able to do it. Knowing it added bitterness to his rage.

"When the others are here, we'll talk about it." His voice was thick with anger and frustration. With a nod at Carlo that said "I'll leave him to you . . ." he followed Felicia to the far end of the beach.

She was picking up small pieces of driftwood and dropping them into a coarse willow basket. The contrast between her elegantly long-legged full-breasted body and her clothing touched him deeply. Her skirt was the remains of a tablecloth. Her blouse had been a chicken feed sack. For warmth she wore a vest of rabbit skin with the fur on the inside. Before, they had laughed over this costume, but now Andrew saw it as another indignity, not at all on the level of Donald's attack but somehow related to it. He had always thought of Felicia as completely self-possessed. Her poise had always been unassailable. Until this exile on Phoenix, he had never seen her cry. Suddenly he knew what was moving him so strongly now. After all these years, he was discovering that Felicia was vulnerable.

He limped across the gravel beach, lifted her basket of

firewood with one hand, and placed his free hand gently on her arm. "That will do for now. Are you warm enough? I'd like to sit here for a while."

She nodded and let him guide her up the sloping beach to a rocky ledge where the swimming pool had been. They sat down, and for several moments neither spoke. Andrew's fury and bitterness had not diminished, but the focus of his emotion had shifted from Donald to Felicia. With her hand held tightly in his, he said, "Did he hurt you?"

She shook her head. "Not . . . not really."

"Not physically."

She nodded, tried to speak, choked on the word, and stopped.

He put his arm around her and held her against his body. "I don't know how to help you. I know how I feel, but I don't know how you feel. You've hardly spoken. Would it relieve you to talk about it?"

"No—yes, I think it would."

"Please do. I want to hear." Still she didn't speak. With a flash of insight, he knew why. "I've never been good at listening, have I, Felicia? No, don't shake your head. I know it's true. But I've been learning, here on Phoenix. You talk, and I will listen, *really* listen. I won't walk away, or pick up a book, or look out the window with my mind on something else. And please understand . . ." He paused, put one hand under her chin, and turned her head so that his eyes were looking directly into hers. "Please understand that I love you. That I've always loved you."

"Always?" Her green eyes were unwavering, her voice was steady. "Even when you came into my bedroom and found me naked, making love to another man?"

The words and the memory they invoked hit him like an invisible fist. Perhaps they did have to talk about it sometime. Perhaps it was inevitable, a true *scène à faire*, the confrontation that would raise a ghost in order to banish it forever. But *now*, when he had expected to deal with the trauma of Donald's attack?

He felt short of breath as he forced himself to reply. "Did I love you when I found you with that man? Ah, Felicia . . ." He closed his eyes in brief acceptance of pain. "At that one particular moment? No, how could I? Or I should say, Yes, I still loved you, but love was submerged by anger and pride. And guilt. Because even at first I knew I was responsible. I wanted to think of you as an unfaithful wife. I held onto that image long enough to get out of Washington. Underneath, I always knew it was my failure as a husband that had created the infidelity. The shock at finding you with another man was the shock of recognizing my own inadequacy."

Felicia remained in the circle of his arm but freed her hands and turned her head so that she could speak to the vast and empty sea. "You have no idea what a long time I took to accept the role of an unfaithful wife. Even when you moved into the second bedroom, I clung to the righteous notion that even if my husband didn't make love to me, I was a 'good wife' and of course would not turn to someone else." She paused for a long moment.

"I had quite a debate with myself," she continued, with a small rueful smile. "It was just like the debate I went through as a young girl. I was still a virgin when most of my friends had long since given up the prize. It was different, you know, back in the early sixties. Girls were having sexual intercourse, all right, but they still felt they had to offer some philosophy that excused their folly or explained why it wasn't folly at all. What stopped me was not so much a moral credo that said sacrificing a mucous membrane would be 'wrong.' What stopped me was an instinct to hold onto something I could give up only once.

"It was the same, Andy, when you no longer came to my bed and my body ached to be loved. I was still the hesitant virgin. Taking a lover for the first time was like a second loss of virginity. I fought it off as long as I could. Not because I was afraid of getting caught, though I did, didn't I? . . . Not because I'd get pregnant or a house detective would knock on the door or some friend would recognize me in the lobby and report to you. I hadn't been afraid of those things as a young girl, either. No, in both cases, I hesitated to commit the irrevocable. One is never *almost* a virgin, nor *almost* a faithful wife."

She sighed. "You *are* listening, aren't you, Andy? I'm grateful, because there's more." She was silent for a moment, studying her hands with their scratches and rough skin and broken fingernails. He waited, holding her but not pressing her. When she began again, her voice was calm. "I am a very physical person, Andy. I should say, a passionate person. As a young virgin, I held it in until one night on a grassy slope above a river, the floodgates broke and I gave myself willingly to a young man who was probably as surprised as I was that it happened. That night in Washington, when you came home early . . . that was my first affair. And it was much the same as that midnight incident by the river. I was starving. You had given me ample justification. And still I held back, even when I was attracted to other men. I didn't pretend otherwise. The desire to be touched and made love to was so dammed up inside me that I'm sure the men who approached me were drawn by some kind of chemical reaction. I fled from them, scared by my own need. Until finally, that night you came home from Paris. The dam broke. I allowed the young man to see me home from the dinner party. I allowed him to come up to the apartment for a nightcap. When he took my hand and led me down the hall to the bedroom, I went of my own free will. And I undressed myself. He didn't have to help me."

Andrew retrieved her left hand, held it firmly between his own and pressed it for emphasis. "I've said it before, and I mean it now, Felicia. That was a long time ago. A long, long time ago."

Felicia shook her head. She avoided his eyes but Andrew could see that her own were brimming with tears. "That's just it, Andy. *That's* all over, of course. It was all over for me only a few weeks after it happened. But I am still a woman with a body that needs fulfillment. There have been other men since.

"There's a connection, you see. Between all this past history and Donald's attack this afternoon. In the motel on Wolf Island, before your boat brought me to Phoenix, Carlo and I made love. Somehow Donald found out about it and once or twice he's threatened to tell you. But that's part of the past, just as much as that young man you saw in the bedroom two years ago."

She paused, drew a deep quivering breath, and turning, looked into Andrew Held's deep-blue eyes. "Everything before Phoenix is past. It's the present I'm trying to live with. I am still a passionate woman. I *yearn*. And I have a guilty feeling that stupid Donald Campbell sensed it. He's an animal, yes. When I let myself dwell on what he tried to do, I feel terribly angry. Worse than that, I feel . . . crazy *mad.* But I am an animal, too. I didn't want *him.* My God, no. But I *want,* and he knew it."

Andrew said quietly, "Felicia, do you want me?"

Startled, she searched his face. Her green eyes misted over as she whispered, "Yes, Andy. Oh yes. More than ever."

His old fear of impotency stirred but quickly sank beneath a new and exhilarating sense of Felicia's need for him. In only a few minutes, the past had become irrelevant. Here beside him now was a woman he had never known so intimately as he had during these three months on Phoenix. Years before he had thought he knew her body, but in the furious pace of the sophisticated urban world it had been revealed to him only briefly for the specific act of intercourse, and then it was withdrawn, once more excluding him from its mystic rituals . . .

The thought stumbled, tripping over a fragment of the whole truth he had subconsciously tried to skip over. Was it Felicia who had withdrawn from him, or had it been the other way around? If she had retreated after the act of love, literally to her own bed and figuratively into her own thoughts, wasn't it because he had shut her out? Mystic rituals? He had been totally absorbed by his own. His scientific experiments. His political involvements. His writing and teaching and lecturing. In his pride and in his eternal striving, he had spent every ounce of his creative energy, until finally there had been nothing left for Felicia. No, she hadn't excluded him. The wall between them had been built from his side. Here, on Phoenix, that wall had been destroyed gradually by the impact of a new and binding intimacy.

In Washington, Felicia had always locked the door when she went into the bathroom, whereas on Phoenix, he had made her sanitary napkins out of spaghnum moss and scraps of cloth, and she accepted them without self-consciousness. In Washington, an impersonal third person called "a doctor" had taken charge when she was ill, but on Phoenix Andrew had held her while she vomited. If Felicia had been stripped of her dignity, what was left was a warm human being, vibrant with life and honest about her needs. Deep in his groin, Andrew felt a surge of excitement. Even the smell of her skin excited him, driving out self-doubt and flooding him with desire.

Andrew stood up, taking Felicia's hand and lifting her to her feet. Without speaking, he led her up the beach to the path. His pulse was rapid as they climbed the hill and entered the shadowy privacy of the dormitory. Neither of them needed to speak. The way she clutched his hand, the pressure of her breast against his arm— these were a message plainer than woods.

Hidden by the thatched shelter over and around Andrew's bed, they lay side by side. The responsive curving of Felicia's body went through Andrew like an electric charge. He raised himself on one arm, and with one finger gently traced the curve of her slightly parted lips. "Be patient with me," he whispered hoarsely. "But oh God, let me love you now."

Her head lifted slightly and their mouths met. He tasted the sweet moisture as her searching tongue caressed the roof of his mouth. His body throbbed against its restricting clothes. His mouth still pressed against hers, Andrew removed her fur vest and her shirt and then, with trembling fingers, striped himself to the waist. He lifted his head. With her lips still parted, Felicia held her breasts with both hands, pressing them upward as the nipples swelled and hardened.

Desire was coursing through him in a hot tide, and with it, a sense of triumphant strength. He lowered his head and softly licked around a nipple. He was hard to bursting, but he could feel himself strengthen even more when Felicia began to moan, very softly, arching upward to receive him. Somehow he drew off the rest of their clothing. He released her breast and slid down, licking her navel, running his tongue gently along the curve of her lower belly. Anticipating him, she cried out, "I want *you*, Andy!"

He spread her legs and softly, rhythmically, stroked the sensitive folds. "You bring me in," he said hoarsely, and gasped with unbearable excitement as her hands found him and pressed him against the damp entrance. He thrust, pulled back slowly, and thrust again.

"Love me," she moaned. "Love me, love me . . ."

"Felicia . . . Oh God, I can't wait."

"Don't wait. I'm ready."

In furious haste, his hands moved under her buttocks and lifted her. He was deep within her, impaling her.

Words dropped from his mouth, matching the spasms of pleasure that gripped his body. They climbed and climbed, bound together in an uncontrollable primitive rhythm, exploding together at the peak. Gasping, they fell down softly on the other side.

"Oh my love," Felicia whispered. "My lovely love."

Andrew lay very still, in a sweet half-death, still over her, voluptuously languid, while the after-pulse of pleasure vibrated between them and slowly, slowly faded away.

Carlo had not meant to watch. He was already in the dormitory when Dr. Held and Felicia appeared at the crest of the hill and walked arm-in-arm to Dr. Held's bedchamber. And it had been a legitimate errand, nothing contrived, no intention of following or observing. Why, then, couldn't he move away quickly and flee from the love scene his rapid pulse was already anticipating?

Because he was hungry for a woman. Because he never saw Felicia without remembering every detail of their one night together. Fighting to protect her from Donald hadn't been a pure and unselfish impulse. It was wanting her, remembering her, that had filled him with foolhardy courage. The ugly truth was that he fought Donald because he wanted her himself. Maybe, subconsciously, he believed he would have her when the fight was over . . .

Leave! Get out of here! Hey, bradda, you got no business standing here. That's a nice lady, and you like her. The woman has her man, and it isn't you . . . but he couldn't tear himself away. He stayed, eyes fixed on a man and woman whose bodies were only partially hidden by the shelter over the bed. He stayed and watched, catching glimpses of their lovemaking, muted bits of sentences as they talked to each other. Felicia's full breasts, her long red hair spread out on the ground, her husky voice as she lifted her arms and drew the man down until the two bodies were a white blur dimly seen through dark green underbrush.

Carlo hated what he was doing, but he was powerless to pull himself beyond the reach of the love act he ached to share. Only when the crescendoing voice of Felicia cried out in the ecstatic sob of her climax was he able to turn away. Then he fled, running through the woods to the cove where he so often went alone to bathe. He stripped off his clothes and plunged into the cold, clean water.

Chapter Thirty-One

THE evening meal was always a festive reunion. They ate heartily, chatted amiably, and laughed at—or booed—Warren Brock's impudent questions as to the genera and mating habits of any wild food he hadn't tasted before. But tonight they knew what the subject at the meeting would be. Knowledge of Donald's attack and the fight with Carlo flowed from one to another through an almost osmotic process requiring very few words. They ate without appetite, tense, silent, scarcely noticing what was on their plates. As if the forces of nature had picked up their mood, the wind rose, chilling the air and whipping the sea into angry waves that beat against the cliffs and fell back, foaming, into the dark water.

While the women cleaned the cooking area and the men, grim-faced, combed the beach for firewood, Andrew Held forced himself to face the problem that confronted them tonight.

What should be done to Donald in retribution for what Donald had done to them? The problem of crime and punishment. And it was "to *them*," Dr. Held reflected. Their faces were clearly expressive of the personal outrage that Carlo, alone, had had an opportunity to release.

Andrew Held understood their feelings better than his own. Next to Felicia, he was the one most wounded by Donald's brutish act. Nevertheless, his reactions were not clear-cut. His anger over Donald's act was still bitter. The knowledge that Carlo had made love to his wife was still imbedded in his consciousness like a barb. But this afternoon something had come alive between him and Felicia, and within himself. The first delicate thread of a bond had been spun, and he wanted, more than anything else in the world, to strengthen it.

Dr. Held looked at Donald with revulsion. He did not want to look at Carlo at all. But this woman beside him, who occasionally pressed his hand or turned to look so unblinkingly into his eyes—she was his as she had never been before. The incident at the spa, even Felicia's confession of a one-night affair with Carlo, were events diminished as though seen through the reverse end of a telescope.

Andrew Held opened the meeting with the rite of the calendar. One short, unadorned notch, as if this were a workday-as-usual. Reflecting on the irony of marking this an "ordinary" day, he turned to face the group. "We all know what our business is tonight."

They answered with murmurs or nods, except for Donald, who had taken his seat on a log some distance from the fire—the accused man seated in the dock.

"I have some thoughts as to how we should go about discussing Donald's breach of . . ." Dr. Held paused, rubbing his forehead with his fingers. "How we should handle such a serious offense. I can't pretend to be objective about this, so it is more important than ever that the personal feelings of one individual, in this case *my* personal feelings, do not prevail, or even influence you. Blake, you're our legal expert. May I call on you first?"

On the opposite side of the bonfire, Blake rose. The cold wind ruffled his long hair, and his eyes were masked by the wooden eyeglasses. His gaze traveled slowly around the circle, measuring and recording what he saw in each face. Then he removed his glasses, as if he had no more need for sight. "Well, I . . ." He closed his eyes and rubbed the eyelids with thumb and forefinger. "It's very kind of you, Dr. Held, very complimentary. Kind of all of you to allow me to speak first. However, I can't pretend any special expertise . . . that is, I'm an attorney, of course. But that hardly qualifies me, any more than any one of you. I should say . . . the issue here isn't strictly legal, is it?"

Andrew Held shook his head. "No, of course not. Not in the conventional sense. This isn't a courtroom, it's a family gathering. But the family has been injured by one of its members. The injury is too serious to be ignored. Somehow we've got to sort ourselves out so that we can face the issue and deal with it. If that makes me the 'judge' when I'm not a judge, you are certainly the logical choice as prosecutor."

Blake looked myopically into the black space beyond

the ring of the campfire. "You're saying Donald is on trial."

Felicia's voice broke in angrily. "My God, Blake, what do you think happened this afternoon?"

"I know, and I am angry, too." Blake's voice was so quiet it seemed to deny his statement, but his hands, working convulsively, closed into fists, opened, then closed again. "You see, that's my problem. I want to be objective. As Dr. Held suggested, I am trained to see both sides of every issue. At the same time, I am . . . I am enraged."

"Good!" Felicia snapped. "*I* am enraged, too, and so is everyone else."

Blake regarded her calmly. "Any human being is entitled to a defense. We should not allow ourselves to become . . . a band of vigilantes."

Felicia leaned forward to reply but Andrew Held rested a hand on her arm. "Certainly not, Blake," he said, "but I doubt that we will act like vigilantes. We've been very close to each other since the tsunami. A family, and an unusually intimate family. I am confident that in spite of strong feelings, we will reach a fair consensus. The point is, we've got to talk about it. We're all thinking about it. We're all . . . angry about it. So we've got to bring it out into the open, and come to an agreement."

"All right. I'll try to state the case." Blake paused and looked down at his hands, still caught between his professional training and his personal feelings. "But who will speak for Donald?"

For several minutes the only sounds were the splash of waves against the rocks and the explosive crackle of the open fire. Andrew Held looked from face to face. "Will someone volunteer?"

The silence stretched on. At length, Norma said tentatively, "I should think Donald could speak for himself."

"Donald?"

The big man turned a bruised and swollen face toward his accusers. "What good would that do me?" he asked bitterly. "What kind of games you guys playing? I'm a human being, like Mr. Mansfield said. You all know what happened. You want me to plead, huh? Like guilty or not guilty? Christ, I know more about this business than any of you."

Donald stood up, towering over his judges. "First thing

is, we make a deal. You say 'rape' and I say, No way, you got to offer me something better. So you drop it to assault third and I figure I can live with that so I stand up and say 'Guilty, your honor,' and that's that. I don't need no lawyer. I been there before."

Blake drew himself up to his full height. For the first time the uncertainty was gone and in posture and voice there was dignity and self-assurance. "You're forgetting something, Donald," he said coldly. "The criminal process doesn't end with determination of guilt, admitted or otherwise. After that, there's the sentencing. That's when you really need someone speaking in your behalf."

"Sentencing? What can you do to me?" Donald's battered lips flung the question against the rising wind. "Send me back to the mainland? You can't. Hang me? You ain't got the guts. Huh! I know what I done." His long arm shot out to point first at Carlo and then at Felicia. "And I know what *they* done. But hell, that don't matter, because she's high class. So you all go ahead and decide whatever you want to. I ain't got nothing more to say."

Andrew Held hesitated, studying the faces around the fire. They were angry but they were not vengeful, with the possible exception of Warren Brock whose cherubic mouth was pinched into an expression of undiluted fury. If Felicia, the victim, could feel as much guilt and pity as she had revealed to him earlier in that day, it wasn't surprising that they were all ambivalent. "I think we can accept what Donald has said as a statement of guilt," Dr. Held said quietly. He nodded toward Blake. "Would you continue, please?"

Blake blinked thoughtfully at the curling flames. "I think it might be appropriate . . . as you said, Dr. Held, this isn't a courtroom, it's a family gathering. For that reason I'd like to step out of my role as . . . well, as legal advisor, and bring something personal into the discussion.

"Before the meeting tonight, all through dinner, we were talking about Donald's offense. I overheard, or I should say, I got the impression, that though Felicia is very angry, as she should be, she is also troubled by a sense of . . . of guilt. As if the circumstances, the intimacy of our lives, Donald's unsatisfied need for a woman . . . as if somehow she had *caused* the attack."

Blake looked toward Felicia, allowing her a chance to

speak. Her answer was to look down at her hands and slowly shake her head. Blake continued, "I feel very strongly that this feeling has to come out in the open, because this unusual intimacy is going to continue as long as we're here. The women are not to blame for it, nor for any . . . acts it might inspire.

"Outraged as she is, Felicia seems to feel that the proximity of a woman, when a man needs and wants a woman, is cause for leniency. I'm saying that, legally, there are no extenuating circumstances in this case, at least in that connection. A woman, even a desirable woman whose nearness presents temptation, has a right to choose her partner and a right to live naturally and freely. Unless she clearly invites aggression, her physical attractiveness does not make her responsible for the feelings she may arouse. In short, the circumstances at the spa this afternoon may have been seductive, but Felicia did not seduce. Blame for a violent act cannot be transferred to its victim."

Blake paused, frowning slightly as his weak eyes tried to find Donald's figure in the shadows beyond the firelight. "That's all, I think, Dr. Held. Except for deciding what we're going to do."

"Yes. Thank you, Blake." Andrew Held's gaze traveled slowly around the circle. "I'm sure you all want to conclude this meeting as quickly as possible. Certainly Donald does. He's indicated as much by pleading guilty. So, in terms of courtroom procedure, we are ready to consider sentencing. In that connection, I have something to say. A recommendation. In fact, an earnest request."

He cleared his throat and proceeded in carefully measured phrases. "You accepted me in the role of judge. I appreciate your trust. But in our community of nine souls, no one man should decide what penalty another must pay. We must *all* decide. As an eight-man jury, if you like. Whatever we do to Donald will also affect us. Therefore I cannot accept sole responsibility for the decision. I will accept *my* share of the responsibility. So must each one of you."

His fingers stroked his beard as he stopped for a moment, weighing what he was about to say. Before a gathering of the world's most brilliant physicists, Andrew Held's mind discharged original, accurate, and well-documented scientific theory with the speed and precision of a high-powered automatic rifle. But that was impersonal. Tonight, all around him, his companions in exile stared at the fire, their faces distorted by raw emotion. "Judging by my own feelings," he said hesitantly, "we may have some problems deciding what to do. Back in the city, Donald's offense wouldn't come any closer to us than a small news item in the daily paper. Donald himself would be nothing but a name, meaningless when we read it and soon forgotten. If he was convicted at all, we might have some casual opinion as to whether the sentence was 'lenient' or 'harsh,' but in either case not one of us would know the offender and not one of us would have to carry out the order of the court.

"But here on Phoenix Island, we *do* know the man who is to be punished, and we know him intimately. He isn't a name in a newspaper or a shadowy figure flashed for a few seconds on a television screen. We've seen him eat his food. His bed is near ours. We know his reactions, his weaknesses, his desires, his strengths. In short, he's a person, a living and familiar part of our own daily lives. We can't shove the offender back where we want him—as a statistic, or a class, separate from our sacred selves, different from us, the Good People.

"And there's another reason we'll probably find it hard to sentence Donald. Whatever the punishment, we have to inflict it ourselves. On Phoenix, we can't—what's the expression?—we can't let George do it. We don't have professional jailers and police and prosecutors so that we can keep our distance and say to them, 'You take care of it, that's what you get paid for.' "

Andrew Held's arm shot out as he pointed across the water toward the invisible mainland. "Back there, a criminal is a nonperson we've never seen, who commits an act we don't believe ourselves capable of, and is caught and punished by officials we neither respect nor adequately compensate. But here . . ." He shrugged. "I have said enough. Perhaps too much. But remember, whatever we do, we must all share the responsibility for doing it. Blake, may I ask you to take over?"

Blake rose again, straight, tall, intensely serious. Their heads inclined toward him, their eyes following him solemnly. Viewed from below, his lean figure seemed to be reaching for the sky. His untrimmed beard, trembling in the cold wind, his myopic eyes peering into the unseen, gave him the face of a troubled mystic. "What are the alternatives?" he asked them, looking over their heads toward the unbroken expanse of the sea. "A hundred and fifty years ago, we didn't have prisons. There were only three penalties for crime. Death, maiming, and banishment. It was the Quakers who introduced the idea that placing an offender in confinement for a certain length of time would force him to reflect on his sins and thus become penitent. But we have no penitentiary on Phoenix Island. We have no jail or lock-up. We're back a century and a half. But will you vote for death? I doubt it. Will you vote for maiming?"

A ripple of protest passed along the human circle.

Blake nodded. "Then I suggest we have only one choice. Banishment."

Though it was an orderly discussion, their voices frequently shook with emotion. Andrew Held noted that they seemed as shocked by the suggested punishment as they had been by the crime.

Banishment? The word sounded ugly and cruel. They protested as if Blake had recommended medieval torture. Their eyes kept flicking uneasily toward Donald's bulky form, a shadow in the cold darkness beyond the reach of their voices. They were angry, they were outraged, they demanded justice, but as Andrew Held had predicted, not one of them had faced the fact that this demand would inevitably lead them to rendering it themselves.

Banishment? That wasn't like a prison they would never see. That was a condition they could visualize with painful clarity, a living-in-the-wilderness with all the suffering of their own exile on Phoenix increased a hundredfold by the loneliness and helplessness of enduring it alone.

Except for two or three angry outbursts from Warren Brock, they were solemn, even sad, as they pursued every possible alternative. It was more than an hour before they finally recognized that the only choice they had was between sending Donald away or doing nothing at all. At that point, the discussion faded into weary silence.

Andrew Held asked each of them to vote. One by one, they rose and expressed their opinions. Banishment for one month. They all agreed without hesitation, all except one, Warren Brock.

Brock sat silently, his lips pressed together and his round eyes staring with a malevolence Andrew Held had never seen in him before. "Warren?" Dr. Held asked. "Everyone else has spoken."

"*I* want his blood. I want to hurt him where he lives. I recommend castration." The sculptor shrugged elaborately. "But I couldn't perform the operation, even if the rest of you agreed to it and were able to hold him down. If I can't do it myself, I can't expect someone else to do it, can I? So, having submitted my recommendation, I withdraw it. *Not* out of kindness. Out of cowardice. Like most upper-class citizens, I prefer to let George do it, as you so aptly expressed it, Andrew." He inclined his head ceremoniously. "I bow to the majestic majority. Banishment it is. Yes, make it unanimous."

"You're sure?"

"Utterly," Brock replied, with a small unreadable smile.

Like a sullen child, Donald stood just outside the circle while Andrew Held outlined the conditions of his exile.

"You are banished for a month."

Donald shrugged and stared at the ground.

"For that length of time, you are excluded from our community. You cannot enter this area, for meals or for any other purpose, and you cannot sleep in the dormitory."

Donald growled, "Who says I want to?"

Andrew Held's firm voice continued. "Except for these areas that are out of bounds—the beach, the dormitory, the spa—you may move freely about the island. With one restriction. You are not to approach any of us. When you hear or see someone else, if you do, you must avoid meeting. A voice in the distance, and you go the other way. If you disobey, we will impose physical punishment. Do you understand?"

Donald nodded, still avoiding their eyes. In fact they were all looking at the ground, Dr. Held noted. Donald's disgrace was as painful as a public hanging. "You don't have to leave tonight," Dr. Held concluded. "But you are to move your bed outside the main dormitory area. In the morning, we will give you a pack of dried and smoked food and a gourd for carrying water."

During the long pause that followed, Andrew Held experienced a surge of relief. The judgment was fair, and

Donald had accepted it without a fight. Andrew realized suddenly that he had been afraid all along of what the big man might do. Though Carlo had beaten him that afternoon, Donald was fantastically strong. The humiliation of being judged and exiled, added to the humiliation of his beating at the hands of a much smaller man, could have driven him to the point of striking back regardless of the consequences.

Donald grumbled low in his throat, "Eight against one . . ." and turned to go. Andrew was silently thanking God when Donald stopped, turned back, and blurted out, "I'll go, all right. But I ain't going without my jackknife."

That afternoon, Carlo had dropped the knife into his pocket. It was in his hand now. Donald lunged, fell on Carlo with all his weight, and jerked the knife out of his hand. Holding it in his fist, he backed away from the fire. "Don't nobody try nothing!"

Carlo and Rolf leaped to their feet, jumped over the log, and threw themselves at Donald. Donald fell to the ground. Grunting, he swung at them with both arms and kicked at them wildly. They retreated and he was up, fighting blindly, cursing and panting.

Dr. Held's voice rose above Donald's angry bellowing. "Donald, stop! Rolf, Blake, Carlo . . . back off!"

They obeyed, and Donald, with his shirt half torn off and a fresh cut bleeding over one eye, faced them all with the jackknife in his hand. Laboring for breath, he choked out his threat. "Don't come no closer. I never stuck nobody in my life, but if I got to, by God, I will now!"

"Donald!"

The big man swung around reluctantly to face the commanding voice.

Andrew Held looked directly into the small, pale eyes. In a simple, expressive gesture, he held out his hand, palm up. "Donald, please give me your knife."

Donald stared at him and didn't move, as if the gentle but authoritative tone had paralyzed him. Andrew Held waited in silence, his hand extended.

Donald's bullish head moved slowly from side to side in stubborn refusal.

"If you please, Donald."

Very slowly, Donald lifted his arm, looked at the jackknife clutched so tightly in his fist, took one step forward, and dropped his beloved possession into Dr. Held's out-stretched hand.

"This is the only knife on the island," Andrew Held said quietly. "We need it. We all use it."

"It's mine! It's the only thing that's *mine*."

"Yes, but that's not as important, here on Phoenix, as the question of who needs it most. The eight of us, or you?"

"It's mine," Donald repeated hoarsely. "I *want* it."

"But do you need it as much as we do?" Dr. Held looked around the circle and saw that no one was going to intercede or offer a solution. After the shock and ten-sion of deciding Donald's punishment, they were clearly willing to leave this issue up to him. "Donald, perhaps you are right, after all. I think that, since you will be alone for a month, your need is indeed greater." With a half-smile, he offered the knife.

Donald grabbed the knife, turned, and ran off through the dark toward the dormitory.

Brock moved like a cat through the velvet darkness of the dormitory. The meeting had not been to his liking. They had been too easy on Donald. For what was more brutal than rape?

His own sexual code might be, well, broader than the average citizen's, but it excluded force. He had never had a love partner, man or woman, who did not join him willingly. He abhorred the dumb brute whose lovemaking was a crude release rather than an aesthetic experience. For him, the physical act of love was a form of com-munication, in which one's own pleasure was intensified by giving pleasure. He had been described by a dozen vulgar synonyms for homosexual and he had laughed at his censors, knowing that his love practices were more considerate, more delicate, more civilized than theirs. But the thing this afternoon . . . Thank God he had been spared the ugly details, for he had been nauseated by the simple fact that Donald tried to invade Felicia's body against her wishes. This was the most terrible humilia-tion he could imagine. Donald, he had promised himself during the meeting, was going to know humiliation too.

Brock followed a zigzag course, avoiding the crude lean-tos that sheltered their beds from rain. Obedient to

Dr. Held's order, Donald had moved his bed away from the usual dormitory area. He was isolated by three hundred feet from his nearest neighbor.

Brock approached softly. As his eyes picked up the shadowy profile of the crude lean-to that sheltered Donald's bed, he stopped, listening for the sound of slow regular breathing that would tell him Donald was asleep. There was no heavy breathing, no snores, only the rustle of a body moving restively on a bed of fern and cedar bows.

He slid to the entrance and whispered, "Donald?" The rustling stopped abruptly.

Brock dropped to the ground and crawled under the slanting roof. "Donald, you're awake?" he said softly as he felt the edge of the bed against his side and knew that Donald's outstretched body was parallel to his own.

"What the hell . . ."

Brock placed one hand gently over Donald's mouth. "Sshh, lover. The others are asleep. Let's not wake them, eh?" He withdrew his hand, letting the tips of the fingers dwell for a moment on Donald's lips. "You can't sleep, I can't sleep. I wonder why?"

"I got too much on my mind." Even as a hoarse whisper, Donald's voice quivered with self-pity. "I don't know why *you* can't sleep. Chrissakes, I don't know why you come here."

"Because I feel very badly about the way you were treated this evening. The cold, cold shoulder. Everyone so inhumanly perfect. They sin not, neither do they forgive the sinner. Fiddle dee dee. The lovely Diana is with child. How did she get that way? Norma the prude has been blossoming like a goddess of fertility. And unless my senses deceive me, even our great mentor, the Reverend Doctor Held, has at long last discovered what that thing between his legs is meant for besides the elimination of certain body wastes. But they expect *you* to become a monk. It's not fair."

Donald did not understand much of Brock's monologue but the sympathetic tone was plain. He responded with childlike pleasure. "Yeah, that's right. It ain't fair. That Mrs. Held ain't no angel. She let Carlo screw her, I know. I heard them in the motel on Wolf."

"You *did?*" Brock's hand settled delicately on Donald's throat and moved under his shirt until it found the right nipple. Caressing it, Brock whispered, "Tell me *all* about it."

Donald had often excited himself by recalling that night in the Harbor Inn, the sounds from the next room seeping through the thin wall to awaken erotic images of an act he could not see. Brock's invitation to describe it made his hungry member strain upwards and diverted him from the suggestive pressure of Brock's fingers. "I was in the next room. I couldn't see nothing, but Christ, it was almost as good as seeing. They come over to the bed, it kind of creaked, real slow at first . . ."

"Yes, yes . . ." Brock's hand traveled smoothly along Donald's hairy chest, unbuttoning the front of his shirt, opening his trousers. "What else did you hear?"

"She said, keep the lights on. Oh Jesus, she wanted him to look at her. It was like I could see it happening."

"Like this?" Brock whispered lovingly, his mouth pressed against Donald's ear. His hand encircled Donald's erect member as his tongue darted in and out of Donald's ear.

"Christ, what're you doing?" Donald moaned. "Hey, leave go. I don't have nothing to do with faggots."

"No, love, no. Except when there aren't any girls. What did you do in prison, love? There must have been plenty of pretty young boys. Which way did you do it?"

"Oh God . . ." More erotic images crowded his memory and made his blood pound. "*I* did it. No one did it to *me*."

"Of course. You're big. You're a man. And you're bursting with it, sweetie. You need it so bad you're going to explode. That's the only reason you went after Felicia today. I understand, I know."

Donald's great organ, free of his clothing, throbbed in Brock's hand. "I believe it, Donald. You were the one who did it, I can tell. But it's good the other way, I promise you. And I've been wanting you, I want to get into you . . ." Brock's fingers caressed and pressed while the tip of his tongue teased Donald's nipple. "Let me do it to you, Donald," he begged softly. "I won't let go of this great, beautiful thing of yours. I'll hold it, I'll love it." Brock's hands went around Donald's waist. Gently but insistently he turned Donald's body and pulled it into knee-chest position.

Donald whispered hoarsely. "No, oh God, what are

you doing? No, no, I've never let anyone do it to me. . . ." But he gave no resistance as Brock pulled down his trousers and as deftly and quickly opened his own.

"Feel this," Brock murmured, directing Donald's hand into his bare crotch. Donald's fingers closed convulsively. "Ah . . ." Brock whispered. "You can feel it, can't you? You know how ready I am, lover. So, *so* ready!"

"God damn it, no . . ." Donald moaned, withdrawing his hand. But Brock's warm flesh was rubbing against his bare back, Brock's arms were around his waist, and Brock's fingers, warm and damp with saliva, were stroking him rhythmically.

"Oh God, oh my God . . " he sobbed as Brock separated his buttocks and a throbbing column began to penetrate. Brock's gentle hands kept stroking, Brock's member was entering, and all at once, nothing mattered but to receive, to be pierced, to be taken.

"Lover, lover . . ." Brock's voice crooned as Donald's body lifted to accept him. "There's more, Donald, more. I'll give it to you, lover. There, there . . ."

With bodies locked, the rhythm mounted. A wild torrent of obscenities rushed from Donald's mouth as Brock's hands moved feverishly back and forth and Brock drove himself deeper and deeper. And then, just as Donald's whole body was about to explode in a shuddering climax, Brock's hands released him, Brock's member withdrew, and somewhere in the dark behind and over him, Brock's jeering voice said, "Bye, bye, big boy. Sorry, but you just don't have it, do you?"

Donald groaned as the peaking desire, trapped inside his body, began to knot into a hot ball of pain. "Damn you!" he gasped weakly. "Leaving me like this. Damn . . ."

"You're just not that good, sweetie. No one ever tell you before? Well, *well*. I do *wonder* about all your little chums in the jail. Very polite boys, I'd say. As for myself . . ." He laughed softly as he pulled on his trousers with businesslike precision. "I am discriminating, which means, dear Donald, I know a good lay from a bad one . . . Tut, tut!" he said coyly, ducking the fist Donald sent blindly through the dark. "Better pull up your drawers, Donny boy. Awful thing, pneumonia of the *sitzplatz*." He slipped through the entrance to Donald's shelter like a ghost melting through a wall. Outside, he laughed again. "Ask not what us faggots can do for you, but what you do for us." With a whisper of movement and a rustle of leaves, he was gone.

Donald did not wait for first light. Gathering his clothes, he fled the woods, down the hill to the beach, around the harbor to the south, and on and on until he was lost in a part of the island he had never seen before.

When the night sky began to silver he was as far as he could get from the people he never wanted to see again. His body, bruised and cut by Carlo, shamed by Brock, rebelled against such cruel usage and collapsed like a deflated blimp. As he dropped to the ground, the hard casing of his jackknife pressed into his flesh. One big hand fumbled for the trouser pocket, pulled out the knife. Tears rolled down his scarred cheeks as he buried his face in the crook of his arm and fell asleep, the jackknife clutched in his hand.

In the morning, Andrew Held was the first to leave the dormitory and walk down the hill to their camp and cooking area above the beach. He was the first, therefore, to discover that the buttery, where they kept the smoked and dried foods they had been storing up for the lean winter months, had been raided during the night.

Donald . . . Andrew had passed Donald's relocated bed shelter on his way through the woods. Finding it empty, he assumed the big man would be somewhere around camp, probably making up the pack of supplies they had promised as one of the conditions of banishment. But would Donald, even an angry and ashamed Donald, have done such terrible mischief to food stores he knew were their only hedge against hunger, or even starvation? Donald was to return in a month. Why would he vandalize supplies on which his own life might depend?

The destruction was sickening. Baskets of venison jerky were torn to shreds, dragged through the dirt and abandoned, half empty, some distance from the buttery shelter. Packages of smoked fish wrapped in layers of fern had been ripped open, plundered, and left to spill the rest of their contents onto the ground. Earthen bowls of dried berries had been overturned and broken, sacks of pemmican pulled down from the shelter walls . . . and the shelter itself had been violated, as if fury had been as much the motivation as hunger.

Quite soon the others would be coming down the hill

to the beach. Andrew dreaded the blow this malicious attack would deal. The loss of a third to a half of their food stores constituted a threat to their physical survival, but it would mean more to them than that. His band of industrious and frugal food gatherers would see the destruction as a violation of their rights. The fact that much of the food had simply been dirtied or torn open and then abandoned amounted to a personal insult. Did Donald do this? No, Dr. Held thought. Donald would steal, but he would not waste the meats and fruits and vegetables he had labored as diligently as any of them to acquire and to accumulate.

The evidence was plain, when Dr. Held went back over the splintered doorway and ground nearby. This wasn't the work of a human being. In the toothmarks, the clawing, the careless destruction, he saw a new danger, even greater than the calamity of losing food.

The feral dogs Donald had fled from when he first hunted grouse were no longer staying at the south end of the island. Attracted perhaps by the rich meat odor that had been drifting up and away from the smokehouse for the past few days, they had ventured outside their usual territory.

The evidence also suggested that Donald had already gone into exile, but without his survival kit of jerky and pemmican. It was reasonable to assume he had left before the invasion of the dog pack, for if he had seen the ravaged buttery, he would have run for the protection of the group on the hill, not so much to sound an alarm as to save his skin. Why Donald had departed in the night, which direction he had taken, or why he had not waited for the promised backpack of supplies, were questions Andrew Held could not answer. For the moment, they did not concern him. He had to deal with the immediate situation, and quickly.

Donald had possession of the all-important jackknife. The remaining eight had lost their strongest man as well as their most effective weapon. They could rebuild the buttery and to some extent they could replenish their food supplies, but this beach community and the nearby dormitory were no longer safe. Dogs bold enough to invade this part of the island would certainly grow bolder now that they had discovered and glutted themselves on camp food. It was time, Andrew Held decided, to reveal his plan.

He had already used five or six of the soft clay tablets Brock made for him, etching designs into their surfaces with finely pointed sticks. He would bring them out this morning, introducing and explaining the project that had occupied his thoughts for several weeks. There were some unsolved problems but in any case he would not have waited much longer to present the plans, for the weather was already changing from the golden warmth of a long Indian summer to the steel-gray chill of approaching winter. Yesterday, he would have called his project "advisable." Today, with the menace of feral dogs settling over their camp like a heavy frost, he could call it a matter of life and death.

BOOK III

Chapter Thirty-Two

A MORNING meeting was recognized as an emergency session. It was significant, Andrew Held reflected, that he'd had no reason to call one for at least two months. Ironically, that cheerful fact was one of the reasons for the group's bleak mood today.

Everything had been going well. There had been problems, but in finding solutions, they had discovered in themselves new dimensions of imagination and inventiveness. And now, in less than twenty-four hours, the harmony of the group had been shattered by violence from within, and a ferocious outside force had threatened their safety and destroyed food stores on which their survival depended.

The mildest term Dr. Held could think of was "setback." Emotionally, it was more of a cataclysm, a sudden terrible drop from prosperity into black depression. And the weather was contributing its share of gloom. The prevailing southwester had retired as the wind shifted around to the north. The air was heavy with the threat of frost, and the morning light was gray and misty. Phoenix Island was a derelict ship drifting on an angry sea beneath a threatening sky.

Rolf piled drift logs onto the fire and sat down next to Diana with his arm encircling her protectively. Blake pulled off his tattered woolen shirt and draped it around Norma. Felicia, at Andrew Held's side, leaned toward the fire with arms extended to the flame and said, "Andy, let's get on with it. Anything you have to say will be more cheerful than what we're all thinking. I haven't felt so terrible since the day after the tsunami."

The clay tablets on which he had engraved his plans were resting on Andrew Held's knees. But there were other issues to be dealt with first.

"We won't mark the calendar this morning, unless some of you think we should. Let's hold that for the evening meeting." Dr. Held paused and, hearing no protest, launched into the subject he knew was uppermost in their minds. "I think it's obvious to us all that Donald has left. And as far as I can tell, without the survival kit we expected to make up for him this morning."

Warren Brock's Cupid lips parted in a malicious smile. "Tsk!" he breathed. "He must have been in a godawful hurry."

"Yes?" Felicia asked impatiently. "For some stupid reason, he left without taking any supplies. Well? What can we do about it?"

"He *does* have his jackknife." The expression on Blake's face was partly obscured by the masklike wood eyeglasses but, to Dr. Held, the grim line of his mouth and his careful tone of voice suggested he was still caught between revulsion at Donald's act and the sort of judicial objectivity he felt he ought to bring to the situation. "And undoubtedly his slingshot and his hunting sling."

"He can make it." This came from Rolf, whose normally quiet voice carried a sharp edge.

"Well, *well*," Brock said drily. "You're supposed to be inscrutable, dear boy."

For several minutes they were silent. All right, Dr. Held thought. What is it going to be? Compassion or revenge?

Carlo had been staring into the fire. As he lifted his head, his dark eyes swept the circle and came to rest on Dr. Held. "Nobody has to agree with me, but I'll say what I think. Maybe Donald *can* make it through the month. But he's no Nature boy like you, Rolf. He lived on this island for a year and never got a half-mile from the house in either direction. Of course he did some hunting when he was a kid, and he's had plenty of experience the last few months. So, like I said, he probably can make it—for thirty days." He paused, and a shadow of a smile played around his mouth. "He got beaten by a guy half his size, remember that. That was punishment. And I got a feeling . . ." His eyes flicked toward Warren Brock and as quickly moved back to Dr. Held. "A real *strong* feeling that I'm not the only one got even with him, one way or another. Anyway, that's not the point, at least to me. That package of pemmican and jerky or whatever else was going into it—that was part of the deal, wasn't it? Maybe Donald doesn't deserve it, but it *was* part of the deal."

Felicia was the first to respond. "Carlo's right, I suppose. We ought to make up a package and get it to him, somehow."

Observing the circle of faces, Andrew Held saw that Felicia's stand, however reluctant, had settled the issue.

Brock responded with a careless shrug. "Oh, well, if that's the way you feel, dear heart. After all, yours should be the role of righteous indignation. Personally, I find retribution more fun than pity. But I've had *my* pound of flesh, thank you. So let's make up the Care package. May Donald's kit runneth over."

With a worried frown, Norma asked, "But how will we get it to him? We haven't the slightest idea where he went."

Rolf said quietly, "I do. He went south. I found tracks. I didn't go very far but there were still plenty of signs when I turned around and came back to camp. So I think I could find him, if I go before another rain."

Andrew Held nodded approval. "Good. There are two other matters I want to bring up this morning. As soon as we've finished discussing them, will you put the package together, please, Rolf? And deliver it, if you can."

"Are we through with Donald?" Warren Brock asked. "May I introduce a less dismal subject?

"The floor is yours, Warren," Andrew Held replied.

"Well . . ." Brock threw out his chest, squared his shoulders, and lifted his round chin in comical imitation of a great orator girding himself for his next Olympian utterance. "A long time ago, *eons* ago, right after the tidal wave, when all of us, innocents that we were, thought rescue was just around the corner. Like prosperity during the Hoover administration. You've all forgotten, I'm sure, but at that time I proposed sending a message in a bottle."

Andrew Held smiled. "I do remember, Warren, especially the fact that I was so negative about someone else's idea. I pointed out that we had neither paper nor pencil."

"True, true. You discouraged me, but you did give me a reason. Everyone else simply ignored me. You know, there goes that whimsical little faggot, chattering about sending an SOS in a bottle. Man-child, funny little boy, playing games. Ha. And again, ha, ha. At this point, almost three months have passed and we still haven't been rescued. In three months my silly bottle might have landed on somebody's beach, and we'd be on our way back to civilization right now instead of worrying about being torn to shreds by wild dogs.

"What you fail to realize," he continued, dusting his soft golden beard with delicate fingers, "is that I am never more serious than when I am silly. So let me be silly-serious once again. We *do* have a bottle. Just one bottle, intact and unbroken. We have learned to make ink. As for paper. I've been experimenting with pounding and drying bark. The result is something like papyrus. Or we could write on small clay tablets, tablets narrow enough to slip through the neck of the bottle."

"A cork?" Norma asked. "A waterproof stopper?"

Brock shrugged elaborately. "One of America's most renowned sculptors has been whittling hairpins and knife handles. Why can't he whittle a stopper?"

Norma said gravely, "To make sure water won't seep in, you should dip the neck of the bottle into melted beeswax, both before and after you insert the stopper."

"Excellent!" Brock clapped his hands. "You're never more serious than when you're serious, are you, Norma love?"

Questions had been answered. Issues raised by his seven companions-in-exile had been aired and, in most cases, settled. Now Andrew Held felt free to present his plans.

The large clay tablets were still on his knees, face to face so that their secrets were hidden. "It's time to tell you what I've been working on since Warren made these tablets. Please be patient with me if I turn into a professor in the process. As Felicia knows, I am incapable of saying more than fifty words without sounding as if I were standing at a blackboard with a piece of chalk in my hand.

"So . . . My plan is based on two facts and two premises. See? I'm doing it already."

Felicia laughed and patted his arm. "Relax, Andy. Go ahead and profess."

"Ah . . ." Andrew Held sighed. They were all smiling at him. "Well, I . . . Well, my plan is based on two facts and two premises. The facts are these. We have located our settlement, such as it is, on and near the beach. Partly because this is where the house was—you might say, this is where civilization was—before the tsunami. Like people living on the slopes of Vesuvius, who automatically set about rebuilding their nests on the same old site. And partly because we wanted to remain where a rescue party would be most likely to spot us.

"Fact number two. The weather is changing. We've had a beautiful, warm fall, but winter is approaching. Now, as to the two premises . . ." He stopped abruptly, and turned to Felicia. "Am I worse than usual?"

Her green eyes sparkled with amusement. "You've got us hanging on the ropes, professor. The premises?"

"First, we must have living quarters for cold and stormy weather. And second, our living arrangements, wherever they are located, must include some signaling device that will announce our existence to any ship or aircraft that might come close enough to see it.

"With these factors in mind, I've come to the conclusion that we should build a good solid log house on the site of the old Furness farm. As soon as the rough exterior is erected, we should leave the beach and resettle on the north end."

"No signal fire?" Norma asked anxiously.

"Why not? The farm is on a high point of land. A plane or helicopter would spot a bonfire in the clearing, perhaps more readily than a fire on the beach."

Blake shook his head. "A ship wouldn't, unless it was sailing along the west side of the island. That clearing is surrounded on three sides by a screen of heavy woods."

"The flame wouldn't be visible from all directions," Andrew Held conceded, "But the smoke would, and we have learned how to make lots of smoke, black or white. But I'm not proposing we put all our faith in signal fires. My plan includes a watchtower, a flagpole, and a signal flag, which are better indications of human beings than a column of smoke. Fire doesn't necessarily mean people. Last year a little island east of Wolf burst into flame and half the timber was burned off. No one had landed there for six or eight months. Fires *do* start in the wilderness. From lightning, for example."

Felicia said thoughtfully, "The house you speak of, Andy. A sturdy log cabin, big enough for all of us. It sounds . . ." She looked at him quizzically. "I'm trying to be realistic. I think we've all advanced well beyond that first period of innocence Warren mentioned earlier, when we were either so naïve, or so ignorant, we expected that at any moment a Coast Guard cutter would come steaming into the harbor. But leaving what we have here? The spa, the smokehouse, the buttery, the little shelters in the dormitory . . . Granted, they are all temporary. We built them as simply and as quickly as we could, mostly, I think, to keep our minds off our situation. Certainly not to last. You seem to be saying we must expect to remain on Phoenix for many more months to come. A house . . . A signal tower? It sounds so . . . so *permanent*."

Andrew Held nodded. "I was afraid that aspect of my plan would trouble you. And I'll admit, I chose the old farm as the building site for the same reasons the first Furness picked that area for his homestead. That's where the best supply of sweet water is located. That's where the soil is rich and deep, and the best building materials are close at hand. It's protected from wind and salt spray, while the entire harbor area is exposed to the weather. All this adds up to permanence, yes. But we've got to face it. We don't know *when* we'll be rescued. Sticking stubbornly to our summer camp area isn't going to delay the approach of winter. We've got to get ready for heavy rain, cold wind, nine- and ten-foot tides, even snow.

"We've admitted it, in one way. You, Felicia, and Norma and Diana in particular. Norma asked Warren to make her knitting needles. You asked for a loom. All three of you have been busy making thread and yarn out of all sorts of fibers and you work on animal hides like three seamstresses getting the most out of a bolt of cloth. When you began to feel cold, you began to make warm clothing.

"That's wonderful, but it isn't enough. We need a house, too. The dormitory . . ." Andrew Held paused and smiled at Diana. "The dormitory is not the best place to have a baby. Our house will be snug and warm. Eventually it will have separate bedrooms. The old well, which was nearly Blake's undoing, will provide a water supply only a few steps from the house. And we won't have to give up the bathhouse, *or* the smokehouse. The wooden sections can be torn apart and moved, like prefabricated buildings."

In the silence that followed, Andrew Held tried to

estimate what the impact of his proposal had been. He
didn't have to wait long.

"We've got an ax," Rolf said. "We couldn't do it without an ax."

Warren Brock spoke from the center of a lovely day-
dream. "The house will be *warm*. I'll build a big circular
fireplace in the center of the living room. I can see it,
all glowing and pink. Something contemporary."

Felicia's laugh was almost light-hearted. "Contemporary, meaning Phoenix 'Seventy-seven?"

"Will you build an oven, too?" Norma asked. "The one
here is fine, of course. But something a little bigger, and
well, more . . ." Her serious dark blue eyes suddenly
twinkled with humor. "Something more . . . permanent?"

"Dr. Held?" Diana's lovely wood nymph face and wide
expressive eyes were shining with excitement. She pointed
at the tablets in his lap. "Don't make us wait any
longer, Dr. Held. Please show us your plans."

For an hour they had been studying his drawings and
arguing about a dozen different details of construction.
All happy talk, Andrew Held noted, a delightful diversion
from the grim issues this emergency meeting had been
called to consider. Raising his voice just enough to be
heard above the cheerful babble, he said, "May I bring up
something else? I promise you, it won't take long."

As they resumed their seats, he thought, Indeed it won't
take long. He knew what he was going to do, and he
knew that he wouldn't be able to go through with it if he
didn't do it quickly. He looked at the ground beside his
feet. The big rock was there, as he knew it would be.
He had put it there himself. Why did he keep looking at it,
as if it might have rolled away?

"We've talked before about weapons. We've added
considerably to our store in the arsenal, to the best of our
ability, with so little metal of any kind. The Indians on
these islands were better off than we are, even a hundred
and fifty years ago. They had metal as soon as the white
man began exploring the coast. Without proper maps or
charts, the first navigators kept running their ships
aground or breaking them up on rocks and reefs. The
Indians learned what iron was when the wreckage
washed up on their beaches. Metal . . . we need it, badly.
Every bit we can find, no matter how small." He was

talking too fast. His voice was strained and pitched too
high. I want to do this, he told himself. I've considered it
thoroughly, I've planned it deliberately. Then why am I
running on like this, as if no one could cut off my head
as long as the tongue is wagging?

His voice trailed off with an unfinished sentence about
how every one of them must be armed against the wild
dogs at all times. The moment to start doing what he
meant to do billowed out like a thundercloud and hung
before his eyes. Now!

As they watched, their expectant faces froze into expressions of disbelief and dismay. Before anyone, even
Felicia sitting next to him, could do anything to prevent
it, Andrew Held had removed his prosthetic device, picked
up the large rock he had brought to the meeting for
the purpose, and with one desperate blow smashed the
combination of wood, rubber, and metal which served as
his right foot.

Very slowly—it was going to be hard to keep his
balance now—he leaned forward, picked up the shattered
mechanism, and laid it carefully across his knees. "I think
we can get six or eight spear points out of this. Rolf,
Warren, Carlo . . . I'll leave it up to you to decide. I'd
just as soon . . ." As his voice broke, he picked up the
prosthesis and held it out toward the men. "Here!" he
said gruffly. "Take it. I'm glad to be rid of the damned
thing. It's a nuisance, and always has been. I'd just as
soon not see it again."

Suddenly they were all around him. Diana's wide blue-
gray eyes were looking into his, and they were misty
with tears. That was Norma, the reserved one, hugging
him and kissing him on the cheek. Felicia was murmuring, "You idiot, you sweet, crazy idiot." And the men
were talking all at once about making something to protect the bare stump and build his right leg to the same
length as his left.

Rolf would supply the leather. Warren would do the
carving. Carlo was reminding them that there was still
something left of the inner tube they had used to make
slingshots . . .

"What am I?" Andrew Held protested in a husky
voice. "The queen bee? Santa Claus?" No one seemed to
hear him. A lovely warm feeling settled over him. "I
really meant it. I hate that thing. I always have. Now

I'm free of it. *Free.*" Someone's lips brushed his cheek, and a firm hand pressed his shoulder. He sighed deeply. He hadn't felt so good in a long, long time . . . not, perhaps, since he was a lad, running joyously to leap aboard a moving streetcar . . .

For some time Rolf, with the Care package tucked under his arm, followed Donald's tracks without difficulty. Fresh footprints in the rain-soaked ground and the raw ends of broken twigs were like fluorescent arrows pointing in the direction of his flight.

As Rolf had anticipated, the big man hadn't moved in a straight line. Like all wild creatures, he had let nature dictate his course, circling clumps of brambles rather than pushing through them, walking around a fallen log rather than climbing over it, and speeding his pace, Rolf guessed, only when he came to flat and open ground. Even without such obvious guideposts as footprints, broken twigs, and trampled ferns, Rolf would have been able to trail Donald simply by following the path of least resistance.

Until the dry wash. All definite signs ceased at the top of a steep bank, where rain and melted snow from above had cut into the gravelly soil, scooping out a straight, almost vertical, trench any vacation hiker would identify as a path. Rolf knew it wasn't. With the first heavy rain, the "path" would become a narrow gully, a conduit for water from the upper slope to the meadow below. Many an amateur following a trail through hilly or mountainous country had lost his way by leaving the trail because he mistook such a dry wash for a shortcut.

Though there was no trail on the south end of Phoenix, Rolf guessed that when Donald reached this point, he would automatically follow something that looked like one. There were no footprints in the dry wash or on either side of it, but there wouldn't be, for the bank was composed of gravel and sand. With the ax gripped firmly in one hand and the backpack of supplies secure under his left arm, Rolf descended the steep bank in a crouching position. And there, it seemed, all clues to Donald's whereabouts ended.

He could have proceeded at any angle. The meadow was carpeted with coarse wild grass on which a man's footfall made no imprint. Without any specific goal, the most natural thing to do was to walk straight ahead, and this Rolf did. At the same time, his eyes searched the field on both sides for any sign that Donald had gone off in a different direction. When he reached the woods on the far side of the meadow, he stopped and studied the forest floor. Finding nothing, he moved first to the left and then to the right along the rim of the woods.

Perhaps Donald hadn't walked this far. He might have stopped at the top of the bank, and instead of sliding down the dry wash he might have changed direction, or even circled back.

Rolf recrossed the meadow, zigzagged his way up the gravel bank, and began to search for signs he might have missed before. Tracking means looking down, so when he heard a sound like the snap of a breaking twig, the cause of the telltale noise was caught only briefly in his peripheral vision. A flick of brown disappearing into a mass of dark green. Animal, or man?

Donald?

Rolf's instinct said it was man. A frightened deer would continue its effort to escape and the snap of twigs and swish of limbs would follow its flight. One of the wild dogs? No, for whatever he had glimpsed had been five or six feet off the ground. Donald. Behind the tangled mass of bushes and vines, Donald must be watching.

"Donald?" Rolf called out loud.

Rolf called again and again, pausing each time he repeated the name to listen for a sound that would tell him Donald was retreating through the woods. But the big man neither answered nor evidently moved out of his hiding place.

He was there, no more than twenty feet away. Rolf's senses shouted it as loudly, as if his ears had picked up the rhythm of Donald's breathing or the thud of his pulse. But he wouldn't try to flush Donald out of his protective thicket. They had sent him into exile, and in some way Rolf didn't understand, the defiant Donald of the "trial" the night before had been so upset he had fled in the middle of the night. Rolf recoiled from the idea of forcing him into the open now.

Slowly and distinctly, he called out, "Donald, you left without any supplies. We made up this package for you. It's mostly pemmican and jerky and dried apples. But I put in some fishing line and two wooden hooks, and a fire drill. And there's a deer paunch, so you can carry water."

He waited. A faint rustle, a flicker of color almost indiscernible from the deep green of the underbrush, and then silence. Rolf put down his ax, lifted the coarse basket of supplies with both arms, and wedged it into the scaly crotch of a bifurcated madrona tree. Then he picked up the ax, signaled good-bye with a wave of the hand, and turned north toward camp.

The agenda for the monthly meeting of the Gregory Place Council of Co-Owners included discussion of what should be done about the Mansfield property. Council Member Thelma Thorstad had already made up her mind. Let the others delay a decision, saying the circumstances were so unusual they didn't know what to do. Mrs. Thorstad *did* know what to do because it was all there, in the real estate laws of the state of New York, in the Condominium Purchase Agreement, in the by-laws, and in the requirements of the Department of Housing and Urban Development and the National Housing Act.

"Mr. Chairman!" Mrs. Thorstad always puffed when under stress and her bosom heaved energetically as she pointed out that Mr. and Mrs. Blake Mansfield had violated the by-laws by defaulting on maintenance charges and ignoring the notice of a special assessment. She reminded the Council that housing economists had predicted that fifty percent of the population of the United States will live in some form of condominium housing by 1996, that action should be taken to release all available units, and . . . huffing mightily . . . that *that* meant the Mansfield property could legally be sold at any time the Council so voted.

A young woman with thoughtful brown eyes and prematurely gray hair signaled to the chairman and rose as he nodded recognition. "As you know, Norma Mansfield has been a personal friend ever since she and Blake bought their apartment. It is inconceivable, to anyone who knows the Mansfields, that they would do anything . . . irregular."

Her voice broke off. She coughed, composed herself, and went on in a firm tone of voice. "I have talked with Blake's law partner, Mr. Boyd, and with several of their close friends. Before they went back to London, I talked with the English couple who sublet the apartment while Blake and Norma were on vacation. They all agree that something serious has happened to prevent the Mansfields from returning to New York on schedule. I'm afraid that . . . that something terrible . . ."

"*That* is for the authorities to decide!" To Thelma Thorstad, authorities were very big. "*Our* business tonight is the management of this condominium."

The young woman, whose name was Lucy, had few friends she valued as much as Norma Mansfield. Health foods and wild mushroom hunting had brought them together, but the traits they shared—a reserved manner, a need for the well-ordered life—had secured the bonds. Lucy was badly shaken by everything she had learned from inquiring about her friends.

That Blake was accused of stealing a rented car! That Norma had never written her uncle in Maine! That Blake had not consulted his law partner before extending his stay in the Pacific Northwest! After two nights in the Olympic Hotel in Seattle, a fact confirmed by the Seattle Police Department, they had simply dropped from sight. "Mrs. Thorstad!" she pleaded. "Please! Can't you understand? They have *disappeared!*"

Uneasy murmurs from others members of the Council accompanied Mrs. Thorstad's breathy response. "Rules are made . . . to be followed."

The chairman took charge with a gentlemanly tap of his gavel. "It's only been two months, hasn't it? Let's not take hasty action against owners who have been so entirely reliable in the past. I will entertain a motion that the question of selling the Mansfield property be tabled for at least another month."

Lucy whispered, "I so move . . ." and, excusing herself, she hurried out of the room. Like her friend Norma, Lucy was too well-brought-up to show emotion in the presence of casual acquaintances.

Chapter Thirty-Three

IN one way or another, they all worked on the house. The men felled the trees and hauled the logs to the building site. There the women de-barked them with stone hatchets, a time-consuming effort that told Andrew Held more about their attitudes than any of them admitted. Stripping off the bark would increase the lifespan of the cabin, because it delayed damage from rot and routed the wood-eating insects that made their home under the bark. But if speed was more important than permanence, it was a dubious embellishment. Many an early cabin was made of rough logs. Many a cabin had no floor other than hard, bare ground. These Phoenix builders, however, the men as well as the women, were united by perfectionist and aesthetic instincts. *Their* cabin would have smooth, insect-free walls. Their cabin would have a wood floor. The moment they started to build, their common goal was to erect the best, though something a great deal less would serve the stated purpose of sheltering them for a month or two.

Was it a primeval urge for self-betterment and self-expression, or merely a desire to regain the bodily comfort they had been conditioned to expect as their birthright? Whatever it was, Andrew Held reflected, it had shown itself from the first. They hadn't made many baskets before they soon began to weave in decorative colors and patterns. After only one batch of plain soap, they had begun to experiment with flowers, herbs, and pine needles to add a pleasing scent and color.

Once the logs were trimmed and de-barked, the ends had to be shaped so as to fit into each other. Here Warren Brock surprised them. Though he liked to disclaim knowledge of anything practical, at some time in his career as a sculptor his dedication to the beauty and uses of wood had detoured him into the technique of jointing logs.

"I've done my *best* to forget it," he assured them. "But

the awful truth is that I know a chamfer from a mortise and I could discourse for an hour on the relative merits of square, saddle, and dovetail notches."

On Brock's advice, they chose what he called the "sharp-notch design" because it could be done with the ax alone. With two slashes, the end of the log was transformed from a circle into a pie-shaped wedge. Two smaller cuts on the side opposite the pointed edge created a wide notch. Once they had prepared as much of this rough "lumber" as they estimated they would use, their progress was rapid. Two cabin walls were erected simultaneously by interlocking the logs at right angles to form a corner of the house, with the pie-shaped joints pointing up and the notch underneath each log snugly fitted over the pointed end of the log below it. Chinking the walls with moss and clay was done by the women.

The house seemed to spring up out of the ground. In less than a month, they had laid a foundation of rock that would prevent the logs from rotting on damp ground and allow air to circulate. On this solid base they had erected four walls enclosing enough living space to accommodate them while they were enlarging the house with the gradual addition of more rooms. There was the roof to be raised, and that would require many more trees for the beams and the rafters. Bolts of cedar had to be split into thick reddish-brown shakes. But once these tasks were accomplished, they could live in the unfinished shell. From adzing timbers for the floor to building interior walls, everything else could be done after they moved in.

When they spoke of Donald, it was a reference to how much help he could be in felling trees and dragging heavy logs from the woods to the farm site. Their careful voices betrayed neither anger nor compassion.

Did they miss him? Yes, Dr. Held decided, in the sense that they were keenly aware of his absence. But Donald was taboo for thirty days. It was a verdict they had all had an opportunity to debate and they had all agreed on. Therefore, they seemed to be saying, discussing the absent Donald was taboo as well. What would it do except disinter the corpse of an act they hoped to bury permanently? Not because they could forget it, or were required to forgive it. Just because that was the only practical way to live together in this small and interreliant community.

When he put another mark on the totem calendar at the close of another day, was he the only one who counted the days Donald had spent in exile? Andrew Held thought not. He had often seen expressions of intense introspection, a shuttered look in their eyes, a grimness around their mouths. Then their growing anticipation of "moving day" would take over, and their faces would light up with excitement as they counted the days out loud. Not to the day Donald would return. In happy singsong, they counted how many days they had worked on the house, and how many days they would have to work before they could leave the beach for the warm, dry shelter of a home they had built themselves.

They did not talk about Donald, but they knew he was alive.

Once or twice a week, Rolf and Carlo went hunting. Besides their usual devices for bagging fowl and rabbit, they carried the new and formidable weapons that Dr. Held's sacrifice of his prosthetic foot had added to the arsenal. The prosthesis had yielded enough metal for nine spear tips. Attached to long straight lengths of hardwood, they made lightweight, razor-sharp spears. They had voted unanimously at the meeting that the women as well as the men were to carry them whenever they left camp, so Andrew Held was not surprised when Rolf and Carlo took them along on their hunting trips. But the day they announced they were going to track game in the unexplored south end of the island, he knew instantly that they were concealing their chief purpose.

It wasn't really necessary to find out what sort of game could be hunted in the south, for they were sincerely dedicated to building the log house and plenty of meat could be snared, trapped, or speared en route to the old Furness farmsite. No, he thought ruefully. Vicious weapons for vicious animals. They were out to track down, and if possible to decimate, the roving pack of feral dogs.

When they returned from their first foray into the south, they brought game, but a quick glance at the clean tips told Andrew Held that Rolf and Carlo had had no reason to use their spears. He was caught in a riptide of emotions. Relief, because they were unharmed, and disappointment because they had not encountered and destroyed any of the dogs.

As he dropped his string of grouse, Rolf revealed another reason for venturing into alien land. "We watched for Donald. We came across ashes. So he's been able to make fire. No other sign."

The third time they went into the hills to the south of the harbor, Rolf and Carlo came back with a different report.

"We saw him," Carlo said. "And he saw us, I'll bet you that. But he took off, went the other way."

Andrew Held nodded. "That was the agreement."

"Shu-ah . . ." Carlo acknowledged. "The only difference, we didn't think he would head south. We figured he would stay north of the beach, in the territory he's used to. Especially since he knew where Rolf saw signs of the dog pack. Man, you don't have to be a coward to be afraid of a pack of wild dogs. What is he? Superbrave?"

Rolf said thoughtfully, "Braver than he ought to be. Maybe, because he's so big, he thinks he can handle anything. Maybe he can, but I still wish we could find that pack and wipe it out. It's a matter of getting the dogs before they get him. Or one of us. But right now Donald's in more danger than we are."

Like all building projects on Phoenix Island, the making of a canoe had to begin with the invention of the necessary tools. Rolf's grandfather had often recited the names of the four guardian spirits to whom the master canoe-builder of the old days always appealed for aid. Adze, Wedge, Ax, and Cedar Tree. Thanks to Norma and Blake's discoveries on the old Furness farm, the colony already had an ax, and Ax had simplified the task of obtaining Cedar Tree, for without it Rolf would have been forced to fell a tree with stone chisels or by controlled burning.

With the assistance of two of the four spirits already secured, Rolf was able to proceed to the making of Wedge and Adze. The adze was the more important of the two. Even when the canoe-maker was fully equipped, with mauls, wedges, chisels, wood bits, curved knives, and abrasives, the hand-adze was the jewel of his tool kit because his skill with it was his measure as an artist. Wedges of elkhorn or yew wood, mauls of stone, chisels of bone or shell were used in the felling of the tree and the rough shaping of the hull, but it was the adze that transformed the crudely hollowed log into a graceful canoe and the adze that enabled the canoe-maker to finish his craft with such distinctive markings his work could not be confused with anyone else's.

Diana watched Rolf's progress with a combination of love and anxiety, but Warren Brock observed with a detached and impersonal recognition of canoe-making as an art.

"Very pretty," he said, when Rolf used stone wedges to split the log, hot stones to char the center, and chisels, maul, and wedges to scoop out the burned wood and rough-shape the outside of the hull. But when Rolf reached the stage of final shaping, Brock looked on with frank admiration.

The adze itself was a work of art. Because his grandfather had been a Nootkan, Rolf had heard more about the D-adze common to that tribe than he had about the elbow adze of the north or the straight adze of the south. His had a blade of polished stone and a haft of hardwood carved into a rectangle with rounded corners, a distinct letter D with smoothly whittled indentations to fit his fingers on the side he gripped with his hand. The blade was lashed to the handle with a strip of deer hide.

"Beautiful!" Brock breathed. And as Rolf began to adze the outer surface, cautiously hewing and rehewing until he got the line that pleased him, Brock laughed and clapped like a child at his first circus.

"By my dear sweet Aunt Nellie," he chuckled. "This isn't carpentry, Rolfie boy. This is sculpture. What have I been doing, making attenuated Jesus Christs with skinny beards, and earth-mother nudes with bulbous breasts? If I want to express sex and religion, I should go into boat-building."

As a child, Rolf had tolerated his grandfather's reminiscences as the maunderings of an old man living in a forgotten time. At more than one stage in the shaping of his canoe, he wished fervently that he had listened more carefully. How thick should the hull be? How much should he cut on the outside, how far should he burn and scrape on the inside?

He remembered one formula because his grandfather had repeated it monotonously: A thirty-foot whaling canoe was a finger's width at the gunwale, two fingers on the sides, and three on the bottom. But he wasn't building a whaler. His canoe was approximately eighteen feet long and for that reason could be thicker without being too heavy to carry. With a silent prayer to the guardian spirits, he gambled on boyhood memories.

Using the camp's precious yellow-handled screwdriver, Rolf drilled several holes in the hull. Then he made plugs to fit the holes, and scorched them until they could be distinguished easily from the red-brown of the cedar log. After cutting the blackened plugs into pieces as long as the desired thickness of the hull, he inserted them into the holes from the outside. These were his guides, his warning system. When he was adzing the interior, he knew, as soon as he cut into a dark plug, that he had gone far enough.

"Marvelous, simply *marvelous!*" Brock exclaimed. "Clever chaps, those Nootkans. And clever of you to remember, dear boy. I'm relieved to see that your Welsh blood didn't dilute your native American instinct. Oh, the Welsh are all right, I suppose, if you want to dig coal or sing in a chorus. But boat-building? Stick with your mother's people. They were bobbing all over the North Pacific when your father's antecedents were piling up rocks to hide behind."

Once the log had been hewn, inside and out, Rolf undertook the spreading of the hull. Again he realized he had given his grandfather his respect but not necessarily his attention. It was done with hot water and with sturdy sticks or "stretchers," but if he had ever known the details of the operation they had long since faded from memory.

Carlo, with his knowledge of Hawaiian dugouts, and Brock with his understanding of the temper and strength of wood, came to his rescue. All three of them worked to increase the beam.

First they poured several inches of hot water into the hull and added heated stones until the water came to a boil. At the same time they kept small, slow fires on both sides of the canoe, near enough to warm the outside but not so close that they risked scorching the wood. Every inch of the hull was soaked with hot water to further insure the pliability of the wood.

At that point the hand-hewn boards, or "stretchers,"

were inserted crosswise between gunwales. Gradually, each set of stretchers was replaced by a longer set, and this went on progressively until the hull was spread to the proper width in proportion to its length. The last set of stretchers remained so that the canoe would retain its shape and there would be seats for those paddlers who preferred to sit rather than kneel.

The job was done at last, and Diana was bailing out the last boatload of now-tepid water when Rolf realized that, in the course of building this canoe, his original purpose had changed.

Presumably this dugout was to be used for salmon fishing and for reaching coves and beaches that were more accessible by sea than by land. That had been firmly established at the meeting, when the group had voted unanimously against his trying to paddle across open sea in order to get help. At the time he had agreed, or at least he had bowed to the majority. He had also recognized the risk. But then he hadn't yet built the boat. "Canoe" was an idea, a theory. As the tree became the hull log and the log became a seagoing craft, and this magical transformation took place under his own hand, his imagination had begun to reach out. If he could go out a mile, he could go another mile, and another mile after that . . .

As Diana moved along the canoe, bending to dip water with a wooden scoop, Rolf watched her thoughtfully, forgetting his own chore. She was carrying his child. It was easy to say that she could bear the child without a doctor because Indian women had managed that way for centuries. But Diana wasn't Indian, and as the weeks passed, her assurances that "everything will be all right" did not quiet the anxiety he felt when he began noticing the changes pregnancy was making. Her slender waist was thicker, her breasts were fuller, and in spite of her efforts to hide it, he had seen her grow pale with a sudden attack of nausea.

His own mother had scoffed at hospitals. She had borne six healthy children with nothing more than the brief assistance of a midwife. But Rolf had overheard enough female conversation about women who had "complications" to know that childbirth was not necessarily easy just because it was natural. He had tried to convince himself that small and slender as Diana was, she wasn't delicate.

She was one of those deceivingly tough small people, all muscle and wire. She could run like a deer, climb trees like a bobcat, swim like an otter. But he always got back to it—she was a girl, *his* girl, with his child, and she had never had a baby. How could she be sure, how could anyone know, that she wouldn't have "complications"?

The discovery that a feral dog pack existed on Phoenix had added to Rolf's anxiety. He was realistic about them and therefore afraid of them. But he was a practical and experienced hunter, confident in his ability to avoid or escape them if he wasn't able to wound or kill. The idea that Diana might be attacked was a different matter.

The more he thought about it, the more the idea frightened him. She couldn't always stay close to him. She was armed, yes. Like Felicia and Norma, she never left camp without her dagger and her spear. In addition, she carried a slingshot for hunting rabbits or wild fowl and, through months of practice, she had become such an accurate marksman that she might be able to drive off one dog, providing she wasn't caught by surprise. But a pack? Only Donald had seen the dogs. He had counted four of them, he said. But no one knew how many there might be on the island. The chances were that they moved in a pack, and pack instinct would multiply the viciousness of a single dog tenfold.

Diana poured out the last dipper of water and, panting a little, rose from her kneeling position. For a moment she stood still and breathed heavily with her eyes half closed, like a runner at the end of a hard race.

Rolf's heart contracted. It was so unlike Diana to be clumsy or short of breath. He went to her quickly, took the dipper out of her hand, and dropped it to the ground. With his arms around her, he looked down into her face.

Her wide eyes picked up blue lights from the sky. Her short straight nose was still adorned with the last of her summer freckles, and her satiny skin glistened softly with moisture that smelled like drying hay. Her lips, curving with a smile, were parted a little, barely revealing straight white teeth.

"Diana," he whispered. "I love you. God, how I love you." Their mouths met in a long kiss, and in that moment Rolf knew what he was going to do as soon as his canoe was in the water.

When Norma and Felicia left camp, their purpose was to replenish the buttery in any way they could. At this time of year, it wouldn't be an easy task. In late summer and fall the woods and the fields had been rich with wild foods, and on the old Furness farm there were plants that had stubbornly reseeded themselves and trees and vines that had refused to give in to neglect and had yielded a surprising crop of fruit, berries, and grain. But the harvest was long past. The fields were brown and soaked with rain. Blackberry vines, salal bushes, Oregon grape were bare. Wild growth was still green, for in this corner of the Pacific Northwest only a small proportion of plant life was deciduous, but even evergreen plants and trees, for all their lively color, lay dormant, retrenching against the first frost. However, there were roots to be dug, and some weed stalks that could be peeled down to a tender core. In the Furness orchard a few apples, pears, and plums might still be scattered on the ground. The cedar bark baskets that Norma and Felicia had strapped to their backs would not be empty when they returned to camp.

Norma was the expert on wild plant food. In the gradual drift toward specialization, she had even surpassed Diana, whose inherited folk knowledge she had absorbed very quickly. Felicia came along as Norma's helper, for her own area of expertise was basket-making and weaving. There was another reason for accompanying Norma, a reason neither of them cared to discuss.

It was no longer safe to leave camp alone. Except for the open area around the harbor and the dormitory on the hill, they had agreed to move about in pairs or in threes and fours. They were to be armed, and the women were not to venture into the woods south of camp. So Norma and Felicia set out together on the familiar trail leading north to the farm.

The wild dogs had destroyed or carried off smoked and dried meat and left their store of vegetables and fruit almost intact, so the community's primary need was for meat. But neither Norma nor Felicia had ever hunted. They left that to the men and to Diana, who was expert with bow and arrow and with the slingshot. They would be doing their part if they increased the supply of roots so that meat rations could be decreased.

They were armed, yes, but for self-protection. Neither

of them had ever faced the fact that killing could be a part of protecting oneself. They carried the primitive weapons because the group had so ruled at the meeting. After all, what could happen on the north end of Phoenix, where they had been wandering freely and safely for more than three months?

But what a picture they made! Looking at Norma, Felicia's sense of the ridiculous diverted her from grim thoughts about the weapons they were carrying. "Aren't we lucky there aren't any mirrors on Phoenix?"

Laughing, she pointed to her own costume and to the near-duplicate Norma was wearing. They were clothed in skins. Vests, skirts, leggings, moccasins—all were the pelts of animals, with the fur worn on the inside for greater warmth. Rain capes of woven cedar bark were draped from their shoulders, tied around their necks with rawhide thongs and falling below their knees. Coiffures to match, Felicia thought. Her own long red hair was twisted into a knot and secured at the nape of her neck with several polished cedar pins substituting for the manufactured hairpins she had donated for fishing gear. Norma's bobbed hair had grown long enough to wear in a thick, bouncing pony tail. She brushed it straight back from her fine-boned face and tied it with a wide band of creamy tan rabbit fur.

"Prehistoric women," Felicia said. "All we need to complete our ensembles are polished thigh bones to stick into our hair."

Norma responded with a faint smile. "I know. We've come a long way, haven't we. From Sixty-third Street, and Lafayette Park. But I'm comfortable, except for this." She touched the scabbard at her belt and the protruding handle of the dagger. "And this." Her eyes lifted to focus on the sharp tip of her spear. "I really don't like them."

"Oh, pooh. Neither do I. But we'll take them, anyway."

"You don't suppose . . . ?"

Felicia shrugged. "That those terrible dogs would be up north? That they could have run right through the dormitory and not one of us would have noticed? Of course not. But Andrew . . ." She choked on the memory of the emergency session when Andrew had destroyed his leg. "Remember, Andrew broke up his prosthesis just for . . . He believed . . . " She swallowed hard and began again. "Oh fiddlesticks, Norma. I mean, let's do as we're told."

"Of course. I meant to. It was just . . . just that I suddenly tried to imagine what I would do with a dagger or a spear if something *did* attack me."

Felicia looked into her partner's troubled face and smiled in understanding. "Very simple, dear. You'd attack right back. You'd do that, wouldn't you, even on Sixty-third Street?"

Norma relaxed visibly. Adjusting the shoulder harness to which her bark basket was attached, she said drily, "*Especially* on Sixty-third Street."

"Then let's go dig roots."

Nodding and smiling, Norma led the way.

Norma's sharp eyes and greatly enlarged repertoire resulted in full baskets. Before they left the farm, they took inventory. It wasn't meat, but it would help fill their stomachs. They shouldered their baskets and set out for camp.

At the edge of the orchard, they saw the raccoons. Four of them, half hidden by the tall dry grass. Their heads were down, sniffing the ground at the base of the tree as they searched for the last edible windfalls.

Felicia and Norma approached cautiously, with nothing in mind except to obtain a better view of the animals' comic faces before their presence was detected. They came within fifteen or twenty feet, and still the raccoons seemed to be oblivious to their approach. They were pawing through clumps of grass, retrieving an apple here and there, biting and chewing with concentration that excluded their human observers.

Felicia thought, How cute they are! What a funny waddle. And then suddenly she saw something more than amusing little animals.

This was meat to replace the stores the wild dogs had carried off. This was fur, for blankets and clothing they would need over the winter. The men had killed many raccoons. She had eaten the meat, and she was wearing one of the pelts. Were she and Norma going to stand by while four raccoons ate their fill of apples and then scuttled away into the woods? Food and clothing, the two basic elements of survival, were theirs for the asking. Could she protest, "But I don't like to kill anything . . ."

and at the same time take for granted her right to share what someone else had killed?

She lifted her spear and looked with revulsion at its pointed tip. The way the raccoons were behaving, she would probably be able to catch at least one by surprise. Of course if she made a quick move or a loud sound, she would frighten them away . . . With a sense of vast relief, she entertained the idea of scaring them off deliberately. No one would expect her to hit a running, half-concealed target.

One of the raccoons reared up onto its hind legs. Its pert triangular face was turned toward the two women. Its bright eyes peered out through round eyeholes in its furry black mask. With part of an apple held delicately between its slender front paws, so human in its whole attitude, the little raider surveyed them without a trace of panic. Its expression was curious but amiable. It was surprised but not really resentful of this human intrusion into its orchard. As Rolf had explained many times, animals on Phoenix were not accustomed to being hunted. They had never learned to be afraid of human beings.

Felicia whispered urgently, "Norma! We've got to." It was ridiculous to expect Norma to understand her, but such a terrible taste of bile was rising in her throat she couldn't trust herself to say more. She turned her head.

Norma's face was ashen, her mouth was trembling, but her spear was raised. Norma understood.

The one raccoon continued to study them while the three others, heads down, kept rustling through the tangled grass. Felicia thought desperately, I can't, I can't . . . But she could. The memory of the way the buttery had looked after the raid assured her that she could because she had to. Food stores ravaged, their precious winter supplies strewn along the beach, days and days—no, weeks and months—of hard work lost in one single attack. Yes, she could. Just charge, drive the spear . . .

"We've got to!" she repeated, though she had already begun to cry.

Norma was beside her as they crept toward the animals and then suddenly ran forward. Norma's spear struck one animal only a second after Felicia had driven her own into the soft belly of the upright, curious raccoon.

The two survivors scuttled through the grass. They

were much smaller than the body quivering at Felicia's feet. Norma's kill was also smaller than her own. Then Felicia realized why one larger raccoon had stood watch while the others ate. The little group had consisted of a mother and three kits. She had slaughtered the mother. Norma had speared one of the kits.

Felicia sank to the ground, crying. Norma sat down beside her, reached for her hand, and holding it tightly, whispered, "I know, I know . . ."

At home, Nurse Watkins was Louise, devoted wife of George B. Watkins whose reputation in the small town in southeast Alaska was for fair dealing in his dry goods store as well as in poker games in the back of the tavern on Sunday afternoons. One of the bonds of their marriage was that they were both on their feet all day and both suffered backache and swollen feet.

Pouring two mugs of strong black coffee, Louise sat down at the kitchen table opposite her husband. "I haven't got the strength to change out of my uniform." She slumped over her cup, elbows on the table, chin resting on her hands.

"Your posture is terrible," George commented mildly. He opened the cabinet under the sink, withdrew a bottle of Demarara rum, and poured a generous shot into each coffee cup. "Anything happen at the hospital today?"

She nodded wearily.

"Bad day, huh?" George Watkins patted his wife's capable hand. "Leave your cases at the hospital, honey, like I leave unpaid bills at the store. Otherwise our minds will get as weak as our arches."

"You're right, George," Nurse Watkins agreed. "But the one today really bothers me."

"Must be Sixteen-A."

She sipped her coffee, set the cup down, and leaning back in her chair, closed her eyes. "That's the one."

"She talk some more?"

"She tried to. She tried *hard,* and I stayed right with her. But it was all jumbled, like it's been before. Like a person who's had a slight stroke. It seemed to me that things were clear in her head, but she couldn't get them out. She couldn't communicate."

"Still talking about an island?"

"That's the one word that did come out, good and clear. She said it over and over. Her eyes were practically begging me to understand."

"But no names? Hers, or the island's, or anybody's?"

"None at all. Just island, island, island."

"Huh. Needle in a haystack. Think of how many hundreds of islands there are along this coast. She might not be talking about Alaska. She might come from B.C., or even from Washington."

Louise Watkins sighed heavily. "I just can't get that old wrinkled face out of my mind, especially those frightened eyes."

George said cheerfully. "Oh, come on, lady. You're an old pro. Besides, you said Sixteen-A was getting better. I know it's been three months, but one of these days what she says will hang together. And you'll be right there when it does."

Louise Watkins rubbed the worry lines between her eyebrows. "George, Sixteen-A died today. She tried so hard to talk and then she collapsed. An hour later, she was dead."

"Ah . . . so *that's* what got to you today."

"Now we're never going to know who she is, or where she belongs. Somewhere there's an island . . . but the hospital has already done everything they can to trace her. It's a . . . dead end."

There was a long silence, and then George Watkins got up, refilled their mugs, and picked up the bottle of rum. "Let's have another dollop."

"Yes. Thanks, George," Nurse Watkins said, as her husband tipped up the bottle and added another cheering measure of 150 proof rum.

Chapter Thirty-Four

ANDREW Held no longer questioned Rolf and Carlo when they went hunting on the south end of the island. After their first venture into that area, it was clear why the two young men, both so intent on building the house that they normally worked on it from sunup to sunset regardless of weather, would sacrifice a half day or a day in pursuit of "game." But when they returned, he always asked, "Did you see him?" More often than not, they had. But only a glimpse, a rustling of brush, telling them Donald was near and they were being watched and followed.

Shortly before Donald's term of exile was to expire, Rolf and Carlo announced at breakfast that they were going hunting.

Dr. Held glanced at the totem calendar. "If Donald shows himself, or if you think he's within earshot, tell him we are expecting him on Saturday. That's another six days. I suppose he's tried to keep track, but perhaps not. In any case, hearing it from you will make it definite."

"La dee *da,* Andrew!" Warren Brock grimaced. "Do you *have* to be thoughtful? Worse than that. You're being *kind.*"

"Try it yourself, Warren," Felicia snapped. "You've often said you enjoy new experiences."

"Oh my dear lady," Brock said with a small chuckle, "not if they *improve* me."

As Rolf and Carlo shouldered their weapons and left camp, Mike and Lili, the basset hounds, abandoned their posts near the bonfire and lumbered down the beach, sniffing the hunters' footprints. Andrew Held watched with amusement. Typical hounds, they used their noses instead of their eyes. Rolf and Carlo were only thirty or forty feet ahead of them. If the dogs looked up, they could see and follow easily. But that wasn't a basset's way. With noses to the ground, Mike and Lili trotted along the beach on stubby pronated legs, so absorbed by following the scent they almost bumped Rolf's heels before they lifted their heads. At that point they wagged their tails frantically and uttered baritone yelps of joy at this unexpected reunion with friends from whom they had been separated for a full minute and a half.

Lili's barrel-shaped torso was becoming even more comical than usual, for she was to have puppies in four or five weeks. Smiling at the grotesque bulge of the female basset *enceinte,* Andrew Held directed his attention to the first project of the day. As the morning wore on, he wondered once or twice where Mike and Lili might be, but he was not concerned. The hounds loved everybody in the group and often chose to bestow their joyful companionship on someone else.

When Carlo and Rolf returned shortly after noon, Dr. Held recalled that when he had last seen the dogs they were following the two young men along the beach. With a twinge of anxiety, he asked, "Did you see Mike and Lili? Weren't they with you?"

"Not for long." Carlo's black eyes were troubled. "They acted like they wanted to follow, but when we got to the woods we sent them back."

"They *did* start back," Rolf added. "We never saw them again. I thought they were here with you."

Andrew Held was disturbed by what he saw in their faces. In an effort to contradict, or at least to ignore it, he said reassuringly, "Well, they aren't lost. A basset hound is never lost. It's only his owner who sometimes gets misplaced."

Donald was proud of himself, and it was a good feeling. It would help at the end of the month when he had to go back to camp and face the people who sent him away. He wasn't a woodsman. They had known that when they condemned him to thirty days in the woods. By God, he had done all right.

Sure, the basket of supplies Rolf cached in the madrona tree had carried him through the first few days. The way he had been feeling that first morning, he would have liked to hand the basket right back to him. But that would have meant coming out in the open. Besides, even while he begrudged Them—the eight who had sat in judgment on him, *Them*—even while he resented the fact that They were in a position to be generous, something told him he might eventually be glad they were.

His instinct had been right. For a time, he had ignored the cache, trying to feed himself on raw roots, the cores of cattail stalks, and the few dry blackberries still clinging to evergreen vines. At the end of his second day in the wilderness, he was desperately hungry, as well as frustrated by bungling attempts to start a fire with sticks. So he found his way back to the madrona tree. His hands had trembled as he tore open the basket. In a choked voice, he had cursed his benefactors.

After that, something began to change. A "something" he couldn't identify at first, within himself, and between him and the woods around him.

In the community of nine, Donald had done more than his share of the work, but since there was always at least one person who knew more about living in the wilderness than he did, he had always worked at someone else's direction. And he had never been observant. In a way, he had refused to be. When he was given a job, he did what he was told, and sought the approval of the others by doing it longer and harder than they expected. If someone else got the job—lighting a fire, for example, or shaping a wooden fish hook—he had always felt they didn't give him a chance at it because they didn't believe he could do it. So the hell with them, he wasn't going to watch and see how it was done.

Exiled on the south end, alone and unaided, he had been forced to experiment. He tried, and he failed. With no one to correct his errors, he simply tried again.

The change, the "something" that made him proud, was that he had finally been thinking for himself. He had never been allowed to do this in the county orphanage, nor later in the strict boys' school run by the church. When he was older, in the army and in prison, he quickly learned that the man who thought for himself was the man who spent time in the brig or in the hole for breaking rules. Donald hadn't even been thinking for himself when he got married. Hell, hot as he was for the girl, he wasn't thinking at all. If he had been, he would have known she'd walk out on him the first time a soft-talking guy put his hand on her knee.

In fact he couldn't remember any time in his whole life, except when he was working with engines, that he had known the satisfaction of being praised for something he thought up himself. "Success," when it came, meant he had managed to follow orders. Alone in the woods on the south end of Phoenix Island, it was all up to him, especially after he had finished off the food in the cache. He wouldn't starve if he could think of ways to obtain food. He wouldn't be cold if he could figure out how to build a shelter. Even with the fire drill and the fish hooks Rolf had left him, he did not make fire the first time, and he had lost one precious fish hook before he got the hang of tying hook to line. So his first fish and his first fire had excited him as nothing had since he had last repaired a diesel engine no one else could fix.

Now, after almost thirty days, he was thinner. His long hair was matted and full of bark and moss because he hadn't bothered to make himself a comb. But he was proud. Hell, he almost laughed out loud when Rolf and Carlo showed up this morning and shouted through the woods, "Donald? Donald? In six days, the month will be up. Keep track of it, Donald. Six days . . . six days . . ."

Ha! They didn't need to tell him that! That's one of the first things he thought up. A calendar. The trunk of a tree growing beside the little creek where he got his drinking water. He cut a notch into it every morning when he came to drink and fill his gourd, just the way Dr. Held did every night at camp.

The wild dogs had scared Donald into his finest accomplishment.

Funny thing, he hadn't given the dogs a thought the night he fled the dormitory, stumbled along the dark beach, and went into hiding on the south end of the island. He had been totally confused. He had been sick, as if Brock had planted an ugly growth deep in his gut. So he had run in the only direction he could take without passing through the woods where they were all sleeping, the woods where Brock was laughing at him. He ran blindly, tripping, falling, struggling to his feet and running on, hardly thinking of what was ahead in his reckless desire to leave humiliation behind.

When he awoke in the morning, he remembered, and fear rippled through his aching and exhausted body.

Somewhere on the south end, maybe near where he was lying, during his pre-exile period, four wild dogs had driven him up a tree while he was hunting birds with his slingshot. It was on the south end that Brock had come across the remains of a fawn slaughtered and eaten by dogs, and it was on the south end where Rolf had located the dogs' cave.

Donald reasoned that he would have to take his chances during the day. Dogs or no dogs, he had to hunt and fish and find water. If he had to defend himself, a spear would be a better weapon than a knife, so he had made one by lashing his jackknife to a stick. And he had his slingshot. It wouldn't kill an attacking dog, but under the right conditions—like, if he had time to climb a tree—it might stun the animal and scare him off. Of course the trick was to hear them coming. Listening was his best weapon against a pack of animals. So during the day he would walk softly and slowly, stopping often, ears straining for every sound. But at night?

Donald wasn't sure whether wild dogs roam at night, but he knew instinctively that any danger would be greater after dark. So he needed a safe place to sleep.

He had faced the problem alone. Forced to think for himself, he had come up with an answer. Sleeping safely meant sleeping up high, well off the ground. He would build a tree house.

He had begun it with a solid platform of small drift logs securely tied to the heavy lower limbs of a maple tree. On three sides, a heavy stand of evergreens screened him from the wind. To keep out rain, he had slung honeysuckle vines over a branch above the platform, tied opposite ends of each length of vine to opposite sides of the platform and used these slanting stringers as the warp in weaving a tent-like roof of cedar boughs. He also wove a rope of honeysuckle tough enough to hold his weight. Looped over the ridgepole limb, it served as a ladder. With his feet on the tree trunk and his hands gripping the rope, he learned to pull himself up, hand over hand, like walking up the tree. The roost was so small he had to sleep folded up like a jackknife, but he had carpeted the platform with layers of moss, fern and cedar bows, so he was reasonably comfortable. And reasonably safe from falling if he should move about in

his sleep, for the platform was enclosed by a foot-high
picket fence of green saplings.

He was so pleased with his tree house that when he
realized Rolf and Carlo were hunting in the area, he kept
hoping they would discover it. But they didn't. Once he
watched them walk right under it. Neither of them
spotted it because they were watching for trail signs and
neither of them looked up. In one way he didn't want his
private bedroom to be discovered. In another way, he
was disappointed.

Six more days. Six more nights in his tree house.
Donald's high spirits began to falter as the idea of returning to camp took hold. In a lame effort to reassure
himself, he thought, They're going to be mighty surprised
when they see me healthy as the day I left. From now
on, they're going to give me credit for some brains . . .
He wasn't going to crawl back. He was going to walk
right in, look them right in the face . . .

But his earlier mood of defiance would not be re-
captured. He could see himself walking across the beach
toward the bonfire. All their eyes would be trained on
him, like spotlights in a prison yard. Would Dr. Held say
something? Would anyone say anything? And what was
he going to say? As if the dreaded scene would be visible
if he were facing in the right direction, he turned toward
the north, staring bleakly through the trees. God damn,
he muttered unhappily. God damn, god damn . . . Six
more days, and he was already afraid to face them,
though he knew he had no choice.

Donald was kneeling on the ground skinning a rabbit
when he heard a movement in the underbrush. He
jumped to his feet, dropped the rabbit and, clutching
the handle of his spear, froze in a semi-crouch.

The dog pack? No. There wasn't that much noise.
But maybe wild dogs didn't always stay in a pack. Maybe they hunted alone or in pairs. That's what it sounded
like—one or two dogs. If they had come anywhere near
they would have picked up the scent of freshly killed
game.

The crackling and swish of brush being parted was
getting more distinct. They were coming toward him. He
gripped his spear and, looking around quickly, backed up

against the nearest tree he could climb. If it was the pack, he'd throw them a rabbit and that way give himself time to reach the safety of limbs six or seven feet aboveground. But if there were only one or two of them, he would hide behind the tree, let them find the meat, and then take them on, first with his slingshot and then with his spear. In twenty-four days of exile, he had learned a great deal about how to kill with such simple weapons. He was frightened at the prospect of fighting wild dogs, but he wasn't panicked. Confidence had come as he discovered that even big old dumb Donald Campbell could think for himself.

The noise in the bushes grew louder. Now he could hear the animals themselves. Not growling or yapping, sounds he had associated with wild dogs ever since he had seen four of them while he was bird hunting. What he heard was panting, the labored breathing of dogs who had been running hard.

He bent his knees so that he could pick up one of the rabbits without lowering his eyes. "Come and get it," he thought grimly, tensed to throw the meat the moment the dogs emerged. The palms of his hands were slippery with sweat. The fingers of his right hand ached with the pressure he was putting on the spear handle. He took a step backward, ready to sacrifice the meat and leap behind the tree.

The brush separated. Mike and Lili, tongues drooping from open mouths, plodded into view.

At the sight of Donald, Mike bounded forward, keening with joy. Lili emitted little yelps of recognition and pleasure as she ran to Donald's feet, threw her full weight against his legs, and looked up at him with large adoring brown eyes. Saliva was dripping from the loose folds of skin at the corners of their mouths as their tongues tried to lick his hands and pant at the same time.

With a lump in his throat that hurt like tears held back, Donald sat down on the ground and swept both dogs into his arms. Their prickly muzzles planted wet kisses on his bearded cheek. Their continuing wails of delight said, "We've found you, we've found you . . ."

"Okay, okay," Donald growled as he rubbed their satiny ears. And then, in spite of himself, the tears spilled over and slowly rolled down his cheeks.

For an hour or two, Donald tried to convince himself he had a right to keep Mike and Lili with him. They had tracked him, *they* had come to *him*, and it was a long way back to camp. They would be company, and at night, since he couldn't get them into his tree house, he'd sleep with them on the ground. He'd find a cave . . . But it wasn't any use. He was kidding himself. He had to take them back, today.

In the first place, Dr. Held would miss them and get worried if they weren't in camp before dark. Besides, it wasn't safe for them here. A dog pack that would kill a deer wouldn't be scared off by a pair of friendly hounds who had never had a fight in their lives. He wouldn't take them *all* the way back. Just to the north rim where the hill sloped down to the beach. The dogs would see the people around the fire and run to them while he stayed hidden by the trees. Once they were back with Dr. Held, he would head south again.

He fed them one of the rabbits he had killed that morning, roasted the other one and wrapped it in ferns. After he banked the fire, he put the package of cooked meat and his water bottle into the basket Rolf had used to bring supplies. He strapped the basket on his back like a rucksack, stuffed his slingshot into his hip pocket, and filled his other pockets with smooth round stones he had collected on the beach for ammunition.

"Okay, let's go." He whistled softly.

The hounds, sleeping contentedly by the fire, lifted their heads and studied him doubtfully. *Get up?* When they were so comfortable lying down? *Go?* When this was the warm place, so obviously the place to stay?

Lili's soft upper lip trembled. What had come over their friend? Mike's elephantine ears lifted, as if he were trying to pick up a sound that would justify Donald's peculiar behavior. Then loyalty to man, demented or otherwise, overcame their reluctance. Groaning audibly, Mike and Lili got up onto their fat webbed feet. Their big dark eyes said, "I'm moving, see? I'm moving, I really am . . ." as they lumbered across the grass to Donald's feet.

"You're going home." Donald picked up his spear. "God damn," he said thickly. "God damn . . ." And he set out through the woods. The bassets padded along at his heels, wagging their tails.

They were halfway back to camp when Donald heard the sound. This time he recognized it instantly. This was no deer, for the distant crackling of underbrush was punctuated by the yelps and growls of an excited dog pack.

A month alone in the woods had sharpened his ears and taught him to translate what he heard. There were three or four dogs, maybe even five. They had killed something and they were fighting over it. It might be a deer, for swift as the deer is, a wild dog can outrun it eventually because of his greater stamina. But if it was a deer, there would be food for all. They wouldn't be fighting. So it was something smaller, and they were quarreling over it because they were viciously, murderously hungry.

Just ahead of Donald, Mike and Lili were still as statues. Heads turned toward the strange sound, their ears lifted and hung like flaps from foreheads wrinkled with perplexity. Along their spines from shoulders to tail the short hair suddenly stood on end, a wide bristling strip denoting instinctive fear.

Donald's frantic eyes combed the spot for any sign of protection. Alone, he would have climbed a tree. With Mike and Lili, that was out. They needed a hollow tree or a cave, where they would be beyond the reach of the pack or at least where he would have some chance of taking the wild animals on one at a time. But here, there was nothing. Pine and fir trees, with tall, limbless trunks rising straight up out of the forest floor. There was underbrush, but you couldn't hide from dogs. Not from carnivores so hungry they would fight each other over a rabbit or a raccoon. And they were still fighting. But the shrill howling was no closer now than it had been. Now was the time to run.

"Mike! Lili!" Donald ran between them. "Come on . . ." Over his shoulder, he saw them hesitate, and then, with one last backward glance, they trotted along in his wake.

Donald pushed his way through the woods, grateful for every small clearing or stretch of ground he could cover quickly without the impediment of vines or underbrush. It was easier for Mike and Lili, whose loose hides helped them wiggle through the worst brambles and whose wide snow-shoe feet were designed for crossing mud or marsh.

Every few minutes, Donald paused and listened. As if this were all part of a game, the basset hounds did the same. For some time, it seemed as if they were leaving the dog pack behind. The sound of the fighting became fainter, and then stopped altogether.

To a God he had always claimed never did anything for him, Donald uttered a silent prayer that whatever kill they had been fighting over had been enough to satisfy them, for if they were gorged, they would stop hunting. Then he realized that the sound of fighting could have ceased for another reason. The kill had been small, the dogs were still hungry, the fight had stopped because the pack had united in search of other game. If that was true, he could only hope that they were headed south rather than north.

Donald ran and the dogs followed, panting. Donald rested, and the dogs sat down and looked up at him curiously with their tongues dropping almost to the ground. The sounds he dreaded—the crack of breaking twigs, the whoosh and slap of parted underbrush—were so vivid he felt as if he had them inside his head even when his ears didn't hear them.

And then at one rest stop, he did. Not close, but not very far. And coming nearer.

In panic, Donald looked around. His pulse, already fast from exertion, was hammering the blood vessels in his neck. No trees to climb. No hollow tree where he and the hounds would find protection. But twenty yards ahead, there was a rocky slab, just visible through the tangle of vines and bushes. He ploughed on, ignoring the brambles that scratched his face and arms, shouting "Mike! Lili!" For there was no longer any reason to keep his voice down so as not to attract the savage pack. Because now the frightening sounds of the approaching beasts were so clear he could hear them without stopping to listen. The sharp snap, the whispering movement of brush—they weren't inside his head any more. They were on the outside and coming closer, coming as fast as a dog pack moves when it's following a scent.

Donald's one desperate thought as he stumbled through the woods was to reach the pile of rocks. From eight or ten feet away, he spotted the formation that could save his life. The rock slab he had seen at a distance jutted out of the mossy ground at an acute angle. In the shadow beneath the rock, Donald recognized the opening to a natural cave, big enough to crawl through, though he couldn't tell how large the hollow beneath the rock would be. "Mike, Lili . . ." he gasped, and turned back to get them just as the first wild dog pushed through the underbrush.

Snarling, the wolfish animal padded stealthily across the clearing toward Mike and Lili. And then a second dog, and a third. In the fraction of time that Donald stood frozen at the mouth of the cave, a fourth dog lunged into the open, lowered his massive head and bared his teeth.

Mike faced them all. His long tail, never before used for anything but wagging, stood up stiffly at a right angle to his body as if a battle flag were flying from the white candlewick tip. Lili eyed the strange dogs and backed off, whimpering. As the pack closed in, a low threatening growl rolled up from Mike's throat. And then the moment of paralysis ended, releasing Donald's body and calming his frightened mind. Gripping the handle of his spear, he charged.

Simultaneously the largest of the four dogs attacked. Without growling or yelping. With no more sound than the rustle of paws pressing on dry grass. With no sound at all as his jaws closed and his teeth sank into the soft flesh of Mike's throat.

Oblivious of the other three, Donald ran to the center of the pack and with all his strength plunged his spear into the dog whose teeth were imbedded in Mike's neck. Instead of releasing Mike, the animal shook his head savagely. Mike's blood spurted from his torn throat, coloring his attacker's muzzle a bright red.

In fury so terrible it almost blinded him, Donald thrust his spear again and again. From behind, another of the pack leaped at him, sinking sharp teeth into his thigh. Scarcely aware of the pain, Donald struck out with the handle of his spear and the dog fell back. Once more, Donald drove the knife blade of his spear into the animal that held Mike in a death grip. With a half dozen jagged holes in its body, the dog let go, shuddered, and was still.

He was dead, but he had already killed. Blood poured from Mike's throat. The beautiful satiny head lay in its own thick blood. The sturdy trunk, the stubby crooked legs were motionless on the red-stained ground.

Cursing wildly, Donald kicked the corpse of Mike's killer. Once again, one of the other dogs sprang from behind. A sharp pain struck Donald's ankle as the dog's teeth tore his flesh. Wheeling around, he kicked furiously, catching the animal in the belly with the toe of his boot. The dog yelped, retreated a few feet, and crouched, its yellow eyes fixed on the bodies of the dead dogs.

Donald faced the three blood-hungry dogs and estimated his chances of saving Lili and himself. Lili had crept across the grass and posted herself at Mike's side. She was whining softly, looking up at Donald with wide, unbelieving eyes. Standing between the dogs and the bodies of the others, Donald realized that the small, mean eyes of the pack saw fresh kill and for the moment, nothing else. They would attack him if he stood between them and food, but if he got out of the way, they would rush in to devour the slaughtered dogs. One of their own, and Mike. While they gorged themselves, he would grab Lili and run for the cave.

Leave Mike behind . . . The thought of the gentle hound being torn to pieces made his stomach knot up. No, by God, they couldn't have old Mike.

Facing the snarling pack, Donald took a step backwards, and then another. At the third step, his boot heel hit Mike's body. He stumbled and fell. As if this were a signal, all three feral dogs lunged. Two set teeth into the corpse of their own pack member. The third leaped at Donald's throat, missed his mark, and bit hard into Donald's outstretched arm.

Like an infuriated giant, Donald rose to his feet, dropped his spear and, without a thought for the dog's slashing teeth, grasped the animal around the neck. There was one violent jerk of his powerful arms, the snap of breaking bones, and the dog was dead. Donald dropped the body, secured his spear under one arm, and, kneeling, slid both hands under Mike's body and gently lifted him. "Lili . . ." But he didn't need to call her. As he ran toward the cave, she followed anxiously at his heels.

With every step, Donald expected that one or both of the remaining dogs would attack him from behind. When he reached the cave, he looked back. One dog was ripping open the soft underbelly of the animal with the broken neck. The other was tearing at the entrails of the dog Donald had speared. One of them lifted his head briefly, his bloody muzzle turned curiously toward the cave. Quickly Donald pushed Mike's body through the opening. Lili followed without being told. Stretching out flat, Donald crawled in after her.

Numbness had been holding back the pain. Now the numbness was wearing off. Pain burned his thigh, his ankle, his forearm. Murderous stabs of pain rocketed through his flesh as if his wounds were connected by an internal telegraph system. There was pain in his chest, a fierce ache as if his lungs were being scorched by the air they were fighting to inhale.

For just a moment, he rested his forehead on his arm and closed his eyes. In the dark, Lili's warm tongue licked lovingly at his cheek.

They didn't let Donald tell what happened, not until Norma had cleaned and dressed his wounds and Diana had fed him hot stew and a mug of coffee made from dandelion roots. Then they listened attentively, waiting patiently when his voice faltered.

He couldn't find the right words, not even for what had happened, not at all for how he felt. His voice was strongest when he described how he had killed the last two. Only half glutted, they had abandoned the dismembered bodies of the other pack dogs and followed the trail of dripping blood to the cave. Then the odds were on his side, for the entrance to his shelter under the rock was so small the dogs could attack only one at a time.

Donald's description was brief and matter-of-fact. He had killed one with his spear, then stunned the second with his slingshot before he crawled out and speared it. The last part, the long dark walk back to camp with Mike in his arms, he covered in a sentence. "Then I dragged Mike out of the cave and came back here."

Only then, when he didn't have anything more to say, his feelings rose up so uncontrollably that he blurted out, "I should of saved Mike."

Dr. Held shook his head slowly. "Don't torture yourself with thoughts like that. You did everything you could, more than any of us could have done. And we do have Lili, thanks to you."

Blake cleared his throat. "Welcome back, Donald." Blake's tone expressed the welcome that could not be read in his eyes, masked as they were by his "Eskimo" glasses.

"Yeah, shu-ah," Carlo put in quickly. "Glad you came back."

A sympathetic murmur went around the circle as they all welcomed him and assured him he had done well. Several times he heard "home" or "coming home." His wounds throbbed and his body ached with fatigue, but Donald's mind fastened hungrily on the word. Home. He had come home. They said so themselves.

Well, everyone said so, except Brock. Donald's small pale eyes moved uncertainly toward the sculptor. He was standing apart from the others, arms crossed over his chest and an aloof expression hardening his Cupid face. Their eyes met, and held for so long that the voices of the others dropped off into an uneasy silence.

Brock ended it abruptly. With deliberate steps he walked forward until he was so close to Donald he seemed to be standing in his shadow. Tilting his head so that he looked straight up into the big man's face, he spoke without a trace of his usual mannerisms. "Everything's settled, as far as I'm concerned."

Donald said thickly, "You and me ain't never going to be friends."

"We don't have to be. But it's hard enough for the nine of us to keep ourselves alive without wasting our strength or our talents on trying to destroy each other."

"Okay. You said, everything's settled. All even. Right?" Brock nodded. "Precisely."

"Okay." For an instant, Donald's big right fist moved toward a handshake, but it stopped midair. Brock reached out, grasped Donald's hand, and completed the shake. "Okay," Donald repeated gruffly. "You say everything's settled. Then that goes for me, too."

Chapter Thirty-Five

THEY launched the canoe early in the morning, when their cooking fire still contrasted brilliantly with the first pale light and the rising sun glowed pink and gold along the eastern horizon. The air was cold but the sea was calm and cloud banks forming to the north seemed a hundred miles away.

Nevertheless, Diana was uneasy as she watched Rolf and Carlo stow fishing gear and a lunch basket into the dugout. A lifetime in the Outer Islands had taught her that the weather was changeable this time of year, purring like a tabby cat at one moment and snarling like a cornered wildcat the next. She had tried to extract a promise from Rolf that he wouldn't go out very far. His answer had been silence, a long intent look, and a gentle kiss.

The special care with which they were handling the boat deepened her sense of foreboding. An ordinary canoe or dinghy could be dragged across the gravel beach without being damaged. Rolf and Carlo were lifting the dugout, carrying it to the water's edge, and setting it down so cautiously Diana was reminded of her grandmother packing eggs. Rough-hewn, sturdy as it looked, the canoe was actually a thin wood shell, only two inches thick in some places. She wanted to cry out, to hold them back. But why? They knew what they had made. They were both accustomed to the sea. How could she explain her last-minute panic, or describe an indescribable fear?

Just before Rolf stepped into the dugout, she found her voice. Pointing north, she called, "Those clouds, Rolf. They look like rain."

"Maybe. But the wind's from the west. They won't be coming this way."

His dark eyes gleamed with excitement as he looked out across the peaceful water. Like a Makah whaler on his way to sea, he had knotted his long black hair and adorned it with sprigs of spruce. He turned, holding the long slender paddle aloft in a victorious salute. He was bursting with laughter, bursting with triumph. The canoe was finished, the omens were right. And still Diana was frightened, without knowing why.

The canoe lifted and fell with each shallow ripple. She called again, "Don't go too far out . . ." Carlo in the bow and Rolf in the stern were laughing so much they didn't hear her. Impulsively, she ran down to the water's edge.

Carlo saw her and gestured. Rolf turned. "Diana! What is it?"

Something was pressing against her lungs so that it was hard to breathe. Heedless of everything, she waded into the bitterly cold water and stumbled on toward the canoe.

Rolf dropped his paddle, knelt in the stern and grasped her hands. In the morning light her wide, heavily fringed eyes were purple. Her lips were parted as if to speak, but nothing came out except shallow, trembling gasps for air.

She clutched his hands in an effort to communicate. "I said . . . ." She tried to smile. "I said, don't go out too far."

Rolf leaned forward and kissed her softly on the mouth. "Go back to camp and put on some dry moccasins." His voice was low and confident. "And don't worry. We're coming back."

"You have to." She held his hands tightly. "Rolf, you have to."

His dark eyes looked directly into hers. "I said, don't worry. Go back now. The tide is rising."

Shivering, Diana released his hands. She stood for a long moment, then waded ashore. Slowly she returned to the campfire. She stared into the fire for a long time, so that when she finally looked up, the canoe was already beyond the mouth of the harbor, already moving steadily out to sea.

The omens were right, as Rolf had said. The westerly wind was behind them. The tide was in flood, so that as long as they headed east, it was in their favor. Rolf's paddle was light and smooth, some seven feet long and diamond-shaped, as coastal Indian paddles had often been so that, if necessary, they could also be used as weapons. Being the steering paddle, it was larger than the one Carlo was wielding so efficiently in the bow.

Watching the strong steady movement of Carlo's shoulders and arms, Rolf thanked the gods, as he had so often before, that he had such a partner. For Carlo had spent his life in and on the water. He was not only a good paddler, but being Hawaiian his experience had been with salt-water canoes. As a member of one of the island state's finest canoe clubs, he had taken part in the annual Molokai race, once in the winning boat. He hadn't always agreed with Rolf's design for the dugout, arguing that an outrigger was a safer boat in rough water, but he had bowed good-naturedly to Rolf's urgent desire to finish as quickly as possible.

"Let's get this one into the water," Rolf had proposed. "Then we'll have something to use for deep-sea fishing. At that point we can start on another canoe, at least for two or three hours a day. An outrigger, if you say so. Or how about a sail? Alder for the mast, pegged to the bottom under the forward thwart. Cedar bark mats or animal skins for the sail cloth. A square-sail, probably. Not too big . . ."

"Hey, bradda," Carlo had responded. "The longer you talk, the better you sound. Hokay. This one hurry-up job. Next one, she goan be some kine queen."

In the Indian tradition, Rolf sat on a thwart but Carlo, in the bow, paddled from a kneeling position. They moved swiftly and smoothly across the water, caught up in the rhythm of the rapid stroke. At last Carlo lifted his paddle over his head and waved surrender. "Who we racing?" he asked, laughter tangling with his efforts to catch his breath. "And say now, bradda, where we headed, anyway? Didn't you say the salmon banks would be in close?"

"They probably are." Rolf picked up one of their water containers, the float ball of a giant kelp plugged at the small end with a whittled piece of cedar. He pulled the stopper and offered the bottle to Carlo. Carlo sipped carefully, grimaced at the salty taste, and handed it back.

Rolf's head tilted as he drank. "Ah . . ." Though the day was cold, his face was flushed and his forehead damp with perspiration. He inserted the stopper, set the kelp gourd down on the bottom of the canoe, and dried his forehead with the back of his hand. "I *meant* to go fishing."

The emphasis was slight but distinct and the tone of his voice was challenging. Carlo's habitually happy face and laughing eyes were suddenly sober. "Hey," he murmured, "hey now, bradda . . ." His head moved from side to side in a series of silent but energetic denials of his companion's sanity.

"Everything's right. The wind, the tide. We could make up to four miles an hour."

Carlo shook his head slowly. There was no trace of light-hearted pidgin as he replied, "It's a long way to Wolf Island."

"Maybe we won't have to go that far. There's a shipping lane between here and there."

"You know the odds better than I do. One, two freighters a day along the only lane we'll cross. Even if we happen to hit the right time, who's going to spot us unless we're close enough to be run down? On radar we'd come up like a floating log."

"Beyond the shipping lane, there's a fishing ground."

"Ha!" Carlo's solemn expression was being eroded by an irrepressible grin. "Ha!" he said again, and lapsed into pidgin. "We get dat far, bradda, we goan be *dere*."

Rolf's eyes gleamed. "Okay. Are you with me? Do we go get help?"

"Just one good thing about it. We won't have to paddle back." The answer was thrown back over his shoulder, for Carlo had already swiveled to face the bow and his paddle was poised above the water, ready for the first stroke in a long, long journey.

The westerly wind was at their backs and the flood tide carried them forward. As Rolf had said, everything was right. How long it remained right, they could not tell, for neither had a watch and they were too absorbed in maintaining their pace to spend even a few minutes estimating time by the position of the sun. When Rolf thought of doing so, he realized for the first time that the brilliant early morning sunshine was obscured now by a solid layer of gray clouds.

Calling to Carlo for a rest, he studied the ominous sky. The black layers to the north seemed darker and nearer, billowing out as if driven from behind by an angry Arctic wind. He turned slowly, letting the air against his damp skin tell him if the wind had changed direction.

Like a mind reader, his partner in the bow spoke his

thoughts. "She's shifted." Like Rolf, he was out of breath. His words were staccato bursts from a heaving chest.

"Out of the east," Rolf gasped. "But the tide's still with us. Ready?"

"Am I crazy, you mean? Shu-ah, bradda. Let's go."

Minute by minute, the sea darkened, reflecting the steel gray of the wintry sky. And slowly, almost imperceptibly at first, the wind swung around from west to northeast. With the tide flooding in one direction and the wind sweeping down from another, the surface of the sea, flat as a pond two or three hours before, was breaking up into short chops.

Caught in the rip tide, the stern of the eighteen-foot dugout rose on the crest of one wave while the bow slapped into the peak of another. Lifted and pounded by waves shorter than she was, the fragile canoe seemed to be attacked from all sides.

In the stern, Rolf clutched his steering paddle and fought to keep the boat on course and the bow pointing at right angles to each cresting wave. The wind was hitting them on the starboard quarter. The canoe had little freeboard and some water was already splashing over the bow. If they took too much water, they would lose their buoyancy . . . He watched grimly as an unexpected short chop slammed against the canoe and foamed up white over the bow. Crests of frothy white rode the rough sea all around them. "You all right?"

Carlo gestured with his paddle like a plane dipping its wings.

Again Rolf reassured himself. The wind was against them but the tide was with them. They would go on.

It was the changing shape of the waves that first gave warning of the ever-rising wind. The short chops began to lengthen into long swells. Even without the cold breath of the northeaster biting into his flesh, Rolf would have known that the wind was increasing. The higher the wind, the longer the waves and the deeper the troughs between them.

Should they turn back? Though his excitement at the possibility of obtaining help was still lively, Rolf was not foolhardy. He had proposed this attempt to reach Wolf because the forces of nature had seemed to be solidly on their side. As strong as his desire to obtain help was his desire to get back to Diana. In addition he felt responsible for Carlo, who would be in sight of Phoenix now if it weren't for him. Turn back? Unless he did something crazy, Carlo would leave the decision up to him. It was difficult to make, for even a strong instinct for survival did not supply the data he needed to decide whether safety lay in going ahead or in turning back.

How far had they come? Were they closer to the area where they might be sighted by a freighter or fishing boat than they were to Phoenix? Did survival lie in advancing rather than retreating?

He had no instruments to tell him any of these things, nor to warn him of what evil caprice the once benevolent god of the sea might indulge in. He looked up at the purple-black sky, and the first icy drop of rain hit his cheek.

Superstitiously, Rolf asked himself—is it a sign? He looked at Carlo's beautifully muscled arms and shoulders, moving in perfect rhythm as his paddle dipped into the angry sea. Carlo was wet from the water splashing over the bow. Now cold rain was pelting his bare head and running down the back of his neck.

Did they need another sign? Even as Rolf asked himself the question, one was offered in the form of sudden recognition. For some time—a quarter of an hour, a half hour—he had had to pull harder on his paddle to keep the boat moving ahead. That could mean only one thing. The tide had turned. Now *everything* was against them.

As the canoe disappeared in the early morning mist, the seven at camp reviewed their plans for the day. Except for food-gathering expeditions, such as Rolf and Carlo's trip to the salmon banks today, their primary occupation was housebuilding. There were still hundreds of trees to be felled, the larger ones for walls, the smaller for rafters and stringers. Donald had eagerly assumed the role of Paul Bunyan and now hurried through breakfast in his zeal to sharpen the ax before he set out for the old farm. Andrew and Felicia had taken on the simple but monotonous job of chinking walls that the young muscle trio, Rolf, Carlo, and Donald, had already erected.

Norma and Blake, also working as a team, were recognized as the group's best shingle-weavers. With hammers, chisels, and adzes, all made of stone, they were splitting cedar shingle bolts into shakes for the roof and leveling and smoothing one side of the logs that would eventually be fitted together to form a rough plank floor. Somehow, the pinpoint visual concentration on his work, necessitated by his "Eskimo" glasses, seemed also to sharpen Blake's mental concentration, and he had become an exceptionally accurate and meticulous craftsman.

Like the Blakes, Diana and Rolf usually worked together, for in spite of her pregnancy Diana was strong and agile. With Rolf out salmon fishing, she turned to Warren Brock. "Whatever you're going to do today, would you like a partner?"

"*Love* it." Brock pointed impishly at the small but distinct outward curve of her belly. "If you think it will be all right with *him*."

Diana laughed. "He, she . . ." She patted her stomach lovingly. "Let's say *they* won't mind. No, I'm feeling fine, really, Warren. I don't lift anything heavy, and my grandmother said you shouldn't stretch your arms over your head but I can do anything else."

"I've found a new bank of clay. *Beautiful* stuff. I'm simply *ecstatic*. You could help me, but I'll do the carrying."

As soon as she saw it, Diana guessed that Brock's discovery was the product of the tidal wave. The cliff of raw blue clay looked bare as compared to the weathered and partially grass-covered shoreline on each side of it. It was still topped by a foot-deep layer of soil, soggy now from frequent rains, but at the cliff's edge this centuries-old accumulation of dirt and vegatation seemed to have been sheared off, and so recently that roots of scrub trees and plants were still dangling below the overhanging shelf of turf.

Diana approached the edge cautiously. The bank dropped straight down into the sea. At its base, some twenty feet below, the limbs of uprooted trees were protruding from a giant pile of sand, rock, and soil. Many of their leaves were still green, and here and there a gnarled root system poked through the deposit. "Be careful," she said to Brock. "There's been a landslide here. The tidal wave probably caused it and uncovered the clay."

"Then *blessings* on thee, tidal wave. None knew thee but to love thee, nor named thee but to praise."

"I'm serious. Look, even the edge is tricky. From here it looks solid. But from over there, where I was just standing, I could see that the cliff is eaten away. Clay is slippery. If it's undermined . . ."

"Dear lovely nymph of the woods, you are suffering some kind of anxiety syndrome, no doubt caused by *him*. You're not going down that cliff. You don't even have to get near the edge. I never meant that you should. We'll do it this way . . ."

As he explained his plan, his gestures were so comic that Diana began to laugh. It was true. The uneasy feeling that hit her when they looked down probably had nothing to do with the clay bank. But it wasn't because of the baby. She was anxious about Rolf. Every time she looked up at the sky the dark storm clouds to the north seemed to be nearer. But she was being silly, and there was work to do. "All right," she said when Brock's lisping recitation came to an end. "I understand. You tie the rope to the big tree, and you lower yourself with the buckets. When you've got one filled, I'll pull it up. No, these buckets aren't too big. They won't be heavy, even when they're filled, not one at a time."

Brock's plan worked so beautifully that Diana forgot the threatening sky. They had brought many more empty pails than they could carry full of clay, but that, too, was by design. They would carry what they could and tomorrow, with the help of the others, they would pick up the rest. Three of the alder bark containers had been filled and dragged up the cliff when the light rain they had both been ignoring changed suddenly to a hard, pelting downpour.

Diana knelt at the edge of the cliff and peered down through a film of water that fogged her vision. Brock was digging energetically at the base of the cliff. She called, and he looked up, grinning.

"Yes, I'm all wet," he chortled. "But no matter, water doesn't hurt clay. It makes it better."

Rain was coursing down Diana's cheeks and trickling down her neck. "You'll be soaked through."

"Hi dee ho, sweet. I already am. And so, no doubt, are you. Therefore, there's no point quitting. My, isn't this *lovely* stuff?"

Though a misty fear was collecting along the edge of her consciousness, Diana wanted to respond to his enthusiasm. Rain wouldn't hurt her, she knew that, and thanks to the fur garments and her cedar-bark rain cape, she was still warm. Of course if it turned cold, she would have to insist that they stop and return to camp. Cold, her grandmother had often warned expectant mothers, could be dangerous when you're carrying.

Even when the wind shifted and the air grew colder, she hesitated. It was enough to stay well back from the edge of the cliff, sheltered by the branches of the big tree. A jerk on the rope told her when Brock had filled another pail, and that was the only time she had to leave the protection of the tree . . . so she was on solid ground at the moment when the whole cliff broke loose from the island and slid into the water.

There was no warning—no ominous rumble or preliminary tremor. For fifty feet on either side of the clay bank, the shoreline simply disintegrated. Weakened by the tidal wave, undermined at the back by a strata of gravel and one of the island's many subterranean springs, the clay land mass dropped away as if it were separating itself from an alien body. An avalanche of clay, sand, and gravel roared down the slope and settled with a sound like a human sigh.

In less than a minute, Diana's safe spot under the big tree was only a foot from the cliff's edge. The raw lip of the new shoreline was almost at her feet. Trembling, she dropped to her knees, crawled to the edge and looked down.

For one terrible moment, she thought Brock had disappeared. Then she saw him. Just his head, and one arm, flung backward as if he had tried to escape the landslide by swimming out to sea on his back. His wild backstroke had never been completed. His right arm and his body were completely buried.

He wasn't struggling to free himself. His face was still and his eyes were closed. From above, he looked like a dead creature cast up from the green-black depths, a white water-soaked reject of the sea that would rest briefly on shore, drying and rotting until the next flood tide came in to wash it away. Even during the split second in which Diana tried to decide whether he was dead or alive, a maverick wave crept toward him, licking his head so that his long hair floated on the surface like fine gold seaweed. There was no question of going to get help. She had to bring him up alone, and fast.

She hardly noticed how cold the wind had become, or

that the chilling rain was turning into snow. She was concerned with the rope. One end of it was still secure around the trunk of the big tree, and though several of the tree's long sprawling roots were now exposed and extending straight out over the cliff, the trunk was standing firm. She pulled on the rope to test it. It resisted her, for the lower end was buried securely in the newly formed bank of clay, sand and rubble at the water's edge. It could still help her.

Her vision was blurred by large wet snowflakes clinging to her eyelashes. She brushed them off, rubbed her eyelids and blinked rapidly. Snow had collected on the rough fabric of her rain cape. The cape weighed on her shoulders and made her move awkwardly. She ripped it off and threw it back under the tree. Lying on her stomach with her back to the water, she grasped the rope, and slowly began to inch her way over the edge. While she could still reach the tree trunk and pull herself back, she tested the rope with a series of hard, jerking motions. It would hold.

But would she have the strength to climb up the cliff with an unconscious man? She dismissed the question as fast as it came to her. The water was rising. Before she thought of anything else, she had to dig Brock's body out of the mud and drag him to the base of the cliff. There, for at least an hour, they would be above the reach of the incoming tide. One of her grandmother's favorite themes came to her as she crept down the cliff. "If you want to do things right, you got to do them in the right order."

Slipping down the rope wasn't difficult. In seconds her feet were resting on the soft pile of clay and sand. Before she released the rope, she dropped her full weight onto the mound. Her feet sank a little, but not so deeply that she couldn't walk across it to the spot where Brock lay. She knelt beside him and felt his forehead and his pulse. He was alive. How badly he was hurt she couldn't tell.

She dug furiously with both hands, flinging the mud to both sides and talking to him constantly. When his right arm emerged, she saw that the crude shale shovel he had been using to dig clay was still in his hand. She pulled it out of his fingers. Now she could dig faster. In ten minutes, or fifteen, or half an hour—she wasn't measuring time in minutes, but in how far the tide had risen—she had worked all around his body and lifted the heaviest load of muddy debris off his stomach. Now, if he wasn't hurt . . .

She stood over him with one foot on each side of his body. Leaning forward, she took a firm grip on both his shoulders. As she pulled, his eyelids fluttered. She spoke to him, and he groaned. "Are you hurt?" she asked him. "Where do you hurt?"

He seemed to have slipped back into unconsciousness, for his eyes closed and the upper part of his body was dead weight, straining against her effort to lift him out of the mud. "Brock!" she said again, more loudly.

He stirred, and his body came alive as he lifted his head and opened his eyes. "Hurting all over," he murmured, "but not hurt."

"Can you stand up?"

"Try to . . ."

With Diana's arms to steady him, he pulled himself to his knees. In that position he rested, fighting to catch his breath. "Feel like truck sat on me. Okay. Now. Upseedaisy . . ." Holding Diana's hands, he moved first one foot, then the other, and slowly straightened up. With arms around each other, they staggered across the mud bank to the foot of the cliff.

Brock sagged against the wall of rock and clay and looked groggily at the rope.

"Can you make it?"

Like an unhappy drunk declining to get up off the floor, Brock solemnly shook his head. "Not a chance. Arms gone all soft. You go."

"And leave you? No. We're not very far from camp. I'll start yelling. Someone might be near enough to hear."

"Save your breath. No use, in this wind."

He was right. Close as they were to each other, they were almost shouting to be heard. In the woods above, the rising wind was howling through the tree tops. Their weak voices were nothing against the rage of the storm.

"Diana, love," Brock said weakly. "Go. Be a good girl and go. If you run across the marines, send back a platoon. But go, *now*."

"I can climb the rope. If you hold onto me, and I hold onto the rope . . ."

Brock managed a faint parody of his usual gesture toward her swelling abdomen. *"Him.* That wouldn't be good for *him."*

"All right. I'll go get help."

Just then, she noticed two things. One was comical. It was the way the snow was collecting on Brock's beard and hair, so thick and white he looked like a chubby Santa Claus without his hat on.

The other thing she noticed was terrifying. It was a feeling in her body. A small, gnawing pain, a stirring.

"Oh, no!" The words weren't spoken. They echoed in her head like a sound trapped on the inside. "Oh, no . . ." the silent voice cried again, as she gripped the rope and, wincing with a sudden twinge of pain, began to pull herself up the cliff.

Chapter Thirty-Six

THE relentless wind, the wind-driven rain, the ebbing tide —they were fighting them all. Eventually the struggle would wear them out. Rolf knew that the only way to take advantage of wind and tide was to reverse their course and pray that the forces of nature would help them return safely to Phoenix.

He shouted "Carlo!" His partner looked over his shoulder. "Back! Back to Phoenix!" He gestured wildly. Carlo's head, dripping rain, nodded in understanding.

Turning a canoe in such a heavy sea was risking their boat and their lives. But it was the lesser risk, and they both knew what to do. Moreover, they had confidence in each other's knowledge. "Paddle like crazy," Rolf recited silently as they began to circle. "Keep the stern on . . ."

In Carlo's frenzied stroke, Rolf read his own fear of what could happen, but they kept the canoe on her keel and brought her around and suddenly the wave that might have killed them was lifting the stern and thrusting them forward toward their destination. "Thanks, brother," Rolf called, but the north wind snatched his voice and tossed it away.

Now that they were headed back, they had a following sea. The dugout rode forward on mountainous swells, lifted higher and higher as the giant bank of water curled up under them, held aloft for a breathless moment on the foaming white-capped ridge, and then cast downward into the dark valley between waves.

The sea was driving them back to Phoenix, but there was a price for its help. The wind was behind them, but it was fiercely cold. The waves carried them forward, but with such violence that Rolf and Carlo had to paddle with demonic fury to keep the dugout's stern at a right angle to each oncoming breaker. And there was no respite. The waves kept rolling, the wind kept rising, and the cold rain hit them with stinging force.

With their backs to the advancing waves, they were often caught without warning when a particularly high wall of water overtook them. When this happened, it was too late to shout or even to think. Years of practice had imbedded the knowledge of what to do, so deeply they might have been acting by instinct.

As a large wave threatened to roll the boat over, Carlo and Rolf threw their bodies toward the upper side, sank their paddles deep into the water, catching the water and forcing it under the boat and, with the same strokes, pushing her forward with all the speed they could muster. They did not have to remind each other that life depended on keeping the bow on into the swells and the stern at ninety degrees to the advancing wall of water. To be twisted broadside was to lose control. The sea was with them while they had the strength and knowledge to channel her formidable power into the course of their own survival. If they used her wrongly, if they failed to pursue their course in spite of her furious efforts to unseat them, she would swallow them whole.

As the storm mounted, the swells grew higher and the troughs between them deeper. On the peak of a wave as tall as a house, the cedar canoe poised for the shuddering descent into the trough. For an awful moment Rolf and Carlo looked down into a hell of black water thirty feet below, and gripped their paddles in anticipation of the sudden wrenching drop. Again and again they survived it, gasping as the icy spray lashed their bodies, stroking in frenzied rhythm as they fought to emerge from the depths and ride forward on the swell.

When did the cold rain turn to snow? Neither of them noticed until the flakes were so thick and sticky that the wind no longer blew them off their faces. Fighting for breath, they opened their mouths, and the air they sucked in deposited snow on their lips and tongues. Snow collected on their eyebrows and eyelashes and clung damply, blinding them so effectively that they had to risk brushing them off even when that meant taking one hand off the paddle. The world around them was a storm-enclosed cave, all black and white and filled with turbulent motion. The roaring black sea cast up spumy white crests, the black sky spewed white snowflakes, and the dugout plunged from the height of a boiling whitecap to the bottom of a black hole in the sea.

"Phoenix!" Carlo's one shouted word carried back to the stern in spite of the howling wind. Rolf hunched his shoulder forward to brush snow off his face without releasing his grip on the paddle. It was Phoenix Island, all right. A shadowy dark shape, humped up at the north end, dropping into a saddle and rising again to the south in a series of lower hills. A lone island, erupting from the violent sea like a mystical creature coming up for air. Phoenix, Diana, safety. In spite of straining muscles and chest aching with the effort to breathe, Rolf felt a surge of power. Now they weren't moving blindly with the storm. Their goal was visible. They could reach what they could see.

Carlo was shouting again. But this time, he turned back toward the stern and heedless of the danger of lifting his paddle out of the water, he pointed to the floor of the dugout. Rolf blinked and wiped his eyes. Squinting against the cold, he saw what Carlo was trying to show him. An ominous crack had opened up down the center of the canoe. There wasn't enough luck in the world to hold this dugout in one piece. Not unless he could lash it together.

His glance darted to their fishing gear, stowed next to the water bottles on the bottom of the dugout under the center thwarts. There was line enough to encircle the dugout in two or three places. With the hull wrapped and tied tightly, the crack would close. Such patchwork repair wouldn't last, but at the speed they were traveling, it would get them to Phoenix.

Should he put down his paddle and do the job, relying on the bow man to keep them headed into the swells? Or was it more important to keep the steering paddle moving in the stern, and try with shouts and signals to show Carlo what must be done? He hesitated, and the maniac sea took command.

A huge wave smashed against the dugout. Caught at a slight angle, the canoe began to broach. In the stern, Rolf struggled vainly to keep her from swinging around broadside, but by now the crack was widening, and water was coming in through the crack as well as over the gunwale. The damaged shell, once so responsive, had become heavy and unwieldy.

As the boat rose sideways on the ridge of the wave, Rolf saw the fishing gear break loose and slide across the bottom of the dugout. If it went over the side, they would lose the only lashing they had and their only chance of holding the canoe together. He leaped for it, groped wildly as the dugout cracked and shuddered before the murderous blows of the wave. The gear escaped him, grazing his fingertips as it slid by with the roll of the boat and disappeared over the side.

Blinded by a burst of spray, Rolf crawled back to the stern and groped for his paddle. Even before the great green comber subsided and he could see clearly, he knew it was gone. In his attempt to rescue the fishing gear, he had let go of the handle.

In desperation, he set out to do the only thing he could think of that might help them stay afloat. Brock had carved a bailer out of cedar. It was a large wooden scoop with a leather thong strung through a hole in the handle. Rolf untied the thong and began bailing in a feverish effort to relieve the canoe of her burden of sea water.

He was on his knees when the crack opened up wide and the canoe split into two pieces, as cleanly as if giant hands had pulled it apart.

He heard a cry from Carlo, and then the sea swept over him, and he was fighting it, beating his arms against the rushing water, kicking his feet, praying for breath.

At first the pain was vague, an undefined cramping sensation coming at such long intervals and retreating so quickly that, in between, Diana told herself it was gone for good. Her first instinctive recognition of the pain's origin persisted, but dully, like a bruise that can be ignored because of more demanding injuries.

She had to get help for Brock. He might not drown, but unless he was rescued quickly he could die of shock and exposure. This thought drove her on, with the bitter wind at her heels and the thick wet snow collecting on her eyelashes and eyebrows. When she stopped for breath, cold blew into her open mouth and desperate tears burned her eyelids. It wasn't only Brock. It wasn't only the pain. It was fear for Rolf.

As she ran, and stopped, and ran again, the image grew of Rolf and Carlo, safe on land and warming themselves at the campfire. By the time Diana reached the hill above the beach, the hoped-for scene and the imagined feeling of Rolf's arms around her were more vivid than the real spasms that now racked her body every ten or fifteen minutes. She looked down, and the dream picture melted. Donald was alone by the campfire.

Trembling violently, Diana called "Donald!" and dropped to the ground, her arms crossed over the torment in her belly. He was beside her before she collected the strength to lift her head and call again.

His questions and her answers were a nightmare conversation of broken phrases that made sense one minute and the next tossed about insanely on a new flood of pain. But she understood what Donald was doing. He was picking her up, carrying her down the steep hill, placing her gently on the ground near the fire. He was covering her with furs. He was propping up walls of the dismantled smokehouse so as to shelter her from the wind and snow. He was holding a cup of water to her mouth . . . And he was talking. His gruff voice rumbled through her head. He was saying the same things over and over, with his eyes begging her to understand. She tried, struggling against a new assault of pain.

The terrible knot loosened once more and her head cleared. She understood, and she nodded, trying to tell him that she did. Donald had built up the fire as a beacon for Rolf and Carlo. Donald knew where the Mansfields were and he would bring them to her before he went for Brock. She was to lie still, to sleep . . .

She wasn't sure, after that, whether she was truly awake or had slipped into sleep, dragging the fear and the pain with her. She had no sense of time, except for brief moments of intense clarity when she opened her eyes and saw the fire was brighter and all the world around was getting darker. She was aware of murmuring voices, and after a time, Brock's was among them. She was conscious of Norma sitting beside her, and she knew, more clearly than anything else, that Rolf had not come back.

Donald carried her up the hill to the dormitory and put her to bed in the Mansfields' shelter. Norman covered her with furs and then she and Blake lay down beside her, enclosing her in a cocoon of body warmth.

Through a haze of pain and terror, Diana felt and saw everything that was happening, and as the reality of the people and the place came into focus, she realized that within her something was changing. The cruel contractions were diminishing, as if her body had expelled the pain.

Suddenly she was wide awake. In the hollow between her legs, a warm fluid was collecting.

"Norma!" It was an anguished whisper.

Norma's hand pressed her arm reassuringly. "I'm right here."

"I'm bleeding!"

"Yes. I expected it. Don't be afraid."

"That means the baby . . ."

Norma said softly. "Probably. But not always. Don't think about it. Just rest and sleep."

"I'll make a mess."

"No, no. While you were asleep, I covered you with bandages. But what if you did? Don't worry about it."

"The baby. I *wanted* the baby."

"But you'll have one, Diana. This happens to thousands of girls. Millions, probably. But they try again, and they have fine healthy children."

"Did it ever happen to you?"

Norma's throat tightened. This was a forbidden subject, something she and Blake never talked about. An old grief that had grown a scab without healing underneath, suddenly exposed by this child-woman's urgent question. "Yes . . . yes, it did."

"But you didn't have a baby . . . afterwards."

"No," Norma said, and now she was speaking as much to Blake as to the girl who lay between them. "Blake wanted to, but I . . . I was too much of a coward."

"But you *could* have."

In the dark, Norma nodded sadly. "Yes, I could have. And you will, Diana. You're braver than I was. I know you'll be all right."

Softly, weakly, Diana began to cry. For the baby she was losing, for Rolf who was out at sea. Norma held her close and wiped her face with a small square of clean cotton torn from the colony's only tablecloth.

"I know, I know," Norma whispered, and wanted to weep with her. For what could she say that would soothe away grief for a lost baby? And how could she quiet Diana's greater fear, that tonight she had lost Rolf as well?

Rolf knew he was drowning. But no, he wasn't. Something was pulling him up. Gasping, his head broke through the dark water, and he felt himself suspended by a hard rounded surface. He groped for it, encircling it with his arms as if once more he was a little boy floating down river on a log. Through a mist of sea water he saw Carlo, and knew it was Carlo's strong hand that had pulled him up and lifted him onto the log. But it wasn't a log. It was half of the canoe. Carlo was stretched out on the other half.

Despite the dark and the freezing cold, admiration swept through Rolf, driving out the feeling of being lost forever. Carlo was indeed a "bradda." He accepted life as it is and people as they are. If they got out of this alive, Carlo would not blame him for the foolish risk they had taken. *If* they got out of it alive. Rolf realized that Carlo knew as well as he that, even with Phoenix in sight, they had very little chance of surviving.

Fortunately, the split hull could be ridden like a pair of surfboards. Lying flat on their bellies and paddling with their arms, they would move forward. But only as long as they had the strength to keep in motion. They were already wet to the skin and the water sloshing over them was only a few degrees above freezing. It would become harder and harder to move their arms and, eventually, the cold would exhaust them so that they couldn't move at all. If they could keep active, they might have half an hour. Were they going to drown? Or would they freeze? And with Phoenix in sight!

With snow collecting on their heads and salt water washing over their bodies, Rolf and Carlo propelled themselves toward Phoenix. Instinctively they stayed close to each other, but they did not try to communicate, for the numbness spreading through their bodies was slowly working into their minds.

What you can see, you can reach . . . That thought had come to Rolf when they first spotted Phoenix. Now it occupied him fully. His arms and feet moved mechanically, even when they ceased to have any feeling. His awareness of being alive was gradually dimming, as if the freezing cold were swallowing him piece by piece, leaving only his head, with the eyes on the outline of Phoenix and the stupefied brain repeating "What you can see, you can reach."

When he saw the light, flickering against the dark background of the island, Rolf wanted to shout, "Carlo! See! They've got a fire. They're waiting for us . . ." But the dead weight of his numbness had risen to his throat. He felt like crying. At the same time he wanted to go to sleep. He could rest his head on the log . . .

With an enormous effort, he lifted his head. Had he actually dozed? The bonfire seemed more distinct now, the flame lighting the way into the U-shaped harbor. He turned his head. Carlo? His partner was motionless, arms hanging limply on both sides of the split hull. While the meaning of what he saw worked its way into Rolf's mind, Carlo's body slipped sideways, dropping heavily into the water.

A cry for help formed in Rolf's throat but he could not force it out. With the last of his strength and the last of his sense of where and who he was, he released his cedar float and plunged into the water after Carlo.

It was a blind and frantic effort, expended without any understanding of how far they were from shore or how long it took him to find Carlo. But he did find Carlo, only slightly submerged beneath the surface, and held his inert form above the water with an arm that was no longer connected with his body, splashing and slapping the sea with his other arm and thrashing his legs.

Just before he slipped into unconsciousness, Rolf's legs dragged across a hard surface. Something in his head told him—the rock floor of the bay, you're scraping the bottom of the bay. Stand up, you fool! You're here! You made it!

But everything he had was used up. His body was lead, his senses were frozen, his mind was empty. Sleep . . . He sank, with Carlo under his arm, and the darkness closed in around him.

Chapter Thirty-Seven

AN involuntary shiver rippled through Andrew Held's body. The camp area on the beach was enclosed by a circle of wooden windbreaks. Bright flames shot up from the driftwood fire and garments of fur and bark preserved his body's heat. But nothing could shut out the December wind, and Dr. Held's eyes teared as a sudden cold gust struck his face. Two weeks before Christmas . . . He looked thoughtfully at the totem calendar. He knew every line and every pictograph. They offered a clear record of four months in exile, but no prophesies. Nevertheless, his forefinger traced the most recent carvings as if his tactile sense had the magic power to coax from this sculptured diary of past events some helpful foreknowledge of things to come.

The chill of winter was stinging his nose and cheeks. His eyes were watering from cold. Omens enough, he thought ruefully, at least for the immediate future. There was no need to look further because the forces of nature would keep them busy for the next few weeks. Nothing clairvoyant about the proposal he was going to make at the meeting tonight. Just as well, he mused, for no wondrous knowledge was flowing back from the totem calendar through his fingertips.

The notches told him today was Saturday, December 11th. The delicate bas-reliefs Brock carved to commemorate special events reminded him that in the past six weeks a great deal had happened to this band of nine diverse personalities and that most of it had tested them severely, both emotionally and physically. Fortunately, their mutual losses and trials had drawn them together, as tonight's cold wind brought them close to one another around the campfire. The bonds were real.

In the beginning they had been bound by raw necessity. Whether they "cared" about their partners in disaster, whether they felt "concern" or "love," what happened to one to some extent happened to them all. They had stuck together in order to survive. But during the past six weeks, he had noticed an enrichment of the community bond, a new dimension. Though he disliked the preachy word "share" almost as much as did Warren Brock, Andrew Held had observed privately that from the enforced sharing of physical experiences—hunger, injury, sickness, accident—they had gradually become sensitive to the emotional impact these experiences had on the others. The killing of his beloved basset hound Mike had hit him harder than anyone else, but they had all identified with his grief. Damn it, Warren Brock's hyper-sophistication notwithstanding, they had all *shared* his loss, Warren as much as anyone.

And when Rolf and Carlo had failed to return from their first venture with the canoe, who had cared "most"? Diana, of course, weeping bitterly while her body was gripped by the spasms of miscarriage. But they had all been frightened when the storm came up and they had all mourned as night descended on the beach and the absence of the two young men took on a new and terrible meaning. Norma and Blake had retired to the dormitory to shelter and comfort Diana, but the others had stayed by the campfire, unwilling to give up the watch even when it seemed hopeless.

"I'm not really *doing* anything," Felicia said, speaking for them all. "But going to bed would be like saying I've stopped believing they'll come back." So they had waited, Felicia, Warren, Donald and Dr. Held himself, silently sharing an act of faith.

Donald had been restless. Even when the flames were leaping high, he got up to throw more wood on the fire. A shadowy movement, the slightest whisper of a sound made him leap to his feet and hurry off to investigate. Twice he thought he heard the wild dogs, and he picked up his spear and strode along the beach to the south. But most of the time his attention was drawn to the harbor. Again and again his imagination created an object or a shape and sent it floating on that dark expanse. Again and again he stumbled through the dark to the water's edge, where he stood peering into the thick night for ten or fifteen minutes before he returned to the bonfire and stared just as hopelessly into the flames.

At first the others followed, but after a while the futility of it was obvious and they remained by the fire, hoping against hope for a shout that would tell them Donald had actually sighted something this time. So no one moved or spoke when, once again, Donald stood up. "I'm going to take another look. A good look, like I should of before."

He picked up a dry stick and thrust it into the flame until the end caught fire. With this torch held high over his head, he charged down the slope.

Felicia said uneasily, "Do you think . . . perhaps this time . . ."

Andrew Held rose slowly and took Felicia's hand. "Like you, I *do* want to believe. Let's go see."

"Let's!" Brock leaped nimbly over the log he had been sitting on. "At least we'll see whether we're seeing anything."

When they reached the water, Donald had already waded into the bay. His torch cast dancing reflections on the waves as he swung his arm left to right, scanning the surface. Suddenly he shouted. "It's them!"

He plunged ahead, his torch trailing ribbons of fire. Far to his left, something white emerged briefly from the shadow and then vanished again into the misty black. An arm? A face? "Rolf! Carlo!" he bawled, splashing frantically through the icy waves. "I'm coming . . ."

The arm . . . he saw it again, floating like a crooked log. And another arm, and a leg, and finally the dim outline of two bodies, with gray faces just barely showing above the shallow water. With a rending sob, he stumbled toward them. The toe of his boot caught on the uneven surface of the bay. He tripped and fell, dropping the flaming stick as he instinctively thrust his arms forward in an effort to break his fall.

The torch hissed and went out. In total darkness, Donald struggled to his knees, pulled himself up and waded blindly toward the spot where he had glimpsed the bodies. Again he tripped and fell, but this time his outstretched hand met something soft. An arm . . . Then, like a giant picking up a doll, he scooped up Rolf's dripping body and tucked it under his left arm.

Carlo was a few feet beyond. Donald dropped to one knee and groped with his free hand. In spite of the dead weight and the burden he was already carrying, he plucked Carlo out of the water and secured him under his right arm. Two large, limp dolls in the hands of a powerful child.

It was this frightening but comic picture that had emerged from the dark and struggled up the gravel slope toward the three people waiting fearfully at the edge of the water. Brock had fired a torch and was holding it aloft like an angelic but jittery Statue of Liberty. Dr. Held limped forward and, with Donald, half-dragged, half-lifted the soggy bodies to the campfire.

"They're still breathing," Donald said gruffly as they lowered Rolf and Carlo to the ground.

"Thank God," Dr. Held murmured. "Thank God the water wasn't any deeper when their strength gave out."

Without a word, Felicia and Brock began removing the young men's clothing and stripping off their own dry outer garments. Turning to Donald, Dr. Held said simply, "Thank you, Donald. Thank you very much." And Brock spoke to Donald for the first time since their conversation the night the big man returned from exile. "No one else could have done it," he said quietly. "No one but you."

Later, Dr. Held marveled that so few words of thanks were spoken by any of them. They hadn't been necessary. Donald had understood perfectly that Felicia's curt command—"Don't just stand there! Get into dry things before you freeze!"—had expressed sincere gratitude. When Brock quipped, "Can't you see our Donald when Atlas comes up to him and says, 'Here, hold this for me for a second, will you, old chap?'" Donald had no idea he was being compared to Hercules, but his big battered face had broken into a happy grin. As before, they had all felt the impact of this near-disaster. There had been a natural difference in the degree of their feelings, but they had *all* experienced Diana's fear before the rescue, and Diana's joyful gratitude when, though she was weak, sick, and half dead with fatigue, she heard Norma whisper, "Rolf is safe. He's down by the fire but he'll be with you in just a little while."

What forges stronger bonds, Andrew Held had often asked himself. Good fortune or bad, prosperity or adversity? Whatever the universal answer, here on Phoenix it was disaster and near-disaster, rather than their occasional streaks of luck, that had developed tolerance and understanding.

When Diana lost her baby, Warren Brock had shown a tenderness they had never glimpsed before, and the last remnant of Norma's self-conscious reserve had dissolved as she took on the earthy duties of nursing the younger girl through a miscarriage. Warren had come to accept a part of himself he had studiously rejected, the loving, serious-minded, vulnerable part. Norma had learned to accept rather than ignore or alter the human body when it was soiled, the human spirit when it was mean.

Donald's fight with the pack of feral dogs had left several ugly scars on his arm, leg, and hand, but it had healed the older wound and brought him back into the group. Since the day he had stumbled into camp with Mike's body in his arms and Mike's blood mingling with his own, they had begun for the first time to accept poor dumb Donald for what he was.

Acceptance. That was the word. If it is true, Andrew Held reflected, that love is the ability to accept another human being as he *is*, then in fighting for survival this little colony has been learning love.

As a group they had never discussed what Andrew and Felicia privately called Phoenix Island's quiet evolution of the soul, but physical changes were visible and on several occasions they had talked about them during meetings.

Muscles had tightened, stomachs were flat, thighs were firm. They had all lost weight, except for Norma and Diana, who had been too thin, and they had gained, for the same regimen of diet and exercise that had made seven persons slender had rounded out the teen-age-boy bodies of the two younger girls. The firmness of their bodies went with a general improvement in health. Though they had all been sunburned, cut, scratched, and chapped, and Carlo, Rolf and Donald had been seriously injured, they healed with remarkable speed. Their skins glowed, their eyes were alert and clear.

The change in Felicia amused and delighted Andrew Held, for she, more than anyone else, had been a hothouse flower. She had always "taken care of herself." Her bathroom scale was her confessional. Her dressing table was an altar where—morning and night—hair, skin, and nails were revered in joyless rituals. Looking at her now, as

supple and smooth-muscled as an athlete, Andrew Held
realized that in the city she had been soft even at her
thinnest.

And her natural beauty had been hidden as much as
enhanced by chemically compounded substances applied
on the outside. She had substituted massage, which was
done for her and to her, for exercise, which she would
have had to do herself. But now, after four months of
what any of her friends in Washington, D.C., would surely
view as ghastly deprivation, four months in which her
"cosmetics" had been extracted from seaweed and bark
and lichens and wild flowers, Felicia's real beauty had
emerged. Her body was firm. Even on a dull day her red
hair shone as if it were reflecting sunshine. Her fingernails
had once needed special treatment to keep them from
breaking. Now they were so strong she claimed she could
use them to uncap a bottle, a boast that could not be dis-
proved because they had no bottles. Her skin radiated a
subtle fragrance that was like a personal signature.

Norma, their acknowledged health authority, traced
both weight loss and improved complexion to the sea.
At a meeting one night she enlarged her theory in one of
the longest speeches she had ever made.

"Exercise has helped us lose weight. So have our
cooking methods. We have so little fat or grease that we
never fry anything. We have no sugar and we have to
conserve our small supply of honey, so we rarely eat anything sweet. Even so, I think our weight loss is mainly
due to what we've been forced to eat, rather than how
we've had to prepare it.

"How many of us used to eat fish more than once a
week? It seems to me that most Americans, Catholic or
Protestant, still think of fish as something you have to eat
on Friday as a penance. I've read that the average person
eats six to ten times more meat and poultry than fish.
But here we eat fish every day, sometimes twice a day.
Plus clams, crabs, oysters, mussels, chitons, barnacles,
and abalone, so that we're probably consuming twenty
times the amount of fish and shellfish we'd have under—"
she paused and smiled as she continued "—under *normal*
conditions. Hence the weight loss. Fish has half the calo-
ries of meat, as well as being low in cholesterol.

"Even more important, we're swallowing tremendous
quantities of minerals and vitamins. Even our salt is better

for us than the table salt we used in the city. You've seen me make it, filling a flat dish with sea water, heating it in the oven until nothing remains but white powdery crystals. Well, that natural sea salt is full of minerals as well as iodine, whereas salt sold in stores has been processed to make it pour more easily, and minerals and elements have been removed.

"And don't forget seaweed. We put it in all our soups and stews. Remember the candy Carlo taught us to make? That was mostly *kombu,* or algae. So if it's true, Andrew, that our hair is shinier and our complexions are clearer, we owe thanks to the sea. Sea spray is good for us. Salt-water baths are good for us. Our glands are in beautiful shape and we'll all live to be two hundred."

Warren Brock's round eyes opened wide. "You don't *say!* Well, in that case, I may be able to finish my statue of the Aphrodite of Phoenix. There is *hope.*"

"Do you suppose . . ." Andrew Held tapped his lower lip with his forefinger and looked around thoughtfully at his companions in exile. "We have injuries, and Diana has suffered a miscarriage, but I'd call them accidents rather than indications of our physical condition. It seems to me that our general health is remarkable.

"Remember two or three years ago when a Japanese officer finally came out of hiding in the Philippine jungle? After thirty years in the wilderness, thirty years in a daily struggle to survive, he was in better shape physically *and* mentally than his urban contemporaries, what with all their nervous tensions. What's happened to our own tension ailments? Norma, you've mentioned having migraine headaches. Blake has suffered from chronic asthma. Those symptoms seem to have vanished."

"And *I,*" Brock put in brightly, "haven't been constipated since I had to do it in the woods."

"What is it?" Dr. Held asked with a smile. "Does the hard life on Phoenix exhaust us so completely that we fall asleep before our headaches and our asthma and our palpitations can catch up with us? As another example. Have you realized that in four months, not one out of nine has come down with the so-called common cold? Perhaps that wasn't surprising during August and September, when sunshine compensated for our lack of clothing and shelter. But during the past two months we've all been chilled and soaked to the skin and repeatedly exposed to elements that life in the city protected us from, yet there hasn't been a sniffle or a cough among us. It's our isolation, I suppose. The germs have no way of getting to Phoenix. I predict that the day after the rescue team finally arrives, we'll all come down with nasty colds."

Norma shook her head. "Not necessarily. We may not be building up immunity, but our bodies are more resistant. We'll be all right in the city if we take plenty of seaweed with us, and plenty of sea water."

"We can't, Norma," Blake said quietly. "Remember? You can't take it with you."

"I was joking . . ." But Norma's smile had faded, and her voice was touched with sadness.

The totem calendar had been notched, a few minor issues had been raised, discussed, and settled. By popular demand, Rolf and Diana recited their latest verse, as they had done many times since the others discovered that they composed poems or bits of poems whenever they worked together.

> I wrap myself in the magic cloak of sleep;
> It lifts me and it carries me into a purpling sky;
> My silvery bed of clouds is soft and deep
> And a thousand brilliant star fires twinkle by . . .

There were smiles and applause, and then a long silence as they warmed their hands on mugs of rose hip tea and sipped the hot liquid carefully, with sleepy eyes fixed on the bonfire.

As leader, Andrew Held routinely waited until everyone else had spoken before he presented his own ideas. "Anything more? Anyone want the floor?" Gestures and murmurs assured him they had said all they meant to say. "Well, then, let's talk about moving day."

He rose, limped across the circle to the totem calendar and pointed to a slash several inches above the one he had cut tonight. "Here's where we started work on the house. November first. Not quite six weeks ago, and of course it's far from finished. But the outside walls are up for the first section. The planks are ready for the floor. Shakes for the roof have been split.

"We can't complain about the weather. For the most part, it's been good to us. But it is December. Our luck can't hold out." His finger dropped to the freshly cut notch. "December eleventh. Two weeks before Christmas. We should be able to lay the floor and put on the roof in a few more days. I propose that we be settled in our house, spa, buttery, apothecary and all, before Christmas."

Felicia exclaimed, "Oh, Andy, that would be great!"

"If we don't take time to go hunting," Rolf said, "maybe we can make it."

In one voice Norma and Felicia said, "We've got enough food for a while." And Diana added, "We can manage."

Andrew Held nodded. "We've got to get under cover, but after that, we can take our time about finishing the interior. So once we've moved, you'll be free to hunt."

Brock glanced at Diana. There was apology in his voice as he said, "I hate to mention clay, but I can assure you that the central fireplace will be finished within the week. It will keep us warm and we can use it for cooking while I start building Norma's ovens."

"Dr. Held?" Donald's scarred face was troubled. "I want to work on the house, like everybody else. But what about them wild dogs? I was going to go back to the south end and try to kill the last of them bastards."

"That's important, I agree. But it's dangerous." Andrew Held's face was grim. "When you hunt for the dogs, you shouldn't go alone. You and Rolf and Carlo should go as a team. Even so, it may take some time. It's my feeling . . ." He paused, hesitating to state a personal conviction as if it were a command. "It is my personal feeling that unless we enter their territory, the dogs present less of a threat right now than winter storms and high tides. We're camped in a low-lying, exposed beach area. I think we will be warmer and safer up on the north end and in our log cabin, unfinished as it is. But I leave it up to you. To all of you."

In a few minutes it was clear that everyone was excited at the prospect of an early move into their house. After a week's illness, Diana's eyes looked enormous and dark in a small, pale face, but they sparkled when Felicia suggested they plan a celebration for Christmas day.

"Thanksgiving went by unnoticed. And no wonder. Mike's death was just too fresh in our minds, no one had the heart for it. I still . . ." Felicia's hand rested affectionately on Andrew Held's knee. "I still have a hard time realizing . . . Well, we've had some troubles these past few

weeks but we now have the time and the means to cele-
brate, and we certainly have enough reasons. Diana is
getting well, and Carlo and Rolf got back safely—thanks
to Donald—and in another two weeks Lili is going to
present us with a wide selection of basset puppies. You,
Andy, will have the pick of the litter."

At the sound of her name, Lili lifted her head and
looked at Felicia expectantly. Seeing no food in Felicia's
hand, she dropped her head to her paws, sighed deeply,
and closed her eyes.

Warren Brock gestured delicately toward Lili's belly.
"*There* is a considerate female. She's not only providing
Michael the Second for you, Andrew. Within that grotesquely distended womb, there must be something for
everyone. Dear comrades, each of us will have a puppy of
his own. As for a Christmas celebration . . . ah, Felicia,
you look like every caveman's pin-up girl, but the instincts
of the capital city's most gracious hostess still lurk within.
A Christmas celebration. Excellent! I'll provide the
smokes."

"We'll have a banquet," Norma said. "A real feast.
Warren, do you suppose a spit could be built into the
fireplace?"

"Why not? I'd make you a bastable, if I could." Brock's
round mouth twisted into a mock grimace. "All I ask is
that the menu include something that isn't *healthy*. How
will we know we've had fun if we don't have indigestion
afterwards?"

Carlo laughed. "Shu-ah, bradda. We goan eat. We goan
smoke. Maybe I get finish making guitar, and we have
music. Guitar not finish, we still goan make music."

"And play some games." Rolf turned to Diana. "You
ever play smetali? Or we could have a spear-throwing con-
test. We've all gotten pretty good with our spears."

"Gambling games, I trust?" Brock said happily. "No
doubt our red brothers bet even when they threw spears."

Rolf smiled so that white teeth glistened between shaggy
black mustache and full beard. "Gambling was a way to
get wealthy. In any game the loser paid off in something
he owned. Anything from an arrowhead to his best wife."

Donald said gruffly, "Well, okay, I go along with doing
the house first and going after the dogs later. And I got
something for the Christmas party." Voices hushed and
all eyes turned his way. He shook his head. "No, I ain't

saying what it is. I'm just saying, I'm making something and we can have it on Christmas."

Andrew Held leaned forward and patted Lili's head. "Is it agreed, then? All efforts concentrated on construction. House, lookout tower, and signal flag." His head inclined toward the totem calendar. "On the night of December twenty-first, we'll sleep in our house."

Norma's uncle, Cabot Sterling, refused the hand-wrapped cigar Simon Boyd offered him. It seemed to him that Blake Mansfield's law partner had expensive tastes and that bothered him. Original oils on the walls, an authentic Kerman on the floor. He had been pleased to note that Blake's office looked more like a place of work. "It's a hard thing to accept," he said in the severe tone of voice he always used when he was in danger of showing emotion. "But since all our inquiries lead to the same conclusion, I think we must."

Simon Boyd bowed his head thoughtfully. His manner combined courtesy for the older man and sorrow for their mutual loss, with genteel reluctance to dwell on the unpleasant. "I spent a week in Seattle. Several of the authorities I talked to, by the way, had already received letters from you. I did manage to get that ridiculous auto theft charge dropped, but I accomplished little else. As far as turning up any proof at all that your niece . . ." he cleared his throat and finished firmly, ". . . that your niece is alive, the conclusion that she and Blake suffered some sort of fatal accident was inescapable."

Out of consideration for the feelings of the deceased's closest living relative, the attorney did not enlarge on the question of what sort of fatal accident had been mentioned during that week in Seattle. The police had held to the theory that the Mansfields picked up a hitchhiker who robbed, killed, and buried them and then went off with their rented car. The automobile rental company concluded that a car that had not shown up anyplace in the continental United States in three months' time was in Mexico with a new paint job. Civil defense officials had made a connection between the probable date of the Mansfields' disappearance and the known date of the tsunami. But not having talked with Norma's uncle at the time, Simon Boyd had had no reason to believe that Norma and Blake, the most conservative of travelers, would have strayed so far beyond conventional tourist circuits as to have been caught in any of the remote coastal areas devastated by the tidal wave.

"Had I known that Norma was carrying a letter of introduction to Dr. Held . . ." He paused again, for death caused by a freakish killer like a tidal wave was as frightening as death at the hands of an armed hitchhiker. In a way it was more shocking, because the odds against it were so much greater. "I would have gone to the Outer Islands if I had known of any connection between the Mansfields and Andrew Held. Phoenix Island, you said?"

Cabot Sterling pulled a clean handkerchief from his breast pocket and carefully blotted his lips. "You would have learned nothing more than I've been able to discover through letters. They did take the ferry to Wolf Island, which is the terminus of the ferry line. They did spend two nights at a motel there and the motel register indicated they were driving a rented car. If they went on to Phoenix, it would have been by private boat, either Dr. Held's boat or a boat they chartered on Wolf. In any case, they had left Wolf Island before the tsunami struck. If they reached Phoenix . . ."

Cabot Sterling refolded his handkerchief with great care and returned it to his pocket. "We know from the Coast Guard what happened to Phoenix, and to anyone who might have been on Phoenix on August fourth. The only possible alternative is that they were lost at sea." He rose, smoothed his vest with the palms of his hands, and ventured a quick nod that was meant to express gratitude. "I'm indebted to you, Mr. Boyd. For making the trip to Seattle, even if it wasn't fruitful. For your many inquiries among Norma's friends here in New York. For handling that business with the condominium association." A thin smile softened his habitually rigid expression. "An old physics professor is not in a position to handle real estate on the east side of Manhattan. I was distressed at the thought that Blake was breaking a contract, though, of course . . ." he added firmly, "through no fault of his own. Thank you for taking over."

Simon Boyd's gesture swept aside the suggestion that he had done anything of importance. "No, really. I've just taken care of one or two technicalities. Avoided some problems before they materialized, you might say. The condominium association probably wouldn't have taken action for six months or so. Meanwhile the assessments are paid and there's no breach of contract. If Blake and Norma haven't returned by the end of six months, their bank will probably be appointed trustee and I'm confident I'll be named co-trustee, so we'll have no problems there." He rose, walked around the desk and extended his hand. "In any case, Dr. Sterling, I'm just holding the fort until they get back."

Cabot Sterling gripped the attorney's hand, gave it one strong all-inclusive shake, and said, "No need to be kind. I can face the truth and you'd better do the same, unless you want to run this law business by yourself. Norma and Blake aren't coming back, Mr. Boyd. It may take the law seven years to admit that, but my training has been in science and I know that if you work a formula correctly, you're going to get the same answer every time. We've got the facts, and we've got the answer. Good-bye, Mr. Boyd. I'm going back to Maine. Glad to see you if you ever come down."

They had never worked harder and they had never worked together so harmoniously. Meanwhile, nature, Andrew Held noted, was manipulating the odds for and against their race to move into the log house by December twenty-first. Against them was the immutability of the winter solstice, for they had chosen the shortest day of the year as moving day. In their favor was an unseasonal spell of dry and windless weather, as if nature were rewarding their industry with the only gift available to her at this time of year.

They worked all day at the farm site. At night, by the campfire, they continued working on household equipment until, in the interests of preserving their health, Andrew Held decreed a ten o'clock curfew. Twentieth-century man, Dr. Held reflected, measures "success" and "happiness" by the ratio of work to leisure. The greater his leisure in relation to the time he must work to acquire it, the more successful he is and, therefore, the "smarter" he is. Perhaps it was their mutual and compelling desire to finish the house that was reversing their values, for clearly they had never been happier. Every log that was perfectly notched, every rusty nail they found and straightened, was proof of their success.

"Or it may be," he confided in Felicia, "that we need

some new definitions. Leisure means recreation, right? But here on Phoenix, what's recreation? Millions of people in noisy polluted cities spend fifty weeks a year in order to buy two weeks on a camping trip or two weeks in the country. But we're already *here,* as the Boston lady said. And what do we call work? Fishing and hunting. Pottery and weaving and wood carving. Isn't that what we used to do for recreation? No wonder everyone's getting along so well with everyone else. There's no thunder in Paradise."

With soft mud in one hand and moss in the other, Felicia straightened up and looked appraisingly at the space between logs she and Andrew had been chinking. "Paradise," she said drily, "would provide an equal number of men and women."

By December twentieth, the house was roughed in. Roof nailed and lashed, floor planks in place, rough doors at the entrances and crude shutters at the windows. The large circular fireplace was finished and dry and Warren Brock's pride, a fieldstone chimney, was ready to carry smoke out through the roof.

Though they had been speaking of moving day as if it were comparable to a massive troop movement through the Alps in winter, there was very little left in the beach area, for no one walked to the old Furness farm without carrying a maximum load. All food supplies in the buttery had been stored in a lean-to beside the cabin's back door. The contents of the apothecary, the armory, and the warehouse were stacked inside the house. The spa and the smokehouse had been dismantled and their component parts carried to the farmsite where, in due course, they would be reassembled. Nothing was left for moving day except the last of the cooking utensils and the beds and bed coverings in the dormitory.

They would rise, make their last fire on the beach, cook their last breakfast on the low saddle of land above the harbor. They were already calling it "summer camp," as if they expected to return to it in five or six months. They had been so careful to save and transfer every scrap of potentially useful material—every rag, broken bottle, and bit of rusty wire, every straight stick and sharp-edged slice of shale—that by December twenty-second, every clue to their four months' occupation would be erased. The area where Andrew Held's fine house had stood, where powerhouse and swimming pool and boat dock had created a small but visible pocket of civilization, would be as bare as the tsunami had left it.

In their fever to finish and move into the log house, they had not neglected the signaling system that would take the place of the bonfire on the beach. As Dr. Held had promised, their signals on the site of the Furness farm were an improvement over the beach fire, for they had both signal fire and lookout post.

The fire was laid on top of the mound of fieldstone which the first Furness settlers had created when they tried to clear the rocky ground. By leveling off the peak, they created a stone pyre like a small Aztec pyramid. On the flat surface at the top they built a bonfire and ignited it by carrying a lighted stick from the hearth fire in the house. As they had for the bonfire on the beach, they took turns tending the fire overnight, for its flame was the only signal sure to be seen after dark.

For daylight hours, they placed their hope for rescue on their lookout. The field around the log house was rimmed on three sides by fir trees. They chose the tallest of these for their "tower," and began work at the same time construction started on the house. First there was a ladder, with two saplings as the verticals and short limbs, lashed to the saplings with honeysuckle vines, as crosspieces. Rolf and Carlo, vying with each other, had skinned their knees and hands and suffered several falls before the ladder was firmly tied to the tree trunk and one man could climb to the top in relative safety.

Then they lashed a flagpole to the topmost limbs. From this crow's nest a flag, their cherished tablecloth, was to fly. They drew straws for the privilege of hanging the flag and everyone gathered at the foot of the tree while Carlo, the winner, ascended like a drunken monkey, secured the mast, and attached the flag.

For a moment it was motionless, falling lifelessly in a mute signal of defeat. Then a burst of icy wind swept across the tops of the trees, catching and lifting the cloth. "Hal-lo deah!" Carlo shouted as the ragged edge of the material flapped and stiffened. "She fly!"

At the foot of the tree, upturned faces broke into delighted smiles and seven voices joined in a cheer. Only Donald was silent. His small eyes cast one brief, hostile glance at the flag and then he looked away. "You guys cheer all you want," he said sullenly. "I got work to do." He turned and plodded across the field toward the log house. No one noticed he had left, except Andrew Held, whose thoughtful blue eyes followed the hulking figure until it disappeared into the house.

Warren Brock's mother sipped her glass of sherry and wondered how best to comfort this poor boy. He was so self-centered in his grief. He would know, if he could get outside himself long enough to think about it, that as Warren's mother she was feeling the loss at least as much as he. His pain would stop. Hers would go on as long as she lived. But meanwhile, he was suffering blindly, and alone. Except that he obviously did want to talk about it. She could listen, for in a sense the details of Warren's death did not disturb her. They were incidental, almost meaningless against the monstrous truth that she had lost her only son. So she would nod, and listen, and nod, and sip sherry.

"The worst part was going through the house." Kirk Aspinwall shivered. "I think it was because there was nothing *wrong*. I mean, by that time I had already talked to the new deputy sheriff, and the Wolf Island postmaster, so I knew Warren was . . ." He choked, cleared his throat, and said firmly, *"dead.* But I thought that somehow, his house would look different. I mean, there would be something . . . dead about it, too.

"Everything outside was the same, except that his car was gone. That gave me a funny feeling because my first reaction was, 'He's run down to the village. He ought to be back in an hour.' Of course right away I realized that, well, psychologically I was refusing to accept the fact that he was dead. I suppose that's why I went up to Wolf in the first place, even when you'd already received the official notice. And why I had to go look through the house, as if, in spite of everything they told me, I would go in and there he'd be, working in his studio, wearing old bluejeans and a faded sweatshirt and composing silly verses while he carved."

"Obscene verses," Mrs. Brock said, nodding her neat, china doll head. "But witty. Never unpleasant."

"Oh, yes!" The young man agreed with her eagerly. "Never really *dirty*. Well, I knew where he hid the extra house key. Under a flowerpot at the back door. So I let myself in. And that's when it began to be . . . difficult.

"Nothing was disturbed. Everything was in perfect order, the way he always kept it. The worst tidal wave in fifty years, they called it. And it hit the waterfront just below the house. Out the front window I could see where the shoreline had been smashed and cut back by the storm. He had been drowned, he might have died a horrible death, and yet his house was exactly the same, waiting for him to come back. There was even an open book beside his reading chair. It seemed that at any minute he would walk into the room and pick it up and start reading where he left off.

"I couldn't stay. I looked around, because I knew you'd want me to. To see if the windows were locked, things like that. And when I went outside, I watered the garden, because there were still a few roses in bloom. Then I left. It was a beautiful day. Bright sun, warm. But I kept shivering."

The little woman's large round eyes were sympathetic. "You were very good to make the trip. I wouldn't have asked you to do it, but when you volunteered, I realized I couldn't quite believe those official reports, either. I, too, wanted to see for myself, but I didn't have the youth and strength to face it." She raised her sherry glass to her Cupid mouth and took a long swallow. "I've left the arrangements with my attorneys. There's nothing to do, really, but wait. For seven years, I think it is. Or is it five? Think of that! At my age, I am to wait seven years before my son is officially dead." She blinked rapidly, set down her sherry glass, and steadied her hand on the carved oak arm of her chair. "Or is it five? Perhaps it's only five. I keep forgetting."

Chapter Thirty-Eight

FELICIA awoke slowly. Drugged by warmth and suspended between dreams and reality, she lay absolutely still, wondering where she was. Gradually her eyes focused and her surroundings began to have shape and substance. She and Andrew were in the log house, in a little cubicle surrounded by pine-bough screens that had once been the walls of their night shelter in the dormitory. They were wrapped together in coverings of fur and woven cedar bark and his body was warm against hers, vibrant even in sleep. She could hear the crackling of the hearth fire, soft footsteps, whispering voices. One, two, three . . . And last night, their fourth under a roof, had been Christmas Eve.

Now she was fully awake, but she snuggled down into her warm chrysalis and sleepily recalled the events of the night before. The trimming of the tree had been a cooperative effort in which all nine insisted on taking part. Nine excited children, Felicia reflected. Simultaneously joyful and solemn in the performance of their ritual. Decorating the fragrant fir had been attended by so much laughter and confusion that it was soon obvious that any one or two of them could finish the job in half the time, but still no one would relinquish his part. When they finished, they stood back while Donald, the tall one, attached a singular decoration to the tip of the tree.

It was a dove in flight, a miniature of the real bird Warren Brock had fashioned out of white feathers and fireweed cotton. It perched at the top of the dark green tree and winked at them all with miniscule black pebble eyes. Below, the slender limbs bent gracefully under decorations taken from the wild. Long tendrils of silvery gray-green moss hung from the limbs in place of tinsel. Fibrous white moss lay along the tops of the branches like patches of "snow." Chains of cherry and ruby red rose hips encircled the tree in flowing loops. Some sort of natural object swung on a thread at the tip of every branch. Seashells of all kinds, cones of different sizes, from fir, cedar, and pine, tiny dried starfish like six-pointed stars.

For several minutes they admired their creation speechlessly, more awed by their handiwork than they would have been by the most glittery confection in a department store window. Felicia thought of her own Christmas trees in her apartment in Washington, D.C. She had been "known" for them. The Washington newspapers had photographed her standing beside her latest "original and innovative holiday creation," and invitations to the cocktail party unveiling were highly prized. Last year the tree had been sprayed with silver and powdered with gold sequins. Brittle glass icicles dripped from its branches. Original, innovative! Felicia smiled at the memory of the caption. It had been, yes, to the degree that it had been rendered unnatural. But it hadn't been her own creation, for every year she commissioned a topflight interior decorator to do it for her. And she had hired a madrigal group, dressed in Old English costumes, to entertain her guests with Christmas carols.

Felicia sighed pleasurably and decided to allow herself another few minutes in bed. How different their caroling had been last night!

Carlo had introduced his latest and most successful attempt at making a guitar. The moment he began to strum chords, someone began to hum, and in minutes they were all singing "God Rest Ye Merry Gentlemen" with such gusto that, when they came to the end of the song, gasping and laughing, Warren Brock exclaimed, "I win! I finished first!"

Immediately, they began "A Partridge in a Pear Tree," dum-dee-dumming when they didn't know the words, and from there progressed to every Christmas song any of them could hum or whistle well enough for Carlo to pick out the harmony. If their voices didn't blend, at least they joined. As in the trimming of the tree, there were no spectators.

When they grew sleepy, they banked the fire and Felicia recited the program for the following day. A special breakfast, planned by Norma. Midmorning, they would exchange gifts. The Christmas feast would be in the late afternoon, preceded by Donald's "surprise," the nature of which he stubbornly refused to reveal. As they were separating to prepare for bed, Rolf and Diana called them back.

"We have a plan for tomorrow." Rolf's low voice was a muted but vibrant drumbeat. "We'd like to invite you to our wedding."

Between their exclamations and murmurs, he explained that he and Diana had composed the ceremony but that all of them would be asked to take part. So that was scheduled for one o'clock, after the breakfast and exchange of gifts, before Donald's surprise and the Christmas dinner. It was going to be a long, beautiful day . . .

Felicia sat up straight, freed herself from the covers as gently as she could and tucked them around Andrew's sleeping form. The cold air was fragrant with wood smoke and the spicy aroma of fresh cut cedar. She dressed quickly. First, her feed sack shift, an outer garment during warm weather and her "lingerie" for the winter. God bless Farmer Dick and his Better Chicks. Next, a pair of men's swim trunks, cinched in at the waist with a piece of twine. Over these supremely modest undergarments, she wore a leather skirt, belted with a strip of rawhide, and a rabbit skin vest. Finally, she slipped her feet into moccasins.

Now for a thorough soap and water scrub, with warm water if the early morning firebuilder had put some on the hearth, plus brushing her teeth with a sponge of stiff white moss. Finally, one hundred strokes with her hairbrush, providing Warren Brock's most recent experiment with seagull quills and cedar would hold up that long. Then, *voilà!* she thought, laughing inwardly. Madame would have finished her *toilette*. Madame would be ready to assume her responsibilities as Chairman of Phoenix Island's Christmas festivities.

Ever since they began construction of the log house, their meals had been Spartan, as much to save time for work as to use food supplies sparingly. Breakfasts had been a bowl of hot porridge made from starchy roots and dried berries, prepared quickly and eaten hastily in the half-light of early morning winter. Now, on Christmas morning, they ate slowly, relishing the delicacies Norma had prepared in honor of the day.

There were hoe cakes, baked on hot stones near the fire, cooked to a deep gold because the flour consisted of equal parts of ground cattail tubers and bright yellow cattail pollen. They spread the cakes with a thick, rosy jam, made with wild plums and honey. The rarest treat was smoked venison sausage, spiced with peppery mushrooms, wild mint, and powdered seaweed. The loop of sausage that Norma simmered in a little sea water and then cut into nine steaming and fragrant pieces was one of several she and Diana had made and stored in the buttery, the only survivors of the raid by the dog pack.

"This is *special*," Warren Brock exclaimed as he picked up his portion between his fingers and delicately bit off a small piece. "Mmm! Yes, *indeed!* But of course it *would* be delicious, wouldn't it, because Norma says meat is bad for you."

"I didn't," Norma protested. "I said fish is better."

"Don't quibble, dear girl. I can tolerate what's good for me, but I *adore* what's bad." He was about to take a second bite of sausage when Lili attracted his attention. She was sitting at his elbow, her front paws turned out like a ballet dancer in second position. Her large brown eyes followed every movement of the hand that held the sausage while her tail thumped hopefully on the rough plank floor.

"Tsk!" Brock said. "Aren't you supposed to want dill pickles and ice cream? You're pregnant, you know. And don't you know the house rule—no dogs in the dining room? Oh, well, I know you're eating for ten." He put the sausage between his front teeth, bit it into two pieces of equal size, and handed one of them to Lili. "Don't *tell* me," he said as Norma began to speak. "I know, I know. Your mother never allowed you to feed dogs at the table."

"True." Norma smiled wistfully. "But that isn't what I was going to say. I was going to call Lili and give her a piece of mine."

Felicia laughed. "So much for our Puritan mothers, eh? Well, so was I."

Tail wagging, Lili made the rounds, while her meat-hungry benefactors licked their empty fingers and sipped from mugs of dandelion root coffee.

When Felicia first submitted her plans for Christmas day, they had all been disappointed because there was no reference to Christmas presents. "Presents?" she asked, astonished by the unanimity of their protest. "Isn't that a little childlike?"

"Perhaps we *are* a little childlike," Andrew Held had answered cheerfully.

So an exchange of gifts had been scheduled to follow breakfast. As soon as the remnants of the meal had been cleared away and the dishes washed, they gathered around the fireplace and Norma filled their mugs with fresh hot tea.

They were all making awkward attempts to conceal their gifts. Several had bulky objects wrapped in their bedclothes. Some hid the gifts under pine boughs or holly-like sprigs of Oregon grape. Donald, grinning self-consciously, emerged from his room with several odd shapes bulging under his shirt.

Felicia's anxiety about the distribution of gifts melted away as they proceeded with the exchange. They had so many things to give away; there really would be something for everyone. In any case, the mood of anticipation seemed to rise from their desire to surprise one another rather than from eagerness to see what they might receive. "How shall we do this?" she asked. "All at once? One at a time?"

A half dozen voices rose in instant and unequivocal response. "All right," she said laughing. "One at a time." She turned to the stack of firewood and snapped off a handful of twigs. "Nine twigs. I'm breaking them into nine different lengths. Now, we'll draw. The one with the shortest stick goes first."

One by one, they revealed their handiwork. There were useful things, like baskets, bowls, and a large smooth rock and stone roller to be used like a *metate* for grinding seeds, wild wheat kernels, and roots. There were things to be worn. Belt buckles carved out of wood, rabbit fur' for leggings, ponchos of woven cedar bark. But most of the gifts, Andrew Held observed, were not utilitarian. Something special, for people whose daily lives were shaped by urgent necessity, was ideally something they didn't need.

There were corsages for the women, and strings of beads made from tiny pine cones and ruby red hips of the wild rose. Shaving was certainly a luxury but Rolf presented the men with razor-sharp clam shells and promised to demonstrate the old Indian method of shaving and cutting hair. For the group as a whole, Dr. Held's gift was basically practical. A detailed design for a potter's wheel. But for Felicia he had made a coronet wreath of winter greens and bird feathers. He placed it on her head.

The feathers swept back from her temples like the head-dress of a Valkyrie and the crown of glossy leaves contrasted vividly with her shiny red hair and brought out the sea-green of her eyes.

They gave each other many small treasures of the wild, things that were to be looked at and touched and felt. Abalone shells with gleaming mother-of-pearl interiors in soft shades of lavender and pink. Dried starfish in deep purple and striking combinations of orange and green. Opalescent agates—Donald had one for everyone in the group. For Carlo he had several lengths of dried animal gut.

"You said you was going to make another fiddle or guitar or whatever that is you been working on. These ought to make good strings."

Among the presents were two games. One was a dice cup and a pair of large wooden dice. The other was a checkerboard of clay on which the "black" squares were cross-hatched with scratches and the "white" were smooth. Small round slices of wood were the checkers, half of them stained a dark brown.

Warren Brock's gift for Diana was the last to be revealed. It was a small statue of a nude female with hands crossed over her abdomen and a secretive smile on her face. "Fertility symbol," he said brightly. "Rub her nose every night before you go to bed. You're such a lovely wild thing, Diana. Make another baby. And if someone like me has a cliff fall on him, pray for him, if you *must*, but don't go after him."

Early in the afternoon, Rolf and Diana approached Dr. Held. They were holding hands like children clinging to each other for reassurance and their eyes shone expectantly.

"Dr. Held," Diana asked. "Would you be the minister?"

"The minister?" The question was totally unexpected and brought a curious lump to Andrew Held's throat. Years before, when he had been called up to receive the most coveted award the international scientific community bestows, he had felt more in possession of himself than he did right now. "I . . . I am deeply honored. I will do the best I can." His Hungarian accent was pronounced, as it often was when he was caught up by emotion. "You have planned the ceremony?"

Rolf nodded. "Yes. We've been talking about it for several days. We've made up a poem, and we know what we want to do. But we'd like you to bring everybody together, and say a few words."

"Do you think we should have a rehearsal?"

"No . . ." Both young people shook their heads energetically. "That would spoil it," Rolf said. "But would you come outside for a few minutes, so we can talk?"

An hour later, Felicia called Norma from the kitchen and Donald and Blake from outside. When they were all together, Andrew Held arranged them in a semi-circle with their backs to the hearth. Rolf and Diana were side by side, facing the group, while Dr. Held took a position between the young couple and the others.

First Dr. Held addressed the half circle. "Brock, Felicia, Norma, Blake, Carlo, Donald. We are witnesses this afternoon to the wedding of our friends Diana and Rolf. We have seen them live and work together. We have seen that they live in harmony and in love. They want to make some promises to each other, in our presence." His deep blue eyes rested on Felicia. "Would you get the wreaths, please, Felicia?"

Felicia disappeared into the young couple's cubicle and came out with wreaths of glossy madrona leaves. She approached Diana first, placing a wreath on top of her dark hair, then turned to Rolf and put the second crown of leaves on his head.

As Felicia stepped back into the semi-circle, Dr. Held glanced at Diana and Rolf. "Which one of you will speak first?"

Rolf drew Diana's arm through his and looked down into her face. "You begin."

Diana's sensitive mouth trembled for an instant and then began to curve into a smile. Facing the group, she said, "We love each other. We respect each other. We are not *one*. We are not two halves that make a whole. We are two individual, separate human beings, who choose to live and work together."

Rolf's eyes left Diana's face and, like Diana, he addressed the people near the hearth. "I will always take care of Diana, and I will always love her. I will protect her, but I will never own her. She is a whole person. She cannot be *mine*."

Diana spoke. "I want you all to know that I love and

respect Rolf. He gives me strength and courage. I trust him."

Their heads turned and, as they looked into each other's faces, Diana said, "I want to have your child."

"I will love and care for our child, but I will never love anybody more than I love you."

"I want a house, a small house, that is all our own."

"I want to build a house for you, with my own hands."

"We will build a house together. Your hands, and my hands, will make our house."

Again their eyes moved back to the circle of their friends. "I, Diana Lindgren, pledge that I will be Rolf's loyal wife."

Rolf's deep voice trembled. "I, Rolf Morgan, pledge that I will be a good and loving husband."

Slowly, together, they removed their wreaths and exchanged them. Placing Rolf's wreath on her own head, Diana said, "Now I am married to you."

"Now I am married to you," Rolf repeated, lifting Diana's wreath and adjusting it on his own head.

Dr. Held said quietly, "This is a solemn pledge. We all witness this pledge, and respect it. You are truly husband and wife."

There was a moment of complete silence, and then Rolf's head bent and their mouths met in a kiss.

Andrew Held motioned to Carlo. "Now, their song."

Carlo left the circle, picked up his guitar and stepped toward Diana and Rolf.

"This is an original song," Dr. Held explained. "None of the poems they memorized in school seemed to fit the occasion, so Rolf and Diana have composed their own. It's called 'The Song of Phoenix.' Carlo worked out the accompaniment."

"It isn't very good poetry," Rolf said, smiling so that his white teeth gleamed beneath his shaggy black mustache.

"It's better than my music, bradda!" Carlo replied, laughing.

"But it's personal, and it's your own," Andrew Held added. "We'd like to hear it."

Carlo ran his finger across the strings, plucking out the first notes of the melody. With their eyes on each other, Diana and Rolf began to sing.

> *I followed my sweetheart across the deep water,*
> *The silvery moon was my Heavenly guide.*
> *Deep in the blackness I came on an island*
> *Rising like a Phoenix from white foaming tide.*
>
> *Phoenix, our Phoenix, you sheltered my sweetheart*
> *And out of the darkness you beckoned to me,*
> *Your shores and your forests, your streams and your*
>   *meadows*
> *A world strange and lovely thrust up from the sea.*

This time Carlo's melodious baritone strengthened and blended with the young couple's voices as all three repeated the chorus:

> *Phoenix, our Phoenix, you sheltered my sweet-*
>   *heart . . .*

The chorus ended, Carlo's fingers ran through the first few bars of the melody. Slowly, softly, Rolf and Diana sang the second verse.

> *My sweetheart was waiting, her arms were around*
>   *me,*
> *The earth was beneath us, the forest above;*
> *In peace and in beauty we whispered our promise*
> *To give and to nurture, to cherish and love.*

Then they began the last chorus, and one by one, the other voices joined in. They were uncertain at first, but gradually gained confidence, so that when the chorus ended Carlo instinctively began it again. All nine sang out so energetically that "The Song of Phoenix," awkward and amateurish as it was, filled the cabin with bursts of happy sound.

> *Phoenix, our Phoenix. . . .*

As it ended, they smiled, and with Rolf's arm around Diana, they walked toward the group. No rehearsal had been necessary, no explanation was needed. As if they had always known that this was the proper ending to a wedding ceremony, each person extended a hand as the young couple moved along the line. First Diana, then Rolf, clasped the hand, and said "In love and harmony."

Then they were all talking at once, and Felicia was hugging Diana fiercely, unaware of the tears running down her cheeks.

For four months, they had eaten their meals like campers, sitting on logs and balancing their plates on their knees. For their Christmas banquet, Felicia had decreed, they were going to have chairs and a table.

Building the log house and the crow's nest lookout and ladder had left no time for making furniture. That was to be their communal project now that the signal flag was flying from the lookout and the cabin was roofed over. Nevertheless, they did achieve a table of sorts, and they did have something to sit on.

The "chairs" were upended cedar bolts that were to be split into shakes as the log house was gradually enlarged. Their "table" consisted of planks like the flooring, resting on a base of small logs notched and criss-crossed like a miniature cabin. Primitive as it was, Felicia set the table as if her only concern was whether to use the Spode or the Wedgwood.

A centerpiece of evergreen ran the length of the table. Seashells of all kinds nestled in the dark and fragrant greenery. Each place setting included a plate, a bowl, and a drinking cup, all of Brock's hand-modeled slate-gray pottery. They would eat with their hands—"If we did have cutlery," Blake commented, "I'm sure we'd find some better use for it than merely eating with it"—but they would eat by candlelight, for Norma had cast two beeswax candles and set them on wooden pedestals amid the decorative bows of fir and cedar.

When Felicia announced that dinner would be ready in an hour, Donald said gruffly, "Well, it's time for my surprise." He left the cabin and returned in a few minutes with a deerskin pouch.

"Can that be *full?*" Brock inquired with a lift of his blond eyebrows. "Of some divine elixir?"

Donald grinned. "That ain't what we called it over at the place. We called it pruno. But I think you got the idea." He caressed the taut surface with rough but surprisingly gentle fingers. "I been having a helluva time keeping this stuff hid. And hid where it was warm enough to work. It ain't been easy to leave it alone, either. That's the trouble with bootleg. Testing it all the time, you finish her off while she's still green."

"Bootleg!" Brock breathed ecstatically. "Donald, you're a prince of a man."

"You better wait till you taste it," Donald said modestly. "It's made of honey and apples, and some of the yeast stuff Norma uses to make bread."

"Is this some fine old recipe, inherited by generation after generation of Campbells?"

Donald's laugh was a short growl. "I *in*-herited it, like you say. From an old con who was always smart enough to get himself a work assignment in the kitchen. Next to the hospital, that's the best spot in the joint. Some of the younger guys called him 'K.P.' and kidded him about dishwater hands. What they didn't figure was that wise old K.P. had got himself located where he could swipe sugar and fruit or whatever he needed to make pruno. OJT, the social workers called it. On the Job Training. I'll say it was! K.P. got trained to make liquor out of raisins and potato peels. He fermented one batch by hiding it behind a light fixture in the ceiling." He grinned at Brock. "It ain't Old Granddad. It's old WSP. Washington State Penitentiary. Maybe you won't like it."

"I'll like it." Brock danced to the dinner table and picked up two pottery mugs. "Let us gather, and drink a toast to good old K.P. and that grand old alma mater, WSP."

"Alcohol . . ." Andrew Held brought his right hand up in a salute. "Donald, you've got the solution."

Donald grinned self-consciously. "Me? To what?"

"The energy crisis." Dr. Held pointed to the deerskin pouch. "Our most brilliant scientists drink it, and have themselves rubbed with it, but they haven't done anything useful about making it."

"Maybe they never done any time. Anyway, it don't taste like bonded stuff."

"Ha!" Andrew Held smiled. "Neither does gasoline or coal. The point is, when you think of alcohol as a fuel, the taste doesn't matter. You've brewed this liquor from plants that can be grown in abundance. You say it can be made from such waste products as potato peelings. Think of it! Energy from corn stubble and grain. From waste paper or trash. From . . ." he laughed ". . . potato peelings!"

"But Dr. Held . . ." Norma's smooth forehead was creased by a puzzled frown. "Are you serious?"

"Never more so! We should benefit from the lesson the Germans learned during the Second World War. They were faced with a critical oil shortage, so they substituted alcohol. As a fuel, it's more efficient, cleaner, and safer than gasoline."

"But the last time we talked about the energy crisis you seemed so positive that deuterium is the solution."

"Dear Norma," Brock said with a little moué, "as a virtue, consistency is *highly* overrated."

Andrew Held's shaggy eyebrows lifted in an expression of surprise. "Oh, there's no contradiction here. Deuterium *is* the ultimate fuel. Our long-range goal must be the construction of thermonuclear fusion power plants utilizing our almost limitless supply of deuterium. When I sing out in praise of alcohol, I'm speaking of an immediate step we can take to reduce oil consumption. Moreover alcohol burns without polluting the atmosphere, which should make it popular with our most zealous ecologists." He paused and smiled. "Most important, every man can make it in his own backyard. I'll admit, however, that the vigilantes in the tax division of the Internal Revenue Service might have a problem convincing our backyard fuel maker that he's supposed to pour the stuff into his automobile instead of his stomach."

"I'll drink to that," Warren Brock said, prodding Donald's arm with his mug.

The crude home brew was sweetish and raw and burned as it slid down the throat, but they sipped the dark liquid and praised Donald's ingenuity and drank toasts to each other, to the newlyweds, to themselves—one and all, to Phoenix Island, and to their rescuers, wherever they might be. When they finally sat down to dinner, they were suffused with loving kindness and a sense of wonderment at the beauty of the day.

The dinner was in three courses, each served after an interlude in which Donald ceremoniously refilled the cups. Diana called it a sit-down dinner, and the old-fashioned term immediately inspired comparisons with their last meal at table, Andrew Held's party for his house guests the night of the tsunami.

Norma and Blake recalled that there were four courses

and, with Diana's help, recited what they were. Brock remembered nothing about the food but everything about the wine and the cognac and especially the champagne they never got to drink because Carlo burst into the living room shouting "Tsunami!" Felicia alone had total recall. China, silverware, linens, and menu, course by course and sauce by sauce.

"Beluga caviar. Lobster. A center-cut *filet* of beef, mushroom caps, salad of artichokes and endive, and for dessert, candied chestnuts, followed by an excellent camembert." Felicia picked up a leg of Dungeness crab, removed the cracked shell and bit off a morsel of the milky meat. "The menu you planned was faultless, Andy. A *grand* dinner, in every way. Remarkable that your cook—Mary, was it? poor thing—was as faultless as the menu, right down to the *sauce bordelaise*. At the time, I wondered how she did it. She had lived all her life in the Outer Islands, hadn't she? She couldn't have had much experience with South African lobster tails, or basting a *filet* with Madeira and cognac, or Italian olive oil and endive and all the other imported ingredients that went into that dinner. Because nothing we ate was really native to these islands."

Andrew Held sipped his mug of pruno. Repressing a grimace, he set the cup down and picked up a piece of crab. "Nothing as remarkable as the dinner you and Norma and Diana have prepared for today." He held the crab leg aloft. "This is a *real* delicacy. Straight from the sea and onto our plates. Never frozen, stored, packaged, shipped, or airmailed. You point out that Mary, my cook, was a stranger to South African lobster tails. Like the nine of us here on Phoenix, poor old Mary had to make do somehow with large quantities of Dungeness crab that had been pulled out of the ocean the day before. Then there's the caviar. The night of the tsunami, we had beluga which had come all the way from the Caspian Sea and which anyone would know was delicious because it cost, roughly, two dollars per spoonful. Tonight we have caviar, too. Salmon caviar we made ourselves, from fish we caught ourselves. Let's go on to our second course for today . . . Yes, I've been snooping around the kitchen, I admit it . . . Next we are to have roast grouse, stuffed with a kind of pilaf of wild wheat, wild onions, and herbs. This, I take it, makes us underprivileged."

With flushed cheeks and blue eyes sparkling, Norma said gaily, "But not underdeveloped."

"I should say *not*." Brock's large dark eyes rested appreciatively on Norma's mid-section. "When we came to Phoenix, my dear Mrs. M., you were built like a malnourished twelve-year-old. I wasn't sure at first, but at this point, you are *definitely* a girl. I'm counting on you to be my model for Aphrodite of Phoenix."

"And after the grouse," Andrew Held continued, "or perhaps with it, there is a casserole. Am I right?"

Felicia nodded. "Jerusalem artichokes and mushrooms. Of course the mushrooms are nothing like the domestic breed, those pallid white caps one buys in grocery stores. Thanks to Norma's six-bite test, we've enlarged our mushroom repertoire so that it includes fifteen or sixteen varieties, and each one has a distinctive flavor." She indicated Diana with a smile and a nod. "Wait until you hear what us poor folk are going to have for dessert. Sorry, no candied chestnuts from France. A strictly local product, created by Diana."

Diana laughed softly. "There's really no name for it."

"Pooh!" Felicia said. "We'll make one up. Ingredients: dried apples, hazelnuts, and honey."

"Fantastique!" Warren Brock lifted his mug. "More of this excellent . . . uh . . . brew of yours, Donald lad. Let's all drink to our beggarly condition. Caviar, crab, grouse, mushrooms, artichokes, hazelnuts and honey. I can hardly wait for the search party to come and save us from privation. No doubt they'll bring plenty of K rations."

Felicia drew gently on her pipeful of Brock's favorite blend of kinnikinnick and reflected that a formal dinner dance at a hundred dollars a plate could not equal this party today. From the special breakfast which they had eaten while the early morning light was still wintry pale to the after-dinner songfest of Christmas carols as the sun was going down, it had been a day of unbroken celebration. Everything had been extraordinary. The food, the gifts, the wine, and above all, the wedding ceremony. Leisure so sweet that necessary household chores had been accomplished without anyone being aware of doing work. At the end of the long, beautiful day, Donald's *heimgemacht* and Brock's tobacco had only heightened the euphoria. They had not caused it.

Admittedly, they were all a little high. With dreamy expressions, Carlo and a combo made up of Rolf, Diana, and Norma were plucking, blowing, or drumming their primitive instruments as they experimented with revised versions of "The Song of Phoenix."

"I followed my sweetheart across the deep water . . ." Blake was singing along joyfully, undeterred by his failure to hit the same key the rest of them were using. During pauses in the music, Brock was creating limericks on the spot and reciting them with appropriate gestures. Even Donald was taking part. His characteristic scowl had been replaced by a faint, somewhat secretive grin. As he listened to the song, he kept turning his cup of cheer between his palms and gazing into it as if an important message might be visible through the dark liquid.

The mood had caught Andrew Held as well. He was lying on the floor with his hound pressed against his side, and he hadn't moved for half an hour except to comfort Lili when she yipped softly in the throes of a canine nightmare.

Felicia looked at him affectionately, thinking how different this peaceful man was from the kinetic husband who had moved so restlessly through their luxury apartment, the man who came home late and reluctantly and applied himself to required amounts of eating and sleeping in order to be prepared for an early departure in the morning. Even when he had relaxed to the extent of sitting down at his beloved grand piano, he played as if he were driven. Regardless of the composer's intention, every note was passionate, every chord was a challenge. He had remained locked in combat with the piano until he was exhausted, and then he went alone to bed, perhaps, Felicia had often thought, to continue the struggle in his dreams.

Phoenix had indeed brought him peace. She smiled at the world-renowned scientist, lying contentedly by the fire with a snoring basset hound cradled in his arm. The only evidence of his restless spirit was in his eyes, which were wide open and fixed brightly on the rafters above his head. Felicia recognized the alert but introspective expression. He was warmed by the fire, he was relaxed by the liquor and soothed by the pipe, but ideas were moving in his head, plans were forming.

Plans . . . She, too, had lived to plan. She had planned for a grand ball at the Shoreham, and she had planned for today. What a difference! It wasn't so much the obvious contrast between the sophisticated entertainment of the city and this island's simple pleasures, but in the degree of participation. In Washington, she and her committee, eight or nine people altogether, had "put on" the elaborate affair for seven or eight hundred individuals whose only contribution had been to pay exorbitant prices. Eight people did something, eight hundred were done unto. Whereas here, all nine members of the Phoenix colony were active participants, in every phase from gathering and preparing the food to creating the entertainment. Even the fire that was keeping them warm and filling the cabin with the pungent aroma of pine was a shared experience, for they all had gathered wood and they all were responsible for keeping the signal fire, as well as the hearth fire, burning day and night.

As if Felicia's thoughts had broadcast a message, Carlo looked up from his guitar and gave the stack of firewood an appraising glance. It was getting low. He stood up, set his instrument on the block of wood that was his chair, crossed the room and opened the door. In the second before he stepped outside and closed the door, Felicia could see the leaping flames of the signal fire, burning at the top of the rock mound like the flame on a pagan altar. Some day, she thought, someone out there in civilization is going to see our fire or spot our column of smoke. Someone will see our flag of distress flying from its fir-tree mast. Then they—they, those impersonal forces, those faceless authorities she had once prayed for so earnestly and now seldom thought of—*they* would come to the rescue.

Then they would all leave Phoenix and everything they had created on Phoenix. They wouldn't have to build the driftwood furniture they were designing, nor make pillows from duck feathers and fireweed cotton. Norma could forget her little hoard of wild wheat seeds because she wouldn't be here to plant them in the spring. Andrew could discard his master plan for a windmill because he could take money out of the bank and hire someone else to make it for him. And she, Felicia Stowe Held, would have two choices. To return to the city without Andrew, in spite of loving him, or to force him, because he loved her, to leave the island which had brought him peace. Or was there a third choice? When rescue came, was it possible that Felicia Stowe Held, Washington hostess, would choose Phoenix Island?

The door closed behind Carlo, shutting out the view of the signal fire. Rolf and Diana were singing "I followed my sweetheart across the deep water, The silvery moon was my Heavenly guide . . ." Felicia felt the heat of the fire against her cheek and watched a puff of green-tasting smoke twist up toward the rafters and slowly dissipate. I love the man, she thought. I love him as I never have before. But when the moment comes, when I have to choose and he has to choose, is that going to be enough?

Carlo wasn't sure what time it was, for in the interest of protecting it from damage Blake seldom wore his wristwatch and they had all got out of the habit of referring to it even when he did. But he could make a good guess. The shadows were deepening, the white sky was turning slate gray, and the rustling day sounds were hushed by the stealthy approach of night. At this time of year it was dark by four-thirty in the afternoon. The misty dusk settling over the farm told him it was now about four o'clock. From now on, he thought, dawn will come one minute earlier every day and sundown will be one minute later. In good time, the willow catkins will burst their coverings and the three-petalled trilliums will bloom in the woods and it will be March.

They had ricked up the firewood in two stacks. Short dry pieces for the fireplace in the cabin. Large green logs for the signal fire, for during daylight they wanted smoke even more than flame. Carlo picked up two freshly cut alder logs, climbed the rock mound and laid them on the pyre. The flame diminished for a few seconds and then shot up again, higher than before.

From his spot on the mound, Carlo could look down the slope toward the water, for timber surrounded the farm area on three sides only and on the west there was no screen of trees to impede the view. Which was a lucky thing, Carlo thought as he faced toward the open sea. The flag and the column of smoke were good distress signals during the day, but at night only a blazing fire would be seen at any distance.

Of course, Brock was still putting his faith in the bottle he had launched. Like the admiral's wife christening a new battleship, he had recited the message sealed inside, kissed the bottle reverently and closed his eyes as it floated out on the tide. Carlo laughed aloud at the memory. He was glad he had been alone when he found the bottle a few days later, in a small rocky cove just around the bend from the spot where Brock had so ceremoniously sent it out to sea. If it had been intact, he would have launched it again, but the neck was broken and the small clay tablets on which the message had been written had been reduced to sticky blue-gray mud. Why bother Brock with such a sad ending to his storybook dream? A message in a bottle would never have brought a rescue party, anyway. But this fire might. Any boat running along the west side of the island could be seen from this spot. Of course, the island was nowhere near the regular trade routes; they had had ample proof of that. Still, this fire ought to be visible to any boat, providing there *was* a boat, and providing it came in close enough. Just in case, he'd lay on another log.

Carlo climbed down, picked up more firewood and was about to carry it up to the fire when he glanced at the tree from which their signal flag was supposed to be flying. At first he thought it was gone. He dropped the fire log and stared out across the field. As his eyes adjusted to the failing light, he saw it. It was hanging, limp and useless, by one corner.

He hurried back to the woodpile, picked up an armload of wood for the fireplace, kicked the cabin door open and went inside. They were just as he had left them. Rolf and Diana singing, Brock and Felicia puffing quietly on their pipes, Dr. Held stretched out with his dog, Blake and Norma talking quietly as they drank from their cups and Donald smiling to himself and saying nothing. Carlo knelt so that he could deposit his load of wood on the floor without disturbing his companions' mellow mood. Then he approached Rolf.

"The flag is down. Looks as if the top corner broke loose and it's caught on a limb. I'm going to go fix it."

His voice wasn't much more than a whisper, but it shocked the sleepy gathering into sudden and complete attention.

"Brother *mio*," Brock twittered. "Surely you're not going to climb that giant of the forest tonight? The very thought drives me back to the bar." He reached for the pouch of home brew and tipped it over his cup. Thick pale eyebrows raised, lips pursed, he asked, "And whom may I serve?"

Donald held out his mug. After a moment's hesitation, Carlo did the same.

"Besides," Brock continued as he poured, "the flag doesn't do us much good at night, does it? Let's just keep the signal fire going, and leave the ascent of Everest for the purposeful morning hours."

Carlo took a long draught of wine. "It's not that dark outside, bradda. I can see to get up the tree. I'm thinking that the way we working on this beautiful stuff, none of us going to feel like climbing trees early tomorrow."

Blake chuckled. "If you feel as I do, you'll climb the wrong tree. AFWI. Ascent of a Fir While Under the Influence. A well-known violation of the Phoenix criminal code. As your attorney of record . . ." A small hiccup interrupted his speech. His fingers flew to his mouth and pressed urgently as a second spasm rippled up from his chest.

Laughing, Norma thumped him between the shoulder blades.

"That won't work," Blake gasped. "You're supposed to scare me."

"Booh!" Norma shouted, as they fell into each other's arms, laughing helplessly.

Felicia went to the hearth and relit her pipe with a splinter of cedar. "That's a scary climb under the best conditions. Bother the flag." Her voice rang with finality. "This is Christmas. Surely those Coast Guard sea scouts get the day off."

"They go when and where there's trouble," Dr. Held said.

"Mighty thoughtless people," Brock stated flatly. "Trying to drown themselves on Christmas."

Carlo chuckled. "Our signal fire isn't meant only for the Coast Guard. We've got to hope for a freighter, or maybe one of those steamers that go out on special holiday cruises. Where we are, way off the beaten track, I'd put my money on a cruise boat. At twenty to one."

"Oh, what the hell . . ." Donald's groggy voice ground to a halt. Elbows on his knees, he glared at the floor.

Rolf stood up. "I'm with you, Carlo. Let's go."

Like children at the heels of the Pied Piper, they all got up and followed Carlo and Rolf out of the cabin. All except Donald, Andrew Held noticed, who turned sullen and stayed by the fireplace with his mug of wine.

"You're not coming?" Dr. Held asked.

"I don't see no point to it."

"There *is* a point, Donald. The flag might attract attention at any time. We have no way of knowing when one of our signals will be sighted, so we have to keep the flag flying and the fire lighted. You understand that as well as I do."

"He's drunk."

"Carlo?" Andrew Held shook his head. "No. If he were, we wouldn't allow him to climb that ladder."

Donald stood up, emptied his mug in one swallow and set it down on the hearth. "I don't have to go just because everyone else does."

Andrew Held smiled. "That's why I thought you'd want to." He turned and limped toward the door. By the time he had caught up with the others, Donald was at his side.

Carlo was at the head of the column, Andrew Held and Donald at the rear. In between, the others straggled tipsily across the shadowy field, laughing and shouting at each other. In the dark and without his glasses, Blake was virtually blind, but Norma had grasped his hand and he plunged ahead, following her lead. The voices of Rolf and Diana rose above the din, singing, "I followed my sweetheart, I followed my sweetheart, I followed my sweetheart and here's what I found. I found Phoenix Island, I found Phoenix Island . . ."

Chapter Thirty-Nine

CARLO leaned against the tree trunk and fought for breath. He hadn't quite reached the top, but he could already see what had happened. The rawhide strips lashing the flagpole to the tree had loosened and the pole had slipped and come to rest among the highest branches. At one corner the tablecloth flag was still fastened to the pole but in several places it had caught on the bark. He would have to free the flag and rewind the lashing.

He steadied himself against the tree as he lifted one foot, found the next rung, and tested his balance before he tried to move again. The slender treetop bent under the weight of his body. Every step was a struggle against sharply protruding branches and the dizzying sway of the tree. He was winded again by the time he reached the top and looked out over the forest to the dark water far below. He look, gasped, and blinked his eyes.

A light, or a twinkling blend of many lights, just barely moving across the water to the west of Phoenix Island. The lights of a ship! For a moment he was so stunned by the possible significance of this apparition that he couldn't make a sound.

A ship? Rescue? It wasn't real, it couldn't be, however much they had planned for it and waited for it. It was a visual trick, like the slow, deadly pullback of water in the bay that had told him, some five months before, that a tsunami was about to roar into Phoenix harbor. During that nightmare moment on the dock below Dr. Held's house, he had been paralyzed by the terror of what he was seeing. The life-or-death necessity of breaking into a run, of calling out the warning, had held him spellbound, just as the vision of offshore lights was doing now. For seconds that were hours his body wouldn't move and his voice was trapped. But this was good news! This was help! Suddenly, the paralysis broke.

"Ship!" he cried hoarsely to the upturned faces at the base of the tree. "I see a ship!"

Suddenly the babble hushed. Andrew Held's voice rose like a sound from a deep pit. "In which direction?"

"To the west!"

"Near? Near enough to see the flag?"

"Not yet. But I think she's coming this way. I'm going to fix it."

Andrew Held's reply was lost in the blur of excited voices. Precariously balanced at the top of the tree, Carlo jerked and pulled on the lashings. They were wet with rain and resisted his feverish effort to untie the knots. He clung to the tree with one hand, working frantically with the other while tufts of fir needles scratched his skin and swaying branches threatened to push him off the ladder.

His head buzzed with the sounds from below. Shrill voices begged him to hurry, and in the next breath warned him to be careful. "Where is it now? Is it coming nearer? How big . . . ?" His foot slipped, he began to lose balance. Somewhere in the darkness below, someone screamed.

Clawing the air, Carlo's hands struck a limb and closed in a desperate grip. Breathing hard, he pulled himself up slowly until one foot, and then the other, touched and found support. He looked up. The flag was gone. In his struggle to save himself, he had ripped off the one corner which had been fast to the flagpole and sent the flag on a slow, irregular fall from branch to branch until it caught on a dead limb just a few feet off the ground.

A chorus of unhappy "oh's" was punctuated by Andrew Held's calm voice, "Carlo, are you all right?"

Though fresh cuts and scratches stung him in a dozen places and his head throbbed from the jolting fall, Carlo called back, "I'm okay, but the flag isn't."

Rolf's deep voice stood out from the disappointed murmuring of the others. "I'll climb up with the flag."

"No use. The way this thing is wrecked, that ship's going to be long gone before I get it fixed."

"Then get down out of that tree!" Felicia ordered. "They'll see the fire. Come on, everyone."

"The fire!"

The word propelled them back across the field, chattering so excitedly that only Andrew Held noticed Donald Campbell wasn't with them. He looked around curiously. Had he gone into the woods, either out of childish pique or because of a simple need to relieve himself?

In the short time they had been standing around the tree, the true blackness of night had fallen. Andrew Held squinted up through the shadows as Carlo's figure descended the primitive ladder. Turning back toward the field, his eyes followed the little group of retreating figures. Dark as it was, Donald's massive head and shoulders would surely stand out above the others, for they were silhouetted against the glow of the signal fire. But he wasn't with them. Where was he, then?

Felicia's voice sang out, "Let's go down to the orchard. We'll get a good view from there!" And Brock trilled, "Hurray, hurray! My ship is coming in!"

It was as good as a battle cry. The victorious troops of Phoenix swung to the west and in joyful hysteria blundered toward the clearing below the orchard where the sea stretched out to the western horizon and they could watch the miraculous approach of the ship which must, within minutes, sight their signal fire.

The moment Carlo reached the ground, Andrew Held sent him ahead and then proceeded slowly at his own limping pace. When he finally caught up with the rollicking band, its mood had changed.

They were all looking toward the west in hushed silence. There it was, the light of a ship, somewhere below the point where the night sky melted into the sea. Ten minutes before, they had been in a frenzy of joy. They had leaped across the field, heedless of the dark, laughing and shouting and hugging each other in a wild dance of exaltation. The ship was there, it was really *there*. The signal fire blazed at their backs and beckoned to their rescuers. Now they were paralyzed by silence. At meetings they had play-acted many versions of their rescue. But the play was over. This wasn't a game. This was serious.

Blake, who couldn't see, was the only one who didn't seem to be mesmerized by the approach of the ship. "I doubt that they'll try to find a harbor tonight," he said solemnly. For the first time in two or three months, Andrew Held heard the undertone of anxiety that had been so noticeable in Blake's voice when he first came to Phoenix. "I assume they know most of these islands are surrounded by rocks. I think they'll drop anchor and a lifeboat will come ashore in the morning."

"Drat!" Warren Brock said. "I'll be sober by then, and in that sorrowful condition, I *hate* uniforms."

"Maybe they won't be in uniform." Rolf's voice was strangely serious, in total contrast with his merry singing of only fifteen minutes earlier. "She'll have to come in closer before we can make out what she is."

"But a freighter, or a trawler?" Norma asked anxiously. "Wouldn't any kind of boat stop and investigate?"

"That depends. On who they are, and whether they know the territory well enough to wonder why there's a fire on this island. That boat isn't on any regular commercial shipping lane."

"Therefore," Norma said firmly, "they wouldn't be coming here if they hadn't been sent. Someone has sent them to get us."

Felicia's hand slipped into Andrew's. "Andy?" she whispered. "I think that this time we are really going to be rescued."

"It seems so, doesn't it? They'll have to come closer to spot our fire, but it's certainly a clear signal and they do seem to be moving in this direction."

"It won't be like the helicopter, flying off without seeing us. Or that other ship, the one that changed course so suddenly and disappeared."

Andrew Held pressed her hand. "No, dear. If we keep that fire burning, they're bound to see it."

"I can't help but wonder . . ." Felicia's voice was wistful. "If they've been sent to Phoenix, who do you suppose convinced them they ought to take another look?"

Andrew Held laughed briefly. "I haven't the least idea. After almost five months without a search effort of any kind? To be truthful, Felicia, I've been convinced for some time that we're all listed as dead. I've taken comfort in the fact that there are so few people to weep for us. We're all childless. At this point, I suspect that our nearest relatives are primarily concerned with the long wait the law requires before an estate can be probated. As for our friends . . ." He paused, nodding in affirmation of the loyalty of friends. "They miss us, of course. But in my case, they have seen me so little for the past two years that my death wouldn't take me much farther away than I was when I was alive."

"And now they'll discover we're alive. Some people," Felicia said drily, "are going to be surprised."

"And some of my colleagues," Andrew Held added tartly, "are going to be disconcerted."

They were so preoccupied with the slow approach of the ship that no one noticed Donald's absence. Once or twice, the question crossed Andrew Held's mind but each time he satisfied himself with the thought that Donald was in the cabin finishing off the home brew. He was sulking, and the reason for it was connected somehow with the signal flag. A senseless and childish mood, best ignored. Ordinarily, Andrew Held read Donald's motivation like a textbook for high school physics. It bothered him a little that he couldn't now. Since his return from exile, Donald had been a happy person. Why this sudden fit of anti-sociability?

When their signal fire dimmed, flickered, and went out, Andrew Held knew why.

"Donald!" he shouted as they all turned their backs to the sea and stared incredulously at the spot which moments before had been so brilliantly illuminated. "Donald!" he called again as the rushing bodies flowed around him, nearly knocking him down.

Felicia's hand on his arm kept him from falling. Then she cried, "My God, he's put out the fire!" and she was running up the slope after the rest of them. And Andrew Held was alone in the dark.

He kept calling Donald's name as he worked his way painfully across the uneven ground, but he didn't see the big man until he had reached the rock mound. Donald was standing alone some twenty or thirty feet from the mound. Their largest water containers, the five-gallon milk can that had been washed up on the beach the morning after the tsunami and the smaller plastic bucket, were on the ground at his feet. At the top of the mound, tendrils of smoke were rising from the blackened remains of the signal fire.

"You bastard!" Andrew Held said quietly. "You dirty, rotten bastard!"

"I don't want no one to come and take me away. When I seen a ship, I got to thinking. I got . . ." His voice cracked. "I got scared."

"They're trying to rebuild the fire," Andrew Held said grimly. "You're going to help them."

"I don't want to, Dr. Held! I soaked it, I soaked it

good. I doused all the kindling, too. God damn it, I ain't going to help!"

It was a pitiful animal cry. Rather than raising his voice, Andrew Held lowered it. "Yes, you are, Donald. Right now."

Without a word, Donald walked toward the woodpile and began to pick up firewood. His face was in shadow, but a moment later Rolf ran out of the cabin with blazing sticks in both hands and, as he passed, the sputtering flames cast light on the big man. In that brief instant, Andrew Held saw that he was crying.

They worked with desperate speed, against heavy odds. The kindling was drenched, the bed of ashes was black mud. They dropped to their knees and scraped the sodden fire area with bare hands. They ran around the dark meadow, looking for dry grass and dead bracken fern to use as tinder. When the new fire failed to ignite the water-soaked wood, they began a frenzied marathon from rock mound to cabin and back again, trying to transfer the hearth fire to the mound. Felicia, Norma, and Diana, Rolf, Carlo, and Brock—all except Blake, who was groping his way back to the cabin for his wooden Eskimo glasses, Andrew who couldn't run, and Donald, whom they ignored—six of them filled pottery cooking utensils with hot coals and raced out of the cabin, across the dark field. Stumbling to the top of the pyramid, each one deposited another small bit of fire and ran back for more.

They worked in silence as thick as the surrounding night. There was the sound of labored breathing, an exclamation or gasp as someone nearly fell, but until the first hesitant flame licked at the firewood and steadied and grew larger, no one spoke. Then there was a sighing exclamation, an invisible wave of verbal sound rippling out from the ring of sweaty, panting fire-makers. As the fire took hold, they began to smile. Donald came forward with an armload of firewood. One by one, the others took a stick from him and laid it on the growing flame.

Felicia was the first to speak. "Now it will burn. Let's go back and watch the boat." She threw Andrew a questioning look.

He responded quickly. "Donald and I will stay here. He'll keep up the fire."

"I'll stay here, too." Blake touched Norma's shoulder

and smiled. "You go watch for our rescuers. I'll wait to meet them personally, now that I'm wearing my glasses. They're going to *love* my glasses."

"I've already seen the ship. I'd rather stay here with you."

Blake shook his head. "No, Norma. Please go with the others. Have another look," and he gave her a gentle push. Reluctantly she followed the figures already hurrying toward the orchard.

Andrew Held sighed deeply, for his right leg was throbbing. "Come along, Blake. Let's go inside and sit down. Getting rescued wears me out. Donald, would you bring the milk can and the pail, please?"

The hint was indirect but firm. With one last look at the new fire he had helped to build, Donald followed obediently.

In half an hour—half an hour according to the curiously accurate time mechanism Andrew Held kept in his head—Norma opened the cabin door and walked slowly across the room. She sat down next to Blake and slid her arm through his. "The others are coming," she said simply. The three men looked at her expectantly, but she shook her head. There was such finality in the gesture that none of them questioned her.

Within a few minutes they were all there, straggling through the door one at a time and silently seeking places near the fire.

Felicia alone remained standing. Arms crossed over her chest, green eyes blazing, she said, "Well, Andrew. We've done it again. Three times and you're out. It seems that the ship hadn't spotted our original fire before Donald, here, put it out. By the time our new fire was big enough to be seen, the ship had continued on its . . . shall I say . . . merry way?"

"Are you *sure?*" Blake's tone was incredulous but not unhappy. "Of course, I couldn't see the ship, but from what you said, Norma . . ."

"We watched, and we waited." Norma's voice was pleasant and matter-of-fact. "Oh yes, Blake. There's no question about it. When we got back to the orchard, that ship, or boat, or whatever it was, was going *away*. And we didn't leave the orchard until it was *gone*. Out of sight. Invisible. Lost forever on the wine-dark sea."

"Oh you poor girl," Blake said sympathetically, as if the question of rescue had nothing to do with him.

"Now we'll never know," Brock said with a small mock frown. "Was it really the fine young defenders of our native shores? Obviously, they couldn't have been coming for us, or they would have kept coming. Ah, me . . . for a while I thought our valiant rescuers would prevent me from starting work on the Aphrodite of Phoenix. It now appears that I will be able to proceed on schedule with the finest sculpture of my career. Unless some frigging search team comes barging in and insists on sparing us from privation. But we ought to be safe for a while now, right? If that *was* the Coast Guard, and anyone asks them about Phoenix, they'll have to report that the island was dark and lifeless, wouldn't they? So unless someone actually stumbles over us, we're as good as dead."

"As good as dead . . ." For minutes the words echoed in a silent room. Finally Felicia spoke. In the tone of a music critic commenting on the rendition of an aria, she said, "That was an extraordinary speech, Warren. You do that sort of thing very well, you know. The declaration of inverted values. Take what we all accept as good and true, turn it upside down, and say—*this* is the good and the true. With the exception of our reverse arsonist . . ." she indicated Donald with an impersonal nod of her head, "we were all thrilled by what seemed to be the end of our life in the wilds. Ergo, we must be correspondingly miserable because once more we've been passed by and our chances of being sought out and found have now reached the vanishing point. That's the truth, that's logic. But you, dear colleague-in-exile, are sitting there with a wise smirk on your pretty face, saying we're lucky to be lost and you're happy about staying lost and *that* seems to be what's true at the moment."

"Never more serious," Norma mused, "than when he's silly."

Warren's shoulders lifted in a dramatic shrug. *"Dear* Felicia. You worked like a Slavic peasant to rebuild the signal fire. But student of human nature that I am, I sensed, in all your frantic running around, that you would not have had to display such fervor for keeping the fire going if you had been absolutely sure you wanted to keep the fire going."

With a dimpling smile, he turned to Norma. "I saw

the same thing in you, Norma sweet. I saw you looking
at the milk can and the plastic pail and the question was
all over your lovely patrician face: Do I want to get more
firewood or do I want to get more water?"

His large brown eyes panned the room like twin television cameras. "Come on now, let's be honest, if not with
ourselves, at least with one another. Andrew, instruct
your encounter group to relax and let it all hang out. I
said I'm glad the stupid ship went away. Anyone wants to
slug me, then go ahead and slug me." He blinked prettily
in Donald's direction. "Except you, old fellow. I don't
mind getting swatted in the name of therapy, but I *hate*
the thought of being squashed like a fly."

Donald said gruffly, "Me, I got no reason to slug you.
I don't want to leave Phoenix."

"That," Felicia said curtly, "is crystal clear. Sometime
you must tell us about your experiences on the mainland.
As for the rest of us . . ." She paused and looked at Andrew. "Don't you want to take hold of this discussion,
Andy?"

Andrew Held chuckled. "I think it's going along beautifully. What can I add to such spontaneous confessions?"

"Your own."

Andrew's bushy eyebrows drew together over intent
blue eyes. "Perhaps the issue is simpler for me than for
the rest of you. I *chose* to live on Phoenix. I have no
intention of leaving it. So for me, the concept of 'rescue'
is not synonymous with being taken away. It means *you*
would be taken away, and I've thought a great deal about
that, never with more pain, or more . . . clarity . . . than
tonight. I want to stay. You want to be taken away, carried off to civilization, returned to the comfortable and
genteel life you're used to. To central heating and high-
powered automobiles and couturier clothes."

Felicia said quietly, "And smog, and polluted rivers,
and gasoline rationing, and inflation, and corrupt government."

"Don't you ever wonder who may take possession of
your Louis Seize drawing room suite?"

After a long pause, Felicia looked directly into her
husband's face. "No," she said, as if her own answer
surprised her. "And I should, shouldn't I? But the only
furniture I've been thinking about is what we're going to
build for this house. We've put together a lot of designs

and I've been looking forward to carrying them out." Her green eyes had a wondering look and she began to smile. "I guess I'm saying I don't want to leave Phoenix until we've finished the furniture. But by then, of course, we'll have ten more wonderful projects, and I won't want to leave until *they're* all carried out, and after that . . ." Still gazing into Andrew's eyes, Felicia began to laugh. At first the laugh was low, almost inaudible, and then it gathered force and depth, and her head tilted as the sound burst from her mouth like a wordless song. All around the room, smiles answered her outburst, and then chuckles, and then they were all laughing, loudly and joyfully.

"Didn't *anyone* want to be rescued?" Diana asked when the room was quiet.

Carlo's dark eyes danced with reflected firelight. "We all want to be rescued," he said, "but bradda, not right *now*."

Norma said, "I've never felt so well. Or so free. I suppose we'll go back sometime. I suppose we'll have to. But for the moment . . ." She took Blake's hand. "For the moment, I'm deeply relieved."

Andrew Held stroked his beard with thumb and forefinger. "Remember the Swiss Family Robinson? When rescue came, they had already won the battle and they didn't want to go back. Survival is a long, difficult journey. By the time help arrives, it's an anticlimax, if you've already reached your destination in your heart."

Rolf said, "Carlo, let's get to work on another boat. Maybe an outrigger this time?"

Carlo didn't hear because on his other side, Blake was explaining how they might make a glass substitute for the cabin windows. So Rolf turned toward Diana, but she had slipped away. "Diana?"

The screens that formed temporary walls for their bedchamber were partially opened. At the sound of her name, Diana appeared and crossed the room with soft, moccasined steps. Her eyes glistened under their thick fringe of black eyelashes and her soft lips opened in a radiant smile. "Lili has had her puppies. On our bed."

Warren Brock exclaimed, "Glory be unto the highest! The day is complete. To paraphrase Tiny Tim, there never *was* such a Christmas."

"How many?" Felicia asked.

"Only six."

Felicia said anxiously, "Oh, dear, how will we divide them?"

Andrew Held, leader, judge, paraclete and moderator, picked up his wife's scratched and work-soiled hand and kissed it gently. "I promise you, Felicia, the decision will not be Solomonic."

Two passengers on the *M.V. Gloria's* "Santa Claus Cruise" ("Christmas on the High Seas—Give *Yourself* a Gift!") were standing at the window of the lounge bar on A deck. One was tall and dressed in mod style, while the stocky man at his side wore Traditional Tourist. The campus at Berkeley versus the mattress factory in Milwaukee. Citizens against Nuclear Terror (CANT) versus Crawford-Langley Post of the American Legion.

"Strange shape, that island out there," the taller man mused. "Like an animal, rising up on its haunches. Know what it's called?"

The man from Milwaukee shook his head. "According to the map on B deck, it isn't even there. You been staring at it too? Maybe we're thinking the same thoughts."

"One thought," the tall man said wistfully, peering through the window. "Escape."

"I'm with you. Escape to an uncharted island. Miles from regular shipping lanes. Hundreds of miles from smog, overpopulation, violence, inflation."

"You mean, no plumbing, TV, sewers, PTA? Living by your wits and ingenuity? Start from scratch with a sharp stone, some leaves and vines, grasses and berries. Live off the land."

"The kids are always talking about that," the older man said. "When I look at that island out there, and then think about what I'm going back to, they actually begin to make sense. And I don't even own a copy of the *Whole Earth Catalog*."

"But you're yearning anyway, right? Your own little patch of wilderness, a hundred miles from the nearest McDonald's. The question is, would you ever really try it? Get rid of your business, pack up the wife and kids and a few tools, and get the hell out?"

Suddenly the stocky man's voice was dead serious. "I'm supposed to be a practical businessman. Would I give up everything I've worked hard to get? The answer is—Yeah, maybe I would. Because I've been thinking, What *have*

I got? Government regulations. Foreign imports. Bidding for contracts. Negotiating with unions. Martinis at one P.M. and six P.M. and Alka-Seltzer the rest of the time." His strong square face broke into a boyish grin. "Hell, I even hate the country club, and it cost me twenty-five thousand and a name change to get into it."

The young man in mod clothing pulled nervously on his beard. "Well, I teach math, and in my field all the really new ideas are coming from younger men. That makes it rougher all the time for me but I'd better quit staring at that island. I'm tripping. Escape to nature. A handful of people who are sick of their own special rat races. An island colony . . ."

The older man nodded. "It would be like a ship at sea. Just our gang, isolated from the world, confined together on an island like passengers on a ship." His gaze moved from the window, wandered thoughtfully around the lounge and fastened on a trio standing by the window at the far end of the room. Two men and a girl, in earnest conversation. "Only I'd want to have more say about who was in our colony than I did about the passenger list for this cruise."

The tall man glanced at the trio and smiled. "Yes, they're pretty antisocial, aren't they? Say, they're really giving our island the once-over. Like people at an auction who know they can top the highest bid. Maybe they're going to beat us to it."

The older man's blue eyes sparked. "Maybe I'm crazy, but just for the hell of it, let's you and I find one of the officers and ask for a compass bearing, or whatever you call it. Getting the name and location isn't signing a sales contract."

With eager steps they hurried out of the lounge bar.

The antisocial threesome at the far end of the lounge were indeed interested in the strangely shaped island, but only one of them possessed such wealth that he could make the last bid on any object he coveted. He was slim, ruggedly handsome, perfectly at ease with a striking young girl on his arm. In an expensive bush jacket, handmade shoes and custom-tailored slacks, he looked like an international banker on holiday. The appearance of wealth was justified. His annual income topped that of the President of the United States by at least a million dollars. The appearance of conservative respectability was questionable, for he was the head of an organization that could never be listed in the "Fortune 500."

The second man projected an image much closer to what he was. He was a rugged blond, with large hands and heavily muscled shoulders, and he was wearing jeans, a T-shirt and a denim jacket. "Believe me, sir," he said, forcing his voice to a near-whisper. "This is important, or I wouldn't interrupt."

The older man said coolly, "Young man, I told *you* to do the scouting. *We're* on vacation. I'll call you when I need you."

The blond man knew very well that "vacation" was a figure of speech. Men like that don't take vacations. But he would never dream of contradicting someone who could easily be rated as one of the ten most dangerous men in the world. "I'm sorry, sir," he said, "but I think that's it! That island over there. It's a natural. I thought you'd want to take a look . . ."

"All right, flyboy, all right. I'll give you one minute flat, no more. And don't point. It's not polite."

The young man stuffed his hands into his jacket pockets. "In the first place, it's not on any map. It's unknown, uninhabited. No one there to watch and ask questions."

Looking out across the water, as the ship continued to approach the still-distant island, the older man said, "And what else? Your time's half up."

"In the second place, it's inside U.S. waters, but it's in easy reach of Canada. A natural jump-off place, a natural stash. I see it this way, my plane from Canada to this island, speedboat to Wolf Island. Then the local ferry, not the international, from Wolf to the mainland, so no customs."

The ship was now changing course, and the young man looked at the island desperately as it began to recede in the distance.

The man in the bush jacket barely inclined his head. "All right, you've done fine. And you've had your minute, *plus.* Now go play and leave the thinking to me."

"Oh, look!" The young girl was pointing excitedly. "Fire!"

Flame flickered faintly over the slowly receding island, and then suddenly was extinguished.

Forgetting his employer's order to move away, the

young man blurted out, "Hey, maybe there *is* someone on that island. Maybe that's some kind of a signal fire."

The older man frowned his displeasure. "Don't be silly! That was just a meteor."

"It's a sign!" the girl whispered, pulling on her companion's sleeve.

"It's a meteor," the expensively attired gentleman said curtly. "Don't either of you know what a meteor looks like?" He patted the girl's hand and his voice softened. "But it's a sign, all right, sweetie. A dollar sign. Flyboy has something. Maybe we'll make a purchase. Like adding an island to our collection."

About the Author

Charlotte Paul, a veteran writer of fiction and nonfiction, lives with her husband on Lopez, one of the San Juan archipelago islands off the northwest coast of Washington.